"*An American Tune* is about the '60s, but it's about now, too. It's about a mother finding herself in her daughter, for better and for worse, and it's about generations of women forever realizing that even though we try our best to prevent them, our children were born to make their own mistakes. Nora will become your honest-to-God best friend because she reminds us of where we've been, what we're doing, and what we are looking for."

MARGARET MCMULLAN, author of *In My Mother's House* and *When Warhol Was Still Alive*

"Barbara Shoup has written a rich and timely story about one generation's outrage and the long reverberations of secrets. Her plot has much to say about the tangle of responsibility and how an ill-advised war disrupts an intricate network of ordinary American lives. A striking and memorable novel warm, sage, and beautifully written."

JOAN SILBER, National Book Award finalist for *Ideas of Heaven: A Ring of Stories* and author of four other books of fiction

"I love *An American Tune,* by Barbara Shoup! She's a wonderful writer with an amazing story to tell to those of us who have been fumbling along trying to gain perspective on a signal moment in our own history. Hers is the first account, in my opinion, that understands the combination of the extraordinary and the banal that characterized the antiwar movement, and yet she's never didactic. The extraordinary and the banal coexist in the seminal moments of any generation, of course, but to those of us who became adults during the Vietnam War years it is still surprising to remember over and over again how self-absorbed, how trivial we were while also making profound decisions."

ROBB FORMAN DEW, author of the novels *Dale Loves Sophie to Death, The Time of Her Life,* and *Fortunate Lives,* and a memoir, *The Family Heart*

"Barbara Shoup's *An American Tune* is an elegant, moving, finely written page-turner that reaffirms and makes fresh again Faulkner's assertion that the past is never dead; it's not even past."

WILL ALLISON, author of *Long Drive Home*

"It's an ordinary day until a man calls your name, a man from the life you've tried your best to leave behind. Suddenly, anything can happen. Such is the case in Barbara Shoup's engaging new novel, *An American Tune.* A story that comes from the heartland and from the heart. I cared about these characters as if they were my own family members. What a moving story of what it is to long for the person you once were, set against the backdrop of political unrest both then and now."

LEE MARTIN, author of *Break the Skin* and *The Bright Forever*

"*An American Tune* kept me on the edge of my seat while at the same time wanting me to savor the evocative, memorable and true sentences along with way. Barbara Shoup's exasperating yet loveable characters felt so real that I longed to lure them into my kitchen for a cup of coffee so I could spend more time with them. Shoup brings the sixties back to life with wry humor and sympathy, reminding us all the while that we have never left its shadow. A haunting, powerful book. I loved it."

ELIZABETH STUCKEY-FRENCH, author of *The Revenge of the Radioactive Lady*

"The story of Jane and Nora – and what happens when these two lives converge – held me in great suspense. This highly readable novel isn't afraid to talk liberal politics during wartime, nor is it afraid to tell an epic love story. I loved everything about Barb Shoup's *An American Tune.*"

CATHY DAY, author of *The Circus in Winter*

"Barb Shoup's new novel *An American Tune* brings to life an important time in our history that young people don't know and older people would rather forget – the idealism and protests of sixties' youth against the war in Vietnam, and the shadow it casts in today's world.

DAN WAKEFIELD, author of *Going All the Way*

An American Tune

break away books

An American Tune

A NOVEL

BARBARA SHOUP

INDIANA UNIVERSITY PRESS *Bloomington & Indianapolis*

This book is a publication of

INDIANA UNIVERSITY PRESS
601 North Morton Street
Bloomington, Indiana 47404-3797 USA

iupress.indiana.edu

Telephone orders 800-842-6796
Fax orders 812-855-7931

∞ The paper used in this publication meets the minimum requirements of the American National Standard for Information Sciences – Permanence of Paper for Printed Library Materials, ANSI Z39.48-1992.

Manufactured in the United States of America

Library of Congress
Cataloging-in-Publication Data

Shoup, Barbara.
An American tune : a novel / Barbara Shoup.
p. cm.
ISBN 978-0-253-00742-1 (pb : alk. paper) – ISBN 978-0-253-00754-4 (eb) 1. Middle-aged women – Fiction 2. Family secrets – Fiction I. Title.
PS3569.H618A83 2012
813'.54 – dc23

2012027221

1 2 3 4 5 17 16 15 14 13 12

FOR STEVE

SEPTEMBER 12, 1965

. . . we come on the ship they call Mayflower
We come on the ship that sailed the moon
We come in the age's most uncertain hour
And sing an American tune.

Paul Simon

PROLOGUE

"Deja Vu"

JULY, 2002

Nora Quillen sat on a bench in People's Park, considering what was lost. The Book Nook was gone and, with it, long, rainy afternoons browsing the cluttered shelves, breathing in the smell of paper and ink. The Oxford Shop, Redwood and Ross, the Peddler were gone, and all the beautiful blue and yellow oxford shirts, the matching Villager skirts and sweaters. Knee socks, the warmth of them on bitter winter mornings.

The SAE house was gone, its big lawn, where you could always count on seeing at least a few cute guys throwing a football, was now a parking lot; the old stadium, the spinning silver spokes of Little 500 bicycle wheels on its cinder track had vanished into green space. There was a Burger King in the Commons, and the Gables, where a young Hoagy Carmichael once sat in a back booth dreaming music, had been gutted and transformed into a Roly Poly Sandwich Shop.

People's Park itself was nothing like it had been in 1970, when students claimed the site after the storefront buildings that once stood there were razed in a fire. In the spirit of Berkeley's People's Park, they brought shovels, lumber, paint, flats of vegetables and flowers, and set out to shape the half-block of mud. Anyone could plant anything, they said. There'd be benches and tables, a playground for children, kiosks announcing every kind of happening. It would be a friendly place, where you could listen to music, fly kites, blow bubbles. Get high. That same spring, Nora remembered – the night Nixon announced he was sending troops into Cambodia – some of the protestors marching from Dunn Meadow toward the courthouse downtown had picked up rocks unearthed from the digging and thrown them, breaking windows in some of the shops on Kirkwood Street.

The warm spring night came back to her, the smell of newly turned earth mingling with sweat and patchouli and marijuana. Chanting overlaid by shouts and laughter, the sound of glass shattering – Tom grabbing a drunk fraternity boy and wrestling a rock from his hand.

But she wasn't going to think about Tom. There was no use in it – and, besides, it was Claire's turn now. Soon her daughter would step into a whole new life here, as she herself had done so many years before.

The park was so tastefully landscaped now, she observed, with neat brick paths dividing the grassy areas into triangles whose points met at the abstract sculpture in its center – a smooth scoop of limestone reminiscent of an open hand. There was a drinking fountain with a brass bowl. Green benches lined the paths, and tables surrounded colorful mosaics that had been set into concrete near the front of the park: fingers on piano keys, cyclists, an eye. There were trees, with commemorative plaques set into the soil beneath them – one dedicated to former chancellor Herman B. Wells: "A Friend of Bloomington's Urban Forest."

Had the chancellor been a friend of People's Park? Nora didn't remember, but she was pretty sure that, at the time, he was as much against the students' occupation of university property as most everyone else. When had it become the Urban Forest, anyway? A stupid name, she thought. If people were bound and determined to rewrite history, they ought to be able to do a better job than that.

That other time simmered inside her, unsettling her, as it had done all too often since the towers came down in New York and the President's intention to hijack the horrific event to further his own political agenda became more and more obvious. Just this morning, there had been another news story about weapons of mass destruction, citing the testimony of a former Iraqi nuclear engineer who claimed that Saddam Hussein would have enough weapons-grade uranium for three nuclear bombs by 2005. God. Couldn't people see through the "Chutes and Ladders" maneuver that had so neatly made Osama bin Laden and Saddam Hussein the same person in their minds and how Bush was using it to justify the buildup toward a war in Iraq that was only vaguely connected to what had happened in New York? One that was likely to be as disastrous, as unwinnable and costly of innocent lives as the war in Vietnam had been?

She could not talk about it, even with her own husband, Charlie, who'd put all that had happened to him in Vietnam, whatever it had been, in a closed-off place and would not even allow himself to consider that anything like it might ever happen again. Nor with Claire, so devastated by the television images: the towers falling in on themselves, the black smoke, people running, screaming. Frantic, grieving loved ones holding up photographs. "Have you seen . . . ?"

"How could this happen *here*?" Claire asked again and again. Nora had heard her, sobbing, on the phone with her boyfriend, Dylan. "How could people hate us so much?"

"Why not here?" Nora would have had to say, if she had said anything. "Why wouldn't they hate us?" But once started, she might not have been able to stop. She might have told them everything, and she was in no way prepared to do that.

Near the sculpture, where the paths converged, a bunch of boys dressed in baggy shorts and Birkenstocks were playing Hacky Sack, rap music blaring from a boom box they'd set on the grass. Rowdy, full of themselves, they hopped and wheeled and backpedaled, ducking and reaching to bounce the little rainbow-colored bean bag off their tattooed ankles, their knees, elbows, wrists, shoulders, foreheads. They scattered a group of chattering girls making their way through the park, careened into trash cans, came perilously close to upsetting a table where a serious-looking young man was drinking a cup of coffee, a book propped before him. When the Hackey Sack landed on the bench where Nora sat, one of the boys darted over, bent and twisted within inches of her face as he scooped it up, and sent it flying again – as if she were invisible.

"Mother*fuck*," another yelled, stretching to bonk it with his forehead. He wore a purple tee shirt with a grinning stick figure on it holding up two fingers in a peace sign.

It should have made her angry to be ignored by them. Or sad. But she was glad to be a middle-aged woman, not even on their radar. She would never want to be young again. The past few days in this place, memories catching her short everywhere she turned, she'd *been* her young self all too often.

Yesterday afternoon, checking into the dorm where parents who had accompanied their children for orientation were staying, she'd been, momentarily, a college freshman again, saying goodbye to her own parents and her little sisters on the day they dropped her off for college, more than thirty-five years before. She could almost hear the stereos cranked up along the corridor, as they had been on that long-ago day. The Beatles, the Beach Boys, the Byrds. The Rolling Stones, inciting them to rebellion. When all her belongings had been unloaded, she'd stood with her family, watching the elevator light blink each floor on its way up, feeling like a can of Coke shaken up hard. Finally, the door opened. Did they hug? Speak? They must have. But all she could remember now was how, suddenly, they were gone. And then flying back to her room, her arms wheeling, her soul rising, wild and joyous. Thinking, anything can happen to me now. Absolutely anything.

The memory had stayed with her all day. And Bridget appearing in her doorway moments later, grinning. Walking across the little bridge onto the winding path she'd walked each day to and from class; the sound of scales drifting from the music building in the humid air; Jordan Hall with its overgrown plants pressing against the steamy greenhouse glass; it was impossible to stay in the present moment. She'd felt Charlie watching her, interpreting her distraction as continuing disapproval of the choice their daughter had made and willing her not to express it. He didn't know she'd gone to IU herself, she'd never told him, so he'd been baffled by her visceral response to Claire's interest in the school last fall. It was a beautiful campus, not terribly far away. It had a better music program than Oberlin, where Claire had originally planned to go. What was the problem?

Claire only wanted to go to IU because Dylan was there, Nora argued – a ridiculous reason to choose a college. She had let him believe her resistance was really about her reluctance to accept that Claire had a serious boyfriend, endured his attempts to persuade her to trust their daughter's judgment. Finally, realizing nothing would sway her, he asked, "Why are you so dead-set against this when it's what Claire wants?"

And she had said, bitterly, surprising even herself, "What she *wants*. In case you haven't noticed, Charlie, you don't get every single thing you want in this world. Or think you want. Nobody does. Now's as good a time as any for Claire to figure that out."

To Claire, she'd said, "Indiana just feels *wrong* to me. If that's irrational, so be it. I'm sorry. But I'm your mother, after all, and – as you'll probably find out yourself some day – you raise kids based on how you feel. It's all you know to do."

It was a stupid-cop-out thing to say. And a flat-out lie. Claire knew it, too. Nora could see it in her face. Eventually, she'd given up. Given in. She'd done her best to be supportive as Claire moved on through her senior year toward graduation, but she could not pretend enthusiasm and so, in the end, had hurt her daughter, the person she loved most in the world, and caused the first real rift between them.

She'd slept poorly in the dorm room last night, tangled in dreams of Tom, waking again and again, her heart racing, half-sick with some terrible combination of joy and grief. She lay on her back, palms up, in the relaxation pose she'd learned on the yoga tape she'd bought, a New Year's resolution mostly abandoned, and concentrated on pushing her breath through her heart, down through the middle of her body, to her toes – and back again. But it didn't help. At five, she got up, put on her clothes, and went down to the dorm lounge, where she sat in a dark corner, trying – and failing – not to think about the past, until dawn broke and other parents began to make their way down to the coffee and pastries that had been set out for them.

She poured a cup for Charlie and took it up to him. "I'm afraid I've got a migraine coming on," she lied. "You take Claire to register for her classes, okay? I'll feel better if I take a walk before the long drive home."

But she hadn't walked far, just the few blocks down Kirkwood Avenue to this place where she'd sat most of the morning, bereft in a way she had hoped she would never have to feel again. She would not indulge in memories of the past, she told herself. Nor would she think about the Minneapolis soccer mom, a doctor's wife, recently wrenched from her suburban life and charged with crimes she'd committed nearly thirty years ago. But when she turned her mind away from these things, all she could remember was arguing and arguing against Claire's coming here, spoiling so much of Claire's last year at home, spoiling something between them.

The clock on the bell tower of the old library struck eleven, and Nora rose to head back to the Union, where Charlie and Claire would be waiting for her after Claire's registration session. The three of them had pored over the class catalogue the evening before, marveling at all the possibilities, making lists and alternate lists so Claire would be prepared to make the best of her scheduled time on the computer. She felt guilty again, thinking that Claire must have been disappointed this morning when Charlie appeared without her.

She walked up Kirkwood Avenue, past a low wall where a scruffy man with a graying ponytail sat strumming a guitar, a battered baseball cap with a scattering of coins in it at his feet. She paused at the Von Lee Theater, its red door padlocked, its marquee blank, its ticket window a makeshift kiosk layered with tattered, rain-spotted flyers. She and Tom had seen "The Graduate" there in the spring of 1968, and she remembered how the audience had stood as one, cheering, when Dustin Hoffman burst into the church, wild-eyed, crazy with love, and Katharine Ross turned, her face luminous at the sight of him.

"Go!" people in the theater yelled. "Fuck it! Go!"

They cheered when she gathered up the train of her wedding gown, stumbling in her high heels as she turned and headed up the aisle, then kicked free of them to run toward his outstretched hand.

It was only a movie. Still, Nora wondered what had become of them. If they had lasted beyond that final frame, there'd have been children, friends and relatives, jobs, cars, and houses to attend to. Long, mind-numbing days interspersed with heart-stopping, unexpected joys. Grief and disappointment with their terrible and wonderful surprises. They'd be looking back, trying to make sense of it all. It made her weary to consider it.

Heading back up the street again, she calculated what time they were likely to arrive home that evening, wondering if their friends Monique and Diane had thought to pick the ripe tomatoes in the garden. Conjuring up her kitchen, the glassed-in sunroom where ferns grew as big as bushes and the begonias and geraniums brought in from the window boxes thrived and bloomed all winter long. The bedroom where she and Charlie had slept together for more than twenty years now. The four-poster bed that his parents and grandparents had slept on before them, the wedding quilt that his mother, Jo, had made for them hung on stretchers above – too beautiful to use. The deep, comfortable easy chair Charlie had bought and set into a cozy corner of the room the day she agreed to move in with him, its red upholstery turned almost coral now from years of sunlight, its arms silky from wear. The oak table beside it cluttered with books.

Just hours now, and she would be there. In the morning, she would walk through the meadow of wildflowers she had sown, toward the break in the trees at the far edge marking the path that would carry her down through the woods to Lake Michigan, where she would fall fully and gratefully back into the life she'd so carefully made.

"Jane? Hey, Jane!"

She stopped short when the voice called out, turned instinctively, and saw that the man with the guitar had followed her. She stood, rooted to the spot, her heart racing.

"Jane?" he said again.

She tilted her head, as if confused. "I'm Nora Quillen," she said, brightly. "Sorry. You must have mistaken me for someone else."

The man raised an eyebrow. "Hey," he said. "Sorry. My bad – "

"No problem."

He nodded. But she felt his eyes follow her as she turned away and walked across Indiana Avenue toward the university gates.

PART ONE

The Expensive Moment

1965–1974

1

"Turn, Turn, Turn"

"Is that the college, honey?" her mother asked, as they turned off the highway toward Bloomington and a big limestone structure came into view.

"Mom, Jeez. That's the *football* stadium."

Jane's father gave a sharp glance to the back seat, but her mother just chattered on. "Janey, do you have the map? Do you know where we're going?"

Jane said the name of her dorm and her mother listened, pointing out street signs, as Jane read from the directions that had been included in her housing packet. It was Mrs. Barth's way not to acknowledge bad behavior but, instead, respond to the rudeness with exaggerated politeness that made Jane simultaneously furious and ashamed. The truth was, Jane didn't know much more about college than her mother did. She had set her heart on it long ago, in the first grade when the thrill of words revealing themselves, unlocking stories, had made her decide she would be a teacher when she grew up. But now that it was actually happening, she felt half-sick with dread. She'd never been away from home, except for overnights with friends and one miserable week at church camp when she was twelve. What if she got homesick? What if she hated her roommate – or worse, her roommate hated her? What if her roommate was rich, and Jane was embarrassed by all she didn't have? The five dollars allowance her mother had promised to send every week would cover only the barest expenses, and it would be awful to add embarrassment to the mix of guilt and resentment she knew she'd feel every time she opened up the envelope and found it here.

She should have let them talk her into going to the university extension at home, she thought, where most of the people from her high school went if they were ambitious enough to want to go to college. She should have been grateful for the opportunity to get any kind of education at all. But she had wanted more, even though she knew going away to college meant that her mother would have to work extra hours at the A&P, where she stood on her feet all day, checking out groceries. Her father would have more cause to stop at the Red Star Tavern each night after work and drink himself quietly, purposefully, into oblivion.

It had been a quiet, awkward trip, the air heavy with all they did not know how to say. Still, Jane felt the weight of her parents' love for her when her father turned the radio to a station that played the music she liked without her having to ask, and in her mother's determined cheerfulness, in the way she fussed over whether Jane had remembered to bring the stamps she'd bought for her and the roll of quarters for her washing. Her sisters, Amy and Susan, huddled near her in the back seat the whole way. Twelve and thirteen, they were sweet, spindly girls with white-blond hair. They'd learned muteness, too. Her brother, Bobby, had simply avoided the situation. When everything was loaded and they were ready to leave, he slid out from underneath the junker he was working on in the driveway, bid Jane a gruff goodbye, then slid right back under it again.

They passed the dorms on Fee Lane and then the new business building, where the street T-ed at the old brick stadium. "Okay, turn left here," Jane said, and they passed more dorms, a little shopping area. "Now right. That's it, there. The first tall one."

There were cars parked every which way, their trunks open. Suitcases, stereos, bicycles scattered on the sidewalk. Skateboarders clattered down the little hill from the dining hall: tanned girls in raggedy cut-off wheat jeans, their long hair flying, dodging frantic parents giving last-minute instructions to daughters who, momentarily, would be free do whatever they pleased.

Jane left her family standing on the sidewalk and, trying to look confident, headed toward the registration table to get her room assignment and pick up her key. There were signs welcoming the new freshmen and student guides to offer help and advice. One of them, a girl named Cindy, guided Jane through registration, then snagged a rolling luggage cart and followed to help unload her belongings.

She was tongue-tied by the girl's friendly questions about her hometown, her major, her hobbies, embarrassed by the inept introduction she made when they reached her family. Transferring her things from the car to the luggage cart, she was acutely aware of what the other girls had: typewriters; stereos and crates of albums; hooded hair-dryers, like the ones in beauty shops; and racks of Villager outfits. Her suitcase was a graduation gift, so brand-new that Cindy could probably tell from looking at it that she'd never been anywhere. If so, she didn't mention it, just chattered on about what a great place this was and how Jane was sure to love it, until she deposited them all at the elevators and moved on to her next good deed.

In the crush of new students and their parents waiting for the elevators, Jane and her family stood in the silence she had left.

"Jane." Amy tugged her sleeve. "Is your room on top?"

"It's on nine," she said. "Pretty close."

"There's eleven," Susan said. "I counted the rows of windows."

"Then can we go to eleven?" Amy asked. "Mom, can we go up and see what it's like at the top?"

A suntanned, freckled girl with long red hair, turned and smiled at her. "You can go all the way up to the roof, if your mom will let you. It's really cool. There's a big wall and you can look over it. You can see the whole campus from there."

"We'll see," Mrs. Barth murmured, before Amy could open her mouth. It was what she always said when she didn't want to say "no" in front of strangers.

The girl shook her hair away from her face and gave Jane a wicked grin. She got off on the ninth floor, too, and Jane watched her hurry off, then disappear into a room near the end of the corridor. She started down the hall, her dad pushing the luggage cart, her mom and sisters following.

"Here it is." She stopped before the closed door of 907. Taped to it was a sign, decorated with little red and white IU symbols that said "Jane Barth & Karen Conklin Live Here."

She placed her key in the lock, took a deep breath, and smiled, preparing to confront her roommate for the first time. But, although Karen had moved in, claimed a bed, a closet, and one of the two built-in desks on either side of the window, she wasn't there.

"Dear Jane," said the note pinned to the bulletin board. "As you can see, I went ahead and put my stuff away when I got here. But if you'd rather have a different desk or whatever, I'd be glad to trade. I've gone out with my boyfriend and won't be back until this evening. I look forward to meeting you then. Karen."

"Well, she's thoughtful," Jane's mother said, reading over her shoulder. "That's something, isn't it? I guess we'll be gone, though, by the time she gets back."

She sounded so wistful and, glancing at her, Jane understood, suddenly, that her mother could not imagine what her life would be like in this place. The truth was, she couldn't imagine it either, and she wished she had the courage to say this to her mother, to admit how scared she was that she'd feel lost and alone in this new life she'd been so insistent upon. No happier than she had been in high school. But she did not. Instead, she let her mother fuss over her, pretended to care which drawer was best for her nightgowns, which for her socks and underwear. Listened, again, to her instructions about laundry and assured her that she had every single thing she needed. When, finally, there was nothing left to do, she walked her family back down the corridor to the elevator and waited, zombie-like, for the moment it would open, swallow them up, and carry them away.

Alone in her dorm room, Jane studied the prom picture on her roommate's bookshelf. Even in a formal dress, Karen looked, well, *average*. Brown hair turned up in a flip, brown eyes. Jane could see in the way she smiled up at her boyfriend that she was the kind of girl who made up for not being pretty by being attentive.

He liked her a lot, in any case. Jane saw that in the way he smiled back at her. He was cute. And a baseball player, too, which she knew because there was a framed picture of him in his baseball uniform.

Karen's high school yearbook was shelved next to her new dictionary, and Jane opened it to the Class of 1965. There she was, the same smile in place, her hair in the same perfect flip she wore on prom night. Karen Conklin: Pep Club (1–4), French Club (1–4), Class Secretary (3, 4), Rotary Scholar.

Not too intimidating, Jane thought. Then she checked out the closet and was relieved to find that, although Karen had more clothes than she did, they weren't particularly stylish. She had a typewriter, which Jane hoped she might be able to borrow sometimes, a stereo, and a stack of albums – Johnny Mathis, Herb Alpert, Barbara Streisand, the first Beatles album. *Not* Bob Dylan or the Rolling Stones. She had a box of scented pink stationery, a makeup bag with tons more makeup than Jane was used to wearing herself – every color of eye shadow, pale lipsticks, and that thick foundation you put on your face with a sponge. There was a white leather Bible with her name imprinted on the front in gold, set on the table beside her bed.

"Snooping?"

Jane whirled around, blushing, and saw the girl with the red hair standing in the doorway. She grinned that same wicked grin, then came right on in and plunked down on Karen's desk chair. "Hey, don't feel bad. I snooped my roommate, too. I'm Bridget Kelly, by the way. 920. You're Jane, right?"

Jane nodded.

"So, what do you think?"

She laughed at Jane's blank expression. "About Karen," she said. "Your roommate? The one whose stuff you were just pawing through? Tell the truth or I'll tell her I caught you mooning over the picture of her boyfriend."

This was so obviously not a real threat that Jane burst out laughing. "She looks a little . . . perky," she said. "That scares me."

"Exactly what I thought when I spied on her moving in. I've been nosing around all day, checking people out." Bridget rolled her eyes. "Mr. Get Up and Get Going, that's the Judge. My dad. We left Evansville at *five*. He and my mom were on their way home by noon. No big deal to them. I'm the last of five kids – all girls. And me a mistake, if you want to know the truth of it. No kidding! My oldest sister, Kathleen, has a kid in junior high. Anyhow, my parents are used to all this. Not to mention ready for a little peace and quiet. We got my stuff unloaded and they were *gone.* Not that I had any problem with that. Man, I've been waiting for this moment ever since we brought Kath here when I was six."

She smiled. "Your little sisters will probably be the same way. Right now, they're probably thinking, I can't wait to grow up and go back there by myself and go up on the roof any damn time I want. That's why I came down. To see if you wanted to go check it out."

"Sure. Okay," Jane said.

They took the stairs, passing the doors to the tenth and eleventh floors to the one that opened out onto the roof, where a dozen or so girls were sunbathing. Jane blinked in the bright sunlight, thrilled by the sudden warmth of the sun on her skin, the scent of Coppertone, the music on a half dozen transistor radios drifting up into the air. Joining Bridget at the wall, she took a tentative look outward, and stepped back, breathless, at the sight of the campus spread out before them like a map of itself.

Later, after they showered and ate their first meal in the dining hall, they walked out into it, toward the Student Union, which Bridget said her sisters had told her was the place where the fraternity boys would come that night to check out the new crop of freshman girls.

They walked along a wooded path that ran aside a creek, which Bridget said was called the "Jordan River." Jane could see some of the old classroom buildings, limestone with leaded windows, and they seemed perfect to her – just like college ought to look. They emerged at Ballantine Hall, where Bridget said some of their classes would be, passed a pretty little stone chapel, where her sister, Colleen, had married in June.

"*Not* a Catholic wedding," she said, sternly. Then laughed.

The Union building looked like a castle to Jane, all peaks and turrets. They entered through an arched doorway and walked along the gleaming corridors, past a bakery and the bookstore to the Commons, where everyone hung out. It was packed, every table taken. But Jane and Bridget went through the line anyway, got Cokes and fries, and a table opened up as they emerged with their trays. They sipped their Cokes, mesmerized by the conversations buzzing all around them, the shouts of greeting, the hugs and even tears as friends reconnected after the long summer.

"Jane! Don't look right this second," Bridget whispered. "But there's this blond guy behind you. He's so *cute*. And he's with this good friend of mine from home. Okay. Now. He's talking to the girl wearing the pink culottes – "

Jane glanced back and knew instantly which boy she meant. He was built like a swimmer, compact and lean, his floppy blond hair streaked by the sun, his mischievous blue eyes full of light. His left arm was in a sling, his wrist wrapped in an ace bandage; there was a huge, painful-looking scrape on his right elbow. As Jane subtly shifted her chair for a better view, he slipped his arm from the sling, bent his legs and held his hands out in a surfer's stance.

"I kid you not," she heard him say. "Fifty miles an hour down that hill on my skateboard. No doubt. And a goddamn little kid comes tottering onto the sidewalk and I jump the curb to avoid him and totally lose it – and what does his mom do? Give me crap for being a bad example."

The girl laughed.

"Hey," he said, reinserting his arm into the sling. "It's a serious injury, man. Major sprain. Plus, it's my writing hand." He grinned. "I need a scribe, so I'm signing up for whatever Gilbert's taking."

"Sucker," the girl said, elbowing the boy standing beside him.

He shrugged and smiled.

"That guy he's with," Bridget whispered. "He's my friend. Tom Gilbert."

He was stocky, with dark, curly hair cropped short. Brown eyes. Out of her league, Jane knew. She glanced at him a second time and blushed, realizing he was looking at her. He smiled, but she turned away as if she hadn't noticed him. *Don't,* she thought. But of course Bridget waved and gestured him over to their table when the girl they had been talking to went on her way.

"Hey, Bridge." He pulled a chair over and sat down. "What's up? Who's your friend?"

Bridget introduced them, then to Jane's relief chattered on about moving in to the dorm and other people from home she'd already run into. From the corner of her eye, Jane watched the blond boy, who'd fed some quarters into the jukebox and was now flipping through the music charts, pushing buttons. When "Wooly Bully" started to play, he turned, zeroed in on Tom, and headed their way. Pete was his name.

"What happened to *you,*" Bridget asked when Tom introduced him, then listened, rapt, as he told the story they'd just overheard. She batted her eyelashes at him. "You poor thing," she said. "You need a nurse *and* a scribe."

"Job's open." Pete sat down beside her.

Boldly, Jane thought, Bridget took his bandaged hand and examined it. "I actually can do this," she said. "Wrap, I mean. I took a first aid class at the Y. For life guarding." She grinned. "You have no idea how talented I am."

"Yeah?" Pete grinned back. "Can you dance?"

Bridget gave her beautiful red hair a shake. "Tom," she said. "Tell him."

"She can dance," Tom said.

"Excellent," Pete said. "Party tomorrow night. Sig house. Want to come?"

"I'd love to," Bridget said.

Into the sudden, awkward silence that followed, Tom said, "Jane?"

"*Of course,* Jane's going," Bridget said.

"Do you want to?" Tom asked.

"Sure," Jane said, trying to sound nonchalant. "Yeah, okay."

She was mortified when, entering the dorm lobby the next afternoon, she saw him picking up the telephone – to call another girl, she assumed; one he actually liked – and she took a step backward, hoping to avoid him.

But he saw her and put down the receiver. "Jane! Hey, I came over to make sure about tonight. Bridget can be so – " Then, surprising her, he blushed. "I just wanted to make sure you really wanted to come to the party."

"I do," Jane said.

"Good. Well, then. Seven."

He grinned, offered his hand; they shook.

And he was gone.

Jane stood for a long while, still feeling the warmth of his palm against hers, elated, a little afraid to know that he had come in search of her.

"That's just like Tom," Bridget said when Jane told her. "Honest to God. He called me this morning and said, 'Do you think Jane really wants to go tonight?' I said, *Yes*. But I knew he didn't believe me." She laughed. "Man, you guys are perfect for each other. You think he's being polite and doesn't really like you, he thinks you're being polite and don't really like him. It's a damn good thing I'm around, that's all I have to say. Here – " She offered Jane a blue and maroon plaid madras shirt that still had the price tag on it. "This will look great with your hair. It's cool that we're exactly the same size, don't you think?"

"Bridget," Jane said. "This is brand new. You haven't even worn it yet."

Bridget rolled her eyes and pressed it upon her. "*Jane*. Here. Really. My sister Colleen took me shopping and we went totally nuts with my mom's charge card. She just graduated, Colleen did. So she knew exactly what everyone would be wearing, and she told my mom I *had* to have it all. So, *God*. There's plenty for both of us."

She said it blithely, as if the dismal state of Jane's closet had only to do with the lack of an older sister to help her shop for the right things.

The shirt *was* perfect, nicer than anything Jane had ever worn. And it did look good with her hair, which was sun-streaked from the summer. Perfectly straight, it had grown to her shoulders, finally, and she'd had it blunt-cut – like a surfer girl's. When she leaned forward, it felt like a silky curtain against her face.

"Okay," Bridget said, settling on a starched blue oxford, buffing her Weejuns with a damp towel. "I give up. Pete can take me or leave me." Then she threw herself backward onto the bed and lay, her arms and legs flung out in an X. "Aargh, I'm a wreck," she said. "A total nervous wreck. Are you?"

"*Yes,*" Jane said.

The party was in the attic of the Sigma Chi house, where no girls were supposed to be. James Brown was blaring on the stereo. People were dancing, the floor slick with spilled beer. Along one wall, there was a row of battered couches where sorority girls perched, laughing, on their dates' laps. The room was smoky, close. The red tips of cigarettes glittered in the dark corners.

"Watch out." That's what Karen Conklin had said the night before, when they were getting acquainted and Jane told her that she and Bridget had been invited to a fraternity party. "Those boys are wild," Karen said. "John – that's my boyfriend – he told me they ask out freshman girls, get them drunk and then – well, you know."

But Jane nursed a single beer most of the evening, and Tom didn't seem to notice. He talked to her. He held his cigarette between his thumb and index finger, taking deep drags. He blew the smoke out evenly, careful as a little kid trying to make perfect soap bubbles. He talked about school, about the guys he lived with. About mornings, hunting with his father – how the fog sat in little pockets in the hollows and his feet went numb with cold and time stopped. He talked for so long it seemed he'd been saving these things all his life, waiting for the moment she would walk into it so he could tell them to her.

Later, in his room, he pulled her toward him. *Now,* Jane thought. She hadn't dated much in high school; she'd never had a boyfriend. Mostly, she had obsessed over certain unattainable boys, shocked speechless on the rare occasion one of them ever said word to her. She had no idea what Tom expected of her now, or what she would say or do if it seemed wrong to her. She tried to concentrate on the bookshelves in the built-in desk they leaned against. Fat, leather-bound business textbooks. *A Farewell to Arms, The Catcher in the Rye.* The books made her feel a little better, but the dark shadow of the bed still frightened her.

He kissed her – a good kiss. She knew enough to know that. Then in what was almost like a dance step, he pushed her away so that they stood apart, just holding hands. "Don't be scared, Jane. I'm not in any hurry here."

"I'm not scared," she said.

"Yeah, you are. Hey, I don't bring girls up here all the time. This isn't a game with me." He lit a cigarette and blew smoke rings that dissolved into the room's gray corners. "Come on. Smile."

And she did, in spite of herself.

"Good." He smiled back.

She laughed a little, drifted over to the window. Outside the street lamps shone, and she could hear the music from the party. She felt him move closer. He stood behind her, not touching her, but so close that she could feel the rhythm of his breathing. There was the faint odor of tobacco mixed with the scent of English Leather. They stood there for a long time. Jane thought that if she raised her arm, his arm would raise, too. If she made a quick feint sideways, he would follow. She let out a deep sigh, and he encircled her.

"*Well?*" Bridget said, when they got back to the dorm. "I, personally, am besotted. Pete told me he'd teach me how to ride his motorcycle, can you believe that? My parents would kill me if they found out!" She threw up her arms in glee. "But they won't! They can't! I swear to God, I've waited *forever* to get here and tonight I realized I never even came *close* to imagining how cool it would actually be. Jane! My God, can you believe it? Me and Pete and you and Tom.

"So, okay," Bridget went on. "We've got the boy front covered. Now tell me what you think about Karen Conklin. The *truth* of what you think about her."

They'd fled to the lounge to talk, and Jane dreaded going back to her room where Karen would surely grill her about the party. The night before, she and Bridget had gotten off the elevator singing "Game of Love" at the top of their lungs and there was Karen emerging from 907, carrying a brand new pink plastic bucket with her toiletries in it. She wore a pink robe with roses on it and matching slippers. Her hair was in pink rollers.

"Hey!" Jane said. "Hi. I'm your roommate."

"I was *wondering* where you were." Karen gave her an assessing look. "It's really nice to meet you," she said, practically whispering. "But it's after hours now. Maybe you didn't realize we're supposed to be quiet in the evenings?"

"That would be *after* classes start," Bridget said.

Karen raised an eyebrow, moved past them, and disappeared into the bathroom. Later, she said to Jane, "Listen, I don't mean to butt in, but that girl is wild – *anyone* can see it, and you might want to be careful about hanging around with her. If you wreck your reputation the very first week you're here, *well . . .*"

"Jane?" Bridget said.

"She's horrible," Jane said.

Bridget smiled serenely. "Exactly my thought. And I saw her eating dinner with my roommate, Carla, who's just as big a drag as she is. So I'm thinking, let's switch."

"You can do that?" Jane asked.

"Yep. Colleen told me, 'If you get a dud for a roommate, figure out who you really want to live with and switch.' But she said you've got do it quick, before things get weird. So let's go down and talk to the dorm counselor about it right now. Get things fixed exactly the way we want them to be."

Bridget was a wonder, Jane thought. She convinced the dorm counselor to let them switch roommates. The next day, she marshaled Jane through registration, making sure they got as many classes together as they could. She shared Colleen's advice to think of college as a 9–5 job and, that first week, the two of them made a pact to get up no later than 8:00 every weekday morning, eat breakfast, and head for class or to the library. No napping in the afternoons, no lying around listening to music, no soap operas down in the lounge. Evenings and weekends were their own, free for hanging out together or dancing with Pete and Tom.

High school had been easy. Jane had grown up in a blue-collar town, and classes were pitched to the majority of students, who were there because they had to be, who expected no more out of life than a job at the steel mill that came with insurance benefits, three weeks of vacation every year, and the promise that you could retire to a little lake cottage someday, kick back, and do nothing at all – or, if you were a girl, to get married to someone with a job like that. Memorize, spit back the facts, and you were National Honor Society material. Here you had to think, which Jane found she liked every bit as much as dancing.

She loved staying up all hours with Bridget trying to puzzle out what a poem meant, or how the stuff of a story might be connected to an author's real life. She loved highlighting her copious notes, reducing the Civil War into an outline, then an anagram that held within it everything she knew, so that when she opened her blue book and wrote the letters on the inside cover, thoughts and facts blossomed out and onto the page as she answered the exam questions.

But she loved most walking through drifts of red and orange leaves on campus, her arms full of books, and glancing up to see Tom coming toward her. She still half-believed he'd walk right past, as if he'd never even met her. Never, ever was she prepared for the way his face lit up at the first sight of her. Walking up the steps to the fraternity house with him on Saturday nights, Jane quickened at the sound of music pouring from the open windows of the dining room, the sight of bodies moving in the haze of cigarette smoke. Inside, the long, scarred tables had been pushed against the walls; the band was set up in one corner: a whole family of colored people from Terre Haute, who came with parents and grandparents, little kids. Teenage sisters in short, spangly dresses and go-go boots, singing backup. They played Motown and the Blues so deafeningly loud that there was nothing to do but dance.

There was always a keg of beer hidden in the phone room just off the front hall. At first, Jane had hesitated: only the wild girls drank in high school. But a few beers – if she was careful – what could it hurt? The second one gave her a nice little buzz, the third dissolved her last shred of self-consciousness, and she was whirling, shouting the lyrics along with everybody else.

It was *fun.* She'd never had such pure fun, she thought. She'd never been so happy as she was dancing with Tom – Bridget and Pete circling like satellites. Wild, silly dancing: the Pony, the Swim, the Funky Chicken. Slow dances, feeling the length of Tom's body against her own, knowing soon they'd go upstairs to his room and collapse, kissing, the music coming right up through the ceiling so that it was as if they were still dancing, even then. One night, goofing around, they realized that their school pep songs were sung to the same tune, then that their thighs, pressing against each other, were exactly the same length, even though Tom was a full head taller. He'd caught her hand and held it to his, palm to palm, and they discovered that, though his palm was bigger, her fingers were longer, making their hands essentially the same size as well.

"See," he'd said. "One more reason you should fall in love with me."

The last weekend in October, he took her to see Peter, Paul & Mary in concert at the Auditorium. Just the two of them. Jane loved their music, the way there were *ideas* in it, the way it made her feel at the same time hopeful and sad. She had sat in the dark auditorium, Tom's arm around her shoulders, marveling that they were there before her, *real.* Proof somehow that she belonged in this larger world and that it had been there all along, just waiting for her – with Tom in it. Walking hand-in-hand through campus afterward, her head was still full of music; her heart full, too, for the way he had surprised her with the tickets. His *pleasure* in surprising her. He stopped and drew her to him in the shadow of a gingko tree.

"I love you, Jane," he said.

She couldn't make herself speak, just burrowed into his chest, breathed in the scent of him, her eyes burning with tears, and he held her tighter.

Till then he'd talked to her only in a teasing way about being in love. Love at first sight, he claimed – and she half-believed him, though it seemed incomprehensible to her. But this was different. She was scared, suddenly. Scared to say she loved him back for fear he'd change his mind and what would she do, now that she could no longer imagine her life without him in it? Scared of how loving Tom made her feel.

"Oh, man." Bridget smacked her hand against her head when Jane tried to explain her confusion. "Jane. Can't you see what this is *really* about? You feel guilty because the truth of what's making you so deliriously happy is making out like a fiend with him. Every single night. Wherever, whenever you can."

She hooted at Jane's embarrassment. "You'd have made a great Catholic, you know? Listen. There's not a thing in the world wrong with making out with someone you like. It's totally natural. It's . . . biological! And, *Jane,* Tom's completely trustworthy. You decide where you want him to stop, and he'll stop. You know he will.

"And just in case you're thinking we shouldn't be going up to their rooms like we do because it's against the rules," she added. "Forget that, too. It's not like it's immoral – and besides, what are they going to do if they find us? Send us to make-out jail?"

Jane laughed then. And Bridget was right; as far as Jane could tell, she was right about pretty much everything. Bridget could always tell which of the sorority girls were really nice and which ones were fake. She knew which boys to trust, which ones to avoid. She knew why Pete got too drunk sometimes, knew the meaning behind things he said and did that sometimes upset Jane or made her worry that Bridget might be in over her head with him.

"He's afraid," Bridget would say. "His parents give him all this money, all this stuff. They're competing for him, but they don't really care about him. Until he met me he was completely alone in the world, really – except for Tom, who's his friend. But, you know. Guys. *I'm* the one who understands him. And he's scared of that, you know? He doesn't even realize he's doing it, but he tests me sometimes –

"Like the other night, when he did the Alligator at the party. He wasn't *that* drunk. I know exactly how much he drank, and it wasn't that much. Plus, we'd had that huge pizza. He did the Alligator to see if I'd do it with him. Big deal. You throw yourself on the floor and writhe around to the music and that's supposed to be the be-all and end-all of depravity? I can do that. It's stupid. But funny. Who gives a shit what those sorority girls think?" She grinned at Jane. "You should have tried it."

"And wreck *your* Villager outfit?" Jane said wryly.

Bridget laughed. "Honestly, Jane, the best thing we ever decided was not to go through rush," she said. "I look at all those girls in church clothes lined up outside the houses just waiting for a chance to go in and grovel for a bid so they can join up and get bossed around by a bunch of prudes. Uh-uh. Not me."

"Me either," Jane had said, relieved not to have to admit she couldn't have afforded it.

Happy, utterly present in this new life, Jane began to dread her regular call home on Sunday evenings: the forced cheerfulness in her mother's voice, the eagerness with which she asked about friends and classes. Still, she couldn't have explained why she didn't tell her mother about Bridget or Tom right from the start, or why she let her believe that she and Karen Conklin were not only still roommates, but had become friends and spent all their free time together. Jane liked to think it was because she believed her mother felt connected to Karen, having read her thoughtful note that first day, and wouldn't worry about Jane being lonely. In darker moments, though, she knew it was pure selfishness that made her keep this happiness to herself.

The day before Thanksgiving she climbed on the Greyhound bus, fearful that, once home, the growing confidence she'd felt in the past months, the sense of belonging would completely dissolve. She tried to read, study, sleep, but ended up staring out of the window at what seemed like an endless number of small towns and stubbled cornfields as the bus wound its way north, through Indiana. The sky was gray; even so, Jane saw the cloud of smog hanging over her hometown well before she saw the first sprawl of houses or the tall, spewing smokestacks of the steel mills.

Her father was waiting at the station, smoking a cigarette, shy and awkward as a teenage boy. She smelled whiskey on his breath when he embraced her, his fortification for anxious moments like this one – or maybe just to get him through the day. Walking through the front door of their little tract house, it seemed to Jane as if she was looking through the wrong end of a telescope. Everything looked so small, so close. The worn carpet, the flickering TV screen, the Formica dinette table set for dinner. There were Amy and Susan, wearing the red Indiana sweatshirts she'd saved up to buy for them. And Bobby, stretched out on the sofa, taller, skinnier, and more sullen than she'd remembered him to be.

"I fixed scalloped potatoes and ham for dinner!" Mrs. Barth said. "Your favorite. It's ready any time. You're hungry, aren't you? After that long bus trip – " She stepped back and looked at her daughter. "Oh, honey, I'm so glad you're home. It's so good to see you."

Jane wasn't glad to be home, she wasn't the least bit hungry. What she wanted to do was collapse right where she stood and sleep until it was time to go back to Bloomington on Sunday morning. But she attempted a smile. Be nice, she told herself; pretend you're thrilled to be here. For three days, be the Jane they need you to be. But when she took her place at the dinner table, it seemed to her as if she'd never even been away.

2

"Blowin' in the Wind"

She had watched them on campus in the fall, secretly fascinated by their intensity: long-haired girls; thin, scraggly-bearded boys in wire-rimmed glasses, wearing black turtleneck sweaters and jeans, fatigue jackets, or battered tweeds. Green Army knapsacks heavy with books flung over their shoulders.

"Greenbaggers," Tom and Pete called them. "Baggers" sometimes. They made fun of them when they saw them in the Commons, gathered around one of the big tables arguing about books or politics. Every time they walked past the Students for a Democratic Society's table in the Union, they grabbed a handful of anti-war pamphlets, tore them up and threw them in the trash.

"Goddamn pinkos," they'd say.

But Jane thought they were more like beatniks. She'd read about beatniks, fantasized about visiting Greenwich Village someday, with its clubs and coffeehouses. Imagining college life, she had thought it might be rather like that and, though she loved the life she had walked into the moment she met Tom, sometimes, walking through the Commons, she peered down the stairs leading to the Kiva, the campus coffeehouse where Baggers hung out, talking, listening to folk music or reading poetry in a haze of cigarette smoke, with a small, secret measure of longing.

She was surprised and a little nonplussed to walk into her honors lit seminar on the first day of the second semester and find a half-dozen Baggers in the classroom, along with the serious, neatly dressed, eager-to-please students like herself. The professor regarded the way the students had divided themselves on the two sides of the room with an expression of wry amusement and made them pull their chairs into a circle.

"There," she said. "At least this way you have to look at one another."

There were just twelve of them, small classes being the greatest advantage of the honors program, Professor Berkovitz had explained to Jane when he recommended her for the seminar. He'd been impressed by her comments during the semester, he said. Her writing skills were excellent. She was clearly capable of a greater challenge.

Back from semester break, she'd gone to the English section in the bookstore and found the shelf where the books for the class were listed: English 103 Honors. The sign alone had made her smile, and she'd taken the books from the shelf one by one and leafed through them feeling connected to the students who had used them before and left evidence of their thoughts and ideas in crabbed margin notes and highlighted passages. She felt proud to have been recognized by her favorite professor, eager to begin the class, which she imagined would be like his class – but even better because everyone in it would care about what they were reading and think about it. Everyone would have something interesting and important to say. This new professor would sit on the edge of his desk, smoking while they talked, as Professor Berkowitz had, commenting now and then, directing the discussion to deeper, more satisfying levels that at the same time made students feel eager to learn, curious – and smarter than they really were.

She hadn't expected a woman, especially one like Professor Farlow. She was tall and stern, her long, dark hair streaked with silver. She was dressed in black, with a colorful, gypsy-like shawl draped over her shoulders; she wore a man's gold watch on one wrist and, on the other, what must have been a dozen thin gold bracelets that jangled whenever she moved. She wore no makeup; her thin lips were colorless, her black eyes snapping with intelligence.

"Well," she said, with no introduction other than having written her name and office hours on the blackboard. "Let's see what you know about Emily Dickinson." She peered at her class list. "John Sargent?"

A boy wearing a Sigma Nu pin sat straight up in his seat.

"You are John Sargent?" Professor Farlow asked.

He nodded.

"Emily Dickinson?" she prodded.

"Um. She wrote poems. She never got married," he said.

Professor Farlow nodded. "Caroline Swayzee?"

"She always dressed in white," a mousy girl responded. "She kept her poems in a dresser drawer and never showed them to anybody."

"She was a recluse," Cathy Crowe, a bagger girl, said. "Kind of crazy."

Professor Farlow raised an eyebrow. "Jane Barth, can you add anything more – literary?"

"Her rhymes – " Jane wracked her brain for the term her high school English teacher had used to describe them. "Well, they don't rhyme exactly? They . . ."

"Aha," Professor Farlow said. "A piece of information about the *poems* of Emily Dickinson. As opposed to the *myth* of Emily Dickinson. Words on the page. That is what we'll be considering for the next eighteen weeks together. Words on the page – and their power." She glanced at Jane. "Slant rhyme, Miss Barth. That is the term you were searching for."

Pens scratched as students wrote it on the first page of their new notebooks.

"As in 'Tell the truth and tell it slant,'" Professor Farlow went on. "Which is the poem we will be considering this afternoon. Page 248 of your text. An excellent introduction to Miss Dickinson's poetry, as you will see."

There was the sound of pages rustling, then quiet, and all eyes were on Professor Farlow, who recited the poem from memory.

She repeated it. "Now look at the words," she said. "What is Miss Dickinson saying here?"

"Lie," said one of the Baggers. Then muttered, "Which is such a load of crap."

Jane was shocked by his response, but Professor Farlow smiled. "In a sense, that is exactly what Miss Dickinson advises. But Mr. – " She glanced at her class list, then splayed her hands, inviting the boy to say his name.

"Dugan," he said, blushing. "Wayne Dugan."

"Mr. Dugan, then. If you will look a little more closely at the first two lines, I think you'll see that's not *quite* it." She leaned forward, holding his gaze in hers, and repeated, "Tell all the Truth but tell it slant – /Success in Circuit lies.' What do the lines actually say?"

"Try to fake people out," he said. "Which is also a load of crap."

"Good. Miss Dickinson does, indeed, advise us to fake people out in the service of the truth. 'A load of crap,' however. Where, in the text, does Miss Dickinson tell us that?"

Several students snickered, and Jane had to bite her lips to keep them from curving into a smile. But she was riveted by the scene unfolding. Wayne Dugan glared at the professor, who gazed back at him with a calm, curious expression.

"She uses all that fancy, flowery language to tell you to lie," he said. "Which I think is a load of crap."

"Ah. *You think.*" Professor Farlow said.

"Yeah. I think."

Professor Farlow waited.

"You're saying I shouldn't think?" he asked. "Or maybe you think I should think what *you* think?'

"Certainly not!" Professor Farlow said. "I am only asking you to connect what you think to the words on the page. The text. I am asking you to explain how you got from Miss Dickinson's advice to fake people out in the service of the truth to – "

"*All* lying's crap," he said. "Look at what they're telling us about Vietnam, for example. Lies. They're telling them slant, all right. So I'm supposed to agree with *Miss* Dickinson that that makes it okay?"

Patiently, Professor Farlow directed him back to the subject at hand. "All lying's crap. Where, in the *poem,* do you see that?"

Wayne blushed brick red.

"In the poem," Professor Farlow repeated.

"It's not *in* the poem," Wayne said.

"Bravo!" She beamed at him with genuine delight. "Yes! You're absolutely right, Mr. Dugan, and in seeing this you have brought us face-to-face with the most crucial aspect of our work this semester: to learn the difference between what's on the page and what we *think* about what's on the page."

She turned away from him, addressed the class. "It isn't easy," she said. "But if you can keep these two things separated, if you can enter into the discourse of literature with an open, curious mind, I assure you that what you think about anything, *everything* will be greatly enriched and all the world will be better for it.

"I commend you for challenging me, Mr. Dugan," she concluded. "I hope all of you will follow this example, testing the limits of your knowledge and understanding during our time together." She took a sheaf of papers from a battered leather bag and set them on her desk. "That is all for today," she said. "Quite enough for you to think about! You may pick up a copy of the syllabus on your way out. Be prepared to discuss the Dickinson poems listed next time we meet." She gave them a dazzling smile, slung the bag over her shoulder, and was gone.

"Whoa," the Sigma Nu said. "I'm out of here. She's crazy."

"Me, too," said the Bagger girl, Cathy. "I don't need this shit, you know?"

"I like her," Wayne Dugan said. "She's not boring. And the literary Miss Barth?" He grinned at Jane, a friendly grin that made her grin back in spite of herself. "What about you?"

She shrugged, half-attracted to him, half-repulsed by him. He was short and skinny, with wildly curly black hair. He wore wire-rimmed glasses and ragged jeans. His green Army bag was stuffed with books and political tracts.

As the weeks went by, he often caught up with her after class and walked as far as Jordan Hall, where she turned off to go back to the dorm. He'd taken Professor Farlow's words to heart that first day and tenaciously pursued the precise meaning of every text they considered, as if it were a game. But he wouldn't stop there. "What this makes me *think* is . . ." he'd say, and connect Emily Dickinson, Shakespeare, Faulkner with what was happening in his own life. In the world. Now.

"So what do *you* think?" he'd ask, walking along beside her. "You're always so quiet in class."

Jane was afraid of him, afraid of thinking the way he thought – though she often found herself pondering the intense discussions that he and a few others had with Professor Farlow in class for days afterwards. Writing the required papers for the class, her mind opened and produced ideas on the page that surprised her – and more than once had prompted Professor Farlow to write "Nice insight" in the margin with her red pen.

"Come on, Barth," Wayne had said after the class discussion on *All Quiet on the Western Front,* which had degenerated into a shouting match between Wayne and one of the fraternity guys about the stupidity of war and, from there, the particular stupidity of the war cranking up in Vietnam. "Admit it. You cannot read that book and not think about what's going on there."

She was too embarrassed to admit that the book hadn't made her think of Vietnam until it came up in class, because Vietnam just wasn't something she thought much about. The war was about stopping Communism, she knew that. Some people thought it was wrong to be there, but she didn't know exactly why.

In fact, what *All Quiet on the Western Front* had made her think about was World War II.

In her high school history class, she had learned about the rise of Hitler, about Pearl Harbor. Her teacher had been a bomber pilot, stationed in England, and told stories of the brave men he had known and the missions they flew. They'd studied diagrams of the D-Day Invasion, the Battle of the Bulge, battles her own father had fought in but would never discuss.

But until she read *All Quiet on the Western Front,* she could not imagine what war – any war – was actually like. Nor had she realized that thinking as if inside another person's head could so drastically change your own point of view. Reading, she became the young German soldier. At the end of his story, herself again, she wept for him. For the stupidity of war, regardless of what side you were on.

Was this what had happened to her father, she wondered? Is this what he *knew?* Why, years later, he lay on the couch each night, anaesthetized? Why he woke at midnight and drove to the Red Star Tavern where others like him gathered to keep from remembering?

The book had disturbed her profoundly, but she did not know how to talk to Wayne or anybody else about it. The next time the Baggers gathered in Dunn Meadow to demonstrate against the Vietnam War she paid attention, though. There were maybe a hundred of them gathered around a makeshift platform, shouting, "Get out now!" Their fists raised, their picket signs bobbing up and down. It was an unseasonably warm day in March, the Moody Blues pouring out of an open window on the second story of the Sigma Chi house, drowning out the words of the ex-Marine who'd taken the podium. She and Bridget sat on the steps, watching Tom and Pete and some others heckle the demonstrators. The boys were laughing, a little drunk already – the demonstration no more than the beginning of Saturday night. They'd filled their beer mugs from the keg hidden in the phone room and they were dancing, half to the rhythm of the music, half to their own obscenities. Before long, they were talking about calling up the Delts and starting an impromptu football game in the midst of the demonstration. Or just going over and cracking some heads.

Across the street, someone fiddled with the microphone and the Marine's words were momentarily clear. "*Look* at what we're doing in Vietnam," he said.

When he finished speaking and stepped down, Jane saw that his right arm was gone, the empty sleeve of his uniform shirt pinned neatly over the stump. The Baggers clapped and whistled. Some took up the chant again, "Get out! Get out!"

"Get *fucked,*" Pete yelled.

Bridget laughed, along with the boys.

"What?" she said, when Jane stood suddenly.

But Jane didn't answer. She was watching Wayne Dugan emerge and move toward the platform, fist raised. In class, he had said it was patriotic to dissent. You were *obligated* to dissent, if you cared about your country and believed it was doing something wrong. It was right there in the Declaration of Independence. He'd read the passage aloud to them.

Now he and some others began to unfurl a large American flag, but the wind caught an end of it, which dipped and dragged along the muddy ground as they struggled to regain control, and this set Tom and Pete moving toward them. A half-dozen of their fraternity brothers followed, a small army of navy blue London Fog jackets, and from the upstairs windows another dozen hollered their support.

The crowd parted to absorb them, then scattered when Pete punched one of the Baggers holding the flag. There was a loud squawk as the microphone toppled over on the platform, then the voice of a campus policeman telling the demonstrators to disperse. In the meadow, the Sigma Chis squared off with the Baggers who remained, Wayne Dugan among them.

Watching them, Jane felt exactly the way she'd felt the day Tom borrowed Pete's motorcycle and took her for a ride, driving so fast that when she looked down, the white staccato lines along the center of the asphalt became one long blur. She held onto him so tightly her arms ached. He glanced back, grinning, and the bike wobbled, righted. *Whaaa.* A car horn bleated, fading as Tom careened around, outdistanced it. She had been furious, thrilled, and scared to death – all in a mix.

She thought, go inside. Don't look. But, rooted to the spot, she watched Tom struggle with Wayne, each of them trying to claim the flag. Tom stepped back for an instant, catching Wayne off-guard, and decked him. Then, as Wayne reeled backward, Tom grabbed the flag, and he and Pete carried it aloft across the street. They ran past the girls, up the steps, into the house. Bridget followed them.

Jane sat outside by herself a while, not sure what she should do. When the sun went down and she felt chilled, she went inside, up the side stairs to Tom's room, where she was not supposed to be. The others had left and he was sitting on his bed, a can of beer in one hand.

He grinned and opened his arms to her. "Jane! Where were you? Man, could you believe that fiasco with the flag? Those asshole Baggers."

She said, "Don't you think they have a right to say what they believe?"

She had to say it twice before it dawned on him that she was serious.

"Are you kidding?" he asked. "Did you see them? Dragging the flag around in the goddamn mud? Okay, maybe things got a little out of hand, but – "

"Out of hand," she said. "You beat the shit out of that one guy. You hurt him."

"Guys fight," he said. "Come on. Have a beer, calm down. It's not that big of a deal."

"I don't want a beer," she said.

Tom stood up, set the can of beer on the table. "What's with you, Jane? What's this sudden deep concern about the Baggers, anyway?"

"I'm not concerned about the Baggers," she said. "I just think – "

"What? You think *what?*" He yanked the flag from the window behind him and threw it at her feet. "If you're so worried about their goddamn flag, why don't you just go take it back to them?"

They glared at each other, then at the flag, which lay in a crumpled heap between them.

Finally, because she didn't know what else to do, she gathered up it up and rushed from the room, down the stairs, out the door. She would not cry. Not until there was no chance anyone could see her.

By now it was dusk, the campus deserted. It felt like winter again, puddles the sun had made icing up at the edges. A light rain began to fall and she shivered in her light jacket. She felt stupid carrying the flag, angry with Wayne Dugan for getting her into this predicament in the first place. He was always so sure he was right – about everything. She crossed the street, glanced to make sure nobody was looking, then left it balled up on a bench at the edge of Dunn Meadow.

Once in her room, she locked the door behind her. She did not turn on the light. She sat on her bed, her back against the wall, her legs stuck straight out, determined to concentrate on the silver slant of rain framed by the window. But she could not stop thinking about what had happened in Tom's room.

What was wrong with her, anyway? She knew nothing about the war in Vietnam, really. Plus, hadn't she been as disrespectful to the flag as Tom had been, dumping it on a park bench because she was too embarrassed to be seen carrying it?

So he had lost his temper. So what? What right had she to judge him over a stupid fight when there were dozens – maybe hundreds – of things she'd seen him do that tipped the balance the other way. The ragged old guy who hung out near the square, looking for a handout. Most everyone just ignored him, but didn't Tom always stop and give him a quarter? Wasn't he constantly out in the parking lot of the Sig house working on the old, beat-up car of one of the cooks, buying parts with his own money because he knew she couldn't afford them? And as for fighting, hadn't he also decked Jack Newley who'd dragged a couple of pledges up in his room, gotten them drunk, and then paddled them with one of those fraternity paddles after he ordered them to do pushups and they collapsed, slipping and sliding in their own vomit?

"Jesus," he'd said afterwards, rubbing his scraped knuckles. "What's the matter with him, anyway? Causing misery just because he *can*."

Jane slid down onto the bed, curled up with her arm over her eyes. She didn't even *care* about the war; it had nothing to do with her. What had she been thinking to risk the only real happiness she'd ever known for some *idea* put in her head by a guy like Wayne Dugan, who as far as she could tell spent his whole life pissed off about everything. She was stupid, *stupid* – and now Tom knew. Already, she missed him so much. But hadn't she known, deep in her heart, that it was just a matter of time before he figured out how pathetic she really was and fell out of love with her?

When the phone rang, she didn't answer it. Bridget, she thought. She wasn't ready to talk to her. But it rang twenty, thirty, forty times and, finally, she picked up the receiver, resigned to it.

"I'm downstairs," Tom said. "We have a date, right?"

She was so shocked to hear his voice she couldn't answer.

"Jane? Jane, look, I – "

"But I'm not ready," she said. "I – "

"It's okay. I'll wait for you."

She threw on some clean clothes, put on some makeup. She waited five minutes at the elevator, agitated, her heart pounding, watching the lights above the door blink as it stopped and started, collecting girls and carrying them down toward their Saturday night dates, then finally gave up and rushed down nine flights of stairs, surprising Tom who was searching for her among the girls spilling out of the elevator.

"Jane!" he said, and she stepped into his arms. For a long moment, he held her so tightly she could hardly breathe. "I'm sorry," he said, stepping back so he could look at her. "You were right. I was a jerk about the flag. I mean it. I'm sorry."

"No," she said. "I was – "

"Hey." Tom drew her close again, cupping her head with his hand. "Forget it, okay? Jane? I don't give a shit about any of that."

"Me, either," she whispered, against his chest.

"Let's go, then. I'm starving."

But he continued to hold her close to him as they walked out into the chilly evening together.

3

"Unchained Melody"

Jane set out for the bus stop every day in the mid-afternoon, the hottest part of the day, carrying a sack lunch and whatever book she was reading. It was a half-hour's walk, through neatly laid out subdivisions of little square houses like the one she lived in with her family, past the swimming pool in the park full of happy, screaming children, past the public library to which she'd ridden her bike most summer afternoons of her childhood. She longed to walk up the steps, into the cool of the little stone building and lose herself reading in a quiet corner. But she trudged on, tired, bored nearly to tears, the hot concrete burning up through the thin soles of her loafers. The new trees lining the streets gave little shade, and she was sticky with sweat, nauseous from the heat by the time she climbed on the wheezing bus and sat down next to an open window.

She clocked in at her summer job at the bookbindery at three and walked through the factory, past the big machines spitting out pastel maps that would be bound into the atlases she would spend the next eight hours packing into cardboard boxes. The work was mind-numbingly repetitive, the factory hot, her fellow workers unfriendly. But a year of college had taught her something about irony, and she could appreciate the image of herself, her own world shrunk to this workstation, her shoulders aching from packing an endless supply of atlases, worlds she longed to see.

At the dinner break, she went to a table in the far corner of the cafeteria and read while she ate the meal her mother had packed for her. She and Bridget had decided to make their way through the list Professor Farlow had handed out the last week of class: "Some Novels Every Serious Reader Should Know." They'd gone to the bookstore and bought used, battered copies cheap. She was at the D's. Halfway through Dreiser's *American Tragedy,* mesmerized by the unfolding story of the young man who dared to dream. The sounds of the factory around her enhanced the effect of the book, so that when the whistle blew she was momentarily both in the book and in the real, grim world of the factory. Herself and the desperate young man in the book who was willing to do whatever he had to do, *anything,* not to fall backward into the small, mean life the world intended for him to live.

When she emerged from the bookbindery a few minutes after eleven, her father was waiting for her, smoking, listening to big band music on the car radio. She could hear it through the open window as she came across the parking lot – Glenn Miller, the Dorsey Brothers. The music of his youth, music he had danced to with her mother when they were not much older than she was now. Happier times, when he could not have imagined himself in a dark car at midnight waiting for a resentful daughter's shift to be over so that he could drive her home, the last place she wanted to be, without a single meaningful word passing between them.

There was music that would always make her happy, too. She would never hear James Brown or the Righteous Brothers without thinking of the smoky dance floor at the Sigma Chi house. The Supremes would always make her think of Bridget, who could not hear them without singing along. The Beatles singing "Things We Said Today" would always be on the radio of the car Tom borrowed the night before she left to come home for the summer, the words of the song tangled up with the words he spoke trying to make her feel better. "I love you. It won't be that long, you'll see."

Just like certain songs would always pitch her into despair. Wherever she was, whoever she turned out to be, she knew that The Mamas & the Papas singing "Monday, Monday" would bring back the loneliness, the misery of entrapment she felt at home with her family this summer. The long, hot walk to the bus stop every afternoon; the high windows of the factory darkening slowly toward night. The sense that she'd found and lost herself, her own real life, the feel of time stretching out endlessly toward the moment when she could return to Bloomington in September.

It occurred to her one night, quite suddenly, that maybe the music her father listened to didn't bring back happy memories at all, but rather wartime memories. The years he and her mother had spent apart. Things that had happened during the war that he'd rather not remember. He'd been in England for a while, then France and Belgium for the worst of it. He never talked about it, though; and the only time Jane pressed him about what he remembered, her mother said afterwards, "Leave him be, Jane. He had a hard time in the war. He just wants to put it behind him."

"But I wasn't asking him about the war," she said. "I was asking about London and Paris. What he saw – "

"Jane."

That's all, just her name, and the war and everything surrounding it became one more thing they didn't talk about. Like the drinking, like money problems, like Bobby's bad attitude, the fact that he'd skipped school so much in the last year that he'd flunked most of his classes, and that his friends were greasers – boys with hopped-up cars and bad attitudes, going nowhere.

"How'd it go?" her father would ask each night when she slid into the passenger's seat of the car after her shift. She'd shrug and look away. If she answered his question, really answered it, she'd have to say, I hate the job. I hate everything about my life here, and if I could figure out a way to leave now and never, ever come back, I swear I'd go.

Sometimes in the silence that fell between them on the drive home, she'd remember standing at the back door of the house they lived in when she was a little girl, waiting for him to come home from work. How her heart lifted when she saw him turn from the bus stop and start down the alley toward home. Her mother, pregnant with Susan, was busy in the kitchen; Bobby was busy playing. But she waited. She wanted, always, to be the first one he saw. Thinking of her five-year-old self, tears sprung to her eyes and grief washed over her.

But wasn't grief something you felt when someone had died? How could it be grief when there was her father, sitting right beside her?

Just get to August, she told herself again and again. She, Tom, and Bridget planned to meet at Pete's house in Indianapolis for a long weekend, and she counted the days as she worked, making each atlas she packed count for a day. Then, when she had counted all the days, each atlas packed and sent along the conveyor belt into oblivion became something that pained or annoyed her. The way her father still cut up her meat each night and handed her the plate, as if in his alcoholic haze he had forgotten she and her siblings were not still little children. Her sisters' bony, sunburned shoulders. Bobby's cracked, dirty fingernails. The bus fare her mother left on the dinette table for her every morning. She fell into bed beside her sleeping sisters when she got home near midnight, then lay, wakeful, until she heard her mother put away whatever housework had kept her busy all evening.

"Hon, don't you want to come to bed?" she'd say to Jane's father, who by then was sleeping – no, passed out – on the couch.

He'd growl at her. She'd stand a moment, looking at him, then go to bed by herself. She was exhausted; she was always exhausted. It was no time before Jane could hear her light snoring. Quietly, she got up, her sisters stirring, sighing back into each other's arms. She got the locked book satchel she kept tucked deep in her closet and crept past her father, away from the smirking, self-satisfied stars on *The Johnny Carson Show,* and out the back door to a battered chaise lounge she'd bought herself when she was in high school for sunbathing in the backyard. She put an oxford shirt on over her cotton nightgown. Who would see her?

Her father, maybe. Often he got up around two, got in the car and drove through the quiet neighborhood. Jane knew he was going to drink somewhere, probably the Red Star. If he said anything to her about being up so late, which she knew he probably wouldn't, she'd threaten to tell her mother. Who also knew where he went. But would do almost anything not to acknowledge it.

She'd lie back on the chaise, staring up at the stars. She'd taken Astronomy last semester and could name the constellations, though they were hard to see in the smoggy air. It pleased her, nonetheless.

There was so much to know. She felt small beneath the stars, but in a good way. Not small in the way she felt here in this place.

In time, she unlocked the satchel with the silver key she kept on a chain around her neck. She brought out her little Hallmark calendar and colored in the whole square of the day with a black ballpoint pen, pressing so hard that the paper became crinkly beneath it. She'd count the days again, though she always knew exactly how many there were to August 4, which she had highlighted in bright yellow. On that Thursday morning, she'd take the Greyhound bus to Indianapolis, Tom and Bridget would drive up from Evansville, and they'd have four days together. After that, there'd be less than a month to endure before school started.

She and Bridget had planned the trip obsessively – down to what they'd wear, what they'd read, sunbathing, what meals they'd attempt to the cook for the boys. They'd bought bikinis the week before they left for summer break. Hers still had the tags on it. It was in the satchel, too, along with Tom's fraternity pin and her journal, and after she'd colored in the square and counted the days, she'd take it out and look at it, imagining herself in a lounge chair by Pete's pool, tanning in the sun. His parents would be in Europe, so it would just be the four of them. They'd sleep with the boys for the first time, she and Bridget had decided. Who'd know? She'd told her parents she'd been invited to a girlfriend's house for a dorm floor reunion.

"Will Karen be there?" her mother had asked.

"Probably," she said, not only continuing to let her mother believe she and Karen were roommates but that they were the closest of friends, continuing to keep Bridget and Tom a secret – able to keep them a secret because the mail came when nobody else was home and she could retrieve the letters they sent before anyone saw them.

Fat letters from Bridget with news about skirmishes with her parents, who simply could not accept that their baby girl had grown up and had her own life now. They set curfews, which she broke – sometimes just on principle. She and Tom would stay out late, talking, for no other reason than to assert her right to do as she pleased. "About you," she wrote. "So in case you worry about what we're up to, don't."

Tom's letters were short, with a summary of what he'd done the past days. Worked at the pool, mowed the lawn, worked in his mom's garden. He wrote about fishing with his dad, hanging out with his high school buddies. He'd always include some funny, outrageous thing Bridget had said or done. "I miss you," he always said at the end. Underlining all three words. "Love, Tom."

Lying under the stars, her body tingled just thinking of him, thinking of where and how he'd touched her and the way his warm breath felt against her skin, his lips whispering endearments as they moved from her mouth, to her ear, her neck, her breasts. She touched herself here, there, something she'd never, ever done before. Something she felt strange and guilty about. Yet she could not stop. She'd lie there on the chaise lounge, her eyes closed, her face wet with dew, and imagine her hands were Tom's. Imagine him there, beside her.

She drifted to sleep sometimes, waking surprised and a little embarrassed to find her hands cupping her breasts or between her legs. She wouldn't move them, though. She'd lie perfectly still, her fingers lightly pinching her nipples or pressing against the warm, wet place between her legs until waves of desire made her body arch up and she shuddered, breathless. It scared her, what she might do to continue to be able to feel this way. She wanted so much. She wanted everything, though she couldn't have said what "everything" meant.

Finally, there he was. He stood, smoking, on the little slice of sidewalk at the edge of the parking bay, and when the bus pulled in she sat for a long moment, looking at him until he saw her framed by the window and her own true self was shocked back into being with his sudden, dazzling smile. He tossed his cigarette to the pavement, took a step forward. She gathered her things, hurried down the aisle and stepped down into his open arms.

"Jane," he said, into her hair. Just that.

She said nothing, only burrowed her head into the dent just above his collar bone that she loved, breathed in the scent of him: smoke and soap and English Leather.

"Jesus, I've missed you," he said.

"Me, too," she whispered. "*I've* missed me." And burrowed deeper into him, squeezed her eyes tight to keep back the tears that threatened to come.

"Let's run away," he said. "I've got Pete's Corvette. He wouldn't care; his dad would just buy him another one. Hell, now that Bridget's here he probably wouldn't even miss it. I haven't seen either one of them since we got here this morning. I've had to sit out by the pool, nursing my beer, all alone."

"Poor baby," Jane said.

He grinned, kissed her, then stepped away and grabbed her hand. "Let's go," he said. "You won't believe Pete's place. There's a built-in beer keg, for Christ's sake. It's amazing."

"Oh!" was all she could say when they got there. She felt embarrassed stepping into the foyer with its marble floor, its crystal chandelier. What would Pete think if he could see her parents' house, the world she'd come from this morning?

She thought of the pile of beautifully ironed clothes her mother had set on her dresser the night before. Jane had meant to iron them herself when she got home from work; she'd told her mother she would iron them. But there they were.

"I didn't have anything extra to give you for your trip," she said, when Jane asked why.

Which shouldn't have made Jane angry, but it did. And, of course, guilty – for countless reasons, not the least of which was that she had lied about where she would be this weekend. She thanked her mother for the ironing, but couldn't make it sound sincere. She couldn't make what her mother had done for her, what her mother wanted and needed to do for her, touch her. If she did that, how could she continue to allow her whole family to make the sacrifices she knew they were making so that she could have this new life? Sacrifices she knew were way too much to ask.

Don't spoil this, she said to herself. *Don't think about her, all the ways you've hurt her.*

How you know you'll hurt her again and again.

Then Bridget appeared, radiantly disheveled, at the top of the beautiful staircase and hurried down into Jane's arms. "God, I thought this weekend would never come," she said. "One more day of teaching swimming lessons and I'd have drowned a six-year-old, just for the pleasure of it. Oh, Jane, I've missed you so much. And here we are!" She stepped back, flung her arms out to encompass the house, the pool that Jane could see through the French doors in the next room.

Pete watched, his hands in the pockets of his khaki shorts, grinning. His sun-streaked hair was mussed, his madras shirt unbuttoned, the shirttails out. He was barefoot. "In case you're wondering about the digs," he said to Jane, "it's all about my mom one-upping my dad, because my stepdad's so much richer. He's an asshole. But filthy rich. I mean, hey, isn't that what really matters?"

"It's really beautiful," Jane said.

He shrugged, ambled away from them and drew a beer from the keg in the utility room just off the kitchen.

"He is *not* okay," Bridget said later, when the boys were out of earshot. "You know I was worried about him all spring. One more semester of shitty grades and he's screwed. I told him he should take a class in summer school, something easy to bring up his GPA a little. But you know Pete. He didn't even get a job. He sleeps half the day, then hangs out with those idiot friends of his from high school. I swear, I hate his parents. I don't even know them and I hate them. Neither one of them gives a shit about him. Not really. They *let* him get away with things to hurt and aggravate each other. Then they get mad when he has problems. Like it's not totally *their* fault.

They were stretched out on chaise lounges by the pool, wearing their bikinis, just as they'd imagined. "I love him so much," Bridget said. "I didn't even realize how much till I was away from him. I didn't know it would be like this. To be in love, I mean. How much it would hurt. How I'd worry about him. How I'd just want to be *with* him. We – "

She lowered her voice. "This morning. When Tom went to get you – "

She didn't finish the sentence, but Jane knew what she meant.

Bridget grinned at her, then whooped, jumped up from her chair and threw herself toward Pete, who was floating on a raft in the deep end of the pool. She was like a child, Jane thought. Sometimes she simply could not contain herself. The two of them like big, beautiful children, wrestling and shouting in the water. Shimmering in the sunlight.

The Lovin' Spoonful was on the radio, a bee buzzed near the bottle of Coke Bridget had abandoned. Jane watched Tom swim laps in the turquoise water. She liked his steady pace and how, when he reached the end of the pool, he made a deft little flip and powered himself off into the opposite direction. Nothing he ever did made her worry, as Bridget worried about Pete. In all the time they'd been together, they'd had only one real argument – about the demonstration in Dunn Meadow in the spring. It still scared her to think of herself, alone in her dorm room afterwards, certain she'd ruined everything. When the phone rang and she heard Tom's voice, she felt much as she did right now, watching him climb out of the pool and come to sit at the foot of her lounge chair.

"Bridget picked me up at five AM," he said. "She wouldn't let me drive, because she said I'd go too slow. I swear to God, she drove ninety the whole way. She's insane. I kept saying, 'Bridge, your dad's a judge in *Evansville.* It won't do you a goddamn bit of good if you get a speeding ticket in Terre Haute.'"

Jane raised an eyebrow. "Scary when you're the voice of reason."

"No shit." He grinned. "On the other hand, getting up at four-thirty is a good excuse to take a nap now."

"Yeah?" She grinned back.

"Yeah. Aren't you tired, too? That long bus ride?"

"Oh, I am," she said, catching his outstretched hand, letting him lead her to the guest room where he'd taken her suitcase earlier.

It was pale pink, like the inside of a seashell, with cream-colored wood shutters on the window instead of curtains. The bedspread was pink and cream striped chintz, turned down to reveal pressed sheets and pillowcases.

"I love you, Jane," Tom said, wrapping his arms around her, pulling her down gently to the bed.

"I love you, too," she said.

All those stupid junior high movies, parents tongue-tied, mortified in the face of it. The threats, the whispering about how boys wouldn't respect you if you went too far – or, heaven forbid, *all the way.* The bad girls who'd done it anyhow and disappeared for a semester, a year maybe, nobody knew exactly where, though there was plenty of talk about them, lots of murmured speculation when they came back, sometimes dull and sad, sometimes wilder, more reckless than they'd been before. Of course, *of course,* they hadn't dared tell what it was really like. The way the world disappeared, the way your whole body sang into the void.

"The nuns said it was addictive," Bridget said, when they came downstairs hours later. She and Pete were curled up on the sofa in the family room, watching a movie on TV. "My, my. Who'd have thought they were ever right about anything?"

They were, though, Jane thought. They definitely were. All their plans for elaborate meals gave way to carry-out pizza and fried chicken. Their plans to go waterskiing and to the County Fair, the books she and Bridget had brought to read dissolved into late, lazy mornings and long afternoon naps. In the evening, they lounged by the pool, the stereo on loud – the hot, humid air, their own hot, sated bodies, cold beer, the Righteous Brothers and Rolling Stones and the Temptations all blurring at the edges.

Only on the last night did she begin to come out of the trance, tensing in Tom's arms, chatter in her head filling her with anxiety about going home.

"Thirty-two days," Tom said, holding her closer. "Come on. It's not that long."

But as she boarded the bus late the next afternoon, the feel of him still against her, the scent of him still in her clothes, her hair, it seemed an eternity before she would see him again, and she could not look back, could not bear to see him there, his hand raised, growing smaller and smaller, finally disappearing as the bus pulled into traffic.

She felt weary, like she imagined her mother must feel after hours on her feet at the A & P, knowing there'd be no rest when she got home, just the endless round of household chores, the squabbles and complaints of her children.

"How was Karen?" she'd ask Jane tonight, her voice eager and bright.

She thought of Bridget laughing, regaling Tom and Pete with stories about Karen's grim, Lutheran disapproval of anything that smacked of fun. How she'd cracked them up, breaking into her best Bob Dylan impression – *I wish that for just one time you could stand inside my shoes / you'd know what a drag it is to see you* – claiming it was all they really needed to know about Karen, anyway.

"That's mean," Mrs. Barth would say.

It was mean, a little. Jane knew that. But it was true, too. Bridget never said anything that wasn't true. It was one of the things Jane most admired about her. And she made Jane feel like it was all right to tell the truth, too – though she never pressed her to tell everything, or made her feel guilty if she didn't. Just smiled and reached out to touch Jane on the hand or maybe the shoulder, as if to say that she was glad to know whatever Jane had told her. It was a gift to know it. Enough.

If Jane told her mother anything true about the weekend, even some small thing, all she would do was worry – or worse. No. It was better to keep on as she had and then, when it was time to leave in September, mention that she would have a new roommate. Bridget Kelly. A girl she knew from the dorm.

"Karen pledged a sorority," she'd say. "She'll be living in the sorority house. I thought I'd told you."

She'd feel guilty, of course. It was wrong to lie to her mother about her friends, her life. But she couldn't imagine how to begin telling her now, or what her mother would say if she knew who Jane had become. She wouldn't understand. How could she? Jane really didn't understand it herself. She could be kinder, though, which would make up a little for lying. She'd paid little attention to her sisters all summer and, with some of the money she'd made working, she'd treat them to the movies, take them shopping for school supplies.

She'd sign up to work extra shifts in the next weeks, which would also help make the time pass more quickly, and when things got tense or she felt lonely or anxious, she'd think about Tom. Right *now* she'd think about him, she decided, and closed her eyes to avoid talking to the stout, grandmotherly woman knitting beside her, to erase the man chain-smoking a few seats ahead of her and drown out the baby crying a few seats behind. She took deep, even breaths until she could see the room where she and Tom had slept. The beautiful, beautiful room. An *extra* room in a house she could not have imagined until this weekend.

She could not have imagined living like man and wife with someone before this weekend either, but she could imagine it now. She and Bridget sang "Wouldn't it be nice" along with the Beach Boys by the pool, only half-laughing at the words. She could not say how it had felt to be with Tom the past few days, what it had meant. But she knew all her life she would remember that first waking into bright morning sunlight, Tom's naked body curved around hers.

The thrill of it shivered through her all over again.

"Dear?" the lady beside her asked. "Are you all right?"

Jane jolted back with her words. "Yes. Fine. Thanks." And flushed with embarrassment, as if the woman *knew.*

Outside, night had fallen. Far out into the country, lamps glowed in the occasional farmhouse, casting quilt squares of light into the yards. There were fields of corn and soybeans on either side of the highway, but they were invisible, and gazing into the darkness made Jane remember the first time she and Tom had driven the winding road out to Bean Blossom Forest at night.

"It's so dark," she said, bemused. Then, "Oh! No streetlights!"

Tom laughed. "City girl," he called her.

Later, in the spring, she had marveled at the daisies growing along the side of the road, and he had pulled over so that she could pick her fill of them. She would live with flowers in her real life, she told him. She would never, ever be without flowers all around her.

He had remembered it, bought a bouquet of daisies for their room at Pete's.

She was flooded with happiness at the thought. And strength.

Her father would meet her at the bus station, just as he met her every night after work. She could manage that. Once home, she'd plead exhaustion and go straight to bed. When she woke in the morning, her mother would have left for work. By the time she got home, Jane would be at the bookbindery. If she played it just right, the rest of her days at home would pass this way – she and her mother never quite connecting.

But when the bus arrived at the station, her father wasn't there. Could he have forgotten the time? Or worse, stopped by the Red Star for just one drink . . . and then another? There were vagrants and low-life types hanging around outside the station, so she sat down on a bench near the ticket counter. She waited five minutes, ten, and was just about to dig in her purse for a dime to call home when she saw him hurrying toward her.

She stood, then sat down again when she saw his face.

"Honey, something's happened. Bobby – " He sat down abruptly beside her. "He's in the hospital, Jane. An accident. It happened Saturday night. Late. The girl with him –

"She was thrown out of the car. She died, Janey. Bobby was in pretty bad shape for a while there. We weren't sure –

"He's okay. He'll pull through. Honey, we tried to get in touch with you – "

The way he looked at her, the sad question in his eyes, made Jane go liquid with dread.

"Janey, the number you gave us."

"What?" Jane asked, though of course she knew.

"You weren't there."

"I – " she began.

But her father stood and said, "It doesn't matter. Not now. I told your mother I'd bring you to the hospital. She won't leave. And I knew you'd want to see Bobby as soon as you got here."

She didn't, really. She wanted to get back on the bus and go – anywhere. To Tom. But when her father picked up her suitcase, she stood and followed him to the car. She sat huddled in the front seat of the car, her teeth pressed together to keep from chattering. It wasn't cold. The air coming in through the open windows was close and warm.

"Eighty degrees," the radio deejay said. "Midnight."

Jane knew it was irrational, but it seemed to her a measure of her disconnection from her family, a kind of punishment, that she hadn't somehow known that something terrible had happened and would have to live forever with the knowledge that, all the while her brother lay near death and her parents were frantic with worry, she had been floating in the pool with Tom in the moonlight, their beer cans in the neat little pockets of the rubber rafts they kept close together by holding hands. But there was nothing she could do about it now, just go where her father was determined to take her and try as best she could to make up for it.

The hospital was shockingly bright inside, the corridors endless and gleaming. Jane walked behind her father, glancing now and then toward the sounds of suffering, the occasional lit room where nurses hovered. The *smell.* It was like that awful green soap the school nurse used to clean scraped knees and elbows, and brought with it that panicky feeling she'd felt when she was a child, hurt, already feeling the sting she knew would come. The tears she would not be able to keep back. *Baby.* She hated crying. Hated the way it made her feel.

"Here." Her father stopped so suddenly at one of the rooms along the hall that Jane had to take a step backward to enter. The first bed in the room was empty, a yellow curtain drawn across the room dividing it from the second bed where Bobby lay, swathed in bandages from head to foot.

He was asleep, Jane saw with relief.

Her mother was not. She sat straight up in the plastic hospital chair that she'd pulled next to Bobby's bed. One hand was on his, holding it. The other she held out to Jane, who had no choice but to take it, thinking that her mother was asking for some comfort. She was shocked off-balance by the force of her mother's grip, shocked to find herself bent over, face-to-face with her.

"Mom," she began, "I – "

"Don't tell me another lie, Jane," her mother said, gripping even harder. "You weren't where you said. Nobody at the number you gave me had ever even heard of you. I was frantic. My God, we thought Bobby was going to die."

She let Jane's hand fall, put her own two hands to her eyes and bent over, sobbing.

"Mom, I'm sorry," Jane said. "I am. It wasn't like I was doing anything terrible. Honest. I *wasn't.*"

"I don't care what you were doing," her mother said. "I don't even want to know what you were doing or who you were doing it with. Not anymore. I don't want to know anything you don't want to tell me."

"But – "

"Don't say another word to me," her mother said. "I mean it. Not one word. Not tonight."

Jane stood, staring at her. It was the last thing she had expected her mother to say.

Mrs. Barth turned to fuss over Bobby, smoothing his tangled hair, tucking the blanket up under his chin. "It's so cold in here," she said to nobody.

"Hon," Mr. Barth said. "Come home. They won't let you stay in the room with him all night, you're not really supposed to be in here now. None of us are. The nurse said Jane could see him, then – "

"I'll just stay in the waiting room," she said. "I'm not going home until I know – "

"Kay, he's all right. The doctor said he's going to be all right. You heard him say so this afternoon."

"I need to be here," she said. "What if he wakes up, afraid? You take Jane home. I know she must be tired."

In the car, Mr. Barth sat a long moment, before putting the key in the ignition. "She nearly lost your brother," he said, his voice tentative and small. "When we couldn't find you, she thought she'd lost you, too. She was scared to death you wouldn't be there when I went to meet the bus tonight. She feels you're lost to us, Janey. Since you went away."

"I'm not *lost* to you," Jane said.

But she was. All she wanted was to get through the next weeks until she could go back to school, which to them might as well have been a different planet.

When her mother finally agreed to come home a few days later, Jane was glad to feel she was invisible to her. Mrs. Barth was consumed with worry over Bobby's recovery, fearful about what would happen to him when he was well enough to face the consequences of his acts. He'd been drinking when the accident occurred; it was considerably after the midnight curfew; and he'd been driving a car that he claimed he'd borrowed with the owner's permission, but the owner said he was lying. At the very least, he'd have to pay for the car, which had been totaled. At worst, he could be sent to reform school. And the girl. Mrs. Barth grieved so for the sorrow Bobby had brought to her family that the doctor had prescribed tranquilizers to help her sleep.

"Why did you lie to Mom?" Susan asked, the only one to bring up what Jane had done after that first night.

"None of your *business,*" Jane said, instantly regretting her nasty tone of voice.

But when Susan responded, stubbornly, "You shouldn't have. You made Mom cry," Jane screamed at her, "Shut up. Shut *up.* Just go away. Leave me alone." And when Susan just stood there, glaring at her,

Jane got up, shoved her into the hallway and slammed the bedroom door behind her.

Alone, in the quiet room, she put her hand to her throat, which hurt from screaming. She had never in her life been hateful to either of her sisters, not like that. She adored them – and only now realized how much she counted on their adoring her back. She lay on the bed, her eyes closed tightly, smarting with tears. She thought of the little matching bowler hats her sisters had worn one year for Easter, decorated with cloth flowers. How, when she'd gotten her driver's license at sixteen, she'd taken them in their pajamas to the drive-in movie, let them sit and eat their popcorn on the hood of the car, something that thrilled them, something their parents would never have allowed. She thought of them huddled up against her in the car on the day she left for college, and of how sometimes those first few months away she woke in the middle of the night missing their sweet powdery scent, the feel of their breath against her skin, soft as feathers. She loved them, felt responsible for them. But she could not make herself get up and go to Susan and say that she was sorry.

She worked overtime, grateful for the exhaustion that made it easy to sleep away any time she had at home and excused her from any more than occasional hospital visits. She did not know what to say to her brother. They'd never been close. When Jane was honest with herself, she knew that it was her fault. That it was because she had always resented him. Bobby had been a bright, funny little boy, easy and endearing. Jane, difficult, intense. Why *wouldn't* her mother love him better? She understood that. But she could not forgive him for it, nor could she help the mean pleasure she had sometimes felt as he grew into an increasingly troubled teenager, constantly testing the boundaries of their mother's love.

Bobby lived under the hood of his junk car, his fingernails filthy, his clothes smelling of oil. He cut classes, hung out with his greaser friends. He *talked* like a greaser, defiantly using poor grammar even though Jane knew he was perfectly capable of speaking correctly. He was smart, probably smarter than she was if the truth were told. Even teachers said he was smart and were charmed by him, at the same time he drove them crazy with his wisecracks and pranks. But he hated school, hated anyone telling him what to do. His single ambition was to get out, get a job, and save up enough money to buy a G.T.O.

It would have been easier if it had been this same Bobby she felt obligated to visit now, she thought. Easier, knowing he'd go back to his cars and loser friends and willful self-destruction as soon as he got well enough to get out of the hospital. But the accident had scared him into a kind of submission she'd never seen in him before. He'd let them cut his hair and he looked as clean-cut as a track star. He was polite to the nurses, wore the old-man pajamas their mother bought him without complaint.

It killed Jane the way his face lit up with shy pleasure when she appeared in his doorway, the way he offered up ideas and thoughts about his future, so obviously hoping for her approval. She could hardly bear to see the clutter of recruitment brochures on his bedside table, visible evidence of how narrow the options for his future had turned out to be. He'd enlist in the service as soon as he'd recovered fully and turned eighteen; this was the deal the prosecutor had offered.

"I've pretty much decided on the Marines," he told her the day before she left to go back to school. He handed her a brochure that showed a young man in dress blues, gold buttons gleaming. "I figure, go with the best. Do something right for once, huh?"

She took it, remembering the former Marine who'd spoken in Dunn Meadow last spring – the empty sleeve of the uniform shirt he wore over his jeans folded and pinned neatly over the stump of his right arm. "Look at what we're doing in Vietnam," he'd said, the speaker crackling around the words. "I'm not saying don't go. All I'm saying is, look first – then decide."

But what choice did Bobby have?

"Absolutely! The Marines," Jane said.

It was the one thing she could do: wish him well. She was sorry he'd been hurt. Sorry, too, for the hurt she'd caused her mother – which she would have made right if she could, if it wouldn't have required stepping backward into the self she had been before she learned what it felt like to be happy.

4

"Tomorrow Never Knows"

Pete had tacked a hand-painted sign on the porch of the old farmhouse: "Land of a Thousand Dances," though it was the Beatles' *Revolver* that he played over and over again. Right now, it was "Here, There and Everywhere." Next would be "Yellow Submarine," Jane knew. Then "Tomorrow Never Knows." It creeped her out, that song. She wanted James Brown or Wilson Pickett. The Stones, the Animals. Wild music to dissolve the last of the summer's unhappiness. But *Revolver* was the only thing Pete wanted to listen to – and he was paying the rent on the party house, so it played constantly, always at full blast.

He had enough money to rent the house in addition to paying for his room at the fraternity because his parents' estrangement had reached an all-time high and, unbeknownst to one another, each had given him full tuition and housing money for the fall. Jane did not know whether to feel sorry for Pete, whom Bridget said actually longed for his parents' attention, or feel envious of how their self-absorption gave him the freedom to do whatever he wanted to do. She loved Pete because Bridget did, and cared about him, but did not know how to think about the sense of entitlement he felt about the benefits of his parents' competition over him or about the thoughtless remarks he made that sometimes cut her to the quick.

"Hey," he said, bragging about the money scam. "It's a game. Parents want to control you one way or another. That's where it's at. Look how stingy your parents are," he said to Jane. "What do you think that's about?"

Jane shrugged. If she had said, "They're not stingy; there's nothing to withhold," he wouldn't have believed it. He couldn't have fathomed the certainty with which she knew her parents would give her anything in the world she wanted, if only they could. Or understood that she loved them, desperately, but no longer knew how to be with them.

Just thinking about her parents made her feel weepy and she regretted, again, the distance between them and how it had deepened after her lie about the weekend was revealed. They hadn't even argued when she said she'd decided to take the Greyhound bus back to Bloomington, her belongings packed in cardboard cartons.

Still, it was so good to be back. Tom had surprised her at the station with the new MG his father had bought him at the end of the summer. Robins' egg blue, with a roll bar that his father, an engineer, had designed to keep him safe in case the little convertible turned over. Then surprised her again with news of Pete's farmhouse. As they pulled into the gravel drive of the farmhouse on that first day, Bridget appeared in an upstairs window. By the time Tom had parked next to Pete's Corvette, she was flinging herself off the porch, running to embrace Jane and dance her around the yard. She wore old, ripped-up cutoffs and a grimy tee shirt. Her hair was pulled back with a bandana. She smelled of sweat and ammonia.

"I know. I'm disgusting," she said, finally letting Jane go. "But I can't help it. I'm so glad to see you. So glad to be *back*. I've been cleaning ever since I got here yesterday. God. This place is so gross. I actually found a perfect little skeleton of a mouse in the front closet. Ugh." She made a face. "But, Jane! It's going to be so groovy when we fix it up!"

"We've got our own room," Tom said, reclaiming her, pulling her close. "It'll be just like it was this summer, at Pete's. Only we won't have to go home."

If her parents *knew,* Jane often thought in the weeks that followed. But they wouldn't know. The house, her whole world, was unimaginable to them. She wrote each week, mainly to avoid talking to them on the phone. Cheery letters about her classes, how pretty it was on campus now that the leaves were turning, how life with her new roommate, Bridget, was going just fine. Her mother wrote back, her letters full of Bobby, passing along his news from Marine boot camp. Each with a worn five-dollar bill folded into it that pierced Jane's heart.

Neither Tom nor Bridget knew exactly what had happened the night she returned from Indianapolis. She'd written to them about Bobby's accident, but not about what had happened with her mother. Bridget would have defended her. Tom would have insisted on driving up to help her set things right. He'd insist on it right now if she told him, a prospect that sent her into a panic just to consider. Anyway, how could she explain? She could still feel her mother's fingernails pressing into the flesh on her wrist, still hear the bitterness in her voice when she said, "I don't want to know anything you don't want to tell me."

Which was the real problem, after all. Jane didn't want to tell her mother about her life – and Tom would never be able to understand that. So she just let him believe that the sadness that leaked out sometimes was all about her brother, the kind of sadness any decent human being would feel.

She wondered sometimes how she could be at the same time so happy and so desolate. Late afternoons, when their classes were through, she and Tom drove out to the farmhouse and spent long, lazy hours making love in the attic room they'd claimed as their own. Jane loved the slanted ceiling, the plank floors dotted with rag rugs she and Bridget had found at Goodwill, the dormer windows. They'd found silk scarves, too, and Jane had draped them over the worn lamp shades so they glowed when dusk fell.

She lay there now, listening to the last cuts of *Revolver,* Tom still fast asleep beside her. It was nearly noon. They'd been up late last night: the usual Friday-night party and, after everyone had left and she and Bridget had made the first pass at tidying up the kitchen, Pete had talked them into smoking grass with him. Sitting in the V of Tom's legs on the floor, her head resting on his chest, Jane had drawn in the smoke and held it as Pete instructed, then lifted her hand so that Tom could take the joint from between her fingers and do the same. A few times around and she felt the world slow down around her and all her cares fall away. She'd felt suddenly giddy – and horny. She smiled, a little chagrined to think of it, but at the same time overwhelmed, again, with desire. She ran her finger lightly down Tom's backbone and he stirred and turned to her, ready, as if he'd been making love to her in a dream.

Downstairs, Pete replayed "Tomorrow Never Knows" twice and started it a third time. The agitated droning, the screeching electric guitars and discordant violins, the unrelenting drumbeat – and underneath the wild whooping that always made Jane think of Alfred Hitchcock's *The Birds,* its terrible black swirling sky.

The idea of turning off her mind, just floating away, frightened her. She didn't want to think about dying.

The music stopped abruptly, replaced by Bridget's angry voice. "Would you quit playing this stupid song?" she said. "I hate it. It's awful."

"Don't be so uptight," Pete said. "What? You can't hear the word 'dying'?"

"It's not the word, it's – the whole idea of it. Like nothing matters."

The song started again, louder. Then there was the shriek of the needle across the record.

"Fuck," Pete said. "You fucking scratched my album. Goddamn – "

"Buy another one," Bridget said. "What's it to you? Ten dollars. Twenty? Five hundred? A thousand? What do you care? You think you're hurting your parents spending all their money? Refusing – "

"Don't start that shit again," Pete said.

The front door slammed; moments later, they heard him rev up his Corvette and screech out of the driveway. Jane untangled herself from Tom's arms, shivering as she stepped naked onto the cold wood floor.

"Stay here," Tom said. "Stay out of it. Let them – "

"I can't," Jane said. "Can't you hear Bridget crying?"

Pulling on her jeans and a sweatshirt, she could feel him watching her, willing her to come back to bed with him. It was what she wanted, too. But her happiness with Tom seemed all the more reason to go to Bridget now, to try to do something to make her feel better. Wasn't Bridget responsible for that happiness, after all? If she hadn't met Bridget, if Bridget hadn't decided instantly, for no reason Jane had ever understood, to befriend her . . .

The trouble was, she had no idea how to help her. Those first euphoric weeks after summer break, the four of them had been like a family, heading out to the farmhouse after their classes were through, disappearing to their rooms, making love, napping in each other's arms, till dusk fell. Then Jane and Bridget would make a simple meal; Tom and Pete would help clean up; and the four of them would settle down to their studies until it was time for Jane and Bridget to go back to the dorm. Fridays, the girls packed duffels and signed out of the dorm as if they were going home for the weekend, but spent the nights at the farmhouse instead.

Then in the middle of October, Bridget discovered that Pete had quit going to his classes and was spending his days hanging out in the television room at the Sigma Chi house.

She was furious with Tom. He should have told her.

"Bridget," he said. "Pete's going to do – or *not* do – whatever he damn well pleases. What am I supposed to do? Handcuff him to my wrist and drag him to the business building every morning?"

"You can make him go," she said. "He listens to you."

"Because I don't nag him. Jesus, Bridge, Pete's . . . He's a little crazy, which is what you *liked* about him in the first place. Now all of a sudden you want to be his mother?"

"I don't want to be his mother. I don't want him to flunk out and get drafted, that's all."

"Nobody wants that," Tom said. "But you can't save him from himself."

Nonetheless, she became consumed with trying. She was ferocious in her misery, stubborn in her refusal to see that her behavior was only making Pete more determined not to do what she wanted him to do. They fought when she tried to make him go to class or study, when she said he shouldn't be drinking in the afternoons or needed to drive more sensibly or was smoking too much grass. Increasingly, Pete disappeared for hours at a time, and they fought when Bridget asked where he'd been.

Jane and Tom could hear them in the room below, though they tried not to.

"I love you," Bridget would cry out, not like Bridget at all.

Jane was almost glad for the respite in the tension that Thanksgiving brought – and the opportunity to mend things at least a little bit with her mother, who'd written to say how much she was looking forward to Jane's visit. Both she and Jane's father had picked her up at the Greyhound station, and she'd kept up the kind of bright chatter Jane had been used to forever. Jane reciprocated with bits and pieces of her life she felt she could afford to share: accounts of football games, random things she'd learned in her classes. Her new roommate, Bridget.

"You actually met her, Mom," she said. "The day I moved in? She was on the elevator when we first went up to see my room. She has red hair and a lot of freckles – "

"Oh," Mrs. Barth said. "The girl who was going to the roof."

"Exactly," Jane said, surprised that her mother remembered, surprised, too, at the pleasure she felt to have given her this small gift.

On the long bus ride back to Bloomington, she felt at peace about her family for the first time in a long while. It hadn't really been so hard to listen to her mother, to eat the meals she'd prepared and say thank you for them, to say what she knew her mother longed for her to say: she was happy at school, but glad to be home for a few days; proud of Bobby, as they were; and looking forward to seeing him at Christmas.

The time apart seemed to have been good for Pete and Bridget, too. He started going to his classes and, relieved, she became, again, his accomplice rather than his keeper. The two of them would cook a holiday feast the night before they all went home for break, they announced – courtesy of the Man.

First, they stole a cookbook from the public library and made a list of what they'd need. The next day, they appeared with a can of cranberries tucked into one of Pete's coat pockets and an onion and some broken stalks of celery in Bridget's purse. They went out again later and scored two cans of green beans, a packet of dry gravy and a loaf of bread for the dressing, then wandered store-to-store stealing potatoes, one at a time, which they thought was hilarious. The day after yielded three bottles of Cold Duck, from who knew where, as well as a dozen dinner rolls, a whole box of butter patties, and a pumpkin pie they'd scammed a waitress at some diner into giving them.

"You did not steal that turkey," Jane said when Pete triumphantly unbuttoned it from inside his parka, and set it in the sink to thaw.

He just smiled mysteriously, tied on a gingham apron they'd lifted from the dime store and started chopping the vegetables, singing tunelessly along with the Beatles, happy as a housewife. Bridget tied on a matching apron and set to work beside him.

When Tom and Jane got back from class the next afternoon, the house was filled with the fragrant aroma of turkey roasting. There were hors d'oeuvres, also filched: cocktail peanuts, a jar of olives, a jar of Vienna sausages. The table was set with a paper cloth printed with sprigs of holly. There were matching paper plates and napkins. And favors: fuzzy Santa hats, each name written in glitter on the front.

Pete had shaved for the first time in days; his blond hair was slicked back. He wore a starched white shirt with his Levi's and served the Cold Duck in beer mugs, a new white dishtowel folded over his arm. Bridget wore a maid's apron. Montovani was on the stereo, a record Jane hadn't heard before. They'd filched that, too, Jane figured.

She should be appalled, she knew. Instead, she was charmed. It was so funny, all of them affecting civilized behavior as Pete and Bridget served the hors d'oeurves, refilled the mugs of Cold Duck with a flourish.

"We are all as God made us," Bridget said, in an atrocious British accent. ". . . only many of us much worse." Spoofing the scene from *Tom Jones,* she reached for a turkey drumstick and devoured it, sucking, gnawing, licking her lips until the others pitched in, hooting with laughter, eating with their fingers, feeding each other, twining their arms to drink from each others' mugs. At the end, when they thought they could eat no more, Pete brought in the pumpkin pie and a can of Reddi-wip, squirting so much on each piece that the wedges of pie disappeared beneath it.

"Open!" he said to Bridget, grinning, holding the can at her mouth.

She did – and let him squirt the cream in, gasping to swallow it. Then she grabbed the can and turned it on him, both of them shouting and laughing, tussling to command it until they both collapsed, exhausted, sated on the living room couch. They'd drunk all three bottles of Cold Duck by then, and who knew how much beer. Fat with pumpkin pie, Jane and Tom pushed away from the table and collapsed as well, Jane on Tom's lap in the easy chair.

She wanted to go bed with him, but she was deliciously tired and couldn't manage to do more than think about it. Maybe she slept, she never knew. Later, when she tried to piece together what had happened, all she could remember was Bridget's piercing scream and Tom standing up so suddenly that she flew forward and had to catch herself to keep from falling.

She saw a field mouse scurry across the living room floor and disappear into the woodwork. Then another. And another. Bridget screamed again, leapt up.

"Jesus, they're just mice," Pete said. Then, "*Shit,*" when two more dropped to the floor, squeaking, from beneath the couch cushion on which Bridget stood. He got up, left the room, and returned with rifle he kept in the back closet for plunking tin cans in the field behind the farmhouse. He gestured to Bridget, who leapt from the couch to the chair, where Jane still sat, and when another mouse appeared, he took a shot that blew a hole in the arm of the couch.

"Pete!" Tom said. "Jesus, what are you doing?"

More mice appeared and scattered. Pete laughed, wildly, and shot again. "I'm going to kill those little fuckers," he said.

"Cut it out," Tom said. "Come on. Somebody's going to get hurt here."

Pete ignored him – and Bridget, too, who was screaming at him.

"Are you crazy?" she said, when he finally stopped. "And that's *my* couch, goddamn it. It was almost brand new. The guy at Goodwill told me it hadn't been there two hours before I got there. I was lending it to you, Pete. You know Jane and I were going to use it in our apartment next year. Now look at it!"

The couch was full of holes, smoking, tufts of stuffing singed brown sticking out every which way.

"You're acting crazy," she said. "I mean it. What's wrong with you, anyway? Every time I think maybe, *maybe* you've got your shit together – "

"Maybe I don't want to get my shit together," he said, quietly. "Did you ever think about that? Maybe I don't even think doing what everyone assumes I should do is what getting my shit together would be."

"Right," Bridget said. "What, exactly, would it be, then?"

"I don't know yet. I just know it isn't fucking college. Not now, anyway." He blew his breath out, set the rifle on the chair beside him. "I enlisted, Bridge. Over Thanksgiving."

Bridget's face turned so pale that, for a moment, Jane thought she might faint. She started to take a step toward her, but stopped when Bridget sank down, safely, on the ruined couch. She turned to Tom, who looked as shocked as Bridget did.

"I didn't know." He mouthed the words.

"But you were going to class," Bridget said. "You were studying."

"I was pretending to study," Pete said. "The thing is, Bridge, I couldn't have made my grades, even if I had studied for real – at which point I'd have been out of here anyway. I figured, enlist. Get it over with."

"You could have made your grades if you'd tried," Bridget said. "You could have talked to your professors and told them you'd be drafted if they failed you. Not to mention the fact that if you really did flunk out your dad could've gotten you a 4-F."

"I don't ask my dad for anything," Pete said. "You know that. Look. I'm sorry I didn't tell you right when we came back, but I wanted us to have some fun before I left. I wanted it to be like it used to be. I was going to tell you tonight."

"Tonight." Bridget said. "As in, 'Oh, by the way, I've enlisted in the Army. Have a great Christmas break.'"

"I'm sorry," Pete said, again.

Bridget stood so she was eye-to-eye with him. "Do you think I'm stupid?" she asked.

"No," Pete said. "Why – ?"

"Do you think I don't know the real, chickenshit reason you enlisted in the fucking army was to get away from *me*? For all I know you flunked out to get away from me. The only person in the whole world who really gives a shit about you? Well, fuck you," she said. "*Fuck you.*" She whirled and rushed out of the room, out the front door, coatless, into the cold night.

"Bridge – " Pete called, but he didn't go after her.

She was halfway across the front yard, walking purposefully toward the road by the time Jane and Tom could throw on their coats and catch up with her.

"Bridget," Tom called out. "Bridge! Hey! Stop."

She turned. Her face was white in the moonlight, her hair wild. When he opened his arms to her, she collapsed against him, sobbing.

When she'd calmed down, he tossed Jane the car keys and went back inside to get their things. Bridget crawled, shivering, into the tiny space behind the seats in the MG; Jane got into the front seat, started the engine and turned the heater on full blast. "Unchained Melody" came on the radio, a song that brought back the long, lazy weekend at Pete's.

Bridget closed her eyes, rested her head on her bent knees. "He doesn't love me," she said, bleakly. "I'm so stupid I wouldn't see it."

"He loves you," Jane said, though she wasn't at all sure it was true. "He just doesn't know how to do it right. He's afraid. You've said that yourself."

"Same difference, isn't it?" Bridget said.

They fell silent then. "Sunshine Superman" came on, oppressively cheerful. Jane watched Tom, framed in the lighted window, talking to Pete – maybe trying to convince him into coming out to talk to Bridget. But when the front door opened, he came out alone.

He got into the car, sat there for a long moment. "Bridge," he finally said, "He said to tell you he's sorry – about everything. It's not your fault."

"Oh, really," she said. "Sorry. Not my fault. Gee, that makes me feel *so* much better. You notice, he didn't say he *loved* me."

Tom glanced toward the window, where Pete stood, looking out. "He has to report on Monday. Do you maybe want to – ?"

"No," Bridget said. "I don't. Gutless fucking wonder. Just go, Tom. I mean it. *Go.* There's no way I'm going back in there and tell him it's okay what he's done. Or beg him to keep on loving me."

5

"Bird on a Wire"

Jane was surprised by the change she saw in her brother when she went home for Christmas. The greaser kid was gone, and the unsettling obsequiousness he'd displayed after the accident had been replaced by a quiet sense of purpose that made him seem older, more mature.

"A blessing in disguise," Jane's mother said, again and again.

The Marines were exactly what Bobby had needed: a fresh start, a chance to excel. All that tinkering with machines, she marveled. Remember how he used to take apart toasters and radios? Remember how he loved Lincoln Logs? And his Erector Set? Then came the car engines! He always did have a head for how things worked, she said. Now he was able to put it to good use.

"Jesus," Bobby said in a quiet moment. "She seems to have forgotten that someone died for this alleged blessing. Not to mention the fact that where I'm going to be putting all this shit to good use is Vietnam. I'm fine with that. I signed up for it, but – "

He blew out his breath. "I used to get pissed off when you'd get so crabby with her, you know? But I've got to say, she's kind of driving me crazy."

"Thank you," Jane said, and they both laughed.

They talked about how she fussed over them, how from the moment they walked into the house she'd started dreading their departure – which Jane felt all the more guilty about since Bridget and Tom had talked her into taking the bus down to Evansville for New Year's Eve and spending the last few days of break at Bridget's house.

"Does she send you money all the time?" Bobby asked.

Jane nodded.

"I told her, don't," Bobby said. "I don't need it. And I don't! I get paid, for Christ's sake. But she keeps sending it anyway, so I send it to Amy and Susan."

"I wish I didn't need it," Jane said. "I feel horrible every time I open the envelope. But the money I made this summer wasn't enough to get me through the year."

"I could send you money," he said. "Seriously. What am I going to do with it in Vietnam?"

"Bobby, you can't do that," she said.

"Why?"

She couldn't answer, for fear of bursting into tears.

"It's no big deal," he said. "Really."

Jane looked at her brother and saw the little boy he'd been. She remembered him sitting on the porch step every afternoon waiting for her to come home from first grade, how she swished past him so importantly with her little book bag full worksheets dotted with gold stars.

"No," she said, in a strangled voice. "You can't."

"Why?" Bobby asked again. "Jane, what's wrong? Why are you crying?"

"I've been such a shit to you," she said. "I always have been."

"Hey, you're my big sister," Bobby said. "That's your job."

"It's not."

"So you're a pain in the ass. So what? Jesus, would you quit crying? You were only trying to keep me from screwing up all the time. Obviously, I should have listened to you."

He leaned over and drew her into an awkward hug. "If I promise not to send you money, will you write to me when I go overseas?"

Jane nodded against his bony chest, laughing and crying until Bobby pulled away and did such a perfect and ridiculous impression of their mother's "Blessing in Disguise" speech that her tears gave way to laughter.

A few times during break, the two of them took the car in the evening and went to the Big Wheel, where they sat, talking over Cokes and fries. Bobby told Jane about boot camp and the buddies he'd made there. She told him about Tom and Bridget, about Pete and how rich and screwed up he was. How he'd enlisted because he was about to flunk out and was probably headed for Vietnam himself.

"He didn't like studying, so he just . . . didn't," she said. "All that money. He didn't even care about going to college, and he's the one who got a free ride."

"Yeah, well, in case you haven't figured it out yet, life's not fair," Bobby said. "As far as I can tell, most of the guys heading for Vietnam are gung-ho morons, guys who couldn't afford college or figure out some other way to avoid the draft, and dumb shits like me who figured it was better than going to jail. It's been good for me, though – getting the hell out of here. San Diego's cool, you know? I'm thinking I might live there when I get out. Maybe go to college," he added, surprising Jane. "There's that G.I. Bill, you know."

"You should definitely go," she said.

"You think I'm smart enough?"

"*Yes.* You're smart enough."

He shrugged, but Jane could tell it pleased him that she thought so.

She wrote to him, as she'd promised, once she got back to Bloomington – about her classes, life on campus. But she also found herself writing about things she'd never shared with anyone, not even Tom – their father's drinking, her conflicted feelings about their mother, the guilt she felt for wanting so much more than they could afford.

He wrote back about his own conflicted feelings about their family, his regret for the behavior that had ended his girlfriend's life and brought down so much sorrow on her parents and theirs. He loved the girl, he said, and regretted, too, that he had never told her so.

Sometimes Jane thought about *All Quiet on the Western Front* and wondered how similar her brother's life was to the lives of the soldiers she'd read about. She wondered about Wayne Dugan, too, and what he'd say to her if he found out she had a brother in Vietnam. She wondered what had happened to him.

When she got to class the Monday morning after the fight in Dunn Meadow, she found one of the Baggers faced off with one of the fraternity guys, having the same argument she and Tom had had about the flag. Her instinct had been to turn and walk away, but Professor Farlow required a doctor's excuse for absences. So she took her seat, opened her book, and bent her head over it.

"You fucking frat boys," the Bagger said, as Professor Farlow entered.

In the utter silence that ensued, Professor Farlow had gone calmly to her desk, set her book bag down, opened it, and taken out a sheaf of papers. "Your essays on *All Quiet on the Western Front,*" she said and began to hand them back.

The fraternity guy's anger morphed when he looked at the grade on his. The essay question had been "Discuss the way *All Quiet on the Western Front* critiques the romantic rhetoric of war, honor, and patriotism." Which was unfair right from the get-go, he said, a setup. To get a decent grade, you had to come to the conclusion that war was wrong – or lie and say you did. The whole point of it – for that matter, the whole point of reading the book at all – was to make them believe what she did.

"Would you recall for us a time during our discussions of the novel that I said I personally believed all war was wrong?" Professor Farlow asked.

"You didn't have to say it," the guy said.

Jane instinctively turned toward Wayne Dugan's place at the back of the classroom, expecting him to counter this idiotic response, but he wasn't there. She had dreaded seeing him today, fearful that he might have seen her sitting at the Sig house on Saturday, known somehow that Tom was her boyfriend. Now it occurred to her that he might have been seriously hurt.

She focused her attention on Professor Farlow, who quietly explained that she had chosen this question for them to consider for the challenge it posed in learning to think critically about a text that questioned the conventional wisdom about beliefs that everyone holds dear.

"The question did not ask you to discuss your personal opinions concerning war, honor, or patriotism," she said, "but to discuss how the experiences of Remarque's fictional characters raise questions about them that are important to consider."

"I don't question patriotism," the guy said. "You do what your country asks you to do. That's what I was taught. That's what my dad did in World War II – and I'll tell you something else. I don't appreciate reading a book that's supposed to make me feel sorry for German soldiers, no matter what war they were in. As far as I'm concerned, they got what they deserved."

Professor Farlow listened. "Love of one's country is a deeply personal, deeply emotional issue," she said when he finished. "I respect your view of patriotism. I honor your father's military service. Nonetheless, your grade in this class is based on your ability to look objectively and analytically at the texts we consider. Your essay on *All Quiet on the Western Front* does not accomplish this. You may see me after class if you'd like to discuss it further. Meanwhile, we will move on to T. S. Eliot's 'The Love Song of J. Alfred Prufrock.'"

> Let us go then, you and I,
> When the evening is spread out against the sky
> Like a patient etherized upon a table . . .

Which was exactly how Jane felt at that moment, numb, not quite there. She had read the poem, struggled through the footnotes trying to understand it, but all she could remember when Professor Farlow called on her was that it addressed the spiritual exhaustion of people in the aftermath of World War I and shook her head, as if unprepared, because she didn't want to draw attention to herself, especially by speaking the word "war."

Wayne never came back. Rumor was he'd been expelled and sent home – or drafted. Some said he was in jail, awaiting trial for assault and battery of an officer, resisting arrest. Others that he'd jumped bail and headed for Canada. Jane was sorry for whatever had happened to him, but glad she didn't have to face him anymore, glad when the class moved on from the literature of World War I to *The Great Gatsby* with its personal, apolitical concerns. She never told Tom that she knew Wayne Dugan, never mentioned the incident at Dunn Meadow again, and made up her mind to forget about the war, which, really, had nothing at all to do with her.

But now that Bobby was in Vietnam, it seemed the war was everywhere: the gruesome body counts; the soundless, grieving peasants; jets zooming low over flooded rice paddies. Once, in the electronics department at Sears, she and Bridget stood, rooted, before a bank of televisions, the same scene unfolding on each screen: bodies of American boys stacked like cordwood, waiting to be loaded onto the helicopter that would carry them back to the base.

Increasingly, people began to question whether the war in Vietnam was a terrible mistake, logistically unwinnable, even morally wrong – thousands of Vietnamese civilians dead in the bombings, the lives and livelihoods of those left wrecked by the scorched-earth policy that had left their land useless for growing. Crowds at the antiwar rallies were bigger than they'd been the spring before, and not only Baggers. Sometimes Jane stood at the edges, trying to make sense of it, trying to figure out what to believe.

"What's it like there, really?" she wrote to Bobby.

"A lot of sitting around, waiting, then some scary shit," he wrote back. "Then you do it again. But, hey, the trucks are cool. I've got my own Jeep. Grass is plentiful. (Don't tell Mom.) Semper Fi."

She made up her mind not to mention her feelings of uncertainty about the war while she was at home for spring break, but when Walter Cronkite reported on the evening news that even LBJ's advisors were beginning to admit it couldn't be won, she blurted out, "And he just keeps on sending kids like Bobby over there. My God, why don't people see that?"

"I'm proud of Bobby turning his life around the way he did," Jane's mother said.

"I'm proud of Bobby, too," Jane replied. "I'm not talking about Bobby doing anything wrong. I'm talking about the war being wrong. He shouldn't be there. Nobody should."

"Well, he is there, Jane." Her mother's voice was quiet, but shaking with anger. "And as long as he's there, it's our job to support him. We have no choice but to believe he's doing the right thing."

She knew better than to respond, but she felt the détente of the past months dissolve into anguished silence. It would be better for everyone if she stayed in Bloomington for the summer, she decided, and Bridget didn't want to spend another long break battling over her independence. So they found a little two-bedroom house just off Kirkwood Avenue, within walking distance of everywhere they needed to go. Working full-time, they could cover their expenses; if Tom moved in and they split the rent three ways, Jane could take on a second job and be able to pay her own tuition in the fall. Within days of moving into the house, she felt right in this new life with Tom and Bridget, the three of them a happier family than her own had ever been.

6

"For What It's Worth"

It was a glorious Saturday afternoon, unseasonably warm for November, and Jane and Bridget lounged on the porch swing, drinking tea, watching Tom wash and wax his MG in the driveway. He wore jeans and a faded blue chambray shirt rolled up at the sleeves. His curly dark hair had grown long enough to brush the top of his collar. Jane liked the way he looked, liked watching him so intent at his task, the last yellow leaves drifting down all around him. Now and then, he stepped back, squinted, and then zeroed in on some little spot he'd missed.

The car looked perfect to Jane. It always looked perfect. Tom's obsession with keeping it that way annoyed her sometimes – he'd wash it again tomorrow, she knew. But on this lazy afternoon, it seemed endearing to her. When he finished waxing the car, he put the top down and the two of them took a drive together, leaving Bloomington behind for the two-lane roads that wound down through Brown County. Jane closed her eyes and felt the late afternoon sun on her face, listened to the music on the radio. Jefferson Airplane, the Doors. Then Buffalo Springfield, "For What It's Worth." The slow tremolo on the electric guitar bending the notes, the dirge-like rhythm of the bass drum brought an odd shiver of fear, a glitch of time in which she was approaching the Business Building exactly as she had last Monday afternoon, carefree, her last class finished for the day, thinking only of meeting Tom.

She thought there'd been an accident when she saw the cluster of police cars where Fee Lane T'd with 10th Street. But there were so many of them, a dozen or more, their red lights flashing. Then, like pieces of a puzzle falling into place, she saw the campus bus sitting outside the building where buses didn't usually stop; police in riot gear guarding the entrance of the Business Building; students rushing toward it, students rushing away, and a growing number of people gathering on the lawn and sidewalk, overflowing into the street. Then the door opened and more police were herding and even dragging students from the building. The students wore black armbands. Some of them were bleeding, Jane saw. There was thudding and cracking, which she realized was the sound of students being struck by nightsticks. Some fell to the grass, some went limp and curled into themselves, protecting their heads from policemen, who kicked or struck them, shouting and swearing. The bench where she and Tom had agreed to meet was at the center of the melee, unreachable, and she was relieved to see him emerge from the crowd and hurry across the street toward her.

"Are you okay?" Jane asked. "My God, what's going on here?"

He pulled a flyer from his jacket pocket and handed it to her. There was a photograph of a clean-cut business student wearing a suit, carrying a briefcase. "Watch your Appearance!" it said. "Are you All-American enough to be interviewed by the makers of jellied death?"

"Oh," Jane said. "Dow Chemical. Because of the napalm. I read they were recruiting here."

"Right," Tom said. "Jesus. It started out, no big deal – a bunch of Baggers sitting around in the hallway outside where they were doing the interviews. Some of them were passing out leaflets. Okay, getting in the way a little. You know how they are. Then all of a sudden there were cops everywhere, everyone was screaming and yelling. But, man, the cops, they were *crazy*. No shit. One of them gave me a shove that almost knocked me down, and all I was doing was trying to get the hell out of his way."

Jane still didn't know how to think about what she had seen that day, or about what had happened the day after, when anti-war demonstrators planted themselves around the Auditorium and heckled the Secretary of State, who was giving a speech there. She had been taught never to be rude. But what were you supposed to do when you spoke peacefully, politely, as the students had done in the Business Building, only to be dragged away and beaten by police who didn't agree with them? How else but through a breach of manners could students get the attention of the President and policy makers in Washington, let them know they would not be complicit in the destruction of Vietnam? She'd thought of Watts burning the summer after she graduated from high school, remembered how white people, her own parents, had condemned the violence. She had condemned it herself. Yet now it seemed clear that most white people had not really begun to take the civil rights struggle seriously until they saw that their own world might be threatened by continuing to ignore it.

She glanced at Tom, comforted by the sight of him there beside her, his hands on the wheel. Just the two of them. Jane was glad Bridget had to work this afternoon, glad to have this time alone with Tom without feeling she was abandoning her, free from the guilt she sometimes felt for her own happiness when she weighed it against Bridget's sorrow about Pete.

She quickened now, thinking of the empty house awaiting them at the end of the drive. It was four o'clock, shadows lengthening across the brown, stubbled fields. The sun went in, and she sank deeper into the leather seat, pulled the stadium blanket up to her chin.

"Cold?" Tom asked

"Freezing," she said.

"I'll warm you up when we get back."

"Yeah?" She smiled.

"Yeah." He shifted, slowing down as they left the country behind them and neared the first stoplight in the city.

They'd take a hot, soapy shower together, Jane thought, as they turned into the driveway. Pull the shades, light the candles she'd melted into the empty Chianti bottles and set them on their dresser. She felt warm and sweet inside anticipating the moment they would slide between the cool sheets and make love. Tom turned off the ignition and put his hand on her thigh for just a moment before opening his door to get out of the car, and she knew he was feeling it, too.

But as they started up the front steps, Bridget opened the front door.

"Oh!" Jane said. "I thought you had to work till nine."

Bridget opened her mouth but could not seem to speak.

"Bridge?" Tom said.

She turned abruptly, went inside. Following her, Jane saw her father on the couch in the living room.

"Janey?" He stood, took a step toward her.

And she knew Bobby was dead.

By snipers, near Da Nang, her father told her. "We just couldn't bring ourselves to give you news like this on the phone. So I came."

"But I didn't see the car – " Jane said, stupidly. "Where – ?"

"Aunt Helen said take theirs. Ours is, well – "

Jane knew. It wasn't reliable enough to make the trip.

"Honey?" He took a tentative step toward her. "Jane?"

She felt as stiff as a mannequin in his arms, and instinctively turned from him toward Tom, who took her hand and held it tightly. She should say something, she knew – at the very least introduce Tom to her father – but she could not speak. She only half-heard Bridget make the introduction, then explain that Jane's father had arrived just as she was leaving for work, and she'd called in sick so he wouldn't have to wait here all alone.

He'd been there more than two hours, Jane thought, and the panic she felt rising inside her was as much about the sudden, stark reality of her brother's death as imagining Bridget and her father together, talking. About seeing the house where they all lived together through her father's eyes.

The batik throws on the couch, the psychedelic posters on the walls, the red silk scarves she and Bridget had draped over the cheap lampshades. The double bed behind the beaded curtain that hung in the doorway of the room she shared with Tom. Would he recognize the scent of marijuana lingering from the night before? Had he been in the kitchen, where, just this morning, Bridget had tacked a new poster on the wall above the kitchen table: War Is Not Healthy for Children and Other Living Things?

It was nearly ten o'clock by the time they got home, but the house was bursting with people. As she walked across the front yard, Jane could see them framed by the picture window: neighbors and relatives, a few of her mother's friends from the A&P. She could see her mother, too, huddled in the corner of the sofa, a handkerchief balled in one hand. Amy and Susan, their faces red and blotchy with tears. She stopped and took in the scene, as if it were something she was watching on television.

She could not go in, she could *not.* All she could think was that the little flag her mother had set so proudly into the corner of the picture window when Bobby left – a flag he'd given her, with a single gold star on a red ground to show that the family of a Marine serving his country lived here – should be removed. And right now, because she simply could not bear to look at it.

She flinched when her father lightly brushed her elbow to set her moving again. Stood, rigid, in the embrace of her Aunt Helen, who met them at the door. Then her mother reached up toward her much as she had the night of Bobby's accident; but this time when Jane went to her she drew her close and held on so tightly and for so long that all Jane's defenses crumbled and, finally, she wept.

Cry. Honey, you cry. You'll feel better if you cry.

She could hear the women murmuring around her.

Get away from me, she wanted to scream.

Instead, she kept her head buried in her mother's lap; let her eyes close, darkness descend. Hours later, she woke in Bobby's room, alone. Had her father carried her there? She couldn't remember. She was still dressed, her clothes rumpled. Her mouth felt sour, her head ached. She was starving.

The house was quiet. She opened the door a sliver and saw the living room was dark. She crept to the bathroom. Then to the kitchen, where she piled a paper plate with food people had brought and stood, eating, by moonlight. Back in Bobby's room –

But it wasn't really his room anymore and hadn't been since he joined the Marines. It was Amy's room now; she was sharing with Susan tonight as she'd done the last time Jane came home – months ago, in April. The curtains and bedspread were pink; there was a pink princess phone on the bedside table. Both Amy and Susan had phones in their rooms, something Jane had never dreamed of having when she lived at home. In high school now, they had bulletin boards, dotted with ticket stubs to dances and ball games, snapshots of their friends. Susan was a cheerleader, Amy the secretary of her class. Both of them popular. Happy.

She had meant to save them: to get through school, get a teaching job, and make sure that they had what they needed when it was time for college. So they wouldn't have to feel guilty about going. But when she had said this to them last spring, Susan shrugged and said, "What if we don't want to be like you?"

They were angry with her for upsetting their mother, arguing as she had against the war; they wouldn't listen when she tried to tell them what she knew. This evening, they had avoided her. She had seen them through her tears, hovering near – as if they were afraid she might hurt their mother again. If they'd been able to choose which sibling to lose, they'd have chosen her, Jane thought. Wasn't she lost to them already?

How long would she have to be here, she wondered. Vaguely, she remembered her father telling her that Bobby's body was being transported from Vietnam. There'd be a calling when it arrived, in a few days; the funeral, of course. She'd read that the caskets of dead servicemen were sealed and could not be opened. Probably because they didn't want you to *see* what had happened to them. She knew what her mother would do: prop that awful photograph of Bobby, all puffed-up and proud in his Marine uniform, against a wreath of flowers. She'd prefer that to looking at his real face, anyway, if he even had a face left at all. It made Jane shudder to think that, made her throat ache with tears – as much for herself as for her brother, because she knew that she would have to find her own way to grieve for him, alone.

When Amy took over Bobby's room, she'd lined up some of his favorite things on the top shelf of the bookcase, which now seemed like a little shrine: his Rin Tin Tin, ratty and threadbare, all the paint worn away from its plastic snout; his cigar boxes full of baseball cards; a model '55 Chevy. Jane had made fun of him for sleeping with the stuffed dog when he was a little boy. And for the simple pleasure he took in the baseball cards, the endless hours he spent organizing them and playing some game he'd made up, throwing dice and moving the cards around an imaginary ball field. The hours he spent gluing and painting model cars and, later, tinkering with real cars in the driveway. How she had hated seeing him there, wrench in hand, his jeans filthy with oil. His greaser friends bent over the engine.

She thought of Tom then, how not even twenty-four hours ago she had sat on the porch watching him wax his MG, amused by his obsession, and it struck her that he and Bobby would have talked about cars if they'd met. Tom would have examined the engine of whatever junk car Bobby was working on, as curious as Bobby was about its problems. He'd have tossed him the keys to his MG and said, "Take it for a spin."

She thought of sitting at the kitchen table with Bobby over Christmas break, laughing about their mother. Of the letters he'd written to her, how touched she'd been when, recently, he asked her to send him some books he thought he should read. It was just so *wrong* that this had happened to him, just when he'd begun to get his life together. Her stomach churned, as if she had eaten something spoiled. She felt agitated. Trapped in this tiny room where he had spent countless hours of his childhood.

She'd unpack, she decided. It was something to do. But when she opened the suitcase Bridget had packed for her and saw the same gray wool jumper and white silk blouse Bridget had lent her for the dinner with Tom's parents when she was in Evansville after Christmas, she closed it and lay down again, overcome with exhaustion. It was a beautiful outfit, expensive. A gift from Bridget's parents.

"Wear it," Bridget insisted that day. "How were you supposed to know you'd need something to wear for dinner at the country club with your boyfriend's snobby mother when you packed for Christmas break?" Though they both knew that even if Jane had known, she wouldn't have had anything nearly as nice to wear for the occasion. She had nothing decent to wear to Bobby's funeral, either – which, of course, was why Bridget had packed the jumper for her yesterday. But the simple sight of it had brought back Tom's mother grilling her about her family in that syrupy, condescending voice, the way she'd introduced Jane to anyone who came to the table as "Tom's friend from school."

"I told you she was uptight," he said, afterwards. "Plus, she was freaked out because, when she asked, I said, yeah, it was serious between us. She'll calm down when she gets used to it. Don't let her intimidate you."

But Jane still cringed every time she thought of the way Mrs. Gilbert had looked her up and down in that beautiful jumper, as if she'd known it couldn't possibly belong to her. Fearful she would somehow find out that Jane's mother was a grocery store clerk and her father was a steelworker who drank away most of his paycheck. That no matter how hard her mother worked, she could not make ends meet and any unexpected expense – a flat tire, a tooth that needed to be filled – would mean going without something else they needed.

Now she'd wear the jumper again, only this time it would be Tom meeting her parents. They'd like him, of course. What wasn't to like about Tom? But, more importantly, Jane knew they'd be predisposed to like him once they knew he was important to her; they'd assume she would be involved with a person of good character. It was the thought of Tom coming to the funeral as he had promised he would and finally seeing exactly where she came from that made her feel sick with apprehension.

It wouldn't matter to him. She knew that, knew what he'd say if she told him how she felt. *They're good people. They love you. Why would you be ashamed of them?*

Still, Jane couldn't help imagining his first sight of her childhood home: the linoleum floors, the shabby furniture, the gold drapes from Sears that her mother had saved months to buy.

She curled up, vibrating with shame and dread and sorrow. Then, finally, slept.

7

"White Rabbit"

Sometimes Jane thought it seemed as if Bridget were the one whose brother had died in Vietnam. She was enraged by what had happened to Bobby. The day after they returned from the funeral, she joined Students for a Democratic Society and threw herself into working against the war. When a letter from Bobby arrived, mailed the day before his death, Bridget took the snapshot he'd enclosed and taped it to the refrigerator: Bobby mugging with his buddies, a cigarette dangling from his mouth, tanned as a lifeguard, his buzzed hair bleached white from the sun.

"We need to remember," she said.

"Bridget," Tom said. "Maybe Jane – "

"No," Jane said. "She's right. We do."

Tom didn't press it. Later, though, when they were alone, he said, "You know, Jane, she shouldn't have done that. How did she know it wouldn't hurt you to see it there?"

She just shook her head. The snapshot did hurt her, but how could she explain that the twist of pain that came each time she saw it was a good thing, something real? Mainly, her own grief oppressed her. It felt less about Bobby's death than about what a terrible sister she'd been to him and how it was too late now to make up for it. About her failure to be a comfort to her family, even to feel as if she belonged to them through the long hours of the calling and even at the funeral.

She thought constantly about the reception at her Aunt Helen's house afterwards, where she had stood awkwardly in the living room, receiving condolences from friends and family.

"Your brother was a hero," her Uncle Bert had said to her. "All those boys over there are heroes. I'll tell you something. I read about that mess with Dow Chemical down at IU last week, and I told your dad if you were one of mine I'd yank you out of that place before you could say 'Jack Robinson.' I hope to hell you were smart enough to steer clear of it."

"I was there," Jane said, quietly. "I wasn't protesting, but I will be next time. I agree with them. I think the war is wrong."

"*Do* you?" he said.

She'd looked at his piggy little face, remembering how he had always had something critical to say about Bobby. Why didn't he play sports? Why did he run around with those hoodlums? Why didn't he clean the grime and oil out from underneath his fingernails? And get a decent haircut?"

"Yeah," she said. "I do."

He snorted. "So, now you're in college you know more than a President and a Congress full of men who've studied foreign policy all their lives."

"I have a right to my opinion," she said. "In case you've forgotten, that's what this country is supposed to be about. You think the war is so great, go ahead and think it. That's *your* right. Go ahead and send your own boys when they get old enough and see what you think when they come home dead, like Bobby did."

"Bert," Aunt Helen said, stricken. "Please. Now's not the time." She took his arm, hurried him into the kitchen.

"*Timing* is not the problem," Jane called after them. "The problem is, it's immoral what we're doing in Vietnam, and if you're too blind, too goddamn smug to see it, God help you. God help you all."

She had realized, suddenly, that she was shouting. All around her, there was a shocked silence. For a long moment, she stared into the roomful of people, most of whom she'd known since childhood. Her own parents and sisters, who looked at her as if she were a stranger.

Then she turned and left, Tom and Bridget in her wake.

"Asshole," Bridget said, brimming with righteous anger. "Let's get Jane's stuff and get the hell out of here."

"He was wrong to say it," Tom said, quietly. "But – Jane, are you okay? Do you want to go back?"

"No," she said. "I can't."

Tom and Bridget had come straight to the funeral, now Jane gave directions to her house – her voice so quiet and small that, more than once, Tom had to ask her to repeat them.

"Are you okay?" he asked again.

She didn't answer.

She hoped he would think grief had stolen her voice. But it wasn't grief, or not only that. Was it possible to be ashamed of being ashamed? If so, that was how she had felt turning into her neighborhood that day, seeing it through Tom and Bridget's eyes. Cracker-box houses falling into disrepair, scruffy kids watching the passage of the unfamiliar car, nicer than any other on the street. The gratitude she felt knowing her neighbors were all at the funeral and would not come out to say, again, how sorry they were about Bobby. This was where she had come from, the secret she'd kept all this time.

"No," she said when Tom offered to go in with her to get her suitcase. "Really, I'm fine." What had they said to each other in the few moments she was gone?

God. Poor Jane.

I had no idea . . .

No wonder . . .

She still couldn't bear to consider it.

She went home for Christmas; what else could she do? But it made her feel crazy listening to her mother speak of Bobby's sacrifice; she was hurt by her sisters' cool indifference toward her, shocked by the medicine bottles of whiskey she found under the front seat of the car, tucked between the sofa cushions, in the toe of her father's worn leather slipper – and returned to Bloomington the first moment she could get away.

In the next weeks – the body count rising, the film footage of the Tet Offensive playing relentlessly on the evening news, the threatened escalation of troops – despair threatened to paralyze her. If she didn't act – do something, anything.

The thought frightened her. The gap between herself and her family was unbridgeable, she could be of no help to them now, but she could work to stop the war that had taken Bobby from them. So she joined SDS and, with Bridget, spent every spare moment manning information tables in the Union, trudging dorm-to-dorm in the freezing weather, working for peace. When Dow Chemical came again in March, they stood in protest, held lit matches to the cloth doll the demonstrators set on fire to mourn all the real children burned by Dow's napalm in Vietnam.

Tom went to the demonstration with them, but he wouldn't join the group, and his acceptance to law school in the spring further strained his already touchy relationship with Bridget.

"It's guys like you who need to stand up," she said. "Get drafted and refuse to go – instead of ducking into law school to save your ass from Vietnam."

"I always planned to go to law school," he said. "But, you know what? If it keeps me out of Vietnam in the process, I'm fine with that. My guess is you'd feel the same way if you really had to put yourself on the line. But you don't, do you? You don't want to admit that the only way to make anything happen is from the inside, either."

"Inside," Bridget sputtered. "*Inside* is the fucking Pentagon. Like anything's ever going to change there. Inside, you're *them*. Inside – remember? '*We've met the enemy and he is us?*'"

Jane could see both sides. But if she agreed with a point one made it felt like betraying the other, so mostly she sat in silence, longing for a domestic peace that seemed, increasingly, as unlikely to occur as peace in Vietnam.

The assassination of Martin Luther King, then Bobby Kennedy in June, had heightened Bridget's resolve, but by then Jane was exhausted and so downhearted that she was incapable of doing anything but the most necessary tasks. Lying in the bedroom she shared with Tom, she could hear Tom and Bridget arguing about her.

"Now's no time to stop," Bridget said. "Aren't you watching the fucking news?"

"I don't give a shit about the news. I give a shit about *Jane.*"

"Like I don't? She'll feel better if she does something. Anything."

"She'll feel better if you stop trying to make her feel personally responsible about Vietnam."

"Oh. Fine. So we all just forget about all that and go out and have some fun."

"What's wrong with having some fun?" Tom said. "It's not the worst idea I've heard."

Fun. It seemed like part of a completely different life, one Jane could barely remember. Yet, suddenly, she longed for it, longed to be with Tom as they had been before all this sadness.

In late July, Pete pulled up in his Corvette. He'd flown in from San Francisco, stayed in Indianapolis just long enough to have a big blow-up with both parents, then headed for Bloomington to spend the rest of his leave.

"I know. I was a dumb shit," he said cheerfully. "Like the Army was going to be better than studying. It was brutal, man. You can't even imagine." He put his arm around Bridget, drew her close. "When it got bad, I'd think of you, Bridge," he said. "All you guys. I'd think, if I get the fuck out of here I am changing my ways."

They had one conversation about the war, in which Bridget set out to convince him that, having been there, having seen the senselessness and destruction firsthand, it was his obligation to join those trying to end it.

"I don't give a flying fuck about the war," he said. "As far as I'm concerned, it *is* over. I'm serious, man. I don't even want to talk about it. I won't."

"Pete – "

But the look on his face quieted her and, to Jane's surprise, she didn't mention the war again.

She quit her job to be with him. She had money in the bank, enough to tide her over until he had to go. Plus, Jane knew, her parents would give her more if she ran out; disconcerted by her stubborn independence, they were constantly begging her to tell them what she needed, pleased at any opportunity to take care of her. The two of them were inseparable while he was there. They *played*. Evenings, they'd sit out on the porch drinking beer, listening to the radio, singing along. Late at night, Jane could hear them making love.

On the last day of Pete's leave, they drove out to Bean Blossom – Pete and Bridget in the Corvette, Jane and Tom in the MG. It was a Monday, the park they liked to visit empty, and they unloaded their picnic at the place by the lake where they used to go. They swam awhile. Laughed, remembering the girl, someone's girlfriend – what was her name? The one whose pet boa constrictor lived under the dashboard of her Volkswagen Bug.

And that Hairy Buffalo the first spring after they'd met: every kind of liquor and cocktail mix poured into a new metal trash can and served up in big Dairy Queen cups, deceptively fruity, but in fact so potent that both Pete and Bridget had passed out on the roof of the shelter, where they'd climbed on a lark. Tom found them, finally – after everyone at the party had searched nearly an hour and had begun to fear something terrible had happened to them.

"I was scared to death you guys had drowned," Jane said.

Pete grinned. "You were scared to death of *everything*," he said. "Man, I still remember lying up there, drunk out of my mind, looking at the stars."

They ate the picnic lunch Bridget had spent hours making: a vast amount of fried chicken, four kinds of salad. "Fucking Donna Reed," Pete teased, pouring from the Thermos of fresh-squeezed lemonade.

When they'd eaten the strawberry shortcake she made from scratch, they threw themselves on the quilts they'd spread out on the grass. Jane was tired; she'd worked a double shift the day before. She closed her eyes and felt the sun on her skin, felt her wet hair drying. Tom lay beside her, not touching her, but she felt preternaturally aware of him, as if her body had lost all its edges. She breathed in the clean scent of the water.

No one spoke. There was just the sound of water lapping at the edges of the lake, a slight breeze rustling in the trees, an occasional birdcall. Odd, she thought, listening to the faint whistle of her own breath. It grew louder, intensifying so that soon what she heard with each breath was like a scream. And her breath itself seemed strange, alive, moving through the tunnel of her body to billow out into the atmosphere, drifting and tangling in the trees above her. She opened her eyes and saw it, like you'd see your breath in cold weather – except it had a pinkish hue. She could see the veins on the leaves, the slivers of green light holding the leaves to the trees by some kind of magic.

She'd read Proust in a literature class last semester, and she might have thought that what she was experiencing was the kind of waking dream he described – but she was absolutely, fully awake. Her eyes open. Her breath, the veins on the leaves, the slivers of light were real, *there*.

What's happening to me, she thought, with some alarm. She wanted her breath back. It scared her, way up there in the trees. She sat straight up, as if to go after it. Then she caught sight of Pete watching her, watching them all – and she knew.

"It's acid, isn't it?" she said. "You put acid in the Thermos."

He smiled, slyly. "Go with it, Jane," he said. "Nice little hit of Blue Cheer from the Haight. Consider it a farewell gift."

She looked at her hands, which had begun to shake – from the acid or from fear of it, she couldn't tell. "You *asshole*," she said. "You don't just – *decide* something like that for people." She stood, wobbly on her feet, and began to gather their things until Tom took her hand and pulled her back to the blanket beside him.

"We can't go now. I can't drive like this." He put his arms around her. "Calm down, okay? I'm right here; I'll stay here with you. But Jesus fucking Christ," he said to Pete. "It *was* a dumb-shit thing to do. Jane's right. You don't just – "

"Hey, lighten up," Pete said. "You're not in law school *yet*."

Jane felt Tom's whole body clench, and for a moment she thought he might go after Pete. Instead, he closed his eyes and sat perfectly still for a long moment. Then said, "Bridge? Are you okay?"

"Groovy," she said.

"Seriously," Pete said. "Don't sweat it, man. It's just . . . *more* of everything. That's all. Good trip, bad trip – you decide. Come on. Bridge – "

He held out his hand and she took it, glancing back at Tom and Jane as they walked toward the woods together.

Jane watched. Color bloomed and pulsed around Bridget as they went, absorbing her so completely that Jane was simultaneously awestruck, broken-hearted, and aware that Bridget had simply disappeared into the trees. What was Tom seeing, she wondered? She might have asked, except for the thought that followed: What is he *ever* seeing? Could it be that, even without acid, the world looked completely different to each one of them?

A wave of loneliness engulfed her, only slightly assuaged when she and Tom lay back on the quilt, wrapped in each other's arms. She concentrated on breathing evenly, trying to ignore the whistle of her breath, the ominous thud-thud of her heart. If she closed her eyes, bright, quivering strings of matter grew from the darkness, drifting into patterns that collapsed into themselves again and again, as if someone were turning a kaleidoscope inside her head.

It frightened her. But it was a kind of kaleidoscope she understood. What terrified her was to open her eyes and watch the sun shatter and fall into the lake – because, with that, came the sudden apprehension that the lake, the woods – the whole physical world as she had known it till that moment – was just one pebble in some cosmic kaleidoscope of what was real. Twist it and you would tunnel through the void to patterns of being that negated – or expanded beyond comprehension – everything you'd always believed life to be.

This was something she did not want to know or even think about. The slow, earnest accumulation of hours leading to the teaching degree she'd staked her whole life on suddenly seemed pointless, absurd. The happiness she imagined it would earn for her no more than an illusion.

Don't think, she told herself. Yet in this new universe, thought was the only recognizable thing and she clung to it like a life raft. How strange that she could look at the bird pecking at the remains of their picnic lunch and see in the fold of its black feathers the very essence of flight – and at the same time think, I'm okay. If I just stay calm, I'm going to be all right.

Later, at home, Tom lost himself until nearly dark washing, then waxing his car. He was thinking, Jane knew, watching him from the kitchen window. Waxing the car was what he always did when he needed to think – in this case, probably about how to deal with Pete.

"He needs to grow up," he'd said on the way home. "And so does Bridget. She knew about the acid. I'd bet money on it."

"No," Jane said, shocked. "She wouldn't – " But then she stopped, because there was a pretty good chance he was right. "Well, if she did, Pete talked her into it. He's so . . . I *hate* the way she always thinks she has to please him. How she's not herself when she's with him."

Tom glanced at her. "You don't always . . . *see* Bridget," he said. "She's your best friend, I know; it's cool how close you are. But I've known Bridget forever, I know her whole family – and, the truth is, she's not that different from Pete, really. It's just, what she wants plays out nicer – or has till now. She wants to save people. She thinks she can save Pete."

"She saved *me*," Jane said. She remembered Bridget appearing in her doorway that first day, claiming her, how every single good thing in her life had happened to her since had been born of that moment.

"Bullshit," Tom said. "You saved yourself. If you needed to be saved, which I don't think you did. Hey, I'm not saying Bridget isn't a great person. She *is*. Jesus, she's got a huge heart. But she's used to getting what she wants – and she wants Pete. She's been living in a fucking fantasy world since he got here, she's conveniently forgotten about how he ended up in Vietnam in the first place. She needs to cut him loose, get over him, live her life. But she won't do it. She won't listen to anyone. She never does."

Now Jane ranged around the house, worrying that they shouldn't have left the park without making sure that Pete and Bridget were okay. It was nearly nine when Pete pulled up in the Corvette and the two of them spilled out into the yard.

Through the open window, Jane heard them call out to Tom. But he ignored them.

"What's he being such a tight-ass for?" Pete asked, when they came inside. "Come on, Jane. It was far out, right? Beautiful. And now here we all are at home, cozy as bugs." He grinned, stretched his arms, cat-like, above his head. "I'm racking out, man," he said. "Bridge?"

Bridget waved him away. "You go. I think I'll sit out here awhile with Jane." She plopped into a kitchen chair, closed her eyes and heaved a deep sigh. "Whoa! Was that some kind of amazing shit, or what?" she said, after he'd gone.

Jane didn't answer.

"Okay," Bridget said. "I know I shouldn't have let him do it. I'm sorry. But, seriously – "

"It scared the crap out of me," Jane said.

Bridget opened her eyes, alarmed. "You're okay, though, aren't you? Jane?"

"Yeah. I'm okay." Jane sat down beside her. "Bridget. The problem is, *Pete's* not okay. He wouldn't have done that if he were okay. He wouldn't have asked *you* to do it. We'd never dropped acid before. How did he know one of us wouldn't totally freak out?"

"But we didn't," Bridget said.

"So what?" Jane said.

Bridget shrugged. "I said, I'm sorry. I shouldn't have let Pete talk me into it. Love makes you stupid, I guess. I mean, what if Tom had asked *you?*"

"Tom would never ask me to do something like that. He'd never do it himself. You know that."

"Of course." Bridget held up her hands in surrender. "Tom: always the good Boy Scout."

Jane flinched, as if she'd been slapped. "I can't believe you'd say that."

"Oh, for Christ's sake," Bridget said. "I love Tom. I love you and Tom together. But, you know, Jane, I don't want what you want. I don't want that kind of – comfort. Shit," she said, crying now. "Not like it even feels like I can choose. I just fucking love Pete, and I always will. The more he fucks up, the more it hurts, the more I think loving him is what I'm supposed to do. The more I think he needs me."

"But he's not good for you," Jane said. "He only cares about himself."

"So what? So *what?* Could we just not talk about this anymore? Please. You don't have any idea how I feel about Pete. I don't think you *can* have."

"Why? Because you think I love Tom *less?*" Jane asked.

Bridget didn't answer.

"Okay," Jane said. "So you love Pete in a way I can never understand – and that means his idiotic idea to put acid in the lemonade didn't freak you out at all?"

"Actually, not that much," Bridget said. "If you think about it, the freaky thing is that we never dropped acid until now."

Jane comforted her when Pete left the next morning, but both she and Tom were glad to see him go. "I'll write," he promised Bridget. But she didn't hear from him – and on Labor Day weekend, Tom got a call from Pete's father. He was AWOL from the Army, he said. Had Tom heard from him? Did he have any idea at all where Pete was, what he might be thinking?

"No," Tom said. "No idea at all."

8

"Everybody's Talkin'"

Jane drove a half-hour each morning in the winter darkness to get to the elementary school where she'd been assigned to do her student teaching – beyond the outskirts of Bloomington into the country, passing farmhouses with lights twinkling inside, a little roadside church, fields and copses, black ponds holding the morning moon. Entering the old brick school, she breathed in the scent of floor wax, chalk dust, paper, and was, for an instant, entering the grade school of her childhood, the one place she had ever felt she truly belonged. The first morning, she had regarded the classroom full of second graders who sat, hands folded on their desks, curious and expectant, and something settled in her. She had known she wanted to be a teacher from her first day in school, but this was a whole new kind of knowing. Like stepping into herself.

The sound of pages turning, the scratch of pencils on paper, the ping of the old radiators brought back the comfort and happiness she had felt in school as a child, the approval of teachers, the small kindnesses that made her believe she might be worthy of their attention. Each morning she watched the school buses lumber in like big yellow animals, her heart opening to whatever the day would bring.

She adored her supervisory teacher, Mrs. Thompson, a maternal, gray-haired lady in her fifties whose common sense and dry wit frequently snapped things into perspective. “There are really only three things you need to know about teaching,” she told Jane during their first meeting. “One, be over-prepared. Two, don’t get overwhelmed by what you don’t have time to teach them. Choose what’s possible and necessary to teach and teach it well. And third – ” She smiled. “You loved school when you were a little girl, right?”

Jane nodded.

“So, think about the class you went through school with. How many people in it loved school like you did?”

“Not very many,” Jane said.

“Exactly,” said Mrs. Thompson. “And that never changes. It’s funny, if you think about it. Most of us go into teaching because we loved school so much – well, and school *supplies,*” she added, laughing. “Anyway. Number Three is, always remember that most kids don’t love school like you did, but you signed on to teach them all. It’s fun to teach children who remind you of yourself at that age, but the real satisfaction is in winning over the reluctant learners. Pick one and I think you’ll see what I mean.”

Jane chose Daniel Pettus, a scrawny, stubborn little boy who often sat hunched over in his seat or even put his head down on his desk when she or Mrs. Thompson was teaching a lesson.

One of eight siblings, he came to school each day dressed in threadbare clothes, his white-blond hair sticking up every which way. Never quite clean, he smelled of greasy cooking and stale cigarette smoke and just a tinge of urine. Some of the children were mean to him; most ignored him. He ate his sack lunch alone in the cafeteria, stood alone at the outskirts of the playground.

“I don’t know,” he would answer if called on during class. Sometimes he refused to answer at all. When Jane spoke directly to him, bringing his attention to something he might enjoy or making a positive comment about something he had done, he shrugged and looked away from her.

He was often kept in from recess for not doing his work and, one morning, she drew a small chair up next his desk. He was slumped in his chair, his jaw clenched, a sullen expression on his face, a page of math problems untouched before him.

“I hate math,” she said in a low, conspiratorial voice.

No response.

"I *really* hate story problems. Jack has six apples and Johnny has five. I always think, 'How come Jack gets more?' Or sometimes I think, 'Who cares?'"

Nothing.

They sat quietly awhile, the sounds of recess drifting in through the open window: kids yelling, balls bouncing. "So what about you, Daniel?" Jane asked. "You don't do the problems because you hate math like me, or because you just don't want to – "

He looked at her then, his blue eyes swimming with tears. "Because I *can't.*"

"Ah," Jane said, resisting the impulse to draw him into her arms. "That's a much easier problem to solve. Here. I'll do one to show you how. Then we'll do the rest together."

When the bell rang, they'd gotten through most of the page. "Would you like it if I called your mom to see if it would be okay for you to stay after school a few times a week, and work on math together?" she asked. "I could give you a ride home afterwards."

He nodded, yes.

"Yeah, well, the government will eventually just use him up as cannon fodder," Bridget said when Jane got home from school that day, thrilled by this first success. "It's what they do with kids like that. You can suck him in and teach him story problems . . . or whatever, but ten years from now there'll be some other stupid war to send him to – if we're not still in Vietnam."

She'd nearly failed student teaching last fall, insistent on bringing politics into whatever she taught, organizing groups of her high school students to participate in the antiwar rallies in Dunn meadow. Now, as spring approached, she was barely passing her last classes, in a perpetual state of rage. LBJ was gone, but Nixon was worse. His promise of an "honorable peace" apparently meant endless negotiations in Paris about what kind of table was suitable for discussion, in lieu of actually talking about the problem at hand, and training Vietnamese troops to fight for democracy, when all they really wanted was for the war to end so they could go back to their villages and live their lives. Meanwhile, American boys kept dying.

What was a bourgeois college degree in the face of that, she said – and boycotted commencement despite her parents' pleas. Jane skipped the ceremony, too – letting Bridget believe she agreed with her when, in fact, not attending was the only way she could justify not inviting her family.

She hadn't seen them since an awkward visit in January, the big framed photograph of Bobby in his Marine uniform on the wall above the couch where they sat. She hadn't written or called since Susan returned the birthday gift Jane had sent to her in February, with a letter that began, "Just in case you're interested, Mom cried for an hour after you left.

"It's obvious you don't want to be part of this family anymore," she went on. "You think Bobby was stupid to die for his country; you're embarrassed by the rest of us. So why don't you just go ahead and live your life with your rich boyfriend and leave us alone. Mom doesn't know I'm writing this and I don't have to tell you she'd be upset if she found out. Tell her if you want, but I think we both know it would only make things worse."

Jane hadn't mentioned the letter to Tom or Bridget, but tucked it away in the shoebox of letters Bobby had sent from Vietnam. Rifling through them, pierced by the sight of his handwriting, it occurred to her for the first time that he might have kept the letters she sent to him, too, and, if he had, they'd have been returned with his personal effects. Of course, her mother would have read them. Jane had written to Bobby about how grateful she was to have gotten away from home; she'd encouraged him to use the G.I. Bill when he got out of the service to do the same – and, worse, she'd shared painful childhood memories about their father's drinking, their mother's refusal to acknowledge it. Bobby's unhappiness, his painful memories were in the letters he'd written to Jane, small, true pieces of himself that their mother would ever know.

His picture remained on the refrigerator, Bridget's call to revolution. But when Jane looked at it now, she saw the bright, rambunctious little boy who'd fallen through the cracks, and she found some measure of comfort in her determination to become the kind of teacher who might have set him on a different path. She had a job for the fall, third grade at the school where she had done her student teaching, and she spent a lot of time that summer in her classroom. "Miss Barth, Grade Three," she printed in the top corner of the blackboard the first day she was there, just so she could look at it. She'd be teaching the kids she'd student-taught the spring before and loved thinking about them walking in on the first day of school in the fall to find her waiting for them. She spent hours working on curriculum, clipping construction paper into letters of the alphabet and bright autumn leaves for her first bulletin board, and poring through professional magazines with articles on everything from art projects to classroom management.

Still, once school started, Jane was so busy that she had little time to do anything but grade papers and make her lesson plans for the next day. It wasn't that she no longer cared about the war. If anything, she felt more heartsick as time went by, every news broadcast with its battle footage and body counts and lying politicians confirmed the belief that her brother had died for nothing at all. When a national moratorium against the war was planned for mid-October, she agreed to help organize it, waiting till the last moment to tell Bridget that she wouldn't actually be attending the event, which was on a school day.

"Take a personal day," Bridget said. "Or just call in sick. What's the big deal?"

"I can't," Jane said.

"Bullshit," Bridget said. "You're a grown-up, remember? You can do what you want."

"I can't do it," Jane said again.

"You mean you *won't*. You're scared you'll get your picture in the paper or your principal or your kids' redneck parents will see you on TV, aren't you?"

Jane didn't deny it. She couldn't say whether the principal and most of the teachers at her school were *for* the war, but knew from the little time she spent in the teachers' lounge that most of them were disgusted by the tactics of the antiwar movement. As for the parents, maybe they were rednecks, but a lot of them also had sons, brothers, husbands, or friends who'd served in Vietnam or were there right now and, like her own parents, felt that not to support the war would be a kind of betrayal. Plus, it was a weird time. It was wrong that undercover police and FBI agents would be watching, taking pictures, taking names, but it was the way it was and Jane wasn't willing to risk her job just to make Bridget happy.

The evening before the moratorium, both Jane and Tom joined the stream of students, faculty, and some townspeople who gathered at Showalter Fountain for the candlelight parade to Dunn Meadow that would begin the event. People talked quietly as they walked along Seventh Street, but fell silent as they approached the meadow, lit by a thousand tiny flames. Soon, voices rose in song. "Give Peace a Chance," "We Shall Overcome." There were a few speeches, then a ripple of agitation ran through the crowd at the news that someone had just been arrested at the Auditorium. There'd been a lecture going on there at the same time of the march and about halfway through the speech, a student in a devil costume leapt onto the stage and threw a cream pie in the speaker's face. He took off running, but the police had wrestled him down. He was on his way to jail right now, people said, and maybe half of the Dunn Meadow crowd headed for the county jail to demand his release.

Bridget was among them, though Jane didn't know it until she walked into the teachers' lounge the next morning and saw her on the front page of the newspaper, her fist raised, her hair wild, her mouth wide open in a scream.

"Look at that girl," one of the teachers said. "So hateful. That's what upsets me most about all this. They talk about peace, but are they peaceful themselves?"

"She's gone off the deep end," Tom said. He refused to talk politics with Bridget anymore and, if she tried, he'd simply declare that his life goal was to be a thorn in the side of the Establishment.

"What the fuck kind of life goal is that, anyway?" Bridget would say. "The war's not funny, Tom. It's not funny the way people's lives get wrecked by what asshole politicians do. If they even survive it."

Jane sat quietly when the two of them argued. She just wanted them to stop. She knew Bridget thought she was naïve and maybe even foolish having come to believe, as she did, that making a child's eyes light up with understanding was in its own small way a political act. Tom thought the same of her for believing that some part of

Bridget was still the lovely free-spirited girl she'd once been. But she loved them both and would not choose. She couldn't. So she avoided talking to Tom about Bridget, avoided talking to Bridget about Tom, and was grateful that, for whatever reason, neither of them pushed her to tip the precarious balance among them.

9

"Ohio"

"Good evening my fellow Americans," President Nixon began.

"'*Good evening my fellow Americans,*'" Bridget mimicked. "Fucker. I swear to God, the very sound of his voice makes me insane."

"Would you just listen," Tom said.

She rolled her eyes at him.

Jane concentrated on the screen: the President in a dark suit, reading from the pages of the speech he held in his hands. "Ten days ago, in my report to the Nation on Vietnam, I announced a decision to withdraw an additional 150,000 Americans from Vietnam over the next year. I said then that I was making that decision despite our concern over increased enemy activity in Laos, Cambodia, and in South Vietnam . . ."

"Meanwhile, bombing the shit out of them," Bridget said. "Like we don't *know* about their so-called secret bombing there."

Tom turned up the television to drown out her muttered commentary as the speech proceeded, though Jane could hear it anyway.

"Look at him," she said when Nixon rose and, with a pointer, delineated areas of troop build-up along the border between Vietnam and Cambodia on a huge map beside him. "Jesus. He's got visual aids. What? Is he going for the 'I am your trusted social studies teacher' effect?"

But even Bridget sat in stunned silence when, after accusations, explanations, and excuses, he baldly stated, "Tonight, American and South Vietnamese units will attack the headquarters for the entire Communist military operation in South Vietnam . . .

"This is not an invasion of Cambodia . . ." he went on. "Our purpose is not to occupy the areas . . . We take this action not for the purpose of expanding the war into Cambodia but for the purpose of ending the war in Vietnam and winning the just peace we all desire . . . We will be conciliatory at the conference table, but we will not be humiliated . . .

"My fellow Americans, we live in an age of anarchy, both abroad and at home. We see mindless attacks on all the great institutions which have been created by free civilizations in the last 500 years. Even here in the United States, great universities are being systematically destroyed . . ."

"Bullshit," Bridget said. "Fucking bullshit. He knows it, too. Look at him. He's sweating like the pig he is. He can hardly read his own lies."

Nixon stopped once to mop his face with a white handkerchief; he paused, clearly having lost his place in the speech, and Jane watched him collect himself, breathe deeply, reconnect – anyone else, she would have felt sorry for.

Bridget stood up. "'Great universities are being systematically destroyed?' Well, *Dick*. Let's get to it." She grabbed a sweatshirt, tied it around her waist. "You guys in?"

"I want to hear the end of the speech," Tom said. "Jane?"

"I'll stay with you."

Bridget looked at them a long moment, shook her head, and was gone.

When it was finished, they joined the stream of people heading for Dunn Meadow, where student leaders stood on a makeshift stage urging a peaceful protest. But the crowd was too agitated to listen and, when a rumor rippled through the crowd about a panty raid going on at Read Center, most of the demonstrators left the Meadow like a flock of birds suddenly turning in the sky and marched to the dorm, where they found a couple of hundred drunk fraternity guys ranging around, yelling up at the girls, who hung out of the windows laughing and tossing out their underwear. Soon cries for panties changed to "Get out of Cambodia" and "To Hell with Nixon." Girls streamed from the dorm, joining the march back to Dunn Meadow, as it proceeded onward, picking up more people along the way.

The balmy spring evening, scented with flowering trees; the absurdity of the panty raid turned protest; the way the crowd swelled and flowed back toward Dunn Meadow as if directed by an invisible hand – none of it seemed quite real to Jane. When they reached the Meadow, news that police had begun to gather at the courthouse set them moving again, down Kirkwood Avenue, toward the town square.

"Let's get out of here," Tom said. "It's a big, fucking party, that's all."

But as they passed the newly dug earth of People's Park on their way home, students began to pick up rocks to break the windows of some of the storefronts they passed. Anti-war protestors, drunk fraternity guys – by then, it was hard to tell the difference. Tom wrested a rock from a kid wearing a Phi Delt sweatshirt and scuffled with his friends, who were looking for a fight. But he gave up, disgusted, and walked away from them. Neither had mentioned Bridget all evening; they didn't mention her now. Jane had spotted her once, among the students leading the protestors toward Read Center, but she'd covered her long red hair in a bandana, which made it easy for her to disappear into the crowd, and Jane hadn't seen her again. She lay awake a long time, waiting for the sound of Bridget's key in the lock, the door closing behind her.

She woke near dawn, nauseated, and threw up repeatedly – something she'd eaten, probably, though it felt to her as if the events of the evening had made her physically ill. She called in sick and took an afghan to the couch, where she slept fitfully into the morning.

Soon after Tom left for class, Bridget appeared, dressed in riot gear: Levi's, long-sleeved shirt, sneakers. She'd tucked a small jar of Vaseline in her pocket, in case she got maced; soaked a cloth in vinegar, for tear gas. She'd taken out her earrings, braided her hair. She'd tied a bandana around her head and one around her neck, in case she needed to cover her mouth and nose with it.

"Right on," she said. "You're cutting school to go? Groovy. You'd better get ready, though. We meet at nine to set our demands."

"I'm sick," Jane said. "In case you didn't hear, I've been barfing for hours."

"Oh." Bridget actually looked at her for the first time. "Sorry. I crashed when I came in. I didn't hear you. But you look okay now. Come on – "

"I can't *move,*" Jane said, grateful for the spasm that sent her to the bathroom again. She didn't want to go. She was scared to death of what might happen.

She stayed on the couch all day, drifting in and out of consciousness. She could hear the whack-whack of helicopters hovering over campus, the sirens, the shouting. The television was on, switching between national coverage of demonstrations happening all over the country to local newscasters reporting on what was happening a few blocks away. Fifteen hundred students marching from Dunn Meadow toward Bryan Hall to present administrators with a list of demands, including a repudiation of Nixon's Southeast Asia policy and the termination of all ROTC programs on campus, had been met halfway by a busload of campus police, who stepped out in riot gear and moved in double-time on their way to protect the building. There was Bridget, screaming in their faces.

A few days later, there was a shooting at Kent State. One of Jane's fellow teachers heard it on the radio and came into the cafeteria, where Jane was on lunch duty, to tell her. Students had been shot, she said. They didn't know how many yet, or if they'd survived. On the playground, afterward, Jane leaned against the cyclone fence in the spring sunshine, shivering.

"Are you cold, Miss Barth?" Daniel Pettus asked.

"I am," she said. "Isn't that crazy? I guess my body still thinks it's winter."

She made herself go through the motions the rest of the day. "Four dead in Ohio," the radio announcer said, as she pulled out of the parking lot and headed home at the end of the day. Jane, Tom, and Bridget sat glued to the news coverage on television. The line of National Guardsmen in gas masks, carrying rifles with bayonets, advancing over the crest of a hill, shooting canisters of tear gas; students yelling and lobbing them back. What looked like a retreat, then a volley of rifle fire dissolving into a chaos of images and voices, smoke drifting up into the spring sky.

"Do you guys get it *yet?*" Bridget asked. "The pigs are killing *us.* They intend to keep killing us. Are you going to do anything about it, or just sit there on your fucking asses?"

In the next days, it seemed as if the revolution she called for might actually occur. Universities across the country closed down. Two more students were killed in riots at Jackson State University, eleven bayoneted at the University of New Mexico by the National Guard. In New York, antiwar protestors were beaten by construction workers wearing hard hats and wielding clubs. A hundred-thousand people mobilized and converged on Washington D.C. to protest the war and the killing of unarmed student protestors. They smashed windows, slashed tires, dragged parked cars into intersections, and threw bedsprings off overpasses into the traffic below. Nixon was removed to Camp David for his own protection.

Then the school year ended. Maybe most people had been as frightened as Jane had been by the events in May, maybe it was as simple as the vacuum left by students leaving campus to step back into the real world of families and summer jobs. But by the middle of June, the energy that had swelled up against the war had been redirected to fighting over parking meters. Would they install them along Kirkwood Avenue? Would they demolish People's Park to build a high-rise apartment with a parking garage?

"The same friendly people who brought us the Vietnam War have awakened the resistance to the value of guerilla warfare," the *Indiana Daily Student* pronounced, suggesting that if the parking meters were installed students might consider filling the coin slots with epoxy glue.

"As if parking meters and people dying in Vietnam were the same thing," Bridget said. "Is there even one single thing in this stupid paper about My Lai? Does anybody think, maybe, we ought to be doing something about *that?*"

She'd become obsessed with the hearings about the massacre, which had begun in the spring – collecting every news story she could find, fingering the pages of photographs in *Life* magazine so many times they'd become soft as cloth. Bodies fallen like Pick-up sticks along a dirt road; people who looked like living death cowering, begging, running; huts bursting into flames. She wouldn't talk about it. There was nothing to say. She lay on the couch hours at a time, stoned or staring at the photographs – keeping them in the forefront of her mind, she said, because what else could she do?

Sometimes Jane could get her to walk and, when she did, Jane walked with her – the two of them winding their way through campus, their conversation ranging from happier times, before Pete enlisted and went to Vietnam, to Bridget's conviction that he would come back and when he did they would tackle the war together and make a difference. He'd sent her a series of postcards since going AWOL the year before – mountains, beaches, rivers, lakes, forests, and deserts, from the Mississippi River to the Pacific Ocean, each with a cryptic, probably drug-induced message. It made Jane furious. If Pete cared about Bridget, why didn't he come back and be with her; if he didn't, why couldn't he just leave her alone?

"He's not coming back," Tom said. "Not like she wants him to, anyway: Poster Boy for the Cause. You give her too much credit, Jane. The truth is, she's pissed off at the whole world. The whole fucking SDS, what's left of it, is full of people just like her. I accomplished more just sitting in the law school library figuring out how to get guys out of going one at a time than they have with their revolutionary bullshit – and she knows it. That's why she gets so pissed off at me."

Then one day near the end of August, Jane and Bridget returned from a walk and found Pete smoking a joint on the front porch. The bedraggled mutt sleeping at his feet woke as they approached the steps and barked twice, then trotted toward them, its tail wagging.

"That's Gandhi," Pete said. "I found him scrounging in a dump near Taos. We've been on the road together ever since. He's a righteous, peaceful companion."

Bridget knelt to pet the dog – maybe to avoid looking at Pete, Jane thought. He was dirty and emaciated, his long, tangled hair pulled back in a bandana, his beard scruffy and unkempt.

"Where's my bro?" he asked.

"Law library," Jane said.

Pete laughed. "Man, is he still doing that gig?"

"One more year. He'll take the bar next July. Which means it would be a real good idea if you smoked that joint inside. Not to mention the fact that I have a teaching job to think about."

"Jane, Jane. Ever the law-abiding citizen." He pinched the burning tip of the joint with his calloused fingers, tucked it in a pocket of his backpack. "So, Bridge," he said "Are *you* glad to see me?"

Bridget didn't answer.

"Come on," he said. "I fucking drove two days straight to get here. Seriously, Bridge. I had this wild dream. Me and Gandhi, we're on this winding road going up a mountain – who the fuck knows where. But there's these women, right? In these far-out hooded robes, man, every color you can imagine. And – dig it! – they're *everywhere,* as far as I can see, walking in front of me and around me and behind me. Like water, man. *Flowing.* It's like they don't have feet, like they're on these invisible roller skates. And there's me and Ghandi just trudging along and I'm so *fucking* tired all I want to do is lie down and go to sleep. Then, whoa! One of the women going by drops her hood and it's you. You give me this walking stick, carved with all this Indian shit. Then, suddenly, I'm all the way at the top of the mountain and there's nothing but sky and clouds and I'm, like, the only fucking guy in the universe. It's all for me. All mine. So I wake up and I'm like, man, I've got to tell this to Bridge. I've got to thank her."

Bridget glanced at Jane, then went to sit beside him on the porch swing.

"So, yeah. Thanks." He grinned. "And Gandhi thanks you." He put his arm around her, drew her close, and she buried her head in his chest. "We need to go find that place, you know? *Be* there. I need you, Bridge. Seriously. Will you come with me?"

Bridget nodded, yes.

10

"Fortunate Son"

She was back before Thanksgiving. They'd driven west, she told Jane – through the mountains in Colorado, then heading north for Wyoming and Montana, searching for the place Pete had seen in his dream. But no place was right. They'd blown most of her savings by the time they got to Yosemite in October. They'd need to settle soon, find work. Pete promised they would, but whenever she brought it up, he turned the music up loud. Lit a joint. Seduced her.

"You want to be like *them?*" he'd say. "The Man? Fuck that. Why not just be together?"

"The thing is," Bridget said. "I didn't give a shit if he worked or not. I could've gotten a waitressing job wherever we were. We'd have been fine. He was better with me, Jane; he *was*. More lucid. He ate the food I fixed for him. He looked like Pete again. And he loved me. He actually, finally said it. He said the best time in his whole life was his sophomore year, the year we were together."

But at night, he dreamed – not rainbow women, not magic walking sticks, not worlds at his feet. He'd wake screaming and shaking, sometimes crying. Once, Bridget told Jane, she was startled awake to find him crouched above her, his hands on her neck. He dreamed he was in Vietnam. That's all he would say. Angrily, as if the dream had been her fault.

Then one day she woke up and he was gone. It was a beautiful morning. Cold. She could see her breath in the clear, crisp air. She was annoyed, but not worried, she told Jane. Pete and Gandhi often disappeared for hours at a time. Mostly, she didn't want to know where they went.

When he hadn't returned by evening, she began to argue with herself. His books, his clothes were still there. His stash. Surely, he wouldn't have just left everything behind. She'd passed a sleepless night in the tent, fearful of every noise, and when after the second night he still did not appear she packed what she could carry in her duffel bag and walked to the highway, where she hitched a ride to L.A. and bought a plane ticket back to Indiana, angrier about the war, more determined to end it than she had been before she left.

Tom and Jane argued about her assumption that she could move back into "her" room.

"She needs to get her own place," Tom said. "I don't want to come home and spar with her every night. And, Jesus, didn't you think it was nice having a little privacy? I like when it's just the two of us. I like coming home at night and being . . . normal."

"I like it too," Jane said. "But – "

"But *what?*"

"She's a mess," Jane said. "She's heartbroken about Pete. We can't just tell her to go."

"Which is such a crock of shit," Tom said. "I've said it before and I'll say it again. Bridget is pissed because she's used to getting every single thing she wants. That's what all this is really about."

"That's not true," Jane said. "She cares about the war. She's given up everything – "

"Bullshit," Tom interrupted. "She decided not to be a teacher because she got pissed off when someone tried to tell her what to do. It took about two seconds for her to forget all about the war when Pete showed up and wanted her to go off and find some magic mountain. Now she's back and it's the war again – which she likes to think wrecked Pete and that's why he keeps leaving her. Bridget wants to be unhappy, Jane. Don't you see that? She thinks she's punishing Pete being unhappy. Jesus, he's dumped her – what, three times now? And she thinks he cares? The guy is fubar, man. Fucked Up Beyond All Repair. She needs to get over it and move on."

As the end of his last semester in law school approached, he pressed harder. "She's so volatile," he said. "I've got the bar exam coming up in July. I need to be able to concentrate. Not to mention her disappearing for days at a time. Who the hell knows what's up with that? Whether or not I pass the bar will become a moot point if the FBI gets it in their mind that we're harboring a goddamn revolutionary. The school board wouldn't like it a whole lot, either."

"Bridget's not – "

"You don't know that, Jane. Not really. Look. I'll be the bad guy. I'll tell her she needs to find her own place; you don't even have to be there. Okay? Jane?"

Jane didn't answer.

He put his arm around her shoulders, turned her toward him. "I know this is hard for you," he said. "But it's time, right? Even you can't talk to her anymore."

"I know," Jane said. "*I know.*"

They were walking home from the law library, where they fled most evenings after their evening meal – Tom, to study; Jane, to grade papers and make lesson plans or just read. Jane felt a moment's reprieve as they approached the house and she saw that it was dark. But inside they found Bridget sitting straight up on the living room couch, lit only by moonlight, her hands folded on her lap.

"I need to talk to you guys," she said.

"What?" Jane took a step into the room. "What's wrong?"

"Nothing. *Nothing.*" Bridget glanced toward the closed door of her bedroom. "I just wanted to tell you there's a . . . well, I mean, I met someone and he's – "

"No problem," Tom interrupted. "Jane? Are you coming to bed?"

"Jane," Bridget said, urgently.

"You go," Jane said, sinking into the battered easy chair across from her. "I'll be there in a little while. So, who is he?" she asked, when Tom had gone.

"You don't know him; he's not from here. I actually met him a month or so ago – " Bridget waved vaguely in lieu of explanation. "The funny thing is, I thought he was a total asshole. He showed up at the SDS office from *wherever* and started bitching at me, like I was personally responsible for the fact that nobody in the whole state of Indiana appeared to give a fuck about the war. He ate shit, slept in his car, but as far as he could tell pretty much everybody else was way more into the *idea* of revolution than the daily grind of it. Blah, blah, blah.

"I said, 'Hey, fuck you,' and gathered up my stuff and walked out on him. It felt good, you know? It beat the shit out of feeling like everything I do is totally useless.

"Anyway. He showed up at the office again today. Penitent. We came back here, I made him some soup, we talked." Bridget smiled, slyly. "The thing is, I knew what was going to happen when he walked through the door of the office. I knew it was why he came back. But before – " She gave a little shrug. "Before – *you* know. Cam – that's his name. John Cameron, actually, but he's called Cam. He said to me, 'Are you with someone?'" She paused and, when she continued, her voice was husky with tears. "I said, 'No. I'm alone.' And, Jane, it was so weird. It was like, when I said it, I felt myself let Pete go. I felt like maybe, *maybe* I might be okay."

She leaned toward Jane, took her hand. "He has work to do here for the next few days, we both do. But after that, I'm going with him."

"Where?" Tom asked, when Jane climbed into bed and told him all that Bridget had said. "She didn't tell me, and I was so freaked out I didn't ask."

"Probably just as well," he said. "Shit. I knew she was getting in over her head with this stuff. My guess is he's with the Weather faction. Or FBI, which would be even worse."

He was cool to Cam when they met the next evening, obviously assessing him.

"My big brother," Bridget said, amused.

"He's beautiful. Isn't he beautiful?" she had whispered when Jane got home from school that afternoon, following her into the bedroom and closing the door behind them. "God, we spent the whole day talking – except when we, well, you know." She flopped onto Tom and Jane's bed and burst into tears. "I'm so *happy*. I feel like . . . *myself* with him. I didn't even know how much I haven't been myself till last night. How I'd stopped being myself ages ago, in the farmhouse with Pete.

"We think exactly the same way about everything that matters," she said. "The war. Our families. Everything. It's like, all this time I've been waiting for him – and he says he feels the same way."

It was true they were electric together, Jane thought, watching them at dinner. And Cam *was* beautiful: tall and blond, athletic, with patrician features. His blue eyes were intelligent, intense as he leaned forward, talking about the work he'd been doing, telling his story. He'd grown up the only child of parents who'd given him everything. All those *things* they'd spent their lives collecting – cars and boats and stock portfolios, paintings that looked like the artist had conceived them as some kind of cosmic joke – hadn't made any of them happy. Still, he said, he'd played by their rules. In high school, he played basketball; he got good grades. At the University of Michigan, he was in the right fraternity, on track to go to work for the family firm.

There was just one small obstacle: the draft.

"I was such a dick then," he said. "*That's* when I started paying attention to the war."

When the sheer stupidity of it became clear to him, he began, suddenly, to notice other things as well. Outside the narrow, easy life he'd led, people were hungry, degraded. He saw them standing at bus stops in tattered clothes, on street corners, begging. For the first time, a barrage of conflicting emotions threatened to overwhelm him. His parents couldn't understand his confusion. What did the existence of poor people have to do with *his* future? Why did the war itself – whether it was *moral* – have anything to do with his decision about the draft?

They hadn't raised him to consider whether things were fair or right, he'd realized, but only whether or not they were expedient. And it was expedient for him not to go to Vietnam.

Cam glanced at Tom. "My old man said law school was the way to go and pulled some strings and got me a 4F. He laughed. "He about shit when I joined the SDS and just walked away."

Listening, Jane argued with herself, the same argument she knew she'd have with Tom later, when they were alone. Wasn't it an exemplary thing to give up everything to fight against the war? Why couldn't Cam have fallen in love with Bridget at first sight? Didn't Tom always swear that he'd fallen in love with *her* exactly that way?

Cam segued into an account of the trip to Cuba he'd made not long after Che Guevara's death, and Jane noticed that his hand had moved from the table to Bridget's thigh, his thumb rubbing small circles high on the inside seam of her Levi's.

"It was so fucking amazing there," Cam said. "The *people*. They sang in the fields."

Tom looked skeptical.

"No shit," Cam said. "It's not at all like what they want us to believe. Debray. I *met* him, man. He knows where it's at: 'The duty of the revolutionary is to make the revolution.' Right on! But you have to do it small. *Foco*. You make a thousand small motors to set the big one going."

"Weather," Tom said.

Cam laughed. "Weather's over, man. I'm talking bigger shit than that."

"Like?"

"I've been looking." Cam glanced at Bridget. "Or I was till now."

"For – ?"

He shrugged. "The right person. The right place."

"That would be me," Bridget said, brightly. "Here. Now."

Tom gave her a long look, then pushed back from the table. "I've got to study. I'm going to the library," he said.

Jane got up, too. "I've got papers go grade. I'll go with you.

"I don't like him," Tom said, closing the front door behind them. "All that Cuba bullshit. He's lying. Régis Debray wasn't even *in* Cuba when Cameron said he was there. He was in Bolivia. In prison. He's a fucking fortunate son, though. I believe that."

He shrugged. "But you know Bridget. Nobody can tell her anything. If she goes, she goes. We can't be responsible for that."

Jane pulled her coat closer against the cold, and they walked the rest of the way to the library in silence. There, Tom bent to his books, fell instantly into deep concentration. She watched him, as she had done so many times, envying his ability to shift so completely from one moment to the next, while she remained caught in an agitated tangle of emotions: relieved that Bridget had made the decision to go, yet fearful about what might happen to her once she was gone.

11

"Gimme Shelter"

Maybe Tom was right in his belief that they were better off not having any contact with Bridget. He probably was right, Jane thought. She still would have worried, of course, but it would have been a different, abstract kind of worry, not the kind born of some small thing Bridget had said during one of her occasional phone calls that burrowed into Jane's mind, mixing with all the other small, disturbing things she'd said since she'd left with John Cameron more than a year before. If Bridget stopped calling, maybe it wouldn't feel as if her volatile spirit lived on in the house, too often edging its way into her relationship with Tom.

If he answered when Bridget called, he handed Jane the receiver without a word. More often than not, she was already talking when Jane put it to her ear.

"Fucking *Idaho,* can you believe it?" she said, when she woke them late one night last summer. "At a truck stop. Cam's got this friend whose parents have this big bourgeois house in Sun Valley and we were up there for a week. Holy shit, you wouldn't believe these digs. And the mountains! We hiked twenty miles every day – and did a hundred push-ups when we got to the top. You should have seen me!"

She rattled on, pausing only to add coins when the phone beeped a warning. "You're okay?" Jane asked. "Are you okay?"

"Yeah, yeah. Listen, I've got to get off. Cam's coming out."

There was a click, and she was gone.

"Idaho," Tom said. "What the fuck are they doing in Idaho?"

"She didn't say."

"Good," he said. "We don't want to know." He punched his pillow a few times, positioning it, and within moments was fast asleep again.

But Jane lay awake. The way Bridget had hung up at the sight of Cam: did that mean she was calling Jane in secret, against his wishes? Or had she hung up to avoid answering Jane's question? Neither of them mentioned Bridget's call in the morning. In an unspoken agreement between them, Jane didn't expect Tom to talk to her about Bridget if he didn't expect her to talk to him about her family, or to spend time with his. In the absence of these tensions, they led what seemed to Jane a fortunate life, happy in their work and in each other's company – and without the money problems that had plagued Jane's childhood and adolescence.

The summer before Jane's third year of teaching, Tom's father had a mild heart attack, and his parents decided to retire to Florida in January. It was a good idea, Tom thought. He'd miss having his dad within easy driving distance, but he would not be sorry to have his mother farther away. Since his graduation from law school, she'd nagged at him about staying in Bloomington, working as a public defender, when any of the good law firms in Evansville would be thrilled to have him. She disapproved of his living with Jane, whom she'd never liked – although she'd never have admitted it.

Tom and Jane had planned to spend the Thanksgiving holiday in Bloomington, as they usually did, and Jane looked forward to the long weekend and the time together. But that year Mrs. Gilbert asked him to come home.

"Our last holiday season in the house you grew up in," she said.

And, "Your dad's health. Well, we just don't know how many more Thanksgivings we'll have together *anywhere*."

"Come with me," Tom said. "We'll get there for dinner and leave right after. Plus, you know my mom – it'll be a cast of thousands. You probably won't even have to talk to her."

Jane agreed because she didn't want to spend Thanksgiving alone. But once they got there, she felt like she always felt in Mrs. Gilbert's presence: awkward and small. She had given up trying to explain to Tom why the little things his mother said and did made her feel that way. He honestly couldn't see why Jane would let them bother her. His mom was a pain. Everybody knew it. He loved her, he guessed. She was his mother, after all. But what she thought meant next to nothing to him.

"See?" he said, when they got in the car to go home. "It wasn't so bad."

But Jane was in a black mood by then and didn't answer. It *was* bad. And didn't he understand that going had made her feel even worse about not having spent Thanksgiving with her own family – or any other holiday, for that matter, since the Christmas after Bobby's death? Five years ago, now. For a few years afterwards, she'd gone home occasionally, just for a day. But the visits were difficult and, in time, she had just quit going at all. Most of the time she managed to keep her guilty thoughts at bay, but the holiday season never failed to bring them to the surface.

She remembered how her mother always went to the bank on the day after Thanksgiving to withdraw the money she'd saved in the Christmas Club that year – two dollars a week, when she could afford it – to ensure there would be something there to alleviate the strain of Christmas expenses. How her father would go out at the last minute, usually Christmas Eve, and come home with some gift with which he meant to please her mother but which, instead, upset her because he had bought it with money that could have been spent on gifts for the children.

Each morning that December, Jane woke full of sorrow that she could not shake until she stood in her classroom, looking over the bent heads of her third-graders, busy at some task. There, among her students, she felt hopeful. *Herself.* This was the one thing in her life that she knew she did absolutely right, the only thing that never, ever disappointed her. It was as natural to her as breathing – and she could be the giver instead of the given-to, as she all too often was with Tom. He loved her too much, she thought sometimes. He believed that the force of his love for her could shelter her and make all things right. But some things just could not be right, not ever. The world! The fact that she'd failed Bridget, broken her parents' hearts!

The children had such extravagant hopes for Christmas, Jane knew – most of which would be crushed when they woke Christmas morning to the few meager gifts their parents could afford. So she threw herself into making the Christmas season at school something special for them. Every morning, she drew a name from a hat to see which student would get to open the door on the advent calendar she had brought. Then the class made some new decoration for the room: candy canes made of twisted red and white pipe cleaners; cotton ball snowmen; angels made from toilet-tissue rolls, with glittery cardboard wings. She read Christmas stories after lunch, taught Christmas customs from all over the world for social studies.

Then, on the Tuesday before Christmas break, days after it had been announced that the peace talks were at an impasse again, news came that President Nixon had ordered the resumption of bombing in Vietnam. Jane saw the headline on an abandoned newspaper in the teachers' lounge when she went there to put her lunch in the refrigerator. She picked it up to skim the story.

Devastating air attack . . . waves of U.S. planes dropped mines in Haiphong Harbor . . . rocket attacks on civilian targets near Hanoi . . . the red glow of fire . . .

"Fuck," she whispered. "*Fuck.*" When she looked down, she saw her hands were shaking.

Through the window, she could see the school buses arriving and she was thankful that the other teachers had already gone to prepare for the children just beginning to spill out of them. She felt nauseous. She thought of going to the office and saying she thought she might be coming down with the flu. But she knew if she left school, sick, the children would find out and worry about her. And it wasn't as if going home would make her feel any better.

They were scheduled in the music room first thing, to practice for Friday's pageant. Usually, it pleased her to lead the children in a long, straight line down the corridor. That morning, though, all she could think was that most of them would spend their whole lives this way: well-behaved, in line, doing what they were supposed to do. Their poor, hardworking parents had done it and their older brothers, as well – too many of whom had ended up in Vietnam. A bulletin board near the principal's office had photographs of a dozen boys in uniform who'd gone to school here and gone on to serve in Vietnam; some had wallet-sized school photos clipped in the corner. Goofy-looking little boys with freckles and crewcuts, grinning.

Tom was working late that night. Jane had intended to have a quiet evening, planning lessons ahead for January so that she'd have Christmas break completely free. But after watching footage of the bombings on the evening news, she knew she would not be able to concentrate. She left a note for Tom and set out walking toward Dunn Meadow, where she found a few dozen people holding a vigil. She took the lit candle one of them offered and bent over the flickering flame to protect it from the wintry air. This was nothing like the demonstration on that spring night after the news that Nixon had ordered the bombing in Cambodia, when thousands of people had gathered to express their rage, to organize, to *do* something. Tonight there was utter silence. No speeches, no signs. Just sorrow as dark as the night surrounding them, and the small comfort of being with people of like mind. Jane recognized only a few of them: Professor Farlow, from whom she had taken an honors course her freshman year; a woman Tom had done draft counseling with when he was in law school; a guy from the public defenders office, where he worked. There was nobody under twenty, except for a group of self-conscious high school kids huddled together against the cold. Jane wondered half-seriously if Nixon had planned it this way: get all the college kids home for Christmas break, then bomb the shit out of Hanoi. Who would protest?

"Who'd protest *anyway*?" Tom said, when she posed the question to him later that evening. "In case you haven't figured it out, the draft lottery killed off all that. You've got to admit, it was a genius move on Nixon's part: once you know *you're* not going, what do you care?"

"But Cambodia. Kent State. They were after the lottery."

"Different," Tom said. "Besides, everyone we knew, everyone with any *history* in this is out of here. They've got jobs. *Kids.* What Nixon does doesn't affect them any more. Students now, all they care about is getting high."

"You sound like an old person," Jane said.

"Maybe," he said. "But what I'm telling you is true."

"So that means we just do . . . nothing?"

"There's not a goddamn thing we can do about Vietnam," he said. "But we're not doing *nothing.* We both do good work, Jane – real work, in the world. That's what we can do, and we're going to keep on doing it – long after we get out of Vietnam. Listen, I'm not saying Nixon's not a fucking asshole. He's a fucking asshole!"

"So we just accept that, and . . ."

But he wouldn't argue.

The last few days before Christmas break began, Jane went through the motions, the news reverberating in her head: *Heaviest bombing in history . . . as of late yesterday, more than 100 B-52's and 500 fighter jets dropped an estimate of 5,000 tons of explosives on North Vietnamese military targets, including sites in downtown Hanoi and Haiphong . . .*

Any kind of social studies lesson she could imagine making of the bombing she'd almost certainly have been fired for, so she didn't mention it to the children at all. Plus, she thought, why upset them? They did math problems; she listened to them read. She walked them down to the music room to practice for the pageant at their scheduled time, but she could not bear to hear the sound of their voices, singing, and fled to the bathroom, where she locked herself in a stall and sat, the heels of her hands pressed against her eyes, until it was time to go collect them.

"Are you sick, Miss Barth?" Judy Unger asked on Thursday.

"No," Jane said, blinking back tears. "I'm not sick, Judy."

"Are you sad, then?"

"Heavens no! It's Christmas!" she said.

Friday afternoon, she walked the children to the gymnasium and settled them into the rows of folding chairs assigned to their class. They wiggled and twisted in their seats, waving to their parents and grandparents, making faces at their younger brothers and sisters in the audience. The gymnasium smelled like sweat and damp wool. It had been foggy that morning, the world no more than the few feet of road her headlights illuminated, and now a dull, gray light seeped in through the high, caged windows. The music teacher took her place at the piano on the stage at the far end of the room, the principal nodded and the curtain rose on a group of sixth-graders in the traditional Christmas tableau. There was Daniel Pettus, a goatherd, in the tunic his mother had made from a burlap bag, and blond Kathy Frank in her mother's Madonna-blue housecoat, bent prettily over the doll in the manger.

"'As it came to pass in those days, that there went out a decree from Caesar Augustus . . .'" began Letty Shoemaker, in her sweet country drawl.

It moved Jane so to see the children she'd taught her first year so grown up, proud sixth-graders now. And the little ones! Kindergartners and first-graders dressed in angel costumes made from white sheets, tinsel halos bobby-pinned to their hair, filed onto the risers and when they began to sing "Away in the Manger," she was glad that the lights had been lowered for the performance, because tears ran down her cheeks and she thought her heart would break at the sound of their high, flutey voices.

One more hour, she thought, and she'd be on her way home, where she could collapse into bed and sleep as long as she wanted to. Days, maybe. Tom would drive to Evansville on Christmas Eve morning and come back that night, but she had decided against going with him. She felt depleted, weak with sadness, more vulnerable than usual to Tom's mother's cool, unspoken disapproval. If the subject of the bombing came up, she did not know how she could keep silent and feared what she might say.

"You go," she told Tom. "Really. I'll be fine."

Though, in truth, when he made up his mind to go, she felt hurt and abandoned.

Jane had made gingerbread men, decorated with icing and sprinkles, and she passed them out just before the last bell rang, along with a wrapped gift for each child: a paperback copy of "The Twelve Days of Christmas" in which she had inscribed "Merry Christmas with love from your third-grade teacher, Miss Barth."

They had brought her gifts, too, which were piled on her desk. She did not have to open them to know what was in them: knick-knacks, perfumed soaps and lotions – things she did not want and would not use. She'd unwrap them and write thank-you notes, then wrap them back up again and deliver them to the nursing home where a friend worked to be given to elderly residents whose families had abandoned them. Still, the thought of the children spending their money on the gifts for her oppressed her, and she was reminded of countless wrong gifts her mother had chosen for her over the years, the edgy disappointment she had felt opening them. If you could have so little, couldn't it at least be something you *want*?

At home, she set the shopping bag of gifts on the kitchen table along with her canvas bag filled with papers to grade and work she planned to do in preparation for the second semester. She'd make a cup of tea, she thought, take a long bath. But reaching for the tin where she kept the tea bags, she heard a sound in the back of the house and froze, the hairs prickling at the back of her neck.

"Tom?" she called out.

But it was Bridget who appeared in the doorway of the kitchen. She'd cropped her hair and dyed it brown. She was so thin, Jane thought. Her bellbottom jeans were dirty, ragged at the hem; her old Shetland sweater baggy, worn at the elbows.

But her smile was the same, wicked and endearing. "Look at *you!* Miss Barth."

Jane went to her then, threw her arms around her.

"Oh, man, I've missed you," Bridget said, hugging her back. "It's okay that I just came in, right? I still had my key, so – "

"Stop," Jane said. "Of course, it's okay you're here. Can you stay?"

"Till Christmas. I've got, well – " Bridget shrugged. "Work. You know."

Jane glanced toward the doorway.

"Cam's not here," Bridget said. "We split for this action that's coming down. But, listen, don't mention it to Tom, okay? The action. I'm just going to tell him that Cam and I have split, period. You know how he is about Cam. I don't want to get into some kind of . . . thing with him. I mean it. I've missed you, Jane. I just want to hang out with you for a couple of days."

Jane didn't ask where Cam was or what action they might be involved in; she didn't want to know. She regarded Bridget, disheveled, running her fingers through her chopped-off hair, and dreaded the arguments she knew would start, as soon as Tom got home from work and found her there – which would be all the worse for the resumption of the bombing this week.

"Well, fuck the system!" Bridget said, the moment he walked through the door. "The time is now."

And they were into it.

Before the bombings had rattled her already fragile hopes, Jane had sometimes been able to believe it was with children like Daniel Pettus, given the skills to succeed, nurtured with kindness and attention, that we'd begin to see how different the world could be. She might even have taken Tom's side in the argument, agreeing that it was only working from the inside that you could really make a difference – even knowing exactly what Bridget would have said in response.

But tonight Jane could not have argued in good conscience that anything anyone did could make any difference at all. So she sat, silent, her stomach roiling, as the argument escalated between them.

"Fucking *murderers,*" Bridget finally said. "Are you aware that they've dropped ten thousand fucking tons of explosives in the last four days? Ten thousand *tons,* Tom! The equivalent of the atomic bomb we dropped on Hiroshima? Jesus!"

"It's a last-ditch effort," Tom said. "I agree. It's insane, morally corrupt, but – "

"But . . . *what*? You think that being a last-ditch effort – if that's even what it is – makes all those Vietnamese people *less dead*?"

"I didn't say that, Bridget," he said.

"Same difference. Just because you didn't say the words . . ."

"Hey, fuck you. Who made you the Queen of Peace?"

"Tom!" Jane said.

"What?" Tom said. "She thinks I'm a sellout. She thinks I've gone over to the dark side because I fucking *think* about things. Are you telling me I'm supposed to listen to that shit?"

"Leave Jane out of it," Bridget said. "And listen, goddamn it – I think, too. I just don't think what you think. I think it's time we actually did something about the war. Something *real.* And while we're on the subject of things we didn't say: *I* never fucking said you were a sellout. You said it. But while you're thinking so hard, maybe you ought to think about that."

Tom gave her a long look, shook his head in disgust, and left the room.

"I'll leave if you want," she said to Jane. "I probably should."

"No," Jane said. "I want you to stay."

But they were awkward together the rest of the evening, talked in fits and starts about nothing that mattered until Bridget yawned and said, "I guess I'll go crawl into my old bed."

Jane showered, took her time to go to her own bed where she knew Tom would be awake, waiting. He put down the book he was reading when she opened the door, folded back the blanket so that she could climb in beside him.

"I'm sorry I got pissed off," he said. "I should know better than to argue with her."

Jane shrugged, blinking back tears.

"Shit," he said, and sighed. He picked up his book, read for a few moments. Then put it down again. "Where's Cameron," he asked quietly. "Why isn't he with her?"

"They split," Jane said.

Tom shook his head. "Bridget doesn't split with people, Jane. Did she tell you why she's here? Really? How she got here?"

"No," Jane said, which was technically true. *Work,* Bridget had said. *Action.* Jane hadn't pressed her for details. "She came on the bus; I don't know where from, though."

"I don't like this," Tom said. "Something's up and I don't want us to get involved in it. Listen, I can't cancel on my parents. I just can't. But would you just come to Evansville with me tomorrow? We won't stay long, I promise. We'll stop somewhere and spend the night. When we get back, Bridget will probably be gone." He glanced at her and saw that she was crying. "Come on," he said, "Jane. We can't help her."

"I *can't,*" she said. "I can't just leave her. And I don't want to spend Christmas Eve with your parents. I told you that. If you're so dead-set on being with them, *go*. But why would I go there so your mother can make me feel like shit again? I don't need that."

"Come on, she's not that bad," he said. "It's not like – "

"She *is,*" Jane said, and turned away from him.

"Well, fuck," he said, and switched off the light. "Fine. Whatever."

Jane felt his tense, waking presence beside her in the dark. The words she wanted to speak formed and dissolved in her mind again and again, but she could not bring herself to say them out loud. *Don't go. Please. Stay here, with me.*

12

"Purple Haze"

When she woke up, he was already gone. He was still mad at her, Jane knew, because there was no note to say what time to expect him back that night. He always left a note since the time, not long after they moved in together, he had decided to go out for a few beers with a friend on the spur of the moment and returned to find her curled up in the corner of the couch, pale and trembling, certain that something terrible had happened to him. It was never anything elaborate, just wherever he was going, when he thought he'd be back, and always, "Love you. Tom." But there was no note this morning.

"I don't blame you for not going," Bridget said when she got up. "Mrs. Gilbert has always been a shit to you. She's never liked you. She actually said that to my mom once."

Jane glanced sharply at her. Bridget had always made fun of Tom's mother – how uptight she was, what a snob. Jane suspected she got a kick out of the fact that Mrs. Gilbert thought she wasn't good enough for Tom, that it pleased her to think she'd personally affronted Mrs. Gilbert, having been the one to introduce the two of them. But she'd never told Jane anything that Mrs. Gilbert said before or alluded to the fact that their relationship was a source of gossip among the ladies in Mrs. Gilbert's circle of friends. Of course, Jane *knew* Mrs. Gilbert must talk about her. But hearing Bridget say so made her feel worse than she already felt, angrier about Tom letting his mother guilt trip him into going home for Christmas Eve.

"I never told you before because I didn't want to hurt your feelings," Bridget said. "I knew how you let her get to you. You always have. But you know, Jane, you really ought to think about where all this is going. If Tom won't say no to her now, what makes you think he ever will? You watch. Ten years, maybe less than that, and he'll be back in Evansville in a suit and tie. You can be one of those wives sitting around the pool at the country club. Or maybe you'll have your own pool in the backyard. Is that what you want?"

"We won't be like that," Jane said.

"Yeah, well. People change. If they don't *think,* if they don't choose, they just drift into some life they never in a million years would have believed they'd be living. Look at my mom. She's got a degree from Vassar, for God's sake. She worked for *Time* magazine in New York. Then one day, boom, she meets my dad and there she is, marooned in Evansville fucking Indiana, with a boatload of kids and bridge club every Wednesday. And she doesn't even *care.* She likes it! Fuck that. Honest to God, she's the smartest person I know. It makes me furious every time I think about what she could have been. *Done.*"

"What's so wrong with being happy?" Jane asked.

Bridget didn't even answer. Just launched into an account of the last blow-up she'd had with her father over her relationship with Cam.

"Fucking Judge," she said. "Nosing around, calling up favors. Like I didn't know Cam's politics myself. Like I was going to say, "Oh, thanks so much, Dad, for checking with the FBI. You know how much I respect the work they do."

She called her sister Colleen once in a while, she told Jane. Fuck the rest of them. Fuck everyone who refused to see what was going on. And the ones who saw and quit trying to do anything about it – fuck them more.

That's me, Jane thought – and at that moment saw herself through Bridget's eyes. The truth was, she'd been deluding herself about everything. Her relationship with Tom, which, when she thought about it honestly, had been tense for a long time now. He didn't, couldn't, understand why she spent nearly every waking moment grading papers, making lesson plans, *thinking* about the children in her class and what she could do to help them. He was growing impatient with her chronic sadness.

Jane needed air, she needed Bridget to stop talking for a while, so she suggested treating her to breakfast at the Ashram Bakery, where she usually went with Tom. Bridget argued against going – she wasn't hungry, it was stupid to waste money in restaurants – and only agreed when Jane said she was going herself, one way or the other. Once there, she headed for a booth at the back and slid into the side where she would be least likely to be seen. She wore a ratty stocking cap pulled low over her eyes, bent over the menu when the waitress came to take her order. As if anyone would have recognized her, Jane thought. She no longer looked anything like herself. When her food came, the waitress had to set it in the middle of the table because she was holding the newspaper up to cover her face.

Christmas Eve and, still, the bombing went on, the front-page story said.

Jane was frightened for her. Bridget ate virtually nothing, gulped down cup after cup of black coffee. She was smoking; her nails were bitten to the quick. She was jumpy, constantly looking at her watch as if waiting for someone to arrive. Cam? Jane had half-expected him to appear once Tom was gone. But there was no sign of him and, as far as she knew, Bridget hadn't heard from him since she'd been there, nor had she tried to call him. Something was up, though, and Jane was also frightened by the possibility of what it might be. There'd been a series of what the Weather Underground called "armed actions" since Bridget left with Cam in the spring of '71. Bombings of the San Francisco Office of California Prisons in retaliation for the killing of one of the Soledad Brothers; The New York Department of Corrections in Albany, to protest the killing of twenty-nine inmates in the prison riots at Attica. The bombing of the Pentagon on Ho Chi Minh's birthday last May after the U.S. bombing raid in Hanoi.

Bridget disappeared into the bedroom after breakfast. To read, she said. But when Jane peeked through the keyhole of the locked door, she was fast asleep, one arm thrown over the duffel she'd set beside her on the bed.

"What's in it?" Tom would have wanted to know. Rightly, he'd point out that if she did something stupid they'd be complicit, having let her stay with them when they knew of her involvement with John Cameron.

"Bridget would never do anything to hurt us," she'd have said back. "She's here because she's in trouble, because she knows we love her and won't let her keep on destroying herself."

She believed this, but what could she *do*? Bridget had spoken of an "action" the day before; she'd temporarily split from Cam, she said, but that didn't mean that he wasn't somewhere nearby. There was an Army recruiting office near the Square, the Armory on the outskirts of town, Fort Benjamin Harrison just sixty miles away, in Indianapolis. It made perfect sense: a Christmas action to make a statement against the unconscionable bombing of Hanoi.

Every time the thought that Bridget might actually have a bomb in her duffel bag made its way into her consciousness, Jane's heart raced with terror and she busied herself with some pointless household task or quietly stepped out into the frigid December air to shock herself into some semblance of calm. She unwrapped the gifts from the children and wrote thank you notes to ground herself and set her mind at ease. She and Tom would take the gifts to the nursing home tomorrow, as planned, all but the Christmas ornament Kathy Frank had given her – a pretty glass angel, which she hung carefully on the tree she and Tom had decorated together. She turned the lights on against the gloomy afternoon, stepped back, and looked at it, remembering the Saturday afternoon a few weeks before when they went out to Kathy's parents' farm to cut it down. Kathy's mother had invited them in for hot chocolate and Kathy had sat, rapt to find herself in the presence of Miss Barth's *boyfriend*. They'd laughed about it driving home, at how surprised children always were to see their teachers out in the real world – as if when school ended every day they stepped into the coat closet and just waited there until the first bell rang the next morning. He'd been so sweet to Kathy. Jane remembered that, too, and how it had made her see, suddenly, what a good father he would be, if –

She thought again of what Bridget had said to her that morning, tried to imagine herself a wife – any kind of wife – but she couldn't. Let alone a *mother*. God. She could barely take care of herself. Even right now she had no idea what to do about Bridget. She longed for Tom to appear and take charge and at the same time bristled with aggravation knowing he'd be perfectly comfortable in that role. Life was so easy for him. He always knew what was right, and she would always be dependent on him, always let him lead the way. How could that be a good thing for either one of them?

Bridget slept into the evening and, when she woke, the two of them sat down to eat the vegetable soup Jane had prepared. She was hungry, ate as if she hadn't eaten, really eaten, for days. They sat at the table a long time, reminiscing. She was calmer, Jane thought. Funny, like she used to be. Telling Jane about the time Tom's mother had gotten lice at the beauty shop and doused everything in the house – including herself, Tom, Tom's dad and the *dog* – with kerosene, she laughed in the old way, simply delighted at the image of Mrs. Gilbert in such a state, not mean-spirited at all.

She'd be leaving in the morning, she said. Time to move on.

"Stay?" Jane asked. "Please?"

She shook her head, sadly it seemed to Jane. "No," she said. "Can't."

She retreated to her room soon afterward, probably to avoid seeing Tom. Jane thought he would be home by nine o'clock, but nine came, then ten and eleven and he still wasn't there. He had bought a bottle of champagne the day before Bridget arrived and put it in the refrigerator. When he got back from Evansville, they'd drink it opening the presents they'd bought for each other, he said. Had he forgotten that? Where *was* he?

It was her natural inclination to worry and, as it got later and he still didn't come, she grew increasingly fearful he'd been in an accident. But what scared her even more than that was the possibility that he'd stayed in Evansville to make the point that he was tired of this shit with Bridget and was no longer willing to put up with it. Or worse, what if his staying away meant that he was no longer willing to put up with her, *Jane,* and turned out to be his first step in leaving her forever?

Jane waited till midnight before going to bed alone. She slept restlessly, waking over and over again to Tom's absence, running through a menu of scenarios ending each time with the image of him asleep in his bedroom at home – the shrine, he called it, untouched since his departure for college eight years ago. A little after three, she woke to the familiar squeak of the floorboards and thought he'd come home, but then she heard the click of the back door closing and footsteps hurrying down the steps. Bridget leaving.

She didn't think – just threw on jeans and a sweatshirt, grabbed a jacket, and went after her. It was five blocks to campus from their house, a straight shot, and she saw Bridget instantly, hurrying in that direction. The windows along the street were lit only by Christmas trees, which cast wavy, colored light onto the yards and, setting out, Jane thought of the children inside, fast asleep in the houses, dreaming toward morning. When Bridget crossed University Avenue and disappeared into the trees on the old part of campus, she remembered the ROTC building. Of course. She looked to make sure the street was empty, then broke into a run to catch up with her.

"Fuck!" Bridget said, wheeling around. "Jane. You scared the *shit* out of me."

But she didn't seem that surprised to see her, Jane thought. Not really.

"What are you doing?" Jane asked.

"Come on," Bridget said, stepping farther into the shadows at the edge of the woods. "You know what I'm doing. It's why you're here."

"I'm here to keep you from doing it. You can't keep on with this, Bridge. It's – "

"What?" Bridget asked. "Wrong?"

"It *is* wrong," Jane said.

"And two wrongs don't make a right," Bridget mocked, and Jane was stung. It was one of the few things she'd told Bridget about her mother: something she used to say when Jane and Bobby were little and fought with one another, something she found herself saying to the children in her class sometimes. But it was true, after all, wasn't it? Like so many sappy, annoying things people said to make a point. *Actions speak louder than words. Fools rush in. He who hesitates is lost.*

"Trouble is," Bridget said, "*their* wrong is killing people. Your own brother, Jane, you may remember. And they won't stop."

"You can't stop them." Jane gestured at the duffel Bridget held. "This won't stop them. Your whole life will be wrecked if you do it – and for what?"

Bridget shrugged.

She started walking toward the ROTC headquarters again, staying close to the edge of the woods. It was an easy target, Jane thought: one of those portable buildings, not unlike a big house trailer, tacked onto the old brick classroom building where her honors English class had met freshman year. Tom laughed every time they passed it and retold the story of how he and Pete, unwilling recruits, had once marched backwards during a military inspection, discreetly making their way to the last row of the last unit, then watched the parade of cadets continue on without them. How Pete had fashioned a removable cast for his leg to get out of marching at all for the better part of the semester.

ROTC was mandatory then; now its ranks were filled by a weird mixture of gung-ho guys and guys who joined with the misguided idea that if they had to go to Vietnam it would be better to go as an officer than a grunt. Stupid fuckers, she thought, surprising herself with the whoosh of rage that shot through her *again*. The lies the Army told students about the training they'd get in ROTC, the way they just ate up people for this war.

Bridget stopped just short of the building, stood listening. She turned slowly, in a complete circle, alert for any movement, any sign of life in the area surrounding them. Jane shivered in the frigid air.

"Look, all this has been prepared," Bridget said in a low voice. "All I have to do is go in, put it in place. It's perfectly safe. It's Christmas, for God's sake. We checked it out. Security is nil. There's someone waiting for me – "

Cam, Jane thought. She should leave, she knew. Go home. Tom would come home in the morning, and she'd tell him she was sorry. She'd tell him, this time, Bridget was really gone. But the bomb was going to go off no matter what she did, and he'd say they had to call the police and tell them Bridget had been staying with them. If they caught her, Jane would have to testify against her.

"Hey," Bridget said. "I can't hang around out here any longer, okay?" She took a wrapped package from the duffel, then handed the bag to Jane. "Five minutes," she said. "I go in, I come out. That's it. Then you decide what to do. Go back. Get real and come with us. Your call."

"I can't – " Jane began.

"You can do whatever you want," Bridget said. "You never have understood that."

She walked lightly toward the building, bouncing a little on her toes. Raised a window that had been left slightly open for her and disappeared into the darkness inside without a backward glance.

Jane felt frozen beneath the vast black bowl of sky, attuned to the wild clatter of her own pounding heart. It was wrong what they were doing; of course, she wouldn't go with them. If she left right now she could call the police from a phone booth. Maybe there'd be time to defuse the bomb, and if... when Bridget was caught the charge would be attempted bombing. Her father would get her the best legal help, and maybe, maybe...

Then there was the blast, the sound of her own voice screaming. And nothing after that, until hours later when she woke in a car beside John Cameron, dawn breaking, Christmas carols on the radio. The same songs her children had sung in the school pageant just two days before.

13

"Paint It Black"

Jane dreamed it for the first time in the motel room with Cam, the night after the bombing: following Bridget out of the icy night into the dark building, the explosion, and Bridget's terrible, surprised expression in the moment before she fell backwards into the flames, her long red hair streaming. She woke, crying, and could not stop. Cam had been slumped, zoned out on the cheap orange chair he'd placed in front of the door to keep her from leaving. Now he stood, and in a step towered over her.

She stopped then, because she was afraid of him. She had deep, purpling bruises on her arms, where he had grabbed her, wrestled her away from the burning building. Jane turned away from him, curled into the fetal position, the dream images tangling with what she actually remembered, her mind scrambling to make sense of it all. She felt punched when the full knowledge of what had happened washed over her again: Bridget was dead; she, Jane, was here in a motel room with John Cameron. She clenched her jaw to keep from making any sound.

She was wearing an old tee shirt of Bridget's that had been in the duffel Bridget thrust into her arms just before disappearing through the open window. It smelled of sweat and patchouli, nothing like the beautiful oxford shirts Jane used to borrow when they were roommates in the dorm with their lingering scents of starch and Shalimar. Vividly, Jane remembered the room they'd shared, moonlight falling across the twin beds where they lay facing each other, talking about Pete and Tom.

Tom.

She closed her eyes and sensed Cam moving away from her, satisfied that she would not cry out again. She was shaking, her teeth chattering. If she had not stupidly followed Bridget, if she had not heard Bridget leaving at *all,* she would be with Tom right now. She crossed her arms on her chest and held tightly to her elbows to calm herself. She would not think about Tom – the Christmas tree they'd decorated with its twinkling white lights, the presents beneath it that they'd meant to unwrap the night before. How he'd have gotten home from Evansville, found her gone, and assumed she'd chosen to go with Bridget. Which, in truth, she had. She saw that now – how she was always choosing Bridget when she should have been choosing Tom.

Even so, he would help her if she could only get back to him.

"It was government property that your friend blew up along with herself," Cam had said. "You were with Bridget; do you think the fucking FBI cares *why?* And if you think I'm going to cut you loose, so you can get your hot-shot lawyer boyfriend to try to make some kind of deal with them, you're crazy."

Jane was terrified. She'd heard stories – who hadn't? – about the FBI bursting into motel rooms, shooting first, asking questions afterwards. Someone, anyone, could have heard the explosion, come out into the street to investigate, and seen them driving away from campus. It would have been logical to be suspicious, to note the model of the car – maybe even the license number. For all she knew, the FBI was waiting in the parking lot of the motel right now. She and Cam would go out in the morning and . . .

But when morning came, they walked out, got into the car, and drove away without incident. At Cam's insistence, Jane was wearing the wig she'd found in Bridget's duffel; with short, brown, curly hair she looked like a completely different person. Cam had chopped off his long, blond hair and used electric clippers to give himself the kind of buzz-cut her dad used to give Bobby when he was a little boy. The short hair sharpened his cheekbones, deepened the effect of his hard blue eyes.

He hadn't said a word to her this morning, except to remind her that when she talked to him – even when she thought of him – she was to call him Terry. Terry Gold. Last night, when they arrived at the motel, he'd given her a driver's license and made her repeat the information on it until she could say it without looking.

Marianne Glazier. 926 Euclid Avenue, Apartment A. St. Louis, Missouri. Birth date: 5/4/47. Marianne was 5'4" and weighed 115 pounds, close enough. She had brown hair, brown eyes. Jane's eyes were changeable, sometimes green, sometimes hazel, sometimes gold, depending on the light, or on what she was wearing – which Bridget had always thought was hilarious. "Jesus, Barth," she'd say. "You're so fucking indecisive even your eyes can't make up their mind what color to be."

Jane felt like weeping. Did Cam feel any grief at all for her? Silent, burning rage was all she'd seen, so far – and directed at *her.* Did he really believe that what had happened was her fault? Was it her fault? Could what he'd said be true: that she'd rattled Bridget, following and confronting her, and caused her to make a mistake that made the bomb detonate too soon? Glancing at him now, his jaw clenched, driving into the dawn, it frightened her to think about what he didn't know: yesterday afternoon, while he stood in an outdoor phone booth, talking, she'd rifled through Bridget's duffel at her feet and found an envelope with a birth certificate, social security card, and driver's license in it. Nora White. Shifting, balling her jacket beneath her head as if to find a more comfortable sleeping position, she'd dipped down for an instant and tucked the envelope just underneath the floor mat. She could touch it right now, a little security blanket at her fingertips, if she weren't afraid that Cam would notice. Next time they made a bathroom stop, she'd loosen the insoles of her chukka boots and, the first chance she got, tuck the documents beneath them. She had no idea what she'd do if he searched Bridget's duffel, looking for them. Maybe Bridget had kept them a secret – in case she ever needed to get away from him. The thought gave her a flicker of hope.

The radio was on, as it had been since they left Bloomington, though Jane tuned it out except for the news at the top of each hour. Nothing about the bombing since the spotty news stories on Christmas Day: there'd been an explosion, a body had been found – that's all. Jane thought of the Weathermen who'd been blown up in the New York townhouse several years before. One had been identified from the print on a severed fingertip, all that was left of her; another had been completely obliterated, identified days later by a Weather communiqué.

"In case you're wondering," Cam said. "They never report this kind of shit. They don't want people to know how many fucking pig institutions we've done destruction to."

"I wasn't," Jane lied.

All yesterday, they had driven back roads going nowhere, it seemed – just *away,* finally landing at the motel on the outskirts of Salina, Kansas, where they'd spent the night. But this morning after they stopped at a truck stop for breakfast and filled the car with gas, Cam had another phone conversation, consulted a map, and headed purposefully north on a two-lane road, up through Nebraska, into South Dakota, and then east toward Minnesota. They reached Minneapolis in the early evening, and he pulled the car into the weedy backyard of a run-down house in a neighborhood at the edge of the city.

"Wait here," he said.

As he walked toward the back door, a light went on in an upstairs window and the curtains parted slightly. Moments later a light came on downstairs. Cam knocked; the back door opened. Jane had taken off her boots earlier; she'd complain that her feet were too warm if Cam said anything, she'd decided, but he hadn't noticed. Now, her heart pounding, she felt for the envelope with her fingertips. Cam was on the porch step talking to the man who'd opened the door, his back toward her – only momentarily, she knew. Quickly, she placed the license and social security card beneath the insole of one boot; folded the birth certificate and placed it beneath the other. Then slipped her feet back into them and tied the laces, all the while keeping an eye on Cam.

Cam. Fuck Terry. He couldn't control what she kept in her mind.

He turned and beckoned her to join him, and the bump of the documents beneath her feet gave her courage as she crossed the yard. It was frozen in muddy ruts, dotted with clumps of dead leaves. Next door, a kid stood near a barrel of burning garbage, poking it with a stick. What if she called out to him, Jane wondered? Or just took off running? But Cam came down to meet her, took her arm. He introduced her to the guy on the porch as Marianne.

The guy nodded. Tim Garret was his name, he said. A lie, Jane knew. His wife – or girlfriend, whatever – was Betsy Dodd. A stupid name for a revolutionary, Jane thought. But, fine. She could play that game. She could be Marianne to them. In fact, as time passed, it was a comfort to her not to be Jane in their presence.

It was Marianne who endured Cameron's rough fury. Marianne who was with him, in another of Bridget's disguises, when he scoped out a recruiting office downtown for friends of Tim and Betsy who arrived a night later, set a bomb there to protest the "peace with honor" agreement that President Nixon had signed, and were gone by the time it went off – safely, this time – in the early morning. Marianne who held the gun he put into her hands, raised it, and fired at the beer can set on the fence post out in the country, near another safe house where some fugitive Weather people stayed.

Tim and Betsy worked nights, cleaning offices. The two of them and Cam slept in shifts in the daytime, so there would always be someone to watch her. Sometimes she woke to the constantly droning television and thought, for a moment, she was back in her parents' house. Then she'd remember where she was and do her best to drift back to sleep again. She slept hours and hours, slept away whole days. When she got up, to go to the bathroom or drag herself to the kitchen to get something to eat, she felt as if she were walking in deep water.

She half-believed Cam was drugging her; but wouldn't she *feel* less if that were true? She could fully wake up if she wanted to – she'd done it. The trouble was, she woke to grief so all-consuming that anything – oblivion – seemed better that trying to deal with it.

Evenings, Cam and Tim would sit at the table in the filthy kitchen, spouting politics, hatching plans that even Jane, in her stupor, knew were pointless and absurd. The war was over. Troops would be withdrawn from Vietnam by the end of March. Which only seemed to make Cam angrier, more bent on destruction. He talked about his father sometimes, the ruthlessness with which he and others like him pursued money and power. Yet it seemed to Jane that he was not so different, after all. The war had provided a means for him to exercise his own kind of ruthlessness, and now that it was ending he was enraged at having been beaten at his own game.

Jane watched Betsy sometimes and occasionally caught a fleeting expression cross her face that seemed very much to her like disgust. She looked increasingly haggard in the mornings when she returned after working her shift, and she and Tim often squabbled over stupid things. Who'd go to the grocery store, who'd be the one to take the car in for the repair when the muffler got so loud it was likely to attract attention?

During the first weeks Jane was there, Betsy was cruel to her in the presence of the men and ignored her when they weren't present. Lately, though, she made a pot of coffee in the mornings and they drank it, sitting at the table together while Cam and Tim slept. She was not a pretty girl. Too skinny, with ropy muscles in her arms and legs. Her skin was so pale it looked blue sometimes. She had sharp, bird-like features. An inch of dark roots beneath her tinder-box platinum hair.

"Listen, I'm sorry about – your friend," she said to Jane one morning in February. She gestured toward the television, where the *Today* host was interviewing Henry Kissinger about the troop withdrawals. "Fuck. What a waste."

"Did you know her?" Jane asked.

Betsy shook her head, lit her fourth cigarette in an hour. "I don't even know – Terry. Fucking asshole. Our luck he ends up here."

Jane waited.

"I have half of a Ph.D. in linguistics," Betsy said. "Can you believe that?"

Jane thought of the children in her classroom. Who was teaching them now, she wondered? How in the world had anyone explained why she'd just disappeared from their lives? She remembered the bulbs they had planted last fall: how she'd sent half the children outside, into the field behind their room and stationed the rest at the windows to call out at them when they reached the far edges of the planting area, which she had told them should be as far as they could see. Then they'd all gone out with trowels to plant the hundreds of bulbs that Jane had bought. Tulips, crocuses, hyacinths, daffodils, anemones. Tears filled her eyes when she thought of them, right now, pushing up through the frozen soil toward spring.

She couldn't tell that to Betsy, though. So she just shrugged, as if to agree with her that for a person with half a Ph.D. in . . . *anything* to end up this way was, indeed, bizarre.

Jane wasn't surprised when she and Tim didn't return from work the next morning. Cam paced, peering occasionally through the front window at the sound of a car. Ten o'clock passed, noon, two. "Fuck this shit. *Fuck,*" he said, kicking the piles of dirty clothes, the trash that had overflowed from the can in the corner of the kitchen. As if Tim and Betsy were accountable to him, Jane thought. As if he owned them.

She wondered if Betsy had been feeling her out the day before, perhaps even contemplating an offer to find a way to take her with them. Then deciding it just wasn't worth the risk. She would go by herself, she decided at that moment. They were alone in the house now. Cam hadn't slept for more than twenty-four hours and, once his rage was spent, he laid down, exhausted, closed his eyes. Jane waited, preternaturally awake, making a plan.

Nora White was still tucked beneath the insoles of her chukka boots. Her parka was in the downstairs closet. Tim and Betsy had taken the grocery money they kept in a coffee can in the pantry, but Jane was pretty sure that Cam had a roll of cash in his duffel. She'd seen it the first night they were in the house together, when Cam left the bag open on the bed – perhaps intentionally, so that she would see the handgun set on top of his clothes and know he wouldn't hesitate to use it.

Then *or* now.

The thought of that sent her into a panic and she lay still, counting her breaths until she calmed down. The minute hand made its way around the face of the clock on the dresser, again, again, again. The window darkened toward evening. Jane watched Cam sleeping until the meanness fell away from his face and she saw his eyelids rippling with dreams. Then she got up. She put her clothes on, then her boots. Cam always kept the duffel near him. Even this afternoon, he had thought to set it within reach, on the chair beside the bed.

Slowly, slowly, she moved the zipper on it, all the while watching him. He didn't stir. There were clothes balled up inside, a sheaf of papers filled with his crabbed handwriting. Jane felt around them, flinching when she touched the gun, moving beyond it to a little inside pocket at one end of the bag where she found the cash. She let a breath out, realizing only then that she had not been breathing.

She stood up, stood perfectly still for a long moment before backing out of the room into the hallway. Shrugging on her jacket in the kitchen, she thought of the click the door of their house had made when Bridget opened it to leave that night and tried, for the life of her, to remember if this kitchen door she'd seen open and close a hundred times made any sound at all.

Her legs felt, suddenly, like rubber. Her heart fluttered wildly, and she blinked her eyes because things went dark at the edges. Resolutely, she put her hand on the knob, turned it, pushed, and the door opened, soundlessly.

The shock of real, almost spring-like air set her moving instantly toward the street. She had no idea where she was, but she couldn't dwell on that, or she'd lose her courage. So she walked briskly towards the city lights she saw in the distance, trying to look like any other person hurrying home at the end of the day.

PART TWO

The Continuous Life

JULY, 2002–JANUARY, 2003

14

"Our House"

She would go through the day, moment by moment, the way she had taught herself to do. Live each moment fully. The sun pouring in through the open kitchen window, catching the prisms dangling among the plants to cast rainbows on the wall. The white bowl of blueberries on the oak table, yellow butter on a blue and white dish. Waffles steaming, the smell of coffee. Charlie and Claire upstairs, getting ready for breakfast. Astro sleeping at her feet.

She would not think about the man who had called out "Jane" the day before. She'd been so rattled, turning toward him, that she hadn't really seen his face. He had a beard, she remembered that. A ponytail. Scruffy, but clean. He was of average height and thin, almost emaciated. A smoker's voice.

She wouldn't think about how she had felt walking away from him. Her legs heavy, her whole body suddenly overtaken by exhaustion – and the headache she'd pretended that morning starting up behind her eyes. The panicky little voice in the back of her mind saying again and again, "You told him your name. He knows what your name is."

Finally, blessedly, the sidewalk had turned toward the Union and carried her out of his sight. Moments later, she sat down on the low wall that ran along the back of Dunn Meadow to collect herself.

It was shady there, the air fresh and green beneath the stand of sheltering trees. There was a platform in the meadow, where long-haired boys were setting up sound equipment. People were covering tables with bright tie-dye cloths in preparation for the summer festival that would begin that afternoon; there was a striped tent for concessions. Students milled on the grass, some lay entangled on blankets, books and notebooks abandoned. Others played Frisbee, threw sticks for their dogs. From where she sat, Nora could see the big white Sigma Chi house on the corner of Seventh and Indiana, its steps painted blue and gold. She looked away. Still, she couldn't help remembering walking down those steps with Tom, on their way to class, to a dance somewhere, to the Pizzeria.

"Nora – "

"Oh!" Her hands flew up and she stepped backwards, into Charlie's arms – and back into her kitchen.

"Caught you," he said. "Daydreaming."

She let him hold her, hoping he wouldn't notice how hard her heart was beating or that she was making an effort to breathe evenly to curb her irritation at him for surprising her.

It wasn't his fault, Nora reminded herself: what he didn't know. He thought her restlessness these past months was all about Claire going away. He'd been restless himself. Countless times she'd heard him remind their daughter of what one of her teachers said the first day of their senior year. "Be kind to your parents when they get weird. They can't help it. They can't believe you've grown up, and they're looking ahead, already missing you." Claire was probably sorry she'd told them, laughing, at dinner that night.

Of course, that was part of it. Nora had already begun to avoid Claire's room, the clothes in little piles where she'd stepped out of them, shoes kicked a few feet away, books and sheet music piled on every free surface. And, worse, plastic crates filled with sheets and towels, laundry supplies, bath soap, shampoo – things she'd been collecting since June to take to college.

The sight of her in the kitchen doorway now, fresh from the shower, pierced Nora's heart. Her blond hair was still wet, close to her head in perfect ringlets. An hour in the sun and she'd look like a girl in a pre-Raphaelite painting. She wore cargo shorts and an orange tee shirt that said "Sleeping Bear Dunes" on the front and "Ask Me about Canoe Rentals" on the back. A woven bracelet on her wrist, exactly like the one her boyfriend, Dylan, wore. She smelled like flowers.

Nora set the first batch of pancakes on the table, and Claire smiled at her. "Poor Mom," she said. "Is your headache gone? Do you feel better this morning?"

Nora nodded. "Honey, I'm really sorry about yesterday. Not helping you register."

Claire rolled her eyes. "Please. I told you. It would only have been worse if you were there. I'd have been horrible to you *and* Dad. God. Dylan told me it would be awful, you just had to gut it out and do it the first time, but I had no idea! He said he and his parents didn't speak for two days afterwards. There was this kid next to me with his aunt and, I swear, he was the only one not being a complete and total jerk. They ought to not *let* parents help when it's actually time to decide on the schedule, you know?" She grinned at Charlie, swooped down to give him a kiss on his cheek before taking her place at the table. "Especially parents who are computer-losers. Or maybe they should mix it up so parents don't get to help their own kids. Then everybody would be more likely to act decent."

"You got a good schedule, though," Charlie said. "You're happy with it, aren't you?"

"Yes!" Claire said, her eyes shining. "I can't wait. I could hardly sleep last night, thinking about, well, just being there. It's so *beautiful.* I knew that from visiting Dylan in the spring. But it was even better than I remembered it. Mom, didn't you just – "

Nora smiled, but her voice cracked when she said, "I did, sweetie. I loved it, too."

When Dylan appeared and the two of them went off to their job at River Rentals together, Nora and Charlie drank a second cup of coffee, as they always did. Usually, they used the time to organize their day, but this morning they sat quietly, lost in their own thoughts.

The ghost of yesterday's headache still lingering behind her eyes, Nora thought about the long drive home, Charlie and Claire in the front seat, talking quietly; Chopin nocturnes on the stereo, meant to soothe her. But they didn't help. She had propped herself in the corner of the backseat, holding the silky eye pillow Claire had given her for her birthday against her eyes to will away the tumble of memory the last few days had brought, to keep from seeing the green Indiana farmland, the little towns rolling past on Highway 31 and, farther north, the cloud of smog drifting above the industrial cities along the lower scoop of Lake Michigan. Just being close to what once had been her home felt claustrophobic and oppressive, as if she had never left high school. She drifted in and out of consciousness, her head pounding. She slept finally, but it was not a restful sleep, and she woke suddenly, disoriented – Jane – until she blinked and saw Charlie at the wheel, heard Claire humming along with the Chopin.

They stopped once, for dinner, near Kalamazoo, where she picked at a salad. Past Grand Rapids, they began to see clouds of purple thistle in the median and along the side of the road. There were silver maples, the pale green undersides of their leaves winking in the breeze, and pine trees planted in lines so straight they seemed like moving spokes as the car flew past. Her headache abated then, perhaps just from the familiar sight of them.

Now she looked out at the meadow she had sown with wildflowers years ago. More purple thistle. And pink coneflowers, black-eyed Susans, daisies, foxglove, goldenrod, phlox – all of it shimmering like a vast Monet in the morning sun. She had made this beauty, she reminded herself. She had made this whole beautiful life for herself, and for Charlie and Claire. It was real.

Charlie sighed. "I can't believe it," he said, pouring a last cup of coffee. "In a month, she'll be gone. Eighteen years, and poof – "

"She's not leaving forever."

"She might be," Charlie said. "Who knows if she'll ever come back here. Oh, summers. Sure. At least next summer. But to live – ?"

"Eeyore." Nora smiled.

"Bloomington just suddenly seems so far away. Driving those last few hours, I thought we'd never get home. I guess I hadn't realized how far away she'd be from us till then. I know," he added. "I was the one who took her side about going."

"Oberlin wouldn't have been that much closer," Nora said. "And you were right, anyway. It's the right place for her."

"Do you really think that?" Charlie asked. "You were so quiet the whole time we were there – and on the way home, too. I know you had a headache. But I was afraid going to the orientation made you mad at me all over."

She put her hand on his, squeezed it. "Charlie, it's okay. It's just . . . strange. I don't know. Sometimes I think it's worse now, still having her with us, than it will be when she finally goes. We'll get used to it, once it happens. People do."

"I'll *never* get used to it," Charlie said.

It was true, Nora thought, watching him walk out the kitchen door toward the kennels. Charlie was a keeper. The barn was lined with shelves of things he couldn't bear to throw away. The worn red leather collar of his first dog, his Davy Crockett coonskin cap, every bicycle he'd ever owned, a collection of Little League caps, scratched 45s and the little record player he'd played them on. The red and white '55 Chevy he'd saved up to buy the day he got his driver's license was parked under the hayloft.

"The Museum of Charlie," Claire called it. And teased him, saying he'd keep all the people he loved there, too, if he could get away with it.

Nora was grateful for the self-absorption of adolescence that kept Claire from knowing how close to the mark she had been about her father's desire to keep her with them forever. It made her feel protective of Charlie, and she followed him outdoors. But she stopped, stepped out of his sightline when she saw him bent over, palms-up to a half-dozen dogs that leapt around him, licking his hands. "Hey, buddy. Here, boy. Hey there, hey," he murmured, his voice throaty with tears.

If only Jo were here, she thought. Still herself. "Now, Honey," she would say – that's all. And he'd grin and say, "I know, Mom. I know." Straighten himself and set forth into the day.

Nora turned, slipped away before he caught sight of her and headed toward the forest, Astro at her heels. Charlie kept a path through the meadow clear with the riding mower, and she walked it now, Queen Anne's lace bowed with dew brushing against her bare legs, toward the wooded trail that led down to Lake Michigan. Stepping onto it through the curtain of trees, her skin prickled at the sudden change in temperature, and she stood in the dappled light falling through the leaves, finally, blessedly invisible. A minute walking, and there was nothing but green as far as she could see, turning in every direction.

She smelled the lake first, then glimpsed it through the trees: teal-blue this morning, choppy little peaks glinting in the sun. Emerging from the forest, she stood at the edge of the high dune as she always did before starting to walk and felt her mind begin to settle. The beach was empty of people, strewn with Petoskey stones smoothed and shaped by the water, a thousand different shades of gray. Gulls squawked, circling and diving. There was a lone sailboat on the horizon.

Astro raced ahead of her, barking at the waves. Nora plunged down the steep dune, the drag of the deep sand slowing her until she reached the water's edge where it was wet and flat. She bent over and scooped up a handful of stones that had come in with the tide, examining each one until she settled on the one she wanted to carry with her. She did this, too, every morning. She liked the feel of the cool, flat stone in her hand. She worried it as she walked, running her thumb and fingers along the surface, exploring the subtle uniqueness of its edges. It made her, well, *happy* to do this – then to throw it as far as she could to be caught by the outgoing tide, drift downward into the blue-green gloom and settle for another thousand years on the sandy floor of the lake. Trudging back up the steep dune to the forest path, her thighs burning, Nora felt that she could face the day.

Monique stood outside the kennels, her hand like a visor over her eyes. She waved wildly when Nora emerged from the woods and started through the meadow, her arms opening to meet her. "Welcome home," she said. "I know it was just two days, but it was weird without you guys here. I'm glad you're back."

Walking back to the house, she told Nora every single thing she'd written in the long note she'd left on the kitchen table, which made Nora smile. Six ripe tomatoes, Astro dragging one of her nightgowns out of the pile of laundry in the utility room and arranging it just-so on his pillow to sleep on, a call from someone in town who might know a lady willing to take the stray mutt they'd been keeping in the kennels since Claire brought it home from the canoe rental several weeks ago. Dinner tonight at their place, she said. They'd taken the tomatoes home, and Diane was making spaghetti sauce even as they spoke.

Monique never changed, Nora thought. She could drive you a little crazy with her relentless kindness, the gratitude she expressed to Charlie again and again – for hiring her to run the kennels when she came home to Michigan in a terrible state, sunk in despair. *She* was the blessing, Nora always told her – arriving as if on schedule just a few weeks after Claire was born to take over the job that was becoming too much for her. But Monique persisted in believing that it was just one more example of Charlie's good character. And swore he was responsible for her happiness with Diane. Hadn't he left Claire to play on the beach with her on that summer day when Diane walked by and Claire toddled after her as if she'd known her all her life?

Mo had been Charlie's girlfriend in high school, though they both laughed a little sheepishly when it came up now. Nora had never asked Charlie if they had had sex together. She thought, no. It was a different time, not required. Monique would not have wanted it, though she probably wouldn't have known exactly why, and Nora could not imagine Charlie being brave enough to attempt it. From what she could tell, they mostly hung out and talked, as they still did – about Tolkien and science and animals. Band geeks, they played classical music together. At night, they might have lain out in the meadow looking up, naming the stars.

She was like a sister-in-law to Nora now, a repository of stories that celebrated and explained Charlie. His fiercest defender – though, Charlie being Charlie, there was little to defend. She grieved over Jo's decline as deeply as Charlie and Nora did and, now, when Nora asked how Jo had been the day before, Monique shook her head.

"She seemed worse. But maybe it was just because she's used to seeing you. I told her where you were, but I think it just confused her."

"Did she know you?" Nora asked.

Monique hesitated, then shook her head. "I don't know. I don't think so."

Nora sighed. "I know it's not *really* connected to Claire leaving. The Alzheimer's takes its own path – Dr. Perry told us that. But I still can't help thinking that every day since Claire's graduation she's slipped away a little more. I'm projecting, probably," she said.

Monique shrugged. "She has, though. Whatever the reason."

Driving to the nursing home to see Jo later that morning, Nora thought, as she had many times over the years, that when she had finally agreed to stay in Michigan and marry Charlie it was in large part because she'd grown so fond of his mother that she couldn't bear the thought of living without her. She loved Charlie. But it was Jo who grounded her, who'd made her feel alive for the first time since she'd lost Tom, hopeful – and forgiven, though why Nora felt this way she didn't know, since she'd never told Jo about her past and Jo had never acted as if she suspected that there was anything for which Nora needed to be forgiven. It was the matter-of-factness of her love that drew Nora to her. The simple gratitude she felt toward Nora for saving Charlie, bringing him back to life after Vietnam, expressed only once, on their wedding day, but which shone in her eyes every moment they were together. Without Jo, there would have been no Claire, for it had been Jo's deep longing for a grandchild that made Nora go against every instinct in conceiving her.

"Grandma, it's me," Claire would say now when she came to visit. "It's Claire."

Jo would smile and repeat her name, but look past her, bemused, as if searching for the little girl she had been. It was wrong, Nora knew, but sometimes she was so angry at Jo that she wanted to take her by the shoulders and say, "Come back. It's not fair. You can't just . . . *change* like this." The real Jo never would have let Nora's stubbornness about IU go as long as it had. She'd have taken her aside before any damage had been done and said, "Her heart's set on that school, Nora. Let her go." And she would have.

Nora might even have told Jo the real reason she didn't want Claire to go there. Everything. She'd always known she could tell Jo the truth about her life, always assumed Jo would be there to tell if she ever decided it was what she needed to do. Jo would listen, her blue eyes brilliant with tears. She'd say, "Oh, Honey, you never had to keep this a secret from us."

This morning she was propped in her recliner, *The Price Is Right* blaring on the television. She was dressed in one of the half-dozen jogging suits Nora had bought her on the recommendation of the nursing staff when she couldn't dress herself anymore. Easy to get on and off, they said. Jo didn't seem to mind them, or the weight she'd put on being so sedentary. But Nora never failed to see her that way without remembering Jo as she had been up to her eightieth birthday just a few years before, dressed in jeans and a sweatshirt, running the dogs in the meadow or rolling out the dough for a pie crust in the kitchen, a force field of energy buzzing around her.

When she tapped on the open door, Jo turned and cocked her head slightly, blinked as if to bring her into focus. Then her face clouded over like a child's might. "Nobody lives in this place anymore," she said in a wobbly voice. "Nobody's been in here to see me all day. I haven't eaten a single thing."

Nora dropped to her knees beside her, took her hand. "Your breakfast tray is in the hall. It looked like you had eaten most everything they left you."

"Oh," Jo said.

"Are you still hungry, though? Mo left you some apples yesterday. There, on the dresser. Or I could go down to the kitchen and see what kind of snack I can find."

"I don't think so," Jo said. "I don't think I'm hungry. I just thought I hadn't eaten and, you know, that I *should*."

"It's okay," Nora said. "You don't have to worry." She moved to sit on the side of the bed and began to tell Jo all about the trip to Bloomington, but Jo looked confused, as if she wasn't quite sure who had taken the trip or why, and she soon nodded off. Nora sat a while, waiting to see if she would wake into a lucid moment as she sometimes did, then gently readjusted the recliner to a position better for sleeping and went on into her day. But making her way through town to do her errands, stopping here and there to chat, she couldn't shake the image of Jo from her mind, and it struck her quite suddenly that she was now almost the same age that Jo had been the summer she came to Monarch, nearly half of her life ago.

She'd been heading for Saginaw, having spent several years drifting her way town-by-town back to the Midwest from California, all alone. Why Saginaw, she wasn't sure. Maybe the Simon and Garfunkel song. Maybe the fact that it was just another medium-sized city where it would be easy to find a crummy job, a small apartment, and just blend in for a while.

She came across Lake Michigan on the car ferry, landing in Ludington and, on a whim, decided to drive north along the coast. It was July, beautiful. If she camped, if she was careful with her money, she could afford a week's delay in her plans. The little lake towns smelling like water, their ice cream and souvenir shops, vacationing families tired and pink from a day at the beach made her feel at the same time calmer and sadder than she had felt in a long while.

Monarch was where her car gave out at the end of that stolen week, where she sat in the Hummingbird Café, her head in her hands, the meal she'd ordered still untouched before her. She didn't have the money to have the car repaired; the smart thing would be to leave it behind and hitchhike. Fine. She'd done it before, though the thought of it filled her with dread. You didn't know who might stop to pick you up. What they might want from you, or wonder. And she was so tired, she realized. More tired than she'd known. At that moment, she simply could not imagine standing up, gathering her bedroll and duffel and walking in the hot sun back to the highway in hope of finding a ride.

Then Jo slid into the booth beside her. "Curt down at the filling station told me about your car," she said. "You by any chance looking for a job? Because I'm really shorthanded here. Darn college girls. They say they want to work, then – " She laughed. "They want you to schedule around their beach time. I've got some shifts, if you want them. There's a little apartment upstairs. It's not much, but you can stay there if you want. Couple of weeks, the worst of my summer rush will be over and you'd have enough to fix the car and be on your way. Wherever you're going."

Nora had just looked at her.

Jo smiled, as if it were the most normal thing in the world to save someone's life. "You'd be doing me a favor," she said. "Really, you would."

Nora had awakened the next morning to the smell of coffee wafting up the stairs to the tidy little apartment where she had slept. The sky was still pink, glittering through the eyelet curtains, and when she stood and went to the window she could see Lake Michigan, blue-gray and calm, dotted with fishing boats, a long black tanker out on the horizon. It was so quiet here, nothing like the places she'd stayed in before. Down on the street, fishermen gathered near the bait shop – dads on vacation, she figured, sharing tips, telling stories. The real ones had been out before dawn. There was a produce truck backed up to the grocery store, a woman sweeping the steps of the ice cream shop. Pinwheels and whirly-gigs fluttered, catching the sun, along the sidewalk leading up to an antique store.

That morning, she'd been determined to earn what she needed to repair the car and be on her way. But it was still high tourist season when the day came and Jo still needed help in the café, or so she said. Okay, Labor Day, Nora told herself. Then Labor Day came and the tourists left, but so did the college girls. There'd be the fall color before they knew it, Jo said. The skiers after that. Could she stay? And so she had.

At the time, she told herself she was just too tired to move on. Why not spend six months in this place, as she had in others before it? Now, of course, she knew that it was because of Jo that she had stayed, just being with Jo who was always smiling, always thinking of some small thing to do for someone else but who knew how to keep her distance, too. Never once did she ask Nora to elaborate on what she had told her after working at the café for several weeks: she was an only child, her parents had died in a car crash not long before she graduated from high school, and she'd been on her own ever since. Nor did Jo mention the sadness surrounding her own life: her young husband, killed in a hunting accident just months after returning from World War II, her only son a virtual recluse since coming home from Vietnam.

Even now, she could not think of Charlie as he had been in those first months she worked at the Hummingbird Café without feeling overwhelmed by tenderness. He'd been painfully shy the few times he came into the café, barely able to carry on a conversation about the weather. But the first time Jo asked her to dinner at the farmhouse, he took her out to the kennels and she was charmed by the transformation she saw in the presence of his animals. There, smiling, his hands held out to receive the dogs' squirming affection, he talked to her about his childhood, how he'd always had a whole houseful of pets and, by the time he was ten, he'd made up his mind that he wanted to be a veterinarian.

When he asked her to see a movie with him, she said yes. Two lonely people. What could it hurt to keep each other company from time to time, Nora had thought. In the next months, they went to movies, to concerts at Interlochen. Sometimes, on her days off, she would drive over to the clinic and help in the kennels. She enjoyed the dogs and surprised herself by being quite good at the office work: scheduling appointments and keeping the books up to date.

"What if I asked Mom if I could steal you to work for me?" he asked one spring day.

"I think I'd like that," Nora said.

That summer, nearly a year after she arrived in Monarch, they were sitting on the beach, watching the sunset, and he lifted her hand from the blanket, kissed it, then drew her to him, wrapped her in his arms. No man had touched her in a loving way since she left Tom, and it was her first impulse to pull away. But she could feel Charlie's heart racing. She knew how shy he was, how lonely – and what the gesture had cost. To pull away, to say no . . .

And it was so lovely to be held by someone safe and kind. Not to be alone.

For just an instant the next morning, waking, she had thought it was Tom sleeping beside her and was filled with such gladness that it took her breath away. But it wasn't Tom, never could be Tom again. Then Charlie stirred and turned toward her, his face naked with longing, and she realized what she had done. Leave now, she told herself. Get up and walk away from him. But she couldn't. Who would she be without Jo and Charlie, without this place she'd grown to love? If she left, where would she go? In time, she stopped thinking about leaving at all.

Life, any life, created its own force of gravity, she saw now. Each kiss and heartache, each meal cooked and consumed, each possession, no matter how small, each garden planted and harvested pulled you toward your own shared center of habit and memory. You couldn't know it would be like this when you started out. You couldn't know what would be expected of you.

And it wasn't as if she regretted staying. No. She loved her life; she'd been grateful every second of every day for it. What she regretted and, increasingly, feared was the secret at its center, which had lain dormant for so long that she had foolishly come to believe it had lost its power to harm her or anyone she loved.

The recent arrest of a Philadelphia woman who had lived underground since participating in a bombing in the 1970s had unbalanced her and brought with it a rush of memories she thought she had put to rest. The impending war in Iraq frightened and enraged her – as much for the way it, too, had begun to dredge up memories of that other time as for the arrogance, the reckless myopia with which it was being pursued. In the last week alone, bombings in Iraq had "accidentally" killed a wedding party, warships were gathering in the Red Sea and now, on the radio, the nasal, self-righteous voice of the Secretary of Defense was asserting, "Measures above and beyond air strikes are necessary to rid Iraq of its supply of weapons of mass destruction." What measures, he didn't say. Or how he knew, for sure, the weapons were even there.

"It scares me," Diane said that evening. They'd finished the meal she and Monique had prepared and the four of them had taken their coffee out to the screened gazebo that overlooked the lake. "My brother's boys are that age," she went on. "Gung ho, the way teenage boys are. Yeah, they'd go in a New York minute, they said after 9/11. And Larry, Jesus! You'd think he'd do everything in the world to convince them not even to *think* about it. But he's like, 'If that's what we have to do . . .'"

"It won't happen," Charlie said.

Diane raised an eyebrow. "Are you kidding?" she said. "We're bombing them already. I'm serious. And the army's holding – " She held up her hands, the first two fingers on each curved like quotation marks. "*Exercises.* In Jordan. What do you think that's about?"

Charlie didn't answer.

Monique gave Diane a stern glance, then in a chirpy voice turned the conversation to the clinic. Old Mrs. Grimes had been in with the awful, yappy Gabrielle, in a panic about a spot on her ear that turned out to be an insect bite. And Bonnie Cato's terrier had eaten three library books. God. Should her stomach be pumped, Bonnie wanted to know?

Diane got up, gathered the empty coffee mugs and took them to the kitchen while Mo chattered on. Music and laughter drifted over from the public beach, where Nora knew Claire and Dylan were playing volleyball – the River Rental team against the wait staff of the Friendly Tavern. Afterward, couple by couple, they'd wrap their beach blankets around their shoulders and hike to a quiet spot to be alone. Her heart ached to think of Claire and Dylan, lying in each other's arms. *Would* the war happen? If it did, how would it change them?

Claire was proud of her father for having served in Vietnam, though she had been virtually unaware of the controversy surrounding the war until her junior year in high school, when her American History teacher assigned a research project on it. In her late thirties, the teacher had vague childhood memories of the sixties, a nostalgic view of the troubles confronting the veterans when they returned from Vietnam, and she believed that by interviewing local men who had served there students could, at the same time, learn firsthand about the war and, belatedly, honor the men through their interest in their experiences. The vets would be invited to a "Welcome Home" party at the high school when students had finished with the unit. They'd be asked to sign an American flag that would be placed in the trophy case in the front hall.

"I don't talk about Vietnam," Charlie said when Claire approached him with the set of questions the teacher had handed out. He had never denied her anything, yet he was adamant in his refusal, immune to her pleas for help. "I put that behind me a long time ago," he told her. "Most of it, I don't even remember. I don't *want* to remember. And if your teacher hassles you about it, you tell her I said she has no business assigning kids to dig around in people's personal lives."

It was so unlike Charlie in every way that Nora was alarmed. "It's for school," she said when they were alone. "Can't you just give her something – basic?"

"Basic?" he said. "*Basic,* like – ?" He shook his head.

"Like what?" Nora asked.

"Like standing outside a surgery tent listening to a couple of intelligence guys torture a Vietnamese kid who'd just gotten thrown 40 feet out of a Huey?" he said. "Listening to the kid scream? Doing nothing? That I think of this every *fucking* day of my life? I could start there."

She stood in shocked silence, let him walk away from her.

He hadn't been the only one to protest the project, and it had fizzled. Instead, the class had a Sixties Day, complete with Beatles music, psychedelic posters, and tie-dye tee shirts. The subject had not come up again, but Nora thought of it now and wondered why she hadn't pressed Charlie to tell her more that day. Why she had let what he *did* say – the first true, deeply personal thing he had ever told her about what happened to him in Vietnam – just float there between them and dissolve.

I didn't want to know, she thought. And, the truth was, Charlie wouldn't want to know what she'd done either. She looked at him, laughing at some long story Monique had launched into, so easily, happily diverted from even the slightest suggestion of conflict or disagreement, and she felt suddenly scooped out, empty to her core.

It won't happen, Charlie had said of the impending war.

It didn't happen, he'd convinced himself of Vietnam.

As if she hadn't done exactly the same thing herself for more than twenty-five years. Believed only in the moment. Now. As if Vietnam had not happened to her, either. Iraq, though, she *saw* – as she'd been incapable of seeing Vietnam in the beginning, when she was young.

15

"Good Day Sunshine"

That night she dreamed of Bridget again. Not the nightmare from long ago that had returned, with different variations, ever since Claire had sent her acceptance to Indiana: Bridget caught in flames, wheeling backwards. But Bridget appearing in the doorway of her dorm room as she had that very first day, suntanned, freckled grinning. She'd dreamed following her up the stairs that opened onto the roof of the dorm – but it was Lake Michigan she saw when she looked over the wall, the view that greeted her each morning.

"Is this groovy, or what?" Bridget said.

Hours after waking, Nora still hadn't shaken the dream.

"Are you all right? Charlie asked at breakfast.

"Fine. Tired," she said.

The tired part was not a lie. Later, walking through the woods with Astro, her legs felt heavy, her breathing was labored. The first glimpse of the lake didn't lift her spirits, but oppressed her. She was Jane looking out at it from the roof of the dorm, shocked to find that the campus had vanished, leaving nothing but water and sky. She cut the walk short, despite Astro's urgent barking when she turned back at less than half their usual distance and was about to give in to a nap when the phone rang.

"Want to float?" Diane asked. "Don't even think of saying no. It's August first. A gorgeous day. If we don't get our float in now, the whole freaking summer is going to get away from us. Do *you* want a summer without a float in it?

"Nora?"

"Yes," Nora said. "I mean, no I don't want a summer without a float. I'll meet you at the launch in twenty minutes."

She threw on her bathing suit and a pair of shorts, stuffed a tee shirt and sunscreen into a beach tote, filled a little cooler with drinks and snacks, and left a note on the table for Charlie: "Floating with Diane. I'll do the bills this evening. N." Monique looked up quizzically from the entry of the clinic, where she was emerging, watering can in hand, to water the window boxes outside Charlie's office window, but Nora just waved as she drove past – still a little aggravated by the way Mo had manipulated last night's conversation away from the Iraqi controversy as if to protect him.

She reached Riverside Rental before Diane got there, signed them up for two of the oversized inner tubes with plastic bottoms, then sat on the deck of the little general store in a puddle of sunshine. The store had been built in the forties, Charlie once told her, and had been added on to so that there was an assortment of nooks and crannies inside, stuffed with fishing tackle, sunscreen, beach toys, groceries, and every kind of tacky souvenir. Outside, it looked like an overgrown cabin, with cedar siding and a stone chimney. A life-size wooden Indian, its paint chipped from years of weather, guarded the front door with the help of a huge, motley teddy bear sitting on a blue deck chair. There was a big white ice chest, a stack of neatly bound bundles of wood for campfires. There were bins of flip-flops and water toys and Frisbees in garish colors. A strawberry ice cream cone the size of an eight-year old child tipped out from the roadside Riverside Rental sign.

"Want one *dat* big," Claire had said, throwing out her chubby arms and grinning, her first joke at barely two.

Now there she was, grown, navigating the happy confusion on the bank below. Nora watched her help a young couple and their children into their canoe, waving as they set off, then turn in search of the next task. The canoes were stacked in silver pyramids under the trees at the edge of the launch area, bouquets of paddles sprouted from big wooden kegs. There were dozens of big, green inner tubes heaped in the walk-in basement and orange life jackets in wire bins, organized by size. Pairs of suntanned adolescents in red tank tops duck-walked canoes to the water; others, half-dancing to the music blaring from a boom box in the garage, unloaded slippery tubes from the wire cage built on the bed of a yellow pick-up truck or stood on the piers, tying inner tubes together with bits of rope, then helping patrons launch themselves onto the river.

Claire bent to help a father and daughter connect their inner tubes, whispering something to the little girl that made her smile. What? Nora wondered. Perhaps that she had been down the river a million times herself and there was nothing to be afraid of. Nothing at all! She was radiant in the sunlight, tanned and healthy. Her long hair was caught up in a single braid, damp tendrils curling around her face.

"Did we ever look like that?" Diane said, flopping onto the bench beside her. "I mean, even on our best day? Before we had a clue about, well, *anything*?"

In fact, Diane looked great now – long-legged and slim as a girl herself. She'd pulled her curly salt-and-pepper hair back into a ponytail that was peeking out from the back of her blue "Michigan" baseball cap. She'd been beautiful when she was young, the homecoming queen in high school, sweetheart of her ex-husband's fraternity when she was in college. She was still beautiful, Nora thought. But as Diane liked to point out, amused and a little wistful: looking good at fifty-five is not exactly the same as . . . looking good.

Now she let out an exasperated sigh. "Sorry it took me so long to get here. Mo's mother called when I got to the house. Okay, I know. Why did I answer the phone when I wasn't officially there? Better question: why was Betty calling when she knew Mo would be at the clinic? The woman never has adjusted to the idea of Mo having a job, you know – *wanting* one when she doesn't really need to work. Truth be told, she's still waiting for her to find the perfect husband and *settle down*."

"That would be Charlie," Nora said.

Diane grinned. "Well, yeah. It would. You interloper!" She waved to Claire down on the bank. "Mo and I had a huge fight last night after you guys left," she said. "Because I mentioned w-a-r in Charlie's presence. Were you mad at me? Mo said you were."

"No," Nora said.

"Because I'm sorry if you are. I'd never – "

"I'm not mad. Really."

"Good," Diane said. "To hell with Mo then. And to hell with George W. Bush, too – and his henchmen. For now, anyway. I poured a whole bottle of merlot into an empty cranberry juice bottle for us. Let's float."

Claire met them as they started down the slope toward the dock, Dylan trailing behind her, and threw her arms first around Nora, then Diane.

"Time for the annual river trip," Diane said, hugging her back. "Too bad you've grown up and abandoned us."

"She told me you guys used to float here every summer when she was little," Dylan said.

"Little," Diane said. "Please. We floated till she was – what? Sixteen? Then – ? Like I said, total abandonment. Denial!"

Claire laughed. "They're driving me nuts," she said to Dylan. "I've got, like, *three* moms – not to mention Dad, who's the worst of all – wailing over the fact that I grew up. Like that's *my* fault."

"Yeah, my parents did the same thing last year." He grinned. "Now they don't even miss me."

Claire punched his shoulder. "They *do*. I read that letter your mom sent."

Dylan shrugged, wrestled her, giggling, into his grasp. Stocky and strong, he was about as unlikely a violinist as Nora could imagine, and she smiled when he picked up Claire and carried her down the bank, back to her station. Remembered watching them together at the street dance in town the weekend before: Claire, in overalls and a tie-dye tee shirt, swaying to the music, her arms raised, undulating, lit white in the light beams raking the street. Dylan doing some strange, wild hopping dance around her.

"They're like puppies," Diane said when they'd pushed off and floated out of earshot. She lay back in her inner tube, her face to the sun. "God. This is exactly what I needed."

Nora lay back, too, trailing her hands in the cool water, paddling half-heartedly if they floated too near trees or rocks along the bank. The river was like a wide road, gray-green and sparkling, narrowing to a point on the horizon. The water was shallow, the bottom sandy, littered with smooth gray stones. Silver minnows flitted beneath the surface, an occasional turtle lay, sunning, on a fallen limb. There was a fishy scent and the scent of pine trees. The scent of sunscreen on their bodies: Coppertone, a scent that never failed to fill Nora with vague longing.

"Are you worried about Claire?" Diane asked. "I mean, *sex*? God, the two of them are veritably exuding hormones."

"I talked to her about sex," Nora said. "Before. Dylan, I mean. In the abstract. You know, birth control, being careful, all that. Maybe I should talk to her about it again. I've thought about it, but I feel – I don't know, like it would be intruding. She's a smart girl. I don't know for sure that she's had sex with Dylan – and if I knew for sure they had, what would I say? *Stop*?"

Diane laughed.

"Actually, I'm not really worried about it," Nora said. "Which kind of surprises me."

"Charlie?"

"Who would know what Charlie thinks?" Nora asked. "If I had to guess, I'd say he's convinced himself that Claire and Dylan are really, really, really good friends."

"They do seem like friends." Diane smiled. "In addition to the fact that they can't keep their hands off each other."

"I know," Nora said. "It's nice."

They drifted quietly awhile, occasionally sipping the wine Diane had poured. The sky was blue, with a few cottony clouds; the sun warm on their bare skin. There were houses and cabins here and there along the bank and Nora peered through the green scrim of foliage for signs of life as they passed by, determined not to let her mind reel backward again as it had done since last night with the talk about war.

Diane said, "Sometimes I wonder what that's like, you know? To be in love, the way Claire and Dylan are? When I was that age myself, I'd watch my girlfriends and think, when is that going to happen to me? It certainly didn't with *Bob.* By the time I figured out why it never happened, it was too late to be young and in love. Just – in love, like I am with Mo. Which is plenty lucky, I know. A lot of people never even get that."

She sighed. "Jesus, I don't know what's wrong with me lately. Hormones, I guess. Only not the good, sexy kind. The kind that – I keep . . . *thinking* about things. Like just now. I was remembering looking out of the window of my room in the sorority house, seeing these two girls walking, holding hands, and being just totally overcome with sadness. I was nineteen. I was so out of it I'm not even sure if I knew then that girls could be together sexually. It just seemed so *nice,* the way they were. Now I look back and think, I should have known.

"And, okay, this Iraq thing. Why, I have no idea, since at the time I was almost totally oblivious, but every time I hear about Iraq I think about Vietnam and how we're headed for the same place again and nobody even cares. That's what I got into an argument with Mo about last night," she said. "Mo and I *never* argue about politics. Am I crazy about this, Nora? Tell me if you think I am."

"No," Nora said. "Either that, or we both are. I'd probably be arguing with Charlie about it, too, if he'd even acknowledge it was happening. You saw him last night. He's not going there."

"It *is* like Vietnam, isn't it?" Diane said.

"Yeah," Nora said. "It seems like that to me.

"Fucking Bob," Diane said. "Amazing how I can still get pissed off at him after all these years – and about whole new things. He had me convinced that the antiwar protesters were all drug addicts and hippies out to brainwash our children, but now I think they weren't. They were telling the truth. *They knew.*

"It's what pisses me off about that poor woman from Philadelphia. The goddamn government still won't admit the protestors were right – and, please! She put a bomb under a police car thirty years ago that never went off, that never hurt *anyone* – and she's a 'domestic terrorist'? Give me a break.

"Okay," she said. "I know that's not Bob's fault – and it's not like he set out to brainwash *me* then. I was just shell-shocked from going from life as a shallow, dopey little sorority girl to being married with a set of twins to take care of practically overnight. Jesus. All I really remember from the entire decade of my twenties is being in a permanent state of exhaustion.

"Well. And I remember Bob's mother. Ha! Grace-the misnamed. The only person in the world who was happy when I left Bob and the girls to run off with Audrey Collins, because it meant she could have them all to herself.

"Not going there," Diane reminded herself, smiling faintly. "Anyway, a couple of Bob's fraternity brothers went to Vietnam. Some guys I went to high school with. But nobody whose life really affected mine. Did you? Know anyone who went?"

A dragonfly hovered between them, its blue wings translucent, then swooped away, skimming across the sunlit water.

"My brother," Nora said. "I had a brother who went."

"Oh!" Diane sat up in her tube, nearly tipping it. "Nora. I had no idea . . . I – "

"It's okay. Charlie doesn't even know. Nobody does. It was . . . we were never – close. It was a long time ago."

Diane's eyes filled with tears. "See? All this emotional turmoil," she said. "It just dredges up – *shit.* Things you can't change. Oh, God, I might as well tell you what's really going on, even though I haven't told Mo yet. I don't exactly know how."

"What?" Nora asked, alarmed.

"I had a letter from Carah yesterday. She's pregnant. She wants to come see me. She wants me to come there for the baby's birth, in January."

"But that's wonderful," Nora said.

"I know," Diane said, crying in earnest now. "I know. But since I got the letter all I can think about is myself when she and Rose were babies. How miserable I was. How much I loved them, but didn't know what to *do* with them half the time. How I just gave them *up* because of Audrey. Totally buckled and let Bob and his mother – "

Nora reached across the inner tube and took Diane's hand. "Diane," she said. "Come on. They were seniors in high school when that happened. You were a wonderful mother to them until then. You'd have kept on being wonderful to them, if they'd have let you. If Bob hadn't let his mother poison them against you. Now Carah's pregnant and seeing what she should've seen all along. Isn't this what you always hoped for?"

"Yes," Diane sobbed.

"Of course, Mo will be happy for you. Won't she?"

"Yes," Diane said. "I don't know. I'm scared, Nora. You know how she hates change."

"But a *baby,*" Nora said.

Just then, a long line of canoes approached and they had to paddle madly to get out of the way. Teenagers wearing bright yellow tee shirts with "Got Jesus?" printed on the back.

"I swear," Diane said. "This morning, I read about this Christian camp in Maine where they have Bible verses on the canoe paddles," she said. "All I could think was, 'For God so loved the world,' *smack.* 'Lead me by the still waters,' *smack.* That'll pretty much tell you what kind of state I'm in."

Nora laughed. "A baby," she repeated. "A baby is a glorious thing."

"Yes!" Diane said, smiling through her tears. "My God. Break out the wine again. I'm going to be a grandmother. How bizarre is that?"

They drank a toast, ate the sandwiches Diane had packed and, for the next hour or so, drifted lazily toward Lake Michigan. Nora closed her eyes and dozed intermittently, warmed by the green sunshine dappling down through the pines. There was the small slap of water against the inner tube, the occasional splash of fish, the low buzz of insects.

"I had a brother who went," she had said.

She was grateful that Diane had not questioned her about Bobby, but in the next days could not help thinking about him. Sitting in the booth at the Big Wheel laughing and sharing secrets that Christmas break before he shipped out – and how his time in Vietnam, his death there, had set her on the path that had brought her to this life which, then, she could never have imagined.

16

"(I Can't Get No) Satisfaction"

The first week of August, the litany of Claire's last moments began: last day at work, last volleyball game, last sunset picnic on the beach, last overnight with her high school girlfriends, last cheeseburger at the Friendly. Tonight was the last concert of the season at Interlochen, a tradition since Claire was a baby. Even Jo was going. They'd loaded her wheelchair into Monique's van, then strapped her, muddled but cheerful, into the backseat, Claire and Dylan on either side of her.

It was a beautiful evening, cool and clear, still light as they joined the throngs of people winding along the various wooded paths, all of which led to the Kellogg Arena at the center of the grounds. There were stone and clapboard practice huts set back among the trees, the occasional earnest camper framed in a window bent over his instrument and the strains of music drifting into the evening air, mingling with the sound of people talking.

Charlie and Monique walked ahead a bit under the canopy of trees, chatting as they always did, about their time at the camp as teenagers. The rules were stricter then, they never failed to remember. Campers were always in their uniforms: girls in navy blue corduroy knickers, pale blue shirts and red knee socks; boys in navy blue pants and blue oxford shirts. Now they were dressed in infinite variations of navy blue and red – most only vaguely in uniform, sporting red knee socks with a blue mini-skirt or a blue "Interlochen" sweatshirt over a pair of jeans.

Dylan pushed Jo's wheelchair and Claire walked alongside, chatting to her grandmother who gazed up at her, beatific, as if she could not imagine why this lovely young woman had decided to be so attentive to her.

"It's sweet," Diane said, as if reading her thoughts. "The two of them with Jo." Then smiled. "Getting ready to come tonight, I was thinking about the time we went to visit her and they'd wheeled everybody into the lounge to hear the old guys playing big band music."

"God," Nora said. "The piano player on oxygen!"

"And all those old ladies bobbing to 'A String of Pearls.' Probably feeling twenty. All I could think was that it'll be us in thirty years, only it'll be, what? 'Sympathy for the Devil'? It's so bizarre, isn't it? I think of my mom at the age we are now, and she was *old*."

"*We're* old," Nora said. "In case you haven't noticed."

"Not old like my mom was in her fifties," Diane said. "We don't have that awful helmet hair, do we? We're not wearing knits. I have to keep reminding myself that I'm going to be a grandmother – speaking of which, Carah called today. Both she and Rose are coming. In September."

Nora stopped short and gave her a hug. "They're really, truly coming!"

Diane nodded, blinking back tears. "God. I'm so – emotional about it. I know I'm about to drive Mo crazy. I can't wait, I'm scared to death. We're fixing up Betty's room for them," she said. "Painting. Taking down those hideous drapes and getting blinds that let the light in. We've got a guy coming tomorrow to give us an estimate."

"Wait," Nora said. "You're redecorating Betty's room?"

"It was Mo's idea," Diane said. "You can't get Betty out of Florida with a crowbar anymore, and Mo said, why should we keep that hideous early American furniture just because she picked it out forty years ago.

"*Mo* said that?"

Diane laughed. "She's not saying she thinks we ought to get rid of it. Knowing Mo, she'll make an annex to the Museum of Charlie, and put it there. But she's been so great about the girls coming. She's so happy for me. She totally surprises me sometimes, you know?"

"Mmm," Nora had responded, thinking that she could not remember the last time Charlie had surprised her, or if he had ever surprised her at all. She tried as she had countless times in the past months to remember how it had felt to be happy with Charlie, before Claire's school decision came between them. Days and days, each virtually the same. What a comfort they had seemed to her, unfolding – Claire at the center of them. Charlie kept a shoebox of her baby things out in the barn, along with the mementoes from his own childhood. Her pacifier, a teething ring, a tiny pair of moccasins. Her first bike was there, too: pink, with a flowered seat and glittery plastic streamers. All the images that came to mind when she concentrated on remembering Charlie in those happy times had Claire in them – the two of them often framed by a window or doorway. Charlie bending over to position the awkward baseball glove on her little hand, adjusting the brim of the "Michigan" baseball cap so she could see better, then throwing the softball again and again – from just steps away, so she would be sure to catch it. Charlie sitting beside her on the piano bench, leaning to run one finger across the notes on the score as she played to help her keep track of them and, years later, the two of them making music together – Claire on the cello, Charlie on his old violin.

Clear as anything, Nora saw them: Charlie giving Claire a hand-up so she could climb into his pickup and tag along on some errand with him, carrying her into Lake Michigan, showing her the right way to brush the dogs in the kennel. They'd built countless sand castles together, flown countless kites in the meadow. When she was not quite a year old, Nora remembered, Claire would raise her chubby arms when she saw him and he would walk her in a circle – through the kitchen, the dining room, the living room, and back through the kitchen again – until one day, to his great delight, she let go and toddled away from him.

The memories softened her toward him, made her resolve to be more patient, more understanding – though she could not imagine how she could avoid *feeling* like a cat with its back up in his presence. He was constantly underfoot; then disappeared when she needed him. He was quiet when she wanted to talk, talkative – about things that bored her to tears – when she wanted to be alone. He tried too hard to please her; he didn't try at all.

It was Claire so near leaving, she reminded herself. That's why she felt so restless, why Charlie was driving her crazy. It was being so sad about Jo. But it wasn't only that. It was also the Philadelphia woman, who'd been arrested for crimes committed in the seventies and whose case was regular fodder on the evening news, always accompanied by clips of her stalwart husband, her bewildered teenage daughters. It was the news about Iraq.

It *was* like Vietnam, as Diane had said. Lies upon lies. Just this week, one of Bush's former advisors had spoken out against the impending war. There was scant evidence tying Saddam Hussein to terrorist organizations, he said. Even less evidence tying him to 9/11. And as for the alleged meeting between one of the terrorists and an Iraqi official in Prague, Vaclav Havel himself had "quietly" called the White House, debunking the story.

Yet "proof" of the meeting had been the lead story on last night's news.

Neither of them said a word about it. Charlie just stood, switched off the television and put Yo-Yo Ma's *Goldberg Variations* on the stereo.

"Do we have to listen that *again*?" Nora asked.

He turned to her, confused, the empty CD case still in his hand. "Is there something you'd rather listen to?"

The Rolling Stones, she felt like saying. "Yeah, (I Can't Get No) Satisfaciton." But they didn't even have a Rolling Stones CD in their collection. They never listened to anything but classical music. Though, lately, she'd been listening to the oldies station in the car.

"Oh, forget it," she said. "The Bach is fine."

But once Charlie had settled into his easy chair, eyes closed, to enjoy it fully, she'd gone outside and walked toward the forest until there was no sound but the rustling trees, the chirp and whirr of insects. Then just stood there for a long time, seething at the sight of him framed in the living room window.

Glancing at him now, still chatting companionably with Mo, Nora wondered whether she and Charlie would be so at odds with each other if Claire had decided to go to Oberlin, as she had originally planned? If she hadn't been shocked into remembering her own young self, would the two of them have gone on living more or less as they always had once Claire left, growing older and older until, like Jo, they became doddering, frail ghosts of themselves?

Stop, she told herself. Lately, her mind felt like a grocery cart with a bad wheel, always veering off in some direction she did not want it to go. She focused her attention on the activity outside the arena: teenagers lounging on the benches that circled clusters of big trees, laughing and talking, their instrument cases at their feet. Some held hands, leaning into each other as close to kissing as you could get without actually doing it. A group of tuba players clustered near the information center, fooling around, the comic bellow of the instruments mingling with the "whoosh" of an espresso machine nearby and the crunching sound of blenders making smoothies with fruit and ice.

Inside the open-air arena, it was cool and dim. The last rays of the sun fell first on Green Lake and set it glittering, then slanted across the arena like a wand, illuminating whole rows of seats and the moths fluttering in the red rafters high above. Nora chatted with Diane, who raised an amused eyebrow at Mo and Charlie, who were reminiscing about concerts they'd heard as campers, sitting out on the lawn because they couldn't afford to buy tickets then. Claire and Dylan had disappeared among the young people clustered down front, near the stage. Jo sat beside her, on the aisle, quietly lost.

She perked up, though, when the music began, lifting both hands as if to capture the notes in them, and Nora saw a glimmer of the old Jo in the simple pleasure on her face and in the way she watched a young father who stood nearby, swaying to the music, an infant bound to his chest in a corduroy snuggly. Was she remembering how they used to bring Claire here when she was just a little girl, wondering what had become of her?

She wondered it herself sometimes, remembered Claire at two, three, four, and how it had felt, then, to be all Claire wanted, the center of her life. How she had known Claire absolutely – her needs and moods. Claire had belonged to her in a way Nora had not fully appreciated until she started kindergarten, her own life that Nora could never fully know.

It was natural, of course. There was your life with your parents, and . . . your life. Her relationship with her parents had been unusually distant and strained. But even Jo hadn't been privy to everything about Charlie's life once he left childhood.

A glimpse now and then was probably the best you could hope for, a little window opening. In fact, just that morning, cleaning the kitchen countertops, she had noticed Claire's portable CD player on the countertop and picked it up, thinking she'd set it on one of the piles in the hallway to make sure Claire wouldn't forget it. But on a whim, she put the earphones on and pushed PLAY.

To her surprise, she heard Janis Joplin. "Piece of My Heart." Then "Somebody to Love," "A Whiter Shade of Pale." It was the mix Dylan had made for her, Nora realized. "He's kind of a sixties freak," Claire had said when she told her about it. "Like you couldn't figure that out. Duh. His *name*?"

Perhaps Nora shouldn't have, but she sat down and kept listening – "Revolution," "Light My Fire" – until Bob Dylan's gravelly voice singing "Like a Rolling Stone" undid her, the plaintive harmonica that seduced the truth and laid it bare. Listening to that song when she was young, she had heard it as a taunt directed at those in the older generation who thought they knew everything, who refused change. "Never trust a person over thirty," they said then, only half-joking. Bob Dylan was all about that, wasn't he? At the base of all his mysterious metaphors, wasn't he really just saying, "Get out of the way, old man. It's our world now."

But listening this afternoon, in her own kitchen, what she heard was the terrible loneliness in his words. The sense that everything you believed in and expected life to be could just dissolve – and where would you be then?

She had felt utterly untethered for a moment – and felt it again, now, as night chased the last of the light away and stars punctured the clear, black sky.

17

"Go Now!"

On Claire's last morning at home, Nora stood at the window and watched her walk slowly through the meadow, trailing her fingers among the flowers as she went, then slip through the trees onto the lake path, Astro trotting along happily behind her. Later, Claire stood in the yard, throwing his Frisbee for nearly an hour, ruffling his fur, leaning down to let him lick her face each time he returned and laid it at her feet.

In the afternoon, they went to the nursing home, where Claire knelt beside her grandmother and talked to her quietly, remembering happy moments they'd shared, while Jo gazed at her benevolently, confused. "Is it okay with you if I go over to Dylan's for a little while, to help him pack?" Claire asked, exiting into the sunshine. "He'll give me a ride home in time for dinner."

"Sure," Nora said, and watched her walk up Main Street, heading for the house he was sharing with some other college students for the summer. He had little to pack, Nora knew. A duffel's worth of clothes, a few books, his computer, stereo, CDs. Claire just needed to be with him; they'd been inseparable since he arrived in May, and she probably could no longer imagine a day without him somewhere in it. Maybe she'd talk to him about how it had hurt her to say goodbye to Jo, how she dreaded leaving Nora and Charlie the next morning and just wished it were over, the two of them already in his truck, driving south. Maybe they wouldn't talk at all but would fall into each other's arms and make love in Dylan's room for the last time. Another last, she thought – one she hadn't considered till this moment.

Halfway to her car, Nora turned and headed for Diane's shop, hoping that by this time of afternoon it would be empty – the tourists back in their cottages, napping, the Traverse City ladies on their way home to fix supper for their families. It was. Diane appeared at the door of the storeroom when the bell rang with Nora's entry.

"Hey," she said. "What's up?"

"Show me some paint chips for the girls' room – or *something,* would you?" Nora said. "I swear to God, I'm going to have a nervous breakdown before Claire actually leaves tomorrow morning."

Diane peered at her over the half glasses she wore for reading or working at the computer. "You look all wound up."

"I am," Nora said. "Can you walk? Just a half hour or so. Enough to – I don't know."

"Yeah," Diane said. "Just let me close up here. And, ha! Be careful what you ask for. I do happen to have some paint chips for you to look at."

"Good," Nora said. "Give them here."

Diane fanned out a dozen or so, all shades of green, and handed them to Nora. "Mo says I should stop looking at the names and just look at the colors," she said. "But I mean, really, under the circumstances, don't you think it's a better bet to paint the room something like 'Green Thoughts' or 'Oatlands Spring Kiss,' as opposed to, say, '*Grassy Knoll*'? Even if we *like* 'Grassy Knoll' a lot?"

Nora laughed. "I'm with you," she said.

"Seriously," Diane said. "What do you think?"

Nora looked at the color chips. "'Frosted jade'? 'Grass Root'? I like those. And 'Aspen Field.' It's cheerful, the color of a Granny Smith apple. 'Green Thoughts' is good, too."

"I think, any of those," Diane said. "With a kind of mossy pink trim? Or maybe pale, pale blue?" She rolled her eyes. "I told Mo, 'Grassy Knoll' with red trim. She was not amused."

"I'm amused," Nora said.

"Of course." Diane grinned. "I knew you would be. I counted on it."

She took the paint chips back, set them on the counter near the cash register, then locked the front door and put the "CLOSED" sign in the window. Nora was already feeling better when they slipped out the back door and set out walking. The route to the beach took them past the rundown clapboard house where Dylan lived with his friends. The front windows were open, music pouring out of them – something Nora didn't recognize.

"Claire decided to go over and help him pack after we saw Jo."

"Right," Diane said. "The same three tee shirts he's been wearing all summer? That should take, maybe, twelve seconds."

"I know. I *know.* It's not even like it upsets me, or even worries me that, well, you know. It's – "

"You're jealous," Diane said. "Hey, aren't we all? God. They're just so – *alive.*"

It was near four o'clock and, at the public beach, mothers were packing up their coolers and blankets and beach chairs. Cranky, sunburned children trudged through the sand, laden with buckets and shovels, dragging rubber rafts behind them. At the shoreline, a young woman threw a pink rubber flip-flop into the lake for a shaggy, tail-wagging mutt that plunged into the waves and swam after it.

They headed north, walking at a brisk pace on the narrow strip of flat, wet sand at the water's edge, skipping sideways to avoid the occasional wave that washed up high enough to threaten their dry shoes. The sun was strong from the west, glittering the water where it slanted down. The rainbow sail of the little sunfish skittering by glowed with it. The wet Petoskey stones shone as if someone had polished them.

"So, *you're* a wreck," Diane said, when they'd gone a ways. "How's Charlie doing?"

Nora shrugged. "You probably know more than I do," she said. "What does Mo say? He's not talking to me. Is he talking to her?"

Diane smiled. "They . . . *commune,*" she said. "Honestly, do you think two less verbal people ever lived? I shudder to think what would have happened to them if Betty's fantasy had actually come true and they'd gotten married to each other. Can you imagine it?"

Nora could, actually – and thought Charlie, at least, would be quite content in a relationship that made such small use of words.

"I have to drag things out of Mo," Diane went on. "I swore when I left Bob that I'd never, ever get into those never-say-anything-you're-really-feeling kind of relationships again. Enough! She hates it, but the truth is I'm good for her and she knows it – though, I suspect Betty feels pretty much the same as Bob's mother did about me." She sang a bar of Santana's "Black Magic Woman."

"That's you, all right," Nora said.

Diane laughed. "I shouldn't complain. I sure as hell wouldn't be closing up the shop early to go walk on the beach if Mo weren't so careful with her money. I wouldn't *have* the shop. She wouldn't be working for Charlie at minimum wage. Not that – "

"It's okay, " Nora said. "I know what you mean. And I know Mo's a . . . comfort to him. I'm grateful for that."

"She doesn't talk about him," Diane said. "I'd tell you if she did."

"I know that," Nora said.

Diane looked at her. "Did something happen between you and Charlie?" she asked.

Nora shook her head. "Nothing," she said. "*Nothing.* That's the problem. He's so – quiet. It's like he's not even there."

"He'll come around once Claire is gone," Diane said. "Poor guy. I watch him look at her and, my God, it's like he's looking at someone he knows is going to die. And Jo. That's got to be part of it, too. *None* of us was prepared for that. What I think is, he's been hijacked by his emotions and doesn't have a clue what to do about it."

"I do think he'll be better once she's gone," Nora said. "Different, anyway. He has to be. But how are we going to get used to being just us, without her?"

"You will," Diane said. "Nora, you *will.*"

They walked quietly all the way back to town, both of them lost in their own thoughts. Diane, perhaps, fixing up the apple green room she meant to make for her daughters in her mind's eye. Nora hoping Diane was right, that life with Charlie would get better once their dread of Claire's leaving dissolved into her actual absence.

She fixed an early dinner – fried chicken, tomatoes from the garden, corn on the cob. Warm peach cobbler made from Jo's recipe.

Everything her daughter loved. Claire was beside herself with excitement. She couldn't wait to meet her roommate, Emily. She hoped she hadn't forgotten to pack anything. This time tomorrow she'd be there!

The naked sadness in Charlie's face made any annoyance Nora had felt toward him give way to the urge to protect him, if only she could. Still, people sent their only child off to college all the time. Of course, it was painful. But they'd be fine. She'd make things fine between them. Claire would leave and make her own life, as all young people must, and she and Charlie would find a new way to be together. People did this all the time, too. They had emotional crises, too, rehashing the past, agonizing over what might have been. Eventually, they got it together and moved on. Which was exactly what Nora meant to do herself. It wasn't as if she could actually change anything.

But that night, she lay sleepless trying to imagine *how* she would go on, what this new life with Charlie could be. The digital clock clicked off two o'clock. Then three. Four. Nora got up, shrugged on her robe and padded down the hallway to Claire's room, where she stood in the doorway a long time and watched her sleep, Astro curled up at her feet. The room looked cavernous in the moonlight, stripped of its posters and decorations. The floor was unnaturally bare, the usual clutter having made its way into boxes and suitcases, the occasional shopping bag – all of which were lined up in the downstairs hallway, ready to be carried out to Dylan's truck in the morning. Downstairs, she made herself a cup of tea, sat down at the kitchen table and picked up the *Newsweek* Charlie had abandoned there.

She opened the magazine randomly to a photograph of the Philadelphia swim mom, in prison garb, almost unrecognizable from the beautiful blond woman who'd been arrested months before. Bravely or foolishly, she had spoken out about the impending war, comparing it to Vietnam, and said she did not regret having worked to end that war in the 1960s and '70s. Someone had to do something then; someone had to do something now.

It was a sidebar to the major article about Iraq, which reported that seven out of ten Americans supported military action in Iraq; fifty-nine percent were ready to use ground troops. This despite the fact that even some Republicans warned that the President was rushing the country into war; countries who had supported the Gulf War were unwilling to provide staging areas for U.S. troops; and even if Saddam Hussein did have weapons of mass destruction, it was likely that they lacked the range to be dangerous to American citizens. Not to mention the fact that the Iraqi people had done nothing to bring down the wrath of the United States upon them.

People saw what they wanted and needed to see. Nora knew that. She had been ignorant about Vietnam until Wayne Dugan forced her to think about what was happening there, until she heard the Marine speak at the demonstration in Dunn Meadow. Even then, she hadn't *wanted* to think about it. But after her brother's death, she had been drawn to the fringes of demonstrations, where she stood watching, listening. Waiting, she realized only later, for the moment when it would be clear what she should do.

Resolutely, she closed the *Newsweek* and threw it in the trash. She would not think about what a mess the world was in on this last morning with Claire or worry about sending her out into it. Near dawn, the birds began their agitated chatter in the tall pine outside the kitchen window. Nora sat, watching the meadow and forest beyond emerge, first in silhouette, then in full color. Upstairs, Claire's alarm went off; moments later, Nora heard the sound of the shower.

She roused Charlie, then put the coffee on, and began to fix the blueberry waffles she'd promised. Soon there was the crunch of Dylan's truck in the driveway. Claire burst into the kitchen, flushed with excitement, and met him at the back door, throwing her arms around him.

"I'm here to kidnap your daughter," he said, with a grin.

When they'd finally gone – when Claire had picked a bouquet of wildflowers from the meadow and wrapped it in wet paper towels for her dorm room, thrown one last stick for Astro, run back to give her parents one last hug – Nora and Charlie went back to the kitchen and sat in silence, emptiness humming all around them. Even Astro looked sad, sniffing the air where Claire had been.

Nora was glad when Charlie got up to go out to the clinic. She sat awhile, imagining Dylan's red truck on a map, heading south toward

Indiana. She cried a little. She went upstairs to the computer Claire had left behind in favor of her new laptop and sent her an e-mail: *I miss you already.* Then pulled up Google and typed in the swim mom's real name: Carole Matthias.

But it was her assumed name, Laura Ann Pearson, that popped up as the first entry: a brief biography, some background on the so-called crime she had committed in the 1970s, information about her life as Carole Matthias, and an account of her arrest, as well as what had happened to her since then.

The arrest had occurred in January, and she had pled guilty and accepted a plea bargain. Weeks later, though, she had withdrawn it, stating that she had agreed to it only because she had been convinced by her lawyer that the events of 9/11 made it impossible for an accused bomber to receive a fair trail. She told the judge that she had pleaded guilty in what she thought was in her own and her family's best interest. But it wasn't the truth and she realized she couldn't live with the fact that she had lied."

She added that she had not made the bomb, nor had she possessed or planted the bomb. It was under the concept of aiding and abetting that she pled guilty.

The judge offered to let her testify under oath about her role in the case, but she refused, stating that she wanted a trial. He denied her request, and sentenced her to serve ten-years-to-life, as opposed to the three-to-five year sentence she had agreed to in the plea – and the life she'd known as Laura Ann Pearson was over.

Her family and friends supported and continued to believe in her, and most media were in agreement that she'd never have been arrested in the first place if 9/11 hadn't given the Bush administration a rationale for pursuing the radical right-wing agenda they had wanted to pursue all along. Those who spoke out about the hijacking of civil rights and the invasion of privacy were considered not only unpatriotic but potential "domestic terrorists," which had given the FBI grounds to reopen cases from the sixties and seventies that had long been abandoned – and to fan the flames of fear generated by the attacks.

"Laura Ann Pearson, the wife, swim mom, painter, gourmet cook, aka Carol Matthias, the accused terrorist and former radical fugitive, has pleaded guilty to possessing bombs with intent to murder police officers in San Francisco," one article read. "Her story represents two very different lives. To Pearson's friends and champions, she is a symbol of passion and conviction. To many law enforcement officials and others, this woman – whomever she claims to be – committed serious crimes and owes an accounting.

"Which do *you* think she really is?"

Both, Nora knew.

18

"Teach Your Children"

It worked sometimes to talk softly to Jo about things that had happened in the past, going back in time to when Charlie was a little boy and then reeling her in toward the present, story by story. But today, Nora did not have the heart for it. The stories would lead to Claire; they always did – memories of her infancy and childhood – and it was just too painful to remember those years and years when the demands and pleasures of caring for Claire had occupied them all so completely that there was rarely a moment for contemplation or regret.

How bright and funny she had been! "Songs!" she would cry out, in the car. But she did not want just any song on the radio. At two, she sat in her car seat, her eyes closed, listening to Mozart or Bach. "Mama, more!" she said when a tape ended and silence fell. "No yike," she said to the easy listening music Jo played in her car, which always made Charlie laugh.

She missed Claire so much. She read the e-mails Claire sent over and over, imagining her daydreaming through comp class in Woodburn Hall, walking back to the dorm on the wooded path that ran alongside the creek that wound its way through the old part of campus.

"It's called the Jordan River," Claire wrote. "Someone said the water used to run black behind the Journalism Building, because they dumped the ink there. Is that gross, or what?"

Nora remembered the inky water washing over the stones, how it grew lighter and lighter the farther away it got from Ernie Pyle Hall. She remembered, too, an unseasonably warm, rainy afternoon in March of her freshman year when she and Bridget had taken off their shoes and waded the Jordan River from Ballantine Hall all the way to the SAE House, where days and days of rain had caused the creek to swell into a little pond. Drenched and laughing, cheered on by a bunch of boys watching from an upstairs window, Bridget set her soggy book bag on the sidewalk, walked in to her knees, her shoulders – and finally submerged herself completely, invisible but for her long red hair floating out around her. Then she burst forth, grinning, splattering water everywhere.

She ached, knowing she could not write back to Claire and share these memories. Instead, she kept her up-to-date on news about Jo, Monique and Diane, and what was happening around town. She wrote about Astro, who thoroughly sniffed Claire's room each morning, as if determined to find her there, then curled up and slept on the old sweatshirt of Claire's that Nora had put there to comfort him. About the leaves in the forest turning toward fall.

She printed Claire's e-mails for Charlie, who read them and wrote letters in return. What was in them, Nora wondered? He looked embarrassed if she came upon him, writing, and cupped his free hand to make a little wall around the script. She was tempted by the crabbed handwriting on the envelopes, the heft of the folded paper inside the sealed envelopes he left in the mailbox by the side of the road. She felt, not exactly jealous, but . . . left out, extraneous somehow, when she thought of Claire opening and reading them in her dorm room.

Still, Nora had her own small private life, which included following the news about Laura Ann Pearson and about Iraq. Charlie's lack of interest in Claire's old computer had made it her province. She'd let Diane install the accounting software she'd been trying to talk her into for over a year, making Claire's room an extension of the clinic office, so there was nothing unusual about her climbing the stairs and settling in at the computer each morning after her walk. Overseeing the business end of Charlie's veterinary practice went more quickly, as Diane had promised it would, and there was time before lunch to read the *New York Times* online; then, from there, to check the website Laura Ann Pearson's friends and family maintained to keep her supporters abreast of any news and, ultimately, to Google through a series of political sites, each of which deepened her understanding and alarm about what seemed more and more like an inevitable war with Iraq.

Of course, she said nothing to Charlie about Laura Ann Pearson – and she had resolved to stop talking to him about Iraq. But she could not seem to help herself from trying to startle him from the vague, complacent world-view formed mainly from the five-minute, top-of-the-hour news spots on the classical music station he listened to and the occasional foray through *Newsweek.*

"Are you aware that our new national security strategy relies on pre-emptive strikes?" she had asked him last night at supper. "All they have to do is call it – call *anything* – terrorism and they can do as they please. Doesn't that concern you?"

"You can't change it, Nora," he said. "Why worry about what you can't change?"

"So we're supposed to just trust them?" she said. "Like we trusted them about Vietnam?"

But he wouldn't argue, and they finished the meal in silence. This morning he had been wary, gawky, and tentative as a teenage boy in his eagerness to please her, asking if she might like to drive to Traverse City for a movie on Saturday afternoon, offering to help her plant daffodil bulbs along the edge of the forest, and she felt defeated by such vulnerable stubbornness, despairing and ashamed.

"What should I *do*?" she whispered to Jo, now.

But Jo did not answer, just sat there in her recliner, watching Nora, a curious expression on her face, her eyes bright with concern.

Here was someone she knew she was glad to see – though, clearly, she couldn't quite remember why. Maybe she was confused because it was someone who usually spoke cheerfully but today was teary and silent for some reason. Instinct or perhaps a vague memory made her lean over to pat Nora's hand reassuringly. A few days ago, when Charlie visited, she had tilted her cheek for a kiss exactly as she used to do each morning before he left for elementary school. "You be a good boy now," she said.

Telling Nora, Charlie shook his head, perplexed. "The thing is, she looked so *happy.*"

It wouldn't be the worst thing, Nora had said to him: to let reality unravel you back to the happiest, most real time in your life. Then realized that, for him, that time was almost certainly when Claire was a little girl. Considering her own happiest time, she had had to get up from the dinner table, busy herself clearing the dishes because the image that came immediately to mind was not Claire as a little girl, but herself – *Jane* – at eighteen, dancing with Tom.

She had thought of him too much in the time since Claire had been gone. Just last night, sleepless, she had gone to the computer in Claire's room, pulled up Google and typed his name into the little box: "Thomas Gilbert." Then "Bloomington Indiana." She had sat a long while, her hand poised on the mouse, looking from the letters she'd typed to the AOL icon that, simultaneously, had begun to bounce at the side of the screen: an e-mail from Claire arriving from cyberspace as if to remind her who she was now. Finally, she clicked to make Tom disappear, guilty, a little breathless – as if caught.

She had not looked up Tom's address, maybe she never would. But she felt different since she had begun to think of him and knew it would be impossible to forget him again. Worse, despite her resolution to be kinder and more patient, she'd begun to compare the young, intense Tom she remembered to shy, bumbling middle-aged Charlie. She'd become more rather than less irritable with Charlie as a result – and about things she'd gotten used to years ago. The way he whistled tunelessly when he went about his work, the way he anal-retentively lined up the shoes and boots along the wall in the mudroom and constantly reorganized the kitchen drawers. The Museum of Charlie aggravated her, his refusal to consider any music composed after Gershwin worthy of his attention aggravated her, ironing six nearly identical plaid flannel shirts in a row drove her wild.

"She's probably just missing Claire," she overheard Monique say to Charlie, stepping into the clinic to retrieve a file she needed after their silent breakfast the day before. She had wanted to throttle Charlie for confiding in her and Monique for giving such a simplistic explanation for her behavior. Honestly, Charlie *should* have married her, Nora had thought, bitterly, stepping out again before they realized she was there. What a big, beautiful bubble of a life the two of them could have made together. Then instantly felt remorseful, flooded with countless memories that reminded her of what a good friend Monique had been to both of them.

Jo continued to observe her curiously, unselfconscious as a child, and Nora wondered if, losing her grasp on day-to-day concerns, emptying her head of attachments and responsibilities, she might have gained some silent, incommunicable intuition that allowed her to see the heart of things. Could she know that thinking about Tom as she had in the past weeks made Nora feel as if she were somehow cheating on Charlie? *Was* she cheating on Charlie, living so much, secretly, in the past?

She half-seriously considered talking to Jo now, telling her everything. Whether Jo responded or not, maybe the simple act of speaking the truth would relieve some of the weight in her heart. But the moment passed. Jo had turned her attention to the television and did not even notice when Nora stood and slipped away.

Outside in the bright sunshine of an Indian summer day, she breathed deeply, grateful that the next days would be filled to overflowing with the final preparations for Diane's daughters' arrival and then the visit that would last through the weekend. Diane had planned endlessly, obsessively, determined to strike the right balance of private and group time, activity and relaxation. Carah's pregnancy must be considered, of course. She mustn't overdo. It wouldn't be good for her to become overly emotional. And Rose could be so prickly. If certain charged subjects came up, would it be better or worse to try to steer away from them and remain in the moment or go ahead and tackle them head-on? Should Diane move the gallery of their childhood photos she kept on the dresser in the bedroom she shared with Monique? Would they be touched to see how close she'd kept them to her all these years? What if they were offended to see them there?

She looked like a wreck, Nora thought, walking into Diane and Monique's kitchen: dressed in jeans and a tattered denim shirt, pale as a wraith, her hair unkempt.

"You should know right off that I put all of Claire's photos away this morning," Diane said. "Just for, well, you know. I was afraid – "

"It's okay." Nora set the coffee she'd brought from the Hummingbird Café on the table.

"It's *not* okay," Diane said. "I know that. I know it's a sign of how whacked out I am. But is the fact that I know it and did it anyway good or bad?"

"Just a fact," Nora said. "Listen, if putting the pictures away while they're here makes it easier, I'm all for it. Claire would be, too. You know she adores you. Here, drink this." She pushed Diane's coffee toward her. "Calm down."

"Right, caffeine's just what I need for *that.* On the other hand, how can it hurt?" Diane ran her hands through her hair, deepening her dishevelment. "God. Nora, this is so totally lame, but right now I wish Carah and Rose weren't coming at all, and I could just go on being Claire's indulgent co-godmother."

"You do not," Nora said. "You've been waiting for this moment ever since I've known you. It'll be fine. It's a start."

Diane sighed. "Maybe they'll like *you.* Maybe I'll get some points for that."

"Maybe," Nora said. "They'll like Charlie, for sure. You know you can count on that."

"Yeah." Diane raised an eyebrow. "Unless, like Betty, they decide he should have married Mo."

They drank their coffee, watching the occasional red leaf from the maple at the edge of the yard fall and settle in the grass. The trees atop the dunes hugging the arc of shoreline as far as they could see were more red and gold than green now; in a few weeks, there would be nothing but glorious, fluorescent color, the last gasp of tourists winding up M-22 in a slow parade to look at it. Then it would be winter, Nora's favorite time of year, when she could walk the beach and never see another human soul, curl up in her favorite chair and read whole days into oblivion.

Distractedly, Diane picked the copy of *Newsweek* amidst the clutter on the table and leafed through it, holding it so that Donald Rumsfeld, on the cover, seemed to be casting his smug gaze in Nora's direction.

"Oh, my God," Diane said. "Can you believe this? Here's what that asshole's got on his desk: a bronze plaque with this Teddy Roosevelt quote that says, 'Aggressive fighting for the right is the noblest sport the world affords.' *Sport.* Like this is some kind of game. Plus, ha! Would that be fighting for the right . . . wing?

"Nora!" She dropped the magazine and straight up in her chair. "Fuck! What if they're Republicans? Their father's a Republican. Why wouldn't they be?" Her eyes filled with tears. "Can you believe I don't know that about my own girls? I don't know anything about their lives now. Seriously, what if they show up wearing those rhinestone American flag pins, like those dreadful patriotic ladies from Grosse Pointe who are always coming into the shop? I'll tell you one thing – " She laughed, a little wildly. "You can bet Bob's mother would be wearing one even as we speak – if she weren't *dead.*"

"That's it," Nora said. "Good! Look on the bright side."

They were laughing when the phone rang, and Diane went to answer it.

"Oh," Nora heard her say. "She's not? She can't?" Then, after a moment of silence. "Of course, I want you to come anyway. No. You definitely shouldn't drive alone. Honey, of course, it's okay if Seth comes with you instead. I'd love that. I know. I can't wait to see you, either. Well, yes. I'm disappointed not to see Rose. Of course I am. But it's not your fault she has to work. I know. I *know.* You absolutely shouldn't have to. *You don't.* Sweetie, don't cry. Really. It's fine. It'll be fine. We'll have a good time. Okay, then. Tomorrow."

Nora waited a moment then went to Diane who was standing, stock-still, the telephone receiver still in her hand. Nora took it, returned it to its cradle. Gently, she touched Diane's shoulder and Diane sank into a kitchen chair and put both hands to her face.

"I'm so sorry," Nora said.

Diane looked up. "Rose doesn't have to work," she said. "She never wanted to come in the first place. Never planned to come. I think I knew that all along."

"Carah's still coming, though."

"Yes. Carah's still coming." Diane laughed, harshly. "You know, once, when the girls were little, an idiot woman actually said to me that it must be a comfort to have twins, knowing that if you lost one –

"Oh, fuck," she said. "Nora. I'm not saying I think that's what you meant."

"I know."

"It's just – I feel so bad for Carah. She said to me, 'Mom, I can't choose anymore.' Why should she have to choose? Why can't she choose everyone? I hate that I've made life so much more difficult for her than it ought to be. And for Rose.

"I swear to God, I run this through my mind every single day of my life. I never forget it. What if I hadn't let myself get drawn in to that . . . *thing* with Audrey? If I'd stayed with Bob six months more, until Rose and Carah were out of high school. Or college. Then made a different life. What if I'd left him when they were really small? I knew the marriage was a terrible mistake almost immediately, long before I fully understood why. If I'd left then and taken the girls with me, maybe when I *did* understand, it wouldn't have created such an explosion in their lives. It might even have happened naturally – "

She wiped away tears with the heels of her hands. "Even if the thing with Audrey had happened earlier, when they were small, it might not have been so bad. I know. There'd have been a custody fight with Bob. But, even if he won, I'd have gotten visitation rights. The girls would have *had* to spend time with me. I could have – "

"What?" Nora asked.

"I don't know," Diane said. "Maybe it wouldn't have made any difference at all. I just think that going off to college, throwing themselves into whole new lives, made it easier for them not to deal with what happened. Easier not to miss me. I mean, in a *best*-case scenario, who wants to hang out with their parents while they're in college? I certainly didn't. I liked my parents just fine and I couldn't wait to get away from them."

Nora smiled. "Claire hasn't exactly been homesick herself," she said. "We're down from e-mails every day – sometimes twice a day – to maybe three or four a week. The occasional phone call."

"Exactly," Diane said. "And that's a good thing. It's what you want for your kids. Unless it lets them avoid dealing with something between you that really needs to be resolved. Once they go away, you might never resolve it. The thing is, what you don't realize until it's too late is that once your kids have left home – really, *emotionally* left home – it's pretty much up to them to decide what your relationship will be.

Jo had understood that, Nora thought, driving home. Once, when Claire was just a little girl, Nora overheard Jo tell one of the waitresses who worked for her, "Honey, you had that child because it's what you decided to do. What *you* wanted. If you didn't want a child and got pregnant anyway, it was your mistake. Either way, it's your job to do the best you can for him and let him go. He's a good boy, he knows what's right. You can keep on trying to control him with some idea of what he owes you, but I guarantee it's the quickest road to heartache I know."

At the time, this had struck Nora as absolutely true, and she swore to herself that she would always remember it. Yet, in desperation, she had ignored what she knew when Claire set her heart on going to IU. "We've done *everything* for you," Nora said, "given you everything." And when Claire simply turned and walked away from her, she suffered the heartache Jo had warned against. She'd apologized, but neither the words nor the hurt they'd caused could ever be fully erased. Whatever adult relationship she and her daughter would make over time would in some way be built upon them – and on other hurts and disappointments that would surely come as Claire grew further away from them, into her real life.

It occurred to her that Jo's genius as a mother was to make you believe, as she did herself, that her own life was good and full enough for her, and anything you gave her, any part you wanted to play in it – large or small – well, that was enough, too. Her attachments were fierce, but all blessing. No matter what you did or how far away you went, she'd hold you in her heart. She'd never give up on you. Never, ever let you go.

Her own mother's love had been a burden to her when she was young, her family an obstacle to overcome. After Bobby's death, she could not bear to be in the presence of her father, lost by then in an alcoholic haze. She felt shut out of the bright, long-suffering triumvirate that her sisters and mother made. In time, if things had turned out differently, would she have made her way back to them?

She had thought of her mother often when Claire was small. Countless times, she caught herself saying things to Claire that her mother had said to her, little things: "*Hold your horses,*" she said when Claire was impatient; "*Home again, Finnegan,*" when they pulled into the driveway; "*Good night, God bless,*" each night, when she tucked her into bed. Helpless when Claire suffered some failure or a slight from a friend, she better understood her mother's mute yearning.

Raising Claire had been so easy, she saw now, because all those years they had been able to keep the world at bay. Charlie's veterinary practice had afforded a comfortable income and the two of them, living only in the moment, had no emotional entanglements outside their little family to distract them, no personal ambitions that might have interfered with what Claire needed. The house Charlie had grown up in, the small town, the forest, the lake – another child might have chafed against such an insular universe, but Claire thrived and grew strong in it. Except for Jo's illness and decline, Claire had never known real sadness. So far, there'd been no problem in her life that could not be solved.

Lately, Nora had begun to imagine what it might be like to tell her daughter the truth about her life. She might gather up the courage, she thought, if she could tell Claire the story and know it could be left at that. But what if Claire insisted on meeting her grandparents? Were they even alive? And what about Amy and Susan? Had they forgiven her for all the hurt she'd caused? Would they even want to see her?

And there was Tom. There was no way she could make Claire understand what had made her run away from her life without explaining how she had felt about him. No matter what she told her daughter about that relationship, or how much, something would be changed between them forever, and she couldn't know what that would mean.

Worse, if she told Claire she'd have to tell Charlie. Every time she considered this, she remembered how she'd decided, suddenly, to spend the night before their wedding in the little apartment above Jo's café. It was tradition, she said. The groom shouldn't see the bride until the moment she appeared before him the day of the ceremony. But she could tell neither Charlie nor Jo quite believed her. The wedding they'd planned was hardly a traditional one: a brief civil service at the courthouse in Traverse City, just the three of them. Jo would be one witness and they'd been assured that someone in the office would be glad to serve as the second.

"I'll meet you there," Nora said. "*Really.*"

She had no intention of walking away. She'd run everything through her mind a thousand times, balancing her life with Charlie and Jo against any last chance of going backwards to Tom. She had not been able to forget him. Years had passed and, still, sometimes he would come to her in a dream, or while she was in the midst of some everyday chore. What she said when he appeared in a dream, what she wanted to say in those waking moments, was, "I'm so sorry." Just that. Some door inside her would close if she could just say that to him. Maybe, maybe she could begin to forgive herself for what she'd done.

But to find him, to see him face-to-face, would be to realize fully everything she'd lost – and she'd have to be Jane again to do it, something she simply could not afford. So she went to the little room where what would turn out to be the rest of her life had begun, lit a candle, and in its flickering light rewound her life to the moment she'd met Tom, relived it – joyfully, tearfully – and let it go. In the morning, new snow falling, blanketing the town, the life she'd chosen felt possible again, right. She could not change what happened the night she followed Bridget. What it had done to Tom, to her family, to herself – Jane – she could never, ever repair. To marry Charlie, though, to be the Nora in whose presence he'd come alive again, might begin to atone for it.

She dressed in the pretty, blue wool dress Jo had insisted on buying her for the occasion, drove the winding road to Traverse City her heart as light as the snowflakes skittering across the windshield. It was so *beautiful*: snow filling up the fields, icing the bare tree limbs. The feeling held. Standing beside Charlie in the courthouse, Jo beside them. Later, in the honeymoon suite at the hotel, sated after making love, she could see the snow still falling. Blowing and drifting now, the wind whistling in from the lake, the sound of the snow plows beneath, in the street. Just the two of them cocooned there. Safe. She would keep it that way, she thought. She *did* love Charlie. That's what she could do for him.

She couldn't break the promise she'd made to herself all those years, even if it meant keeping the truth from her daughter. But since Laura Ann Pearson's arrest, keeping or not keeping the secret no longer seemed entirely up to her. Reporters were already dredging up other stories about sixties radicals who'd gone underground and were never heard of again. In a year, it would be the thirtieth anniversary of the Christmas bombing, and it was perfectly within the realm of possibility that a Bloomington reporter would revisit it – perhaps even an *Indiana Daily Student* reporter. Would Claire, coming upon such a story, be struck by the photograph of the girl who'd disappeared that night – a girl who looked uncannily like herself?

19

"The Long and Winding Road"

Charlie's mood lightened with October: a series of cool, golden days and Parents Weekend nearing. He started collecting things to take to Claire: fudge from the candy shop in town, a big, fleecy hooded sweatshirt with "Sleeping Bear Dunes" on the front, a bag of the first Michigan apples. The day before they left, he stopped at the Hummingbird Café to pick up a dozen triple-chunk chocolate chip cookies – Jo's recipe.

"Remember?" he said to Nora. "How, when she was little, she'd sit in a window booth and eat the whole plate of them Mother brought, just watching the world go by."

She did – and hoped Claire would remember, too. Hoped Claire would see how much her father needed her to remember. The eagerness with which he looked forward to the visit pierced her heart and heightened the sense of foreboding that had been building since the day in August when she'd sat in People's Park and her own memories, held tight within her until then, had begun to unravel. This afternoon she'd Googled Tom. She had no intention of contacting him, she told herself. She just wanted to know if he was still there. She clicked and "Thomas M. Gilbert, Civil Trial Law Attorney – Bloomington, Indiana" popped up, as she had been almost certain it would. She did not click a second time to reveal his address or any personal information. She didn't want him to be that real to her.

Still, she could not help thinking about him as they drove south on Friday morning. There'd be no time to look him up, even if she was foolish enough to consider it. But he'd be there, somewhere, and she worried about how this might affect her time with Claire. She worried about the busker who'd called out her name on Kirkwood Avenue last summer, too. She'd avoid that area if she could, keep her eye out for him, and hope that if he saw her with Charlie and Claire he'd have the decency to leave her be.

Thankfully, Charlie was oblivious. In fact, chatting companionably beside her, he seemed more himself to Nora than he had since they had begun to consider Claire's college choice. She loved the funny way he talked about the animals in his care, as if he were in cahoots with them against their often overbearing and unreasonable owners. Diane had talked him into adding a line of pet boutique items, and he spoke almost apologetically about the tartan plaid, belted sweater McDuff, the terrier, would have to forebear this winter and the Harley Davidson collar that Kirk Wheatley had bought for King, his majestic Great Dane. He'd been amused to learn that the Dalmatian, Sheba Louise, had dragged her ratty old pillow from the trash and set it on the new designer bed her owner, Mrs. Otto, had bought for her. Nora listened, dozing and waking to the collection of music Charlie had brought – Vivaldi, Mendelssohn's "Italian Symphony," a reflection of the happy anticipation he must be feeling.

Claire was waiting in the lobby of the dorm when they arrived in the late afternoon and threw her arms around Charlie, talking a mile a minute. "I'm so glad you guys are here," she said. "I couldn't stand waiting in my room, so I came downstairs. Look!" She pointed to a pile of books and papers abandoned on a nearby chair. "I thought I'd study. Ha! All I did was get up and go over and look out the window every three minutes."

Charlie stood, a little abashed, still holding the shopping bag with all her presents in it as Claire turned and embraced Nora, still talking. Her roommate, Emily, was waiting upstairs. Her dad was coming, after all – this evening. So could the two of them come along to dinner, instead of just Emily? And Dylan, of course. He'd be going to the game with them tomorrow, as well. His parents *weren't* coming. She laughed. "They're totally over him, he says. They don't even miss him anymore. Like you guys will be over me next year.

"Just *kidding,*" she said, when she saw Charlie's face. "I mean, really, I'm so fabulous! How could anyone get over *me*?"

Heading for the elevator, she chattered on. She'd gotten an "A" on her most recent paper in composition; she loved her literature class, where they were reading *King Lear.* "Oh, God," she groaned, to find a crowd of people waiting near the elevator door.

Crunched among a half-dozen girls with their boyfriends as the packed elevator made its way upwards, Nora couldn't help remembering the strict rules there'd been when she was a freshman in college. Boys in the room had been strictly forbidden, punishable by expulsion.

"Man in the hall!" the custodians hollered when the elevator door opened, before making their way down the corridor – which Bridget had thought was hilarious. Other girls would scurry to their rooms and close the doors; Bridget loved to wait till the guy who'd hollered figured it was safe, then saunter out of their room, half-dressed, just to see what he would do about it.

She had worried a little about how Claire would adapt. Having had her own spacious room at home, Nora feared she would feel a lack of privacy, living communally for the first time. But within moments it was clear that Claire was as happy living with Emily as she herself had been living with Bridget. They mugged in the clutter of photos on the bulletin board; their conversation was rich with jokes and references to experiences they'd shared in the two months they'd lived together.

At dinner, Emily's father, a genial businessman, drew Charlie out, questioning him about his veterinary practice and about vacation properties in the area. He'd flown directly from doing a business deal in Dallas, he said. He'd expected to be there another week and had been thrilled to finish early so that he could make it for Parents Weekend after all. When he said he planned to walk over to the stadium with them the next day, hoping to scalp a ticket for the game, Nora said, impulsively, "Please. Take mine. Really. You guys go."

"Mom, *thanks,*" Claire said, beaming.

"I don't mind," she said, her heart racing at the implications of what she had just done. "It'll be nice for you girls to go with your dads."

Later, in the hotel room, she shrugged Charlie away when he gave her a hug and whispered how nice it was what she'd done. "It wasn't that nice, given how much I don't like football," she said, more curtly than she had intended.

Saturday morning dawned sunny and crisp and, walking out into it to meet Claire for breakfast, Nora remembered how she had loved football Saturdays just like this one when she was young – how they started out cool enough for a sweater but by mid-afternoon left them all sweltering on the bleachers in the stadium, prime for the moment when Pete would say, "Chianti snow cones," and dispatch a pledge to the concession stand to bring back a cardboard tray of perfect round scoops of crushed ice in paper cones. The wineskins would come out from their hiding places inside the boys' London Fog jackets then, and the sweet, syrupy wine poured over the ice made snow cones that gave them a happy little buzz and made them forget all about the hot sun and the scratch of wool. On the field, the inept Hoosiers fumbled again and again. The cheerleaders cheered nonetheless. The alumni, a massive block of red across the field, cheered with them. But in the student stands, the game was the middle of a party that had begun with lunch at the fraternity house and would continue with a dance that would last till just before all the girls had to be back in their dorms or sorority houses at one AM. Even then it wasn't really over. Back in their room, Jane and Bridget put on the Supremes, curled up on their beds and replayed the day.

How could it still seem so real, Nora wondered now? She was glad she didn't have to go to the game today, glad she didn't have to sit in the stadium all afternoon, remembering, and sent Charlie and Claire off just after noon with the reassurance that she'd be fine alone. She'd take a long walk, she said – which she did. But shuffling through the dry leaves, following the lovely, winding paths through the old, wooded area of campus, she was, from one moment to the next, the person she had been here long ago – Jane, so light, so fraught with possibility that she feared she might simply fly up into the sky. And the person she was now, Nora, too often heavy-hearted, too often overcome with sorrow. In time, she found herself approaching the university gates at the edge of the campus, just a block from People's Park.

She saw the busker on the low wall next to the old Von Lee Theater, but kept going anyway, past him, down Kirkwood Avenue and into the park. She sat on the bench where she had watched the boys play Hacky Sack last summer and watched the world go on around her: music and laughter, traffic passing by, dry leaves pin-wheeling through dusty sunlight, gathering in red and yellow drifts at the edges of the park. Hippie-types, straggly-haired and dressed in baggy clothes, lounged around the nearby sculpture, smoking, talking with their friends; couples sat at the umbrella tables, chatting over coffee from the nearby Starbucks; students, like Claire, showed their parents around and moved on down the street.

It was only when she saw Tom enter the park and head in her direction that Nora knew – or admitted to herself – that she had meant to come here all along. He wore jeans, a navy Shetland sweater with a gray tee shirt underneath it, showing at the collar. His hair was white, cropped close to his head; his face might have been his father's. He wore wire-rimmed glasses. But he was fit – she could see that in the breadth of his shoulders, in the way his torso narrowed toward his waist. In the springy step.

She stood, quite suddenly breathless with longing. Awkward and young as she had felt the night they met and, at the same time, conscious of her own hair, the blond streaked with silver, absurdly apologetic for the strangeness of her own changed face.

A smile lit his face, the one she'd tried all these years to forget. His arms opened and she walked into them. The familiarity of his body against her, the rightness of it, shocked her off-balance for a moment. He caught her, placed his hands on her shoulders and stepped back slightly, so he could look at her.

"Damn." He shook his head. "Jane."

"I'm – " she started to say, "Nora." But in truth she *was* Jane in his presence.

She couldn't have said how they got back to the bench where she'd been sitting, but she knew she would always remember the moment when, sitting there, he touched her hand and her palm turned up instinctively, her fingers folded into his – a gesture she'd made thousands of times when they were together.

A car drove past, hip-hop pouring from its open windows. The sweet scent of marijuana trailed behind a passing boy who looked furtive, his hand curled awkwardly to cup the joint he held between his thumb and forefinger. Nora watched the leaves drift down and thought of home: how leaves there would be drifting to the green floor of the forest, how Lake Michigan would be choppy, shining in the sun. But it seemed unreal to her, dream-like, as if she had lived her entire life in this spot, her hand in Tom's.

"Are you okay?" he asked. "Are you happy?"

She didn't answer.

"Remember that night we found out about the bombing in Cambodia? Walking past here and people picking up rocks and smashing windows? We were thinking about your brother and Pete and the whole fucked up mess of it, but for them it was either a big, wild party or an excuse to act out their revolutionary fantasies. We should have forgotten any idea we had about being able to end the war right then – and any idea we had an *obligation* to try to end it."

Neither spoke Bridget's name. But she was there, between them, as she had been then. And the Christmas she came back. All they'd lost because of it.

"Just tell me one thing, would you?" Tom finally asked. "Did you know what she was going to do that night? Did you decide to go with her?"

"No. *No.* I heard her go out and I followed her. I knew she was going to do . . . *something,* and I thought – "

"Fucking Bridget," he said. "Like anybody could've stopped her by then. She never should have come to see you in the first place. All she really cared about by then was whatever crazy idea John Cameron put in her head."

"I was so scared for her," Nora said. "I thought I could – "

"Save her," Tom said. "I know. You always did."

"I never meant to leave you," she said. "Cam made me – "

"I know that," he said.

"How – "

"I *know.* Never mind how. I also know there was nothing keeping you from coming back here once you got away from him."

"I couldn't. He . . ." She took a deep breath to calm herself. "He made me believe I couldn't – and the thing is, Tom, it was my fault what happened to Bridget that night. I didn't stop her. I was *with* her . . .

"How could I drag you into that? Things weren't all that great between us then, you may remember – and she got me so confused about everything. About *us.* The longer I didn't come back, the easier – "

Anger surged up, catching her by surprise.

"I knew you'd be okay without me," she said. "And wasn't I right? Look at you. You just went right on and made another life."

"What else could I do? I couldn't look for you. Where would I look? And yeah, I have a life. But FYI, I stayed here so you'd know where to find me. Oh, fuck," he said. "I'm sorry. The last thing I want to do is argue about that now."

He put his hand on hers again, but this time she kept her fingers curled in a fist.

"Are you married?" she asked. "Do you have children? Tell me about your life."

He laughed, though not with real humor. "I was married for about ten minutes," he said. "Madeleine was her name. I couldn't really tell you why I married her, other than that I was getting older. She was there; she was nothing like you at all. It was a fucking disaster. My mom had high hopes for us, too – grandchildren, the whole nine yards."

"Your dad?"

"Never knew her," Tom said. "Heart attack got him, after all. Funny – one of the last things he said to me was, 'That Jane was a good girl. You suppose things will turn out okay for her?' I said, yeah, I did. He got it, you know? Eventually. My mom never did. Anyway. *You're* married," he said. "I know that. One daughter, Claire. You live in Michigan –

"Friend in the admissions office," he said. "Don't worry. It was Pete who saw you last summer, by the way. You said your name, that's how we – "

"Pete?"

"I know," Tom said. "He looks like shit. Old. It was Pete, though. I guarantee it."

"But how – "

"You look exactly like yourself," Tom said.

"No," Nora said. "I – "

"Yeah," Tom said. "You do. I've been sitting over at Kilroy's since this morning, thinking you might come, and I knew you the second I saw you. Anyway, Pete – he showed up a couple of years after you left, totally fucked up. I got him into rehab, he got clean. He knocked around, doing odd jobs to get by until his dad died and left him enough money to hang out on Kirkwood Avenue and play his guitar all day. Sometimes I think he's still totally fubar, sometimes I think he's got it totally figured out – chill out, just *be*. He's been a good friend to me, in any case. The only person who knows everything about us."

"Nobody in my life knows," she said.

Tom was quiet a moment. Then said, "That must be hard."

"For a long time it wasn't," she said. "For a long time it felt like a blessing."

"But it's hard now, because of your daughter."

She nodded. "I tried to talk her out of coming here, but of course I couldn't say why, so all that did was get me sideways with everyone I loved. It's the perfect place for her, everyone could see that. I could see it. But I knew if she came here, I'd have to come back, and that scared me to death –

"Not because I thought someone would recognize me," she said. "It seems stupid now, but I didn't really think about that happening. I was scared to *be* here. To be – " Her throat ached with tears. "I was scared to be myself," she said. "I was scared I'd be Jane again. I can't be Jane. Not anymore."

"You don't have to be Jane for me," Tom said. "You can be anyone you want."

She stood abruptly. "I have to go. Really. I can't stay."

He stood, too, caught her hand. "Wait. You need to know some things."

"What?" she said. "I can't – "

But she didn't pull her hand away, and without quite deciding to she found herself walking up Kirkwood Avenue with Tom, through the university gates to a bench in the woods where they used to sit sometimes between classes. It amazed her that it was still there, that the place looked exactly the same. Dusty shafts of light falling down through the thick trees, drenching the carpet of yellow ginkgo leaves with even deeper color; the sky above like a blue ceiling. Thirty-five years had been nothing to the little patch of forest, she thought. She'd live through this time, live her life. In another thirty-five years, it would be all over. None of this would matter.

"Listen," Tom said. "I don't know what you want. Or need. But you came back to the park, so I figure you need something – and this is what I know for sure I can give you." He touched her face and turned it so she had to look at him. "You're not responsible for what happened to Bridget that night."

"I *am.*" She closed her eyes, willing away the sudden rush of memory that came with his words. The blast, the whoosh of flame, the sound of her own voice screaming and then nothing, blackness.

"Feeling responsible, that's something you have to work out in your own mind. And you need to do that. What I mean is, you won't be held responsible – from a legal point of view."

"How do you know that?" she asked.

"Hey, I'm a lawyer," he said. "Remember? I know how this shit works. I knew right from the get-go it was Cameron they really wanted. He was in deep way before he ever came to Bloomington that first time. The ROTC building wasn't the first *action* he was involved in."

"Or the last," Nora said. "Tom, I was with him – "

"I know about all that," he said. "I found out from the FBI. They caught him not all that long after you left, you know. I also knew they had virtually nothing on you. They couldn't even prove you were there when the bomb went off – and it was arguable that Cameron had forced you to go with him, meaning whatever you did when you were with him was done under duress.

"The other thing I knew was that the FBI had fucked up so badly trying to nail most of the other Weather people they arrested that they really needed this one to stick. I never trusted Cameron. You know that. I'd been keeping track of him all along – and Bridget, too. I was in touch with people I still knew from the Movement; there were people in the law school who had contacts, too. So I knew things, useful things – which I traded for the promise that they'd stop looking for you."

"You never told me you were checking up on them," Nora said.

"I know. I should have," he said. "But I knew you'd be pissed. Plus, I figured you wouldn't want to know, you wouldn't have wanted to believe it. I guess I was trying to protect you. Meanwhile, you were bound and determined to save Bridget. Fuck. Look where it got us."

"Oh, God," Nora said. "I'm just so sorry about – *everything.*"

"I know," he said. "I know." He bent and picked up one of the ginkgo leaves and handed it to her, a little yellow fan.

"I'd never seen a ginkgo tree before I met you," she said. "I'd never seen anything."

"You were – "

Nora raised a hand to stop him. They sat quietly for a long moment, the sound of traffic on University Avenue filtering in through the trees. Nora twirled the stem of the ginkgo leaf back and forth between her fingers, concentrated on the crazy little dance it made.

"Jane," Tom said, finally. "Nora – "

She let the leaf float to the ground. "Really. I should go now," she said.

But he put his hand on her arm, to keep her there. "Look," he said. "I loved you the first time I saw you, I never stopped loving you. Or missing you. I never will. I'm not saying I've been sitting around all this time waiting for you to come back. I'm fine. I've got a life. It's good. You've got a life, too – and the smart thing to do would be to leave here and walk right back into it. But – " He took a business card from his shirt pocket and tucked it into her bag. "If you ever want to talk, if you ever want or need *anything,* call or e-mail. Promise?"

"It's not a good idea," she said.

"I said, if you need to."

She nodded. "Okay, then. If I need to I will."

He let loose of her then, freeing her to go, but she felt as if all the air had gone out of her and she sat back down on the bench – Jane. At that moment, she could not imagine being anyone else. Afterward, she thought that if Tom had taken her hand again and led her . . . anywhere, she would have gone. He didn't, though. Just looked at her a long moment, kind of shook his head as if to bring himself back to his own reality, then turned and made his way down the wooded path, alone.

She walked. Threading in and out of buildings, wandering along paths once so familiar to her, she kept moving in constant retreat from herself. She walked to the top of Ballantine Hall, then down again. She peered into the library at Jordan Hall, with its long battered wooden tables where she and Bridget had sat studying before their botany class; walked through the cool, damp greenhouse with its gargantuan tropical plants. So much was exactly the same as it had been then, the tattered notices on the bulletin boards with advertisements for computer discounts and cell phones the only evidence of another era.

Even the voices wafting through the open windows in the Music Building, running up and down the register of scales, were the same. She stood on the path and listened for a long time, transported to a classroom on the second floor of the Education Building on the first day of "Introduction to Teaching," her freshman year. An Indian summer day: sticky, no breeze. She sat at a desk, a brand new notebook open before her, as drowsy as the honey-drunk bee buzzing at the corner of the open window – and then, suddenly, a single ghostly voice singing scales came drifting over from the Music Building next door. She sat straight up in her seat, her scalp prickled, and she was shot through with the visceral confirmation of her own escape.

How could she have forgotten this? Years of listening to Claire practice scales on her cello, and so completely had she buried the person she once was that she never remembered that moment and what it had meant to her. She ached to think of it now and of the sounds from the life she'd escaped that had been its counterpoint: the constant roar of traffic on the interstate highway behind her parents' home, the hiss of her mother's steam iron late at night, the television laugh track.

If she could find that classroom, she could think. It had become a secret place for her all through college, someplace she went in the late afternoons when she was feeling guilty or low. Outside, the Education Building looked the same: limestone, with leaded casement windows and iron grillwork above the high doors. Caleb Mills' words were still there, etched deep into the portals: "A teacher must inspire as well as instruct," and she remembered how it had always made her feel proud to read them and to imagine herself in her own classroom someday, her students lined in neat rows, their faces expectant. But the building was a recital center now, completely renovated to accommodate the overflow of music students. The second floor classrooms had been transformed into a web of practice rooms, recital halls, and recording studios, their doors locked so that there was no hope of finding the window she remembered.

Maybe Claire would be assigned the practice room with her window in it, Nora thought. But that only made her feel more lost and confused, more disconnected from her daughter, her *life.* What would it be like to be able to tell Claire how it had felt to hear that voice singing scales when she was young, she wondered. To say how glad she was that such a sound was not in the least exotic to Claire herself because every kind of beauty had been a part of her life since she was a little girl. This was something she had done right, Nora thought. She and Charlie, together. They'd made a beautiful life for their child.

But all she could think about was how she had lied to her daughter and kept herself apart, how leaving Tom so long ago, determined to punish herself for what happened that night, had set her on the path toward this moment when, finally, she must come face-to-face with all she had lost.

To wish that she had not succumbed to loneliness, to wish that she had held fast and lived her life alone – or, in time, returned to Tom and made a life with him, after all – would be to wish that Claire had never been born. She did not wish that. She could not even imagine it. She just wished that, on the day of Claire's birth, when she and Charlie were so happy, closer than they had ever been or ever would be again, she had gathered up her courage and told him the truth about her life.

20

"Mercy Mercy Me"

Nora felt strange in her own house after the weekend in Bloomington – not unlike she'd felt on acid all those years ago. Scared, clinging to rational thought in exactly the same way. But the world she'd seen on acid was chemically induced, not real, and in time the images had faded. Now both worlds were real – the world she'd made with Charlie and the one, before and beyond, with Tom in it. As for Charlie, he seemed shocked by the fact that Claire really did have a life away from him, that it was her real life now. They'd had breakfast with Claire and Dylan on Sunday morning, before setting out for home, and she'd been embarrassed by his uncharacteristic volubility, the way he'd delayed their departure with anecdotes and bits of advice, even after Claire said, finally, that they had plans to go to Brown County with friends who were waiting for them back at Dylan's apartment.

What? Nora wanted to say to him. You didn't know this would happen?

She missed Claire, too. But there was no surprise in it. She'd known all along that something would be over once Claire was gone – and *more* over for the fact that she'd gone to IU, something she realized she was still angry with Charlie about.

She told herself that, regardless of where Claire had chosen to go to college, the foreboding images of war these past few months, the dissembling of politicians, the inevitable comparisons to Vietnam would have dredged up memories of Bridget and made her wonder, after all these years, what had become of Tom. It was the time of life, too. Wasn't remembering the people you loved when you were young a natural part of the process of looking back at your life, coming to terms with what it had turned out to be? It might have been only mildly disconcerting if she hadn't seen Tom. If she didn't have the image of him now in her mind's eye or hear the echo of his voice speaking her true name.

It was unfair to blame Charlie for this, she knew, but at times she could not help herself. She was short with him when she should have been kind. She was confrontational about the impending war in Iraq. Look! Nora wanted to say . . . about *everything.* But Charlie had no idea that there was anything he needed to look at, anything he didn't know that might threaten what the rest of their lives together would turn out to be. When, increasingly, he withdrew, spending evenings with his nose in a book or listening to music two and three centuries old, it made Nora more, not less, angry with him, less able to remember the ways in which they had once made one another happy.

Still, she was genuinely distressed about Iraq, enraged by the blatant attempts of the media to bring emotions to a fever pitch in service of the President's determination to go to war. The lurid stories about Saddam's lairs, his brutal sons, his crazed followers leaving the voting booth, index fingers raised – red with their own blood that they'd touched to the ballot to show the depth of their devotion. The news that whole divisions of tanks had disappeared from Europe and allegedly had been spotted atop transport trucks in Kuwait; Special Forces had arrived in Iraq to probe defenses; F-16 fighters sat on an airbase in Turkey, locked and loaded, ready for action.

She wondered if Tom felt the same way. She kept the business card he'd given her tucked into the torn lining of her wallet, took it out countless times and looked at it – mostly in the middle of the night. Walking each morning, she carried on a conversation with him in her head – about how much she had loved him, about the mistakes she'd made, and how frightened she was at the way the world she'd made so carefully and lovingly no longer seemed enough. Then spent the whole way back home telling herself that to reconnect with him at this point in her life would be to invite disaster.

November came with its gunmetal skies – and Thanksgiving to look forward to, Nora thought – until Diane tentatively offered up the news that she and Monique had been invited to Carah and Seth's for the holiday.

"Oh!" Nora said. "That's wonderful. Of course you should go."

Diane's eyes teared up, and she engulfed her in a hug.

"Mo *will* be making Betty's cranberry salad for us before you leave, though," Nora said, still caught in the embrace. "And you'll do the corn soufflé. Right?"

She meant it as a joke. But her voice cracked, and Diane stepped back to look at her.

"Nora," she said. "Are you okay?"

Nora waved her hands, she hoped, reassuringly.

Diane looked at her a moment longer, and Nora saw her decide to believe her. In the past weeks, she'd been consumed by her renewed relationship with Carah; if she had noticed that Nora was not herself, she hadn't mentioned it.

When Nora stopped in at the shop, Diane talked about how Carah was feeling and showed Nora some new photo Carah had sent on the internet – of Carah standing sideways to reveal the ever-increasing curve of her belly, or the progress of the nursery she and Seth were decorating together. When the four of them had dinner, Diane knitted afterwards – a beautiful blue bunting taking shape beneath her needles for the baby (a boy, the ultrasound had revealed) to wear home from the hospital – while Charlie and Monique talked about music or the clinic and Nora drifted quietly away from them all, thinking about Tom.

Time after time, she sat before the computer, staring at his e-mail address, which she had typed into the little box on the screen. She might actually have written to him, but she had no idea how to begin. She couldn't even think what to put in the subject box. "In My Life?" "The Things We Said Today?"

Already, she'd been deceitful enough to create an alternate e-mail account. Then she deleted it, realizing that Claire was likely to use the computer when she was home for Thanksgiving break. She wouldn't be able to open any e-mails that came to the address without knowing the password, but she'd notice the new screen name listed there.

Nora willed herself to stay in the present moment. She did not listen to NPR or read the newspaper; she set aside the *Newsweek* with "Top Gun" in a banner across the cover photo of President Bush dressed in ranch clothes, giving the thumbs-up, grinning. She redirected all thoughts of the past to the long list of things she must do to prepare for Claire's arrival.

Focused this way, her irritation with Charlie dissolved. She thought of an article she read years ago in a women's magazine: you know yours is a healthy marriage if, mid-argument, you start feeling sorrier for distressing the person you love than you are angry at him for whatever he's done. Then, the writer said, it's possible to talk about how to make things right between you. It had struck her as true at the time, and still did – though, limited in its usefulness in her relationship with Charlie because, of course, it did not accommodate the idea that one of the partners in the marriage might be keeping a secret that could never be told.

Until she saw Tom in October, she still believed she did not dare tell it to anyone. She was Charlie's wife, Claire's mother, but she was also a fugitive, complicit in crimes that had caused both death and destruction. For years, she had believed that, if caught, she'd be arrested and sent to prison. Now, Tom said, that wouldn't happen. It never would have happened. The life she'd made with Charlie wasn't even what *she* believed it had been.

There had been no need for the distance she'd cultivated between them. If she had told him her most painful truth right from the start, would he have told her his? He had been drafted when he graduated from veterinarian school, and his medical skills had qualified him to be a surgical assistant in a MASH unit; at least once, he'd stood outside a surgery tent, listening to intelligence officers torturing a Vietnamese kid who'd been thrown out of a helicopter. After nearly twenty-five years together, that's all she knew – and that he remembered the boy every day of his life, heard him screaming.

It made her feel more sympathetic towards Charlie to wonder at which moments the memory came. When he stopped suddenly, gazing up into the November sky, was that what he saw? When the dogs whined in the kennels and he bent to feel their real, rough tongues on his hand, was it a way to efface the boy's voice in his head? When

Claire was a baby, sometimes Nora would wake and find him standing at the side of her crib. Now she wondered if he had dreamed the boy on those nights and, in watching Claire sleep, found some kind of proportion.

At the sight of her daughter emerging from the car, hefting the strap of her cello case over her shoulder, Nora felt their world come back into balance. Charlie opened the door and threw his arms around her, cello case, duffel, and all. Her ride, a girl from Traverse City, tooted the horn and backed down the driveway. She was theirs again, if only for a little while.

The next morning, Nora and Claire rolled out the crust for the pies: pumpkin, apple, pecan. Monique and Diane came by on their way to Chicago, bearing the cranberry salad and corn casseroles they contributed to the meal every year.

"I know you were kidding about these," Diane said. "Mo and I wanted to bring them. That way you have to think about us tomorrow."

"Like we wouldn't," Claire said. She was still in her robe and pajamas, her hair wild – and floury, where she'd kept pushing it back with her hands. "We're making the doll pies, too. Look! Just like the ones Grandma and I used to make when I was little. Next year, you guys can take some to the baby. Or maybe he'll come!"

"This summer, for sure," Diane said. "Carah's already promised to bring him. We can slather him up with sunscreen and do the short float, maybe. The beach, of course. He'll be, what?" She counted on her fingers. "Six or seven months, just sitting up. Perfect for pouring sand."

"Did you like Carah?" Claire asked Nora when they'd gone.

"I did," Nora said. "She's a lot like Diane – funny and smart. I liked her husband, too. They were sweet together, so excited about the baby coming – and both wanting Diane to be there when it happens. I was worried, you know. That it wouldn't go well, and Diane would end up feeling worse than she had before."

Claire's face hardened. "I never could understand why Carah and Rose were so mean to her. And Rose still is. I mean, how could anyone be mean to Diane?"

"She – " Nora began. "They were angry. They felt . . . abandoned by her."

"Mom. They were *my* age. It's not like they were little children."

Nora looked at her, disquieted by such certainty. "It wasn't only that she went away, Claire. Not everyone grew up like you did, believing it might be . . . acceptable – even natural – for two women to be together. That was hard for Rose and Carah, too."

"I just don't get that," Claire said. "Whose business is it, really? Why do people care?"

"I don't get that, either. Love – well, it's not all that easy to find, and it's always seemed a blessing to me, regardless of how it happens. But some people just can't deal with the gay thing, even when it's someone that really matters to them. Maybe especially then. Or it takes time – which seems to be what happened with Carah. Finally, whatever she feels – or felt – about Diane being with Mo became less important to her than wanting her mother back again. Probably because of the baby coming. Babies change things."

"Yeah?" Claire asked. "Did I change you?"

"Oh, Honey – " Nora said. "*Yes.*"

"How?" Claire asked. "Before, you were – ? And – then?"

"Before – " Nora began. "You . . . grounded me. That's all I know. Holding you, I knew I was in the absolute right place, right in the world – which was something I hadn't felt in a long time. I loved your dad, of course. I loved – " Her voice cracked.

"Mom," Claire said, alarmed. "God, I didn't mean to upset you."

Nora closed her eyes a moment, collected herself. "You didn't," she said. "Not really. It's just – I'm so glad you're home."

"Me, too," Claire said. "I love school. I *love* it. But I miss you guys. I miss this – " She flung out her arm to encompass the kitchen, the view out the window, sprinkling flour on Astro, who lay asleep at her feet. "You know, I kind of like it that it's just us for Thanksgiving – you and me and Dad. Except I wish Grandma could come. Grandma the way she *was.*"

A light snow began to fall, dusting the meadow, and when the big pies were finished and set out on the counter to cool, Nora and Claire wrapped the little ones in foil to take to Jo. Snow swirled on the pavement, hit the windshield in icy whispers. Tomorrow, after dinner, they'd go cut a Christmas tree, as they did each year, and if the snow kept up they'd carry it back on Charlie's old sled. Jo had been with them last Thanksgiving, still enough herself to remember Christmases long ago when she'd pulled Charlie into the pine forest on the sled, cut down the tree he chose, lashed it to the sled with clothesline rope, and then pulled it home, Charlie trudging along beside her. Now to bring her home at all would just frighten and disorient her.

She'd been sick with the flu in the past weeks, too, still weak with it, and Nora watched Claire closely as she entered Jo's room and saw how frail and lost her grandmother had become.

"Oh!" she whispered, glancing back at Nora. But then went straight to Jo and knelt beside her recliner. "Grandma?" she said, taking Jo's hand. "Grandma, I'm home."

Jo turned her head slowly from the window, where she'd been watching a flurry of birds pecking at each other to get at the seed in the tray of the feeder, and gazed upon her with the frank curiosity of a child.

"It's Claire," Nora said. "All grown up. Remember?"

Jo smiled, a little anxiously. Perhaps, at least, she knew she *should* remember, Nora thought. Though, clearly, she did not. Intently, she watched Claire take the little pies from the basket, unwrap them one-by-one, and set them on the TV tray near her chair.

"I brought you these," Claire said. "Remember? You used to make them for me? For my dolls. When I got big enough, we made them together."

Jo raised her hand, as if to reach for one. Then gave Nora an inquiring look, as if asking for permission.

Nora nodded, offered a fork, which Jo took.

She beamed at her first taste. "Apple."

"Yes, apple," Nora said, through a scrim of tears.

In the morning, Nora stuffed the turkey, trussed it neatly and rubbed it with butter. Then went about preparing the rest of the meal. It seemed odd to be in the kitchen alone – and in charge – on Thanksgiving morning. All those years, she had been Jo's willing assistant – she, Mo, and Diane. Normally, by now, all four of them would be tripping over each other, washing and peeling potatoes, assembling various casseroles, setting out ingredients for gravy, buttering the dinner roles.

"You girls!" Jo would say, finally. "Out!"

And the three of them would flee, giggling, to throw themselves onto couches and easy chairs in the family room to watch the Macy's Thanksgiving Day Parade on TV with Charlie and Claire.

It was so hard without her, Nora thought. When Jo was here, when she was herself, they were all like a big bunch of amenable children who just let her tell them what to do and how to think about whatever problems cropped up and caused them sorrow or confusion. Why wouldn't they have? She was always right.

Still, half to her surprise, the meal was perfect, and it *was* nice – just the three of them. When they'd cleared the table and put all the dishes in the dishwasher, Charlie went out to get the sled from the barn.

"Pull me," Claire said, plopping down on it, her red parka bright against the new snow.

She'd brought her camera and handed it to Nora so that she could take a picture of her on the sled to send to Dylan. Nora snapped one of her alone, then one with Charlie holding the rope of the sled, grinning. Together, they pulled her, laughing, toward the stand of pines at the edge of the meadow – Astro running in circles, barking, at their heels.

All along the highway, there were vast pine forests planted in long, perfectly straight rows by the WPA during the Depression; these pines were haphazard, though – volunteers grown from pinecones dropped and blown, every kind of size. The three of them spread out, tying bits of blue rag on the straightest, most shapely among them, then revisiting each to decide. They looked for the worst tree, too, a Charlie Brown tree to set in the sunroom and decorate with the fading paper chains and cotton-ball angels Claire had made all through grade school. It smelled wonderful in the midst of the pines: sharp and fresh.

It was near dusk when they returned with the trees and dragged them inside. Nora brought the ornaments down from the attic, while Charlie set the big tree in place. He laid out the long strings of bubble lights to test them, then wound each string round the tree, top to bottom – taking forever, as he always did.

When he was finally through, Claire put her own ornaments on the tree: one from every Christmas since she was a baby, each dated with a Sharpie on the bottom – a pink glass teddy bear with "Baby's First Christmas" written in glitter on it, a Snoopy, a cello, a sled, a skier, a snowman. She clapped with delight when Nora produced this year's: a Santa with "IU" on his hat. Nora and Charlie had found it, browsing in the bookstore on the Saturday morning of Parents Weekend, just before Nora had walked to People's Park in search of Tom.

The sky had grown heavy again and, at six, Charlie turned on the television to get the weather forecast. There was the predictable tease: "The day after Thanksgiving is traditionally the year's busiest shopping day, and this year's early Christmas shopping may be white."

Then the news. Film footage showed the first UN inspectors arriving in Iraq.

"It's hopeful, don't you think?" Charlie asked. "The inspectors going in?"

Nora looked at him, first dumbfounded, then furious that he would even mention it – especially at the end of the happiest day they'd had together in a long, long while. "No," she said. "I don't. I think Colin Powell convinced Bush we had to agree to it. To *look* like we want to avoid a war if we possibly can. A few months, big deal. Then W can go in there and bomb the shit out of them, which, if you'd read anything at all about what's going on, you'd know was what he made up his mind to do on about September 12th. So what, if there's absolutely no connection."

She felt her words take all the air out of the day. Claire looked as surprised by what she'd said as she herself, had been surprised by Charlie having mentioned Iraq at all – though whether Claire was surprised by what Nora had said or by the tone of voice in which she'd said it, Nora couldn't tell. Maybe she was just surprised by the fact that it seemed to matter so much, Nora thought. She couldn't bring herself to take the words back, in any case. Stung, Charlie picked up the box of tinsel and started laying it on the tree, strand-by-strand. It was the last touch on the tree every year, his job. He was the only one with the patience for it.

They ate turkey sandwiches and watched *It's a Wonderful Life,* as they always did when the tree was done. But when the movie was over, Claire went up to her room. Finals were coming up in a few weeks, she said, and she had some reading to do if she didn't want to fall behind. Watching her go, Nora remembered how desperately she used to miss Tom when she went home on breaks, how quickly her true home had become wherever he was. Probably Claire felt the same way. Would she call Dylan and tell him about her mother's strange outburst, Nora wondered? Or would she just throw herself across the bed in her dark room, longing to be with him?

Nora went upstairs after she'd put away all the dishes from the Thanksgiving meal and set the kitchen right for morning. She drew a hot bath and lay back against the tub, calming herself with the Ujjayi breathing she'd learned on her yoga tape. Audible breath. She concentrated on moving it through her body. Pure energy. Her chest rose and fell; her hands floated in the water. Still, the thought came: *I can't.*

She probed it like you'd probe a cracked tooth with your tongue. Can't – what?

Lie? Tell? Risk? Keep on?

Can't hurt Charlie anymore.

There was no breathing technique in the world that could stem the sudden liquid flow of darkness through all the channels where her breath had just been. There it was: simple and impossible. Stop hurting Charlie.

But she couldn't go backward, couldn't be the person she had been the moment before Pete called out to her as she left People's Park that day last summer. She couldn't staunch the flow of memory it had set in motion, couldn't remain unchanged by it. She couldn't forget that she had seen Tom and how it had felt to be with him. She could only tell Charlie the truth and hope that, in time, it would heal them. And not the whole truth, not yet. She'd have to find a way to draw him slowly, safely toward it.

Nora got out of the bathtub, put her nightgown and robe on and went downstairs. Charlie was sitting in his leather chair, a book open on his lap. She put a log on the fire, which had begun to die down, and sat down in her own easy chair, directly across from him.

"I'm sorry about tonight," she said, quietly. "But Charlie, the thing is – my brother died in Vietnam."

He looked up from his book with a fearful expression.

"And all this talk about Iraq. I can't help it, I've been thinking about him, and . . . other things from that time. It's one reason I've been – " She splayed her hands. "So – out of sorts lately."

She waited for him to ask, "You had a *brother*? Was this death before or after your parents died in the car crash? Before or after you struck out on your own that summer after you graduated from high school? And what, exactly, do you mean by 'other things from that time'?"

But he said nothing.

"Don't you see it's the same thing?" she asked. "As Vietnam?"

"No," he said. "I don't see it that way, Nora. And I've said this before: I don't see what good it does for you to be so upset over what's happening there. What does it have to do with you? With us? It's not like anything you can do will change it."

"I know I can't change it," Nora said. "God, it's the *opposite* of that. Believe me, I know all too well that I'm completely powerless to do anything that matters. It's just – I know I've been, well, difficult since Claire left. I know I hurt your feelings, and spoiled things tonight – and it wasn't the first time.

"And I wanted . . . Charlie – " She paused and took a deep breath to steady her voice before going on. "It's been hard since Claire left, being without her. Both of us are struggling with that, and I don't know why, but we haven't been able to be much help to each other. And Jo. I'm heartbroken about Jo. We both are.

"But for me it's this war coming, too. It's been on my mind about my brother, I just can't seem to stop thinking about it, and I thought telling you about him might explain, maybe, at least part of why I've been so – I don't know, *blindsided* by the whole thing. I mean, when you see all this stuff on the news, doesn't it make you remember?"

Charlie was quiet a long moment, gazing beyond her at the dark window. "I don't let myself remember," he said, finally. "I want to live my life now. I want *us* to do that, to enjoy what we have together. Is that so much to ask? Look, I'm sorry about your brother, Nora. I – didn't know. But – " His jaw clenched, as it always did when he felt boxed-in and recalcitrant. "Dwelling on it now," he said. "How can it do anything but make you feel miserable? What's the point in that?"

"No point. " She gave a helpless shrug. "But there it is, in my mind. Keeping it or letting it go doesn't feel like an option. Anyway. I thought I should tell you. So you'd know."

Charlie nodded.

She felt dismissed; though, later, he crawled into bed and drew her to him, spooned his long body around hers and held her till he drifted off to sleep, the way he used to when they were happy.

21

"The Things We Said Today"

FROM *JBMI65@aol.com*
TO *TGilbert@gilbertlaw.com*
SUBJECT *Then*
DATE SENT *Sun, Dec 1, 2002 4 PM*

Do you remember that first Thanksgiving in the house, when Bridget and I cooked the turkey and, carving it, you found we'd left the plastic bag of innards inside? How you just stood there, holding it between your thumb and fingers with this expression on your face that made Bridget and me laugh so hard Bridget peed her pants. Which only made us laugh harder. It was just a few weeks after Bobby died. The first thing that had made me laugh since we got home that afternoon and my dad was there to tell me. I remember howling with laughter, feeling almost sick with it and, even while I was laughing, thinking that leaving the giblet bag in the turkey was funny – but not this funny. I could as easily have been crying.

I don't know. You're probably reading this and thinking, all those years of utter silence, and she's e-mailing me about a stupid Thanksgiving turkey? The truth is, it's what I wrote because I couldn't think how else to start. After I saw you a few weeks ago, I told myself I wouldn't write to you, no matter what. The problem is, though, I can't stop thinking about – everything. It's what I said to you about coming back to Bloomington because of my daughter, Claire – how I knew it would make me remember and dreaded that. But it's Iraq, too. Everything since 9/11, really. The way it's so much like Vietnam – and people just won't see. Does it seem that way to you, too? Or am I being paranoid?

You're the only person in my life who remembers what it was like then – and I guess all this about the turkey and how freaked out I am, suddenly remembering so much after all this time, is just to say you're the only person I feel like I can talk to right now. Can I e-mail sometimes? Say no, if you need to. I'll understand.

* * *

FROM *TGilbert@gilbertlaw.com*
TO *JBMI65@aol.com*
SUBJECT *Re: Then*
DATE SENT *Mon, Dec 2, 2002 8:05 AM*

You're not paranoid. Write, talk. Any time.

* * *

FROM *JBMI65@aol.com*
TO *TGilbert@gilbertlaw.com*
SUBJECT *Then*
DATE SENT *Mon, Dec 3, 2002 12:35 AM*

There's another Thanksgiving that I've been remembering, too: the one right before your parents moved to Florida. Thinking about it now, it seems so obvious to me that it's directly connected to what happened that Christmas Eve, maybe more directly connected than my getting so freaked out about the bombing that had started up again. I never could explain to you how your mother made me feel, how when I was around her I began to believe I really was all wrong for you. That you really would be better off with someone else. I see now that it was hard for you to be with them, too. Even though, by then, we weren't involved in anything we might have gotten into trouble for, our politics were the exact opposite of theirs – and, of course, there was their disappointment about what you'd chosen to do after law school. There was a lot you couldn't say when you were with them. But you loved your dad and you'd never have just walked away from him the way Bridget and I did from our families. I admired you for that, but it also made me feel worse about hurting my own parents – and that sometimes translated to being mad at you when you went to see yours, and feeling abandoned.

Still, I should have tried harder to explain to you how I felt. Partly, I didn't because, deep down, I knew it was irrational. You were right: I shouldn't have let your mother bother me. But it was more than that. When Bobby died, you saw where I came from, you knew what my family was like. But I could never bring myself to talk honestly about those things with you.

Why, I wonder now, since from the very beginning I knew there was nothing I could ever do or say to make you stop loving me. I depended on it, absolutely, but it was so – large. I couldn't see what I gave you in return. That was the blessing of it, but I didn't know that then. And I don't want this to be true, but it is: no matter what happens to me now, no matter what and whom I lose from here on in – even if it's my own daughter – I know it won't make me feel as lost as I felt after I left you, knowing I could never, ever come back.

But I've gotten ahead of myself. Already.

What I want to tell you is what happened that night. The truth is, I haven't thought about it myself till now. Not really. Though I dreamed it almost every night for a long time afterward – and began to dream it again when Claire decided to go to IU.

The thing is, Tom, even before Bridget showed up that Friday I was upset with you for deciding to go to Evansville on Christmas Eve. Being there at Thanksgiving upset me more than I let you know – and then, on top of that, the bombing in Hanoi. I was so angry about it. I hadn't been that angry for a long time, and I think the way it kept raging up in me freaked me out as much as the bombing itself. I'd look at the children in my class and imagine them like the children in that awful photograph: you know, the one with the naked little girl running down the road, screaming. All that week, every chance I got, I'd go into the bathroom, lock myself into a stall, and just sit there till I could calm down.

Even so, I'd have been okay – I think we'd have been okay – if Bridget hadn't come. I was so depleted when school finally let out for break that I probably would have spent Christmas Eve sleeping. Maybe we'd have had an argument when you got back from Evansville, but that probably would have been a good thing. People in healthy, adult relationships argue. They negotiate.

Which is something I didn't do with Charlie, either, I see now.

But Bridget –

She came.

You'd told me more than once that I didn't see her clearly, and you were right. I saw what I wanted and needed to see. But even when I knew full well that what she was doing was crazy or wrong, I'd think of how she befriended me that first day, how my whole life changed because of it – and I was incapable of putting any emotional distance between us. Something else I see now is that I loved her as completely and irrationally as you loved me.

When I got home that afternoon and found her at the house, I knew there was something really wrong. Her hair, the clothes she was wearing. The kitchen curtains had been drawn – we always kept them open. There was the fact that she'd come by Greyhound Bus; where was her car? And, of course, that she asked me to lie to you about having split with Cam.

I was stupid. I just wanted us all to be together for a few days, happy – like we were that fall we first met. I longed for that time so much, so often, and couldn't admit to myself that – even then – it was already a lifetime ago. I knew I should have told you the truth that night when I came to bed: that she was still with Cam, that she'd mentioned some kind of "action" coming down. I owed you that. *You* were my best friend, the most important person in the world to me. I trusted you more than anyone. I felt horrible about lying to you, but once I'd done it, it seemed to me I couldn't go back – and I was pissed off at you for thinking the problem of Bridget could be solved by my going to Evansville with you.

Oh, God. It was so long ago. I was so wrong – about everything. Including the ridiculous idea that you should have been able to read my mind. But I still can't help thinking, how could you have not known that I needed you to stay with me?

22

"Helpless"

FROM *TGilbert@gilbertlaw.com*
TO *JBMI65@aol.com*
SUBJECT *Re: Then*
DATE SENT *Mon, Dec 3, 2002 8:12 AM*

I hate to think how many times I've run it all through my head, thinking, what if I hadn't gone? What if I'd come back that night, like I should have? The only thing I know for sure is that if I'd been there and been the one who woke up and heard Bridget leave, I'd have let her go. I was sick to death of her by then – all the fucking melodrama about her love life, her political tantrums, her moral outrage about every little thing. And, okay, since we're coming clean here, I was pissed off at you, too. I just didn't get the thing with my mom; that was part of it. But mainly I was pissed off because you kept taking Bridget in. All the time she lived with us, right from the start, I wanted her to leave.

But if I'd said, "Okay, I'm done. It's me or Bridget," I wasn't sure which one of us you'd choose.

I was glad every time she went away. And, yeah, we were friends in high school. I liked her family; they were always good to me. But I swear to God that, by then, if Bridget had gone and blown herself up that night all alone, I wouldn't have been that sorry.

Even after all this time, there's no way I can explain how I felt Christmas morning when I got home and you were gone. You'd made your choice, I thought – and without even leaving me a note to tell me why. I didn't know about the bombing until a couple of hours later, when the guy next door stopped by with some cookies his wife had made and mentioned it, and the fact that a body had been found. I called the police. What else could I do? I told them that Bridget had been here, that you were missing. For three days, until what was left of Bridget was finally identified, I was afraid you were the one who died – and all I could think was that if it wasn't you and if I ever saw Bridget again I'd kill her myself. I think I would have, too. But then I'd think, if it wasn't you, if you did make it out alive, then you'd gone off with Cameron. Which, it turned out, was true.

You asked how could I not have known that you needed me to stay that Christmas Eve. I did know. You were pissed at me for asking you to go; I was pissed at you for being stubborn about not going with me. Then Bridget came and the whole thing shifted and I felt like you'd chosen to spend Christmas with her instead of me. So, stupidly, I left, mad, and drank too much at the fucking country club and had to stay the night. I blame myself for that.

But here's what I want to know. After you got away from Cameron, why didn't you come back? Didn't you know I'd want you back, no matter what?

* * *

FROM *JBMI65@aol.com*
TO *TGilbert@gilbertlaw.com*
SUBJECT *Re: Then*
DATE SENT *Tues, Dec 4, 2002 1:17 AM*

I knew. There wasn't a moment I didn't want to come back. When I think about it now, it seems totally obvious that I should have called you the second I got away from Cam. You'd have come for me, we'd have figured out what to do together. But then, so many things seem obvious to me now.

This is such a strange age, isn't it? The way, suddenly, you have this long view of your life – like the map of a journey that had no map when were traveling it. You see how clearly one road led to the next and the next. You see what mattered. You, Bridget, Claire. That was it for me – and my mother-in-law, Jo, who was the real reason I ended up where I am. If I hadn't encountered her by chance, I don't know how much longer I could have just wandered, resisting the temptation to come back to you, regardless of the consequences. Because, like you said, I always knew where you would be.

Funny. Now it's news 24/7. You can find out anything, anywhere, any time. Then, we didn't know, couldn't safely try to find out what had actually happened after the bomb exploded. I remember that afterwards Cam had the radio on in the car, listening for news. There was one report in the morning: the damage done, an unidentified body found, not even any speculation about who might be responsible. But the station faded away as we got farther and farther from Bloomington, and was completely gone by the time we crossed over into Illinois. Then, within days, the bombing in Vietnam stopped, there was serious talk of the war really, finally ending – and what Bridget did turned out to be such a small story, after all. Buried in the back pages of the newspapers. She would have hated that.

I was scared to death the whole time I was with him. He convinced me the FBI was looking for me. He made me handle guns and documents so my fingerprints would be on them. The thing is, though, getting caught, going to prison, wasn't what scared me the most – some part of me would have been thankful for a clear punishment for what I'd done. What terrified me was coming back to the mess I'd made of my life. I couldn't even bear to think about it. I knew you loved me, I knew you'd want me to come back, but I couldn't see how I could let you forgive me when I knew I could never forgive myself.

For the longest time after I got away from Cam, I just drifted. Northern California, Oregon, Idaho. I waited tables in crappy little nowhere places. I'd save up a couple hundred dollars, enough to move on. I had to keep moving, I thought. When I thought about all I'd done, all I'd lost, I'd make myself stop – and eventually I did stop. Altogether. Which amazes me now. I mean, all those years. How could I have just . . . forgotten? After Claire decided on Bloomington, I started having dreams about the night of the bombing, but I didn't actually think about it – or what happened afterwards. I didn't dare.

I still wonder if Bridget meant for me to follow her – and, if she did, whether it was to force me, finally, to act on what I said I believed or to make me save her from herself. She never told me what she planned to do or asked me to help – though, of course, she'd used me, used both of us, appearing like she did, knowing we'd be implicated once the bomb had gone off. I was angry and upset with you about Evansville. She knew that. She knew I was distraught about the bombing in Vietnam. Maybe she purposely reeled me in, playing on my guilt for doing nothing about the war, on my worst fears about us – that, ultimately, you'd choose the life your parents raised you to lead. And where would that leave me?

Even so, when I left the house that night, it wasn't a political act, it so wasn't about being angry at you. I followed Bridget to try to stop her from whatever she was setting out to do. When I couldn't stop her, I stayed with her because, stupidly, I believed I could somehow keep her safe.

There's so much I've forgotten. But this part I remember perfectly. I've dreamed it over and over these past months. The vast emptiness of early, early morning. Crisp, cold. The sky black, dotted with stars. Bridget ahead of me, walking at a quick pace, appearing, disappearing under the streetlights. When I realized she was heading for the ROTC building, I took off running after her.

Here's where the dream I have differs from what actually happened: I go into the building with her. I'm there when the bomb goes off prematurely. I hear glass shattering and see the windows blow out. I see the Bridget I first knew wheeling backward, on fire, her beautiful, long red hair streaming.

The thing is, Tom, I've dreamed that dream so many times now, I half-believe I actually was in the building with her. But if I had been there, I'd be dead, too. In fact, we stood outside the building, arguing, until she took a package from the duffel then thrust the bag into my hands just before climbing into the window that had been left open for her.

As for what happened after that, there was a terrible blast. Fire. Cam appeared, as if out of nowhere. I remember that – and that he was rough with me. Maybe I was screaming. I probably was. Like I said before, I remember being in a car with him, but not how I got there. I remember begging him to let me out, let me go. He was furious, raging about Bridget. He'd told her not to contact me – and hadn't that been what killed her, after all? Letting me distract her from her purpose?

I think I would have come back if he'd let me go that first night. But by the time I did get away, it seemed too late. But to be totally honest, there was this, too: I was so tired. There was something easy about accepting, finally, what that little voice inside me had been saying all along. You don't deserve Tom, you never did. You're not capable of being the person you wanted to be. Look at what I'd demanded of my parents, I told myself – then willfully, selfishly broken their hearts. I'd failed Bridget, I'd failed my students, who loved and depended on me. Worst of all I'd failed you and ruined all we might have had together.

I wonder now where such shame comes from, the instinct to turn to shame first in trying to make any sense at all of what has happened to you. All I know is that my whole early life was shaped by it. "Is there anything that satisfies you, Jane?" my mother would ask, when I behaved badly or was moody and sullen. "Is there anything that makes you happy?"

There wasn't, really. I wanted. She didn't understand that. She couldn't see that I just wasn't a happy person by nature. Her deep desire for my happiness, her belief that I could be happy if only I tried, oppressed me. It enraged me, which I knew was ridiculous, even then. What mother wouldn't want her daughter to be happy? What kind of daughter hoarded any happiness that did come her way?

But then.

That first day with Cam, I found a set of documents in Bridget's duffel. Birth certificate, social security card, driver's license. I was smart enough to put them in a secret place, for when I mustered up the courage to get away from Cam. Nora White. I used to think about her: born the same year I was born, in St. Louis. Who was she? Most fake identity papers used names of dead people. I knew that and wondered, how did she die? But eventually she became me: a woman who'd lost everything through her own stupidity, a woman with no life, nowhere to go.

It surprised me, in a way: it's not as difficult to change your identity as you might think. Women do it all the time, even now – changing their last names when they marry. Really, it would be almost as hard to track down a high school classmate who'd moved away and married – maybe several times – as it would have been to find me. By the time I married Charlie and changed my name a second time, it seemed to me that Jane really had died on that Christmas morning.

So much of what happened between then and the summer I landed in Monarch is a blank. Nobody ever questioned the story I told about my parents, dead in a car accident. How I struck out on my own afterwards. Even I didn't question it after a while. I never thought about the past, lived only in the now.

But, really, doesn't that happen to everyone to some degree?

I mean, life happens. Not that so much of it isn't lovely: waves sparkling on the lake in the early morning, the smell of pies baking in your own kitchen, moths batting against the screens on summer nights. A child growing right before your eyes. Sometimes I think I could stack all of Claire's school pictures top to bottom, kindergarten to twelfth grade, flip them like an animator to watch her grow, and the second it would take to do it would seem as long – or as short – as the years themselves took. Where do they go? Old people always say that. But it's true.

But here's what I'm writing to you about, really: remember, I said in the first e-mail I sent you that I told Charlie about Bobby, that it didn't go well? What started it was, he's been upset with me because he thinks I've become obsessed with Iraq. What does it have to do with us? We had a nasty little exchange about it Thanksgiving night, which surprised and upset Claire. I was nasty – after Charlie asked, didn't I think it was a good thing that the inspectors were there?

Well, it doesn't matter what the argument was about. Just that afterwards I felt ashamed of myself for hurting Charlie – and not for the first time in the past months. We've been – not okay, really, ever since Claire decided to go to IU. Worse since she left. And it's been mostly my fault. So after Claire had gone to bed, I went downstairs and apologized – and told him about Bobby. That was three days ago, and he's barely said a word to me since. I'm scared, Tom – I don't know how long I can keep on this way.

* * *

FROM *JBMI65@aol.com*
TO *TGilbert@gilbertlaw.com*
SUBJECT *PS*
DATE SENT *Tues, Dec 4, 2002 2:12 AM*

That day in Bloomington, you said you had a life. That it was good. I'm glad for that. What is it like? Tell me your greatest pleasures.

* * *

FROM *TGilbert@gilbertlaw.com*
TO *JBMI65@aol.com*
SUBJECT *Re: PS*
DATE SENT *Tues, Dec 4, 2002 7:33 AM*

It's pretty simple, really. The law practice – mostly civil rights and kids who get themselves in trouble somehow. I like it: license to fight. Though it's depressing sometimes, how fucked up things are.

Anyway. Work. The gym right after that, then I usually eat out somewhere. Evenings, I read – or watch a movie or sports on TV, depending the season. Tuesday is pool night. Weekends I'm outside whenever I can be. I ski in the winter; summers I go fishing way up in Canada. I've got a house on Grant Street, just off Kirkwood Avenue, a great mutt, Maxine.

Pleasures (shallow): '99 Corvette (red), '97 Ford truck (black), '67 GTO (maroon, mint condition), '91 Harley Sturgis (black). Dad's old aluminum fishing boat. Huge garage, mother of all garages. Probably, this won't surprise you.

Like you said, life happens. Mostly, I'm happy.

Those first couple of years without you were tough ones, though. I'd go over to the Sig house on football Saturdays – you know, the old-fart lunch they always have. A lot of old guys with comb-overs, drunk at noon, talking about how great things were when they were in college. I'd go to remind myself of what I didn't want to be.

Sunday evenings, I'd decide what I was going to do every night after work. I'd make a list, stick it on the refrigerator and fucking do every single thing on it – even when what I really wanted to do was hole up and feel sorry for myself. I said I was going to do that stuff, so I did. I learned how to keep you in a certain place in my mind. I was pretty good at it, too, until Pete saw you that day.

I went over to the house the Saturday after I saw you in October. Same scene, only now the old guys with comb-overs running the wasn't-it-great-then trip are our age. There was nobody there I knew, which was fine with me. I didn't want to see anyone. Just hang out, see what it felt like to be there. I wandered around. Checked out our composite pictures – down in the basement with the rest of the dinosaurs. Pete and I used to think that was hilarious. Like we'd never end up there ourselves. But there we were, so clean-cut, faking it in our suits and ties.

Really, the place hasn't changed much at all. The dining room still smells like bad cooking mixed with sweat and beer. It's still a pit upstairs. Remember the big clothes cupboard you hid in, holding the Bloody Marys, that night the fraternity police came through? It's still in my old room on the third floor. I got a kick out of remembering how we used to sneak around upstairs. You'd have thought it was a federal offense. Shit. Now kids can do anything they want. Where's the fun in that?

Yeah, I know. I sound like those old guys, after all.

Remember Pete when he came back that last time, how he was such a sanctimonious shit about the fact that I was in law school, you were teaching – we had plans for our lives. He was all about "Be Here Now."

Who'd have thought he'd turn out to be right? Trouble is, though, since I saw you, Now and Then feel like exactly the same thing to me.

* * *

FROM *JBMI65@aol.com*
TO *TGilbert@gilbertlaw.com*
SUBJECT *Re: PS*
DATE SENT *Tues, Dec 4, 2002 8:37 AM*

I know. Me, too.

23

"She's Not There"

"I was thinking we should decorate Jo's room for Christmas," Nora said to Charlie. "It might ground her a bit. Or just be something pretty for her to look at."

He shrugged but agreed to drive into Traverse City to the Walmart with her, where they bought a table-top tree with tiny, twinkling lights. They picked up, then put down, a box of miniature glass balls – too dangerous – and bought a bag of candy canes to use as decorations instead. At home, Nora made a batch of the Mexican wedding-cake cookies Jo loved. She packed up the ceramic nativity figures Charlie had made in Sunday School when he was a little boy, the paint chipped from years of use, along with a few other things she thought might feel familiar to her: a nutcracker, a Santa wearing skis, a paper snowflake – brown at the edges now – that Claire had made in grade school.

Charlie carried the box with the tree in it into the nursing home; Nora followed with the decorations and the cookies she'd arranged on a snowman plate. They passed through the lounge, where some of the residents had gathered to listen to a group of kids from the high school, decked out in Santa hats, singing Christmas carols.

"Jo's feeling a little under the weather today," one of the nurses said. "Catching a cold, I think. She'll be glad to see you."

But she greeted them with a blank stare. Her eyes were red-rimmed, her nose rubbed raw. She sat in her recliner, facing the dark window – as if waiting for the birds to come back into her view. The TV was on – the 6:30 news. "Despite Iraq's claim that there are no banned weapons in the country, despite UN inspectors' failure to turn up any evidence of such weapons, 89 percent of Americans believe that Iraq possesses weapons of mass destruction," Dan Rather said.

But Jo wasn't listening.

Nora switched it off, bent and kissed Jo's cheek. "We brought you Christmas," she said. "Look. Charlie's brought you a pretty little tree. And I made some Mexican wedding cakes. You've always loved those." She took the plastic wrap from the cookie plate, but Jo looked past it to her bed, a weary expression on her face that spoke volumes: *please.*

"You set up the tree," Nora said to Charlie. "I'll get her ready for bed."

Gently, she helped Jo to the bathroom and closed the door, knowing that it distressed Charlie to see his mother in such a private way. She pulled down Jo's sweatpants, took off the Depends she wore now, and guided her to the toilet. When she'd finished, Nora wiped her clean with a warm cloth. She took off Jo's top and pulled a fresh, clean nightgown over her head, talking quietly to her all the while – about Christmas and snow in the forecast and how good the cookies had smelled baking in the house.

"Tomorrow you'll have some," she said. "You'll feel better tomorrow."

When they came out of the bathroom, Charlie was sitting in exactly the same place.

"Charlie," Nora said. "I thought you were going to – "

"Oh." He looked at the unopened box beside him.

"Never mind," Nora said. She settled Jo into her bed, then took the tree from the box, set it on the little dining table and plugged in the lights. She arranged the nativity figures beneath it, set the nutcracker and the Santa on the windowsill, and looped the thread on Claire's paper snowflake around the window latch – taking care not to block the view of the birdfeeder, working quietly so as not to disturb Jo, who had fallen fast asleep the moment her head hit the pillow.

"Leave the candy canes till later?" she whispered to Charlie. "I'm afraid crackling the wrappers to open them will wake her."

He didn't answer. He looked at his mother, and for an instant his expression was completely unguarded, bereft. Then he put his head in his hands and began to sob quietly, his bony shoulders heaving.

"Charlie!" Nora said.

He waved her away, and when she went to him anyway, threw off her touch, knocking her off balance, so that she was still reeling when he stood, suddenly, and bolted from the room. All this time, he'd refused to see what was happening to his mother, Nora thought – and how was she any better, dragging him over here with some convoluted idea that making Christmas for Jo would be a comfort for any of them? All she'd done was force Charlie to come face-to-face with one more thing he knew but couldn't bear to know and hasten the speed with which their whole world was falling to pieces all around them. She grabbed her coat and hurried after him, past old ladies making their way back to their rooms after the Christmas program. Outside, sprung from the depressing atmosphere, the students were climbing boisterously into a van that had pulled up at the entrance, their shouts and laughter bright puffs in the cold, crisp air.

"Hey! Mrs. Quillen!" a voice called.

One of Claire's friends, probably. But Nora didn't look back.

Charlie stood, jacketless, his fists clenched, in the parking lot nowhere near where his truck was parked. Nora stopped short of him, and he turned and walked away from her again – this time up Main Street. It was not seven yet, but pitch dark, nearing the longest night of the year. Cars moved slowly in the snow that was just beginning to fall, the beams of their headlights haloed in it. The streetlamps were haloed, too. They looked like a long row of angels.

He was going to the Hummingbird Café, she knew – and he didn't want her to follow him. She went back for his jacket, then walked to the café anyway and stood in front of the steamy window until he looked up from his favorite booth, where he used to sit on summer days at lunchtime when he was a little boy. She raised the jacket, he shrugged. She stepped inside and hung it on a peg in the entry, then walked the few blocks over to Mo and Diane's.

Shivering, not only from the cold, she stood on the sidewalk looking at the two of them framed in the dining room window – like any happy married couple, Nora thought – the remains of their evening meal, a bottle of wine, half-drunk, between them. Talking over the day's events. She had thought . . . she had no idea what she'd thought, really – that they could help her? That they would know what to do? She knew what to do. She just didn't want to do it.

She walked back through the dark streets, into the café, and slid into the booth across from Charlie. His hands were on the table, cupping a full mug of coffee as if for its warmth. He wouldn't look at her.

"Hey, Nora!" said Renee, the waitress. "I never see you guys in the evening. What's up? Coffee?"

"Sure," Nora said, ignoring the first question.

"You've eaten," Renee asked, pouring. "Charlie said he had."

Nora nodded.

"I'm so sorry about Jo," she said to Charlie in a low voice, when she'd gone. "I'm sorry for the way I've been since Claire left – "

"Don't say you're sorry," he said, bitterly.

"But I am sorry," she said. "About Jo, of course. I'm heartsick about Jo. But it's not only that. Charlie, there's something we need to talk about if we're ever – "

"It's about Bloomington, isn't it?" he interrupted. "Why you didn't want Claire to go there."

"I went to school at IU," Nora said. "In the sixties. I didn't want to go back. I just didn't see how I could – "

"Great," he said. "First I find out you had a brother who died in Vietnam. So much for being an only child whose parents were killed in a car crash. Now – " He shook his head. "All those times my mom tried to get you to let her pay for you to go to college. You were too smart not to go, she'd tell me. She felt bad because she thought you were too insecure to give it a try. We both did. And you'd already been."

Nora's eyes filled with tears.

"Don't *cry,*" he said.

The words, spoken low and mean, felt like physical blows to her.

"Charlie, can we go home?" she asked quietly. "Please? Can we talk there?"

"Here's as good as anywhere," he said.

The café was mostly deserted, she was thankful for that – and for the fact that Renee's boyfriend had come in and she was fussing over him.

"Need anything?" she asked, on her way to the kitchen.

Nora shook her head, no.

How many times they had sat here in this same booth over the years, drinking coffee, eating one of Jo's good meals, maybe a piece of apple or cherry pie. If things were slow, Jo would slide in next to Charlie and give him a hug and a kiss, reach across the table to cup her hand over Nora's and give it a squeeze, then fill them in on whatever news of the town had come her way that day. When Claire was a baby, Jo loved to carry her around the restaurant – the coffee pot in one hand, Claire balanced on the opposite hip. Later, Claire spent whole days at the café with Jo, who folded down a waitress apron for her, gave her a notepad, and let her wait on customers when it wasn't too busy.

"Well – ?" Charlie said now.

Nora took a deep breath. "I – lived with someone in Bloomington," she began. "We were together a long time. And I had a friend – we, all three of us, were involved in the antiwar movement. My . . . boyfriend, he was in law school. He did draft counseling. This was after my brother died, and then a good friend of ours went over and – " She paused to collect herself. "I don't know what to say, Charlie. How to explain. You know what it was like then. How – "

She told him about Bridget, her deepening, radical involvement in the movement and how worried she'd been when Bridget left with Cam.

"She was gone a long time," Nora said. "More than a year. And she came back that Christmas when Nixon bombed Hanoi. Remember that? 1972?"

Charlie just looked at her.

"See – " she went on. "And I know I've said this before, but part of why I've been so upset about Iraq is, it seems like it's happening all over. I mean, look! Here it is almost Christmas again and, Charlie, they're moving troops over there. If you go on the internet, there are all these sites. Photographs. Real information about what's happening, and it's nothing like what's on the news. They're lying about *everything.* Sometimes I feel like I'm living in two times at once. I think about what it was like then and – "

"Nora." He leaned toward her, jaw clenched. "How many times do I have to tell you, I don't care what's happening in Iraq? It doesn't have a goddamn thing to do with us."

"But it does," Nora said. "It has to do with *me.* How I feel. How I can't – " A bolt of anger shot through her. "Okay. Fine. *Then.* My friend – Bridget – put a bomb in the ROTC building. I was with her. It went off too soon. She died. And I – " Now her hands were clenched in fists. "I left – "

"With . . . this guy." Charlie said.

"No." Nora shook her head. "Not with him. It was – "

"He's still there, isn't he? In Bloomington. You saw him when we went in October. That's why you gave away the football ticket. That's where you went instead."

"I saw him," Nora said. "I hadn't made plans to see him. But I did. Oh, God. This never would have happened, none of it would've happened, if I'd told you all this as soon as Claire started thinking about going there. I should have told you in the very beginning, or at least when we decided to get married. But I didn't know how – and after all that time went by, where would I start? Plus, come on, Charlie. Would you really have wanted me to tell you?"

"I didn't want you to tell me now, Nora." He shrugged. "But you did. So what am I supposed to do about it? What does it change?"

Nora looked at him, his face pinched and old. "Charlie," she said. "Can't you see? Everything's changed *already.* Claire and Jo are gone. It's just the two of us, day-to-day, from here on in, and we need to figure out what the rest of our lives together will be. We'd have needed to do that anyway, even if – "

"What? Our whole life together hadn't been a lie?"

"It's not a lie," Nora said. "Not what we felt, what we've had. God, Claire's not a lie! Charlie, I love you. I cherish the life we've had together. I don't want – "

She leaned toward him, reached across the table for his hand. But he pulled it away.

"*Who* loves me?" he said. "Isn't that the real problem? I don't even know who you are."

Outside, the snow was coming down harder. The café felt like a cave of light, its blue neon coffee cup glowing in the big front window. Except for the absence of Jo, the Hummingbird hadn't changed since the day Nora wandered in and sat down, wondering how in the world she would manage to pay for the repairs her car needed and get to Saginaw.

If she could go back to that day, what would she do? Any option other than taking the job Jo offered would have played out in a life without Claire in it, which was something she simply could not imagine. She did not want to imagine it. Nor did she want to imagine telling Claire what she'd just told Charlie. But she knew she must.

When Nora walked the next morning, she did not turn back at her usual place but continued along the shoreline until she came to the public beach. It was deserted, gulls flapping and shrieking. Heavy clouds hung low over the lake, promising more snow. The sand in the volleyball pit was frozen in little peaks, edged in ice, and passing it on her way to town she thought of sitting on Mo and Diane's porch, listening to the laughter of Claire and her friends drift up the beach into their hearing. They had come to the edge of an argument about Iraq that summer night, but Monique had veered them all away from it, protecting Charlie from any distress.

He would need Mo now, Nora knew. But he wouldn't ask for help. Last night, when she suggested it, he said had no intention of telling Mo what had happened between them.

"What could she do about it?" he said. "It's just information. She can't change it."

He wouldn't want her to tell Diane, either; nonetheless, Nora turned on to Main Street and walked toward the shop, where Diane would be getting organized for the day. It was that or yield to the impulse to go back to bed and just lie there, paralyzed with grief.

She was freezing when she arrived, her feet soaking wet from sloshing through the wet snow. "Take your shoes off," Diane said, pulling her in. "I'll go make you a cup of tea. And would you look?" Laughing, she gestured toward the computer, where Nora saw a screen-size photo of Carah, standing sideways, dressed only in her underwear to display her pregnant belly.

"She's gargantuan," Diane called, from the back room. "That baby can't possibly be six weeks away, do you think?"

When Nora didn't answer, she stepped back into the shop, teakettle in hand, and actually looked at her for the first time. "Nora," she said. "What's wrong? It's not Claire, is it? Has something happened to Claire?"

"No," Nora said. "It's not that."

"What, then?" Diane asked. She kept two comfortable, chintz-covered easy chairs in the cluttered backroom, and the two of them had spent countless hours there, talking. She gestured Nora into one of them now and sank into the other herself.

"Talk," she said.

And Nora told her everything.

She listened. The time for opening the shop came and went.

"You almost told me all this the day we floated, didn't you?" she said when Nora was through. "When I was a wreck because I'd just found out Carah was pregnant."

"I might have told you. I don't know. But it was before I saw Tom – and I thought then I could work through it in my mind, just get over it. So maybe I'd have chickened out. I probably would have."

"Still," Diane said. "These past months – since that day, really, when Carah's letter came – I've been so – "

"Happy?" Nora smiled.

"Stupidly," Diane said. "Selfishly. Nora, I'm sorry. I've been so wrapped up in Carah and the baby coming that I didn't even see. I mean, obviously, I saw there was tension between you and Charlie. Mo and I both saw that. But we figured it was all about adjusting to Claire being gone, that you'd work it out. You know Mo. She'd never ask. I should have, though – "

She shook her head. "Well, there's no point wallowing around in guilt – either one of us. I'll stop beating myself up over not paying attention if you'll stop beating yourself up about telling Charlie. He's your husband, for God's sake. What else could you have done but tell him? The real question is, what are we going to do now? What about Claire? When does she get home?"

"Friday," Nora said. "And Charlie says I shouldn't tell her. Ever. Those were his last words to me before he went to sleep in Jo's bedroom last night."

"Shit," Diane said. "And you think – "

"I think I can't *not* tell her."

"I think you're right," Diane said. "You have to tell her, and soon. She's a smart girl. She probably knows something's wrong and, believe me, the longer you wait to tell her what it is, the worse it's going to be. God. Where do we get this idiotic idea that being the perfect parent, protecting them from everything is even possible? I mean, you have a kid; you have no idea what you're supposed to do. You don't even know who the kid is – and it's not till way later that you realize that's even a factor. I had identical twins, and it's taken me thirty-four years to figure out that they're absolutely nothing alike – inside! Not to mention that all the time I was raising them I was trying to grow up myself.

"It's interesting, you know? Since Carah and I have begun to talk again, really talk, I see how much of the damage that was done between us – and between me and Rose – was done less because I turned out to be a lesbian than because I didn't tell them I was a lesbian once I knew that's what I was. I didn't even admit it to myself – which is how I got so whacked out that it would make any kind of sense to me to just leave with Audrey. I hadn't been honest with myself for so long I didn't even know what it would look like.

"The thing is, Nora. I know this sounds harsh, and I didn't use to think this at all, but the world isn't easy, and the sooner kids figure it out, the better. Jesus, the other day I was listening to some guy on a talk show – a counselor – who said it wasn't necessarily a bad idea to lie to your teenage kids if you'd used drugs when you were younger. Can you believe that? Like, number one, they'd even believe it. Not to mention that it doesn't help them figure out what to do when all their friends are getting high and it looks like a whole lot of fun. Shit! It is fun. Lying about that is about as stupid as Nancy Reagan and her

'Just Say No.' Easy when you're eight and you have no idea what you're saying 'no' to. Plus, where does that kind of lying stop?

"Sure, you could just not tell Claire – pretend you've never done anything wrong. Pretend you have a perfect marriage. Maybe she'll buy into it. But eventually, when she finds out how hard it is just to live day-to-day, all the negotiation and compromise it takes to stay in a relationship – let alone keep loving the person you're in it with – she'll either be pissed off because you didn't prepare her for it or feel like a failure because she can't be perfect like you are. Or, worst of all, indulge you – which is what most kids do with their parents, after all. They never let them into their real lives."

Diane was quiet a moment; she looked chagrined. "You know, Nora," she said, "you've got to really fuck up big time to get as smart as I am now. So I hope you're listening. Or you could just tell me to just shut up."

"I knew what you'd tell me," Nora said. "It's why I came."

NPR was on the radio in Charlie's office later that day, when she knocked lightly and entered, as she had always done. Could the timing have been worse, she wondered afterwards?

" – looking drawn, years older than she had on the day of her arrest . . ." a reporter was saying. Laura Ann Pearson's appeal had been denied, and she was escorted from the courtroom – glancing back just once at her husband and daughters, left heartbroken in her wake.

Charlie reached over, turned it off, and bent to the stack of papers on his desk, without acknowledging Nora's presence.

"It won't be like that for us," she said.

He didn't look at her.

"Tom – " She paused, jarred by the sound of her voice speaking his name "The . . . person I told you about. In Bloomington. He told me the case had been dropped years ago, so I didn't need to be afraid – "

"Of being hauled off to prison?" Charlie asked, bitterly. "He told you this when? In October? So if that's the case, why tell me anything at all?"

"I had to tell you. I couldn't go on not telling you."

"Which was really all about you," he said. "What you needed. But, for God's sake, why would you want to tell Claire? You said yourself there's no danger of your being arrested – "

"That doesn't mean it couldn't still come out some way."

"How?" he asked. "Come on, Nora. You know as well as I do that the only way Claire's going to find out about all this is if you tell her."

She looked at him, this man she had been married to for more than twenty years, and he looked completely unfamiliar to her. "Charlie," she said. "Please. I'm her mother. I have to tell her the truth about who I am."

"No, Nora. You don't." He stood, put on his lab coat, and brushed past her on his way to the kennels, where the animals awaited him, simple in their needs.

24

"Bridge over Troubled Water"

In the next days, she might as well have been invisible to him. Until Claire came home, he could sit silently through breakfast, take his second cup of coffee out to the clinic rather than drinking it with Nora. He could sit in his easy chair all evening, ignoring her. He could walk upstairs to Jo's bedroom and go to sleep.

Nora could spend hours at the shop, talking to Diane. Or sit in the kitchen staring out the window and tell herself why she shouldn't e-mail Tom – until she couldn't stand it anymore and went up to Claire's room and did it anyway. To have told him about what was happening with Charlie would have felt like too great a betrayal, so, instead, she wrote to him about what she remembered: small things, mostly, moments that floated up and pierced her heart.

Friday morning, she woke full of dread. When Charlie had gone to the clinic, she went into Claire's room and e-mailed Tom.

* * *

FROM *JBMI65@aol.com*
TO *TGilbert@gilbertlaw.com*
SUBJECT *No Subject*
DATE SENT *Friday, December 18 12:46 PM*

Claire's coming home today, and she'll be using the computer so I have to delete this e-mail account while she's here. I'm scared, Tom. I can't imagine how to talk to her, how it can turn out right. But I have to try.

* * *

FROM *TGilbert@gilbertlaw.com*
TO *JBMI65@aol.com*
SUBJECT *RE: No Subject*
DATE SENT *Friday, December 18 12:55 PM*

I understand. Take care.

* * *

She deleted the account and felt for a moment neither Nora nor Jane – nobody at all. She'd stop this thing with Tom for good, she told herself. She had to. She wouldn't e-mail him again – or she'd e-mail him one more time to tell him that she and Charlie had come to an understanding after all. Claire was what mattered, and they'd work together, find a way to be what she needed them to be.

She couldn't help but brighten when Claire burst in that afternoon, so full of life. She talked all through supper – about her finals, which she thought she had done well on, and about Dylan, with whom she was clearly even more in love.

"It's so good to be home," she said, beaming at both of them. If she thought it odd that, moments later, Charlie got up and went out to the kennels, she didn't mention it, but chattered on to Nora about a dozen different things.

Nor was she alarmed when Nora dissolved into tears opening the narcissus bulbs that Charlie gave her on Christmas morning. He got them every year for her; she'd set them on Petoskey stones piled in the bottom of glass vases, water them, and mid-January the whole house would be full of their scent.

"Mom," Claire teased. "Get a grip!"

"They're just always so beautiful," Nora said, thinking, When they bloom, will I be here?

On New Year's Eve – Claire at a party with some high school friends, Monique and Diane in Chicago with Carah – Nora lit a fire and sat down across from Charlie, determined to convince him this time that telling Claire the truth was the right thing to do.

"I want to have a real relationship with her," she said. "And I can't, if I don't tell her the truth about my life. It's her life, too. Charlie, even if things were perfectly normal, our relationship with Claire would be changing. It has to change. We can either keep pretending she's just our little girl or start to try to develop an adult relationship with her."

"She's my child," he said. "I don't want an adult relationship with her. I want to take care of her and protect her, like my mom did for me. That's what parents do – as long as they're able."

Nora started to argue that, if Jo could, she'd tell him that Nora was right, that they had to be honest with Claire – but, quite suddenly, she wasn't at all sure what Jo would say. She'd cared for and fiercely protected Charlie, yes, but in so doing she'd allowed him to be emotionally dependent upon her. In truth, she'd allowed Nora to be dependent on her, too. Why wouldn't she feel the same way about Claire? If Nora had been able to tell Jo the truth, would she have counseled her to keep it a secret from Charlie?

Her mind reeled, she felt half-sick at the rush of thoughts that followed. Jo loved Nora, but that love had been based on someone she was not. She could never know now if Jo could have forgiven her for the harm the lie at the center of her life had brought to Charlie. Could Jo have loved the mix of Jane and Nora she now knew she had to learn to become. Could anyone?

"Charlie," she said. "I have to tell Claire. Help me. Please."

"Help you what?" he said. "Break her heart? I really don't see any good reason to do that, Nora. Unless you have some plan I don't know about."

"What plan?" Nora asked.

She knew from the way he looked at her and shrugged his shoulders that he meant Tom.

"It's not about that," she said. "I don't have any plan. But, Charlie, Claire must know something's wrong between us by now. She's been home nearly two weeks and we haven't said anything but the absolute bare minimum to each other. And you think she hasn't noticed that you're sleeping in Jo's room, but – "

"She doesn't know that," he said. "I'm up and out of there way before she wakes up in the morning. I keep the door closed at night."

"Maybe," Nora said. "But if you intend to sleep in Jo's room forever – "

"I'm not prepared to talk about my . . . sleeping arrangements."

"Well, what are you prepared to talk about?" Nora asked. "We can't keep on this way. I've said I'm sorry, Charlie. I am sorry – for the hurt I've caused you. But I can't take back what you know; I'm not sure I'd take it back if I could. It was wrong trying to pretend what I did never happened. It was there all the time, anyway. I didn't even realize what it was doing to me, to us until I – "

"Spare me the therapy, okay?"

"It's not therapy," she said. "It's true. It's also true that this is the way it is now, and we have to deal with it."

"You deal with it," he said. "Or talk it to death with Diane. Or – " He shrugged again. "Whatever his name is."

"Tom. His name is Tom, but this has nothing to do with him. It's about us – you and me and Claire."

He picked up a magazine from the clutter of them on the coffee table and leafed through it. Claire's *Seventeen.* It would have been funny, Nora thought, the sight of him reading a magazine with the photograph of a teenage fashionista on the front – except nothing was funny between them right now. She went and put a log on the fire, watched it flare up. By the time she returned to her chair, Charlie had put down the magazine and was on his way upstairs. She heard the door of Jo's room close behind him.

She sat awhile by the fire, then put her jacket on and went outdoors, Astro yipping at her feet. He leapt through the knee-deep snow like a dolphin, circling around her as she walked toward the edge of the forest. She had tucked her jeans into her boots, but they were quickly soaked through. Her feet freezing.

It was so beautiful, though. The night was clear, moonlight illuminating the snow in the meadow so that it glittered like a field of stars fallen from the sky – and the old farmhouse, her home, in the center of it all. Though it could not feel like home again until she was right with her daughter in it.

It was just past nine o'clock, hours before Claire would return. Nora walked back to the house in her own tracks, showered to warm herself. She put on her nightgown and robe, made a pot of tea, and sat alone by the fire to wait for her. She felt calm for the first time in a long while, grounded in the moment. It was right, what she meant to do. Necessary. Regardless of what might come of it. It seemed strange to her to think that she'd ever considered any other option.

"Sit, Honey," she said, when Claire came in. "There's something I need to tell you."

"What?" Claire said, alarmed. "Where's Dad?"

"Sleeping," Nora said. "It's not that. He's all right."

"Then – "

"Honey, sit down. Please."

Claire sat on the edge of Charlie's chair. "You and dad aren't – ? I mean, you've been so weird since I've been home. Are you getting a divorce?"

She looked so fearful that, for a moment, Nora thought she couldn't go on.

"Mom – " Claire said, urgently.

"No," Nora said. "It's something about myself I need to tell you. I'm not sick," she added quickly. "I promise. It's something about –

"Remember, I got so . . . upset about your wanting to go to IU?"

"Of course, I remember," Clare said. "But what's that got to do – "

"The thing is," Nora said, "I went there myself. I never told anybody. Because – "

"You went there?" Claire asked, leaning forward. "Mom, what do you mean you went there?"

"To college," Nora said. "When I was a girl, when I was your age. I know. You thought I didn't go to college, but I did. There."

"And you didn't tell anybody?" Claire said. "But why? And why were you so, well, shitty about it when I decided it was where I wanted to go?"

Nora flinched at her words. "I – " She had not meant to cry, but suddenly tears were streaming down her cheeks. "Because I was afraid to go back there," she said. "Because I knew if that's where you decided to go, I'd have to go back."

She paused, collected herself. Claire watched, a wariness in her expression that Nora had never seen.

"I was involved in the antiwar movement in the sixties," she went on. "I got caught up in something that, well, it turned out very, very badly. And I ran away from it. From my life. I thought I could really do that."

"Mom," Claire said. "What are you talking about? What did you do?"

Nora told her, briefly, and Claire stood, lurching, as if she'd been hit.

"You're not – " she began. "I mean, who are you if you're not – "

Nora stood to go to her, but she stepped back. "Honey," she said. "Claire."

"No. Don't talk to me. Don't tell me anymore. I don't want to hear!"

"Claire, please."

But she turned and fled up the stairs to her bedroom.

"I'm going to Dylan's," she announced in the morning. Her voice was cold, firm. "I got my ticket online last night. I've got a ride to the airport in Traverse City. Right now, I just need to be with him."

"Now see what you've done?" Charlie said, when she'd gone – and refused to say another word about it. Claire's anger Nora could accept, and even the precipice of silence she slipped into once she'd gone to be with Dylan. But the quiet distance Charlie so determinedly continued to put between them, the sense that she had become invisible to him, she did not think she could bear.

A week passed. Though the final report of the weapons inspectors would not be in until the end of the month, there was news of troop deployments to Kuwait, aircraft carriers moving toward the Persian Gulf. Rumors of air squadrons departing for bases in Al Jaber, something else Charlie refused to acknowledge, along with the fact that Jo had grown weaker, more distant since her illness in December. She slept more and resisted getting out of bed when she woke, curling away from the nurse or from Nora herself, covering her face with her gnarled hands.

"Charlie, talk to me. Please," she finally said.

But he stood and walked out to the clinic, his breakfast left half-eaten on the kitchen table. Watching through the window, Nora felt as she did in the relaxation part of her yoga tape, no more than the sound of her own breath, uncertain where the edges of her body met the air. But the sensation was not a happy one, as it had seemed when she was using the tape – a reason to do yoga. Instead, it frightened her.

She walked, thinking the feeling would dissolve. But it didn't. She longed to talk to Diane, but didn't want to call her in Chicago, where she'd gone to be with Carah in this last week before the baby's birth.

By lunchtime, she felt a headache coming on and lay down on Claire's bed. Snow had begun to fall and she was grateful for the way it dulled the daylight, darkening the room so that it seemed almost like evening. She slept awhile, dreamed herself, Jane, shouting at her own mother, "I can't be here. I can't listen to you anymore. Don't you see that Bobby died for nothing? Nothing, Mom. Nothing at all."

Jolting awake, she thought of Claire. She got up and went to the computer to see if she'd sent an e-mail. No. Nothing since the brief message she'd sent to say she'd arrived safely in Cincinnati. Had she talked to Charlie, Nora wondered – perhaps called him at the clinic during the time she knew her mother took her morning walk? Had Charlie called her? Nora had no idea what either of them might do. How they might be, who they might be without her. That was when she made a new e-mail account and wrote to Tom. Because he was real, because she knew he would answer her.

FROM *MIJB65@aol.com*
TO *TGilbert@gilbertlaw.com*
SUBJECT *No Subject*
DATE SENT *Thursday, Jan 9, 2003 12:46 PM*

I told both Charlie and Claire everything, and it was a terrible mistake. Claire left the next day and went to be with her boyfriend; Charlie won't talk to me. I can't think. I don't know what to do, just what

I can't do, which is to keep on as if I'd never had a life before I came here.

* * *

FROM *TGilbert@gilbertlaw.com*
TO *MIJB65@aol.com*
SUBJECT *RE: No Subject*
DATE SENT *Thursday, Jan 9, 2003 1:07 PM*

Do you want me to come?

* * *

FROM *MIJB65@aol.com*
TO *TGilbert@gilbertlaw.com*
SUBJECT *No Subject*
DATE SENT *Tuesday, Jan 9, 2003 1:10 PM*

Yes.

* * *

FROM *TGilbert@gilbertlaw.com*
TO *MIJB65@aol.com*
SUBJECT *RE: No Subject*
DATE SENT *Thursday, Jan 9, 2003 1:15 PM*

Heading for Traverse City as soon as I wrap up a few things here. I'll find a place to stay there. Let me know where/when to meet you tomorrow. You've got my cell number. Call if you need to talk before that.

* * *

FROM *MIJB65@aol.com*
TO *TGilbert@gilbertlaw.com*
SUBJECT *RE: No Subject*
DATE SENT *Thursday, Jan 9, 1:25 PM*

Drive to the public beach at Monarch. Walk south, and in about fifteen minutes you'll see a downed tree near the water, and just after that, just before the lake curves, some weird little stone sculptures up on the sand. I always walk in the morning around eight. That's where I'll be.

PART THREE

Unfinished Days

JANUARY–JULY, 2003

25

"Stand by Me"

The sky was blue and cloudless, the sun shining – warm on Nora's face, despite the cold air. She came down from the woods, Astro following, and picked up a stone as she did every morning. Light gray, smooth, and egg-shaped, it fit perfectly into the palm of her hand. When she'd walked a while, she took off one glove so she could feel the stone against her skin, as if it could ground her in this place.

She'd been sleepless the night before, knowing Tom was nearby. She lay in bed thinking of him driving from Traverse City to Monarch this morning, on the two-lane highway that wound up and down through woods and farmland. It was a road she loved in every season – especially spring, when, coming down a hill into blooming cherry orchards, it seemed as if huge pink clouds had fallen from the sky. Today the bare branches of the same trees would be iced with snow, the dried grasses in the meadows bent and broken. The big, white farmhouses along the road always looked the same, cozy and inviting, each with an apple-red silo next to the barn, topped by what looked like a big, round piece of red-and-white striped peppermint candy. Would Tom smile at the sight of them as she always did?

The minutes on the digital clock on her bedside table had whispered away – but so slowly. Moonlight shone through the dark windows, revealing icy patterns on the glass. Near four, Nora threw back the comforter and stepped, shuddering, into the frigid air. She wrapped her robe around her, padded down to the kitchen and sat, drinking coffee, the radio turned on low.

In time, night drained from the window and the edges of the meadow grew pink with dawn. Classical music morphed to news: "Citing inspectors' discovery of twelve empty warheads and documents related to a failed nuclear program's attempt at laser enrichment of uranium, critics of the Bush administration's planned invasion argue that the inspections are working and that they should continue under the terms of 1999 UN Security Council Resolution 1284. They contend that if Iraq still possesses illegal weapons it can be peacefully and effectively disarmed by the inspections process, thus making the argument for war moot. But the Bush administration argues instead that the inspection process has demonstrated that Saddam Hussein is not willing to disarm . . ."

Now, at the shoreline, she picked up her pace, imagining Tom starting toward her from Monarch Beach. Astro trotted along beside her, occasionally stopping to bark at the waves, splashing into the water to chase a seagull, oblivious to the freezing water. He ran around her sometimes, leaping at her knees – which meant he wanted her to find a stick and throw it, she knew. But she kept on.

She slowed when she came to the place, near the point, where there were dozens of huge rocks just beyond the shore, set in place by glaciers thousands and thousands of years before. Sun dazzled them this morning, bounced off their shiny wet surfaces. Rocks the size of basketballs or melons could be seen just under the surface of the clear water, some had washed up, tangled in bright green seaweed, along the shore.

Early last summer, she had passed a young man, nineteen or twenty, wrapping them a dozen or so at a time into a blanket, then dragging it down the beach a ways to dump the stones on the sand. She had thought he was making one of the sculptures that had been mysteriously appearing on the beach in the last year or so, but on her way back she saw that he had lined the rocks in vertical groups and was in the process of forming each group into a letter.

She stopped, curious, and asked, "What in the world are you spelling?"

He grinned, bending to ruffle Astro's wet fur. "Will you marry me?" He waved his arm toward the southernmost letter. "See?"

Nora had thought it was an "M," facing the water, but now saw that it was a "W" facing the lookout point at the top of the steep dune, high above them. Next to it, "I-L-L. Then Y-O-U M-A-R."

"How long have you been here?" she asked.

"Couple of hours," he said. "I still have to get the stones for the rest of the letters, so I figure it'll take me at least another two. Man, I'll tell you what. I'm bringing my girlfriend up here this evening. She better say, yes!"

But he knew she would, Nora could tell, and it had made her feel weepy to think of the girl's first look at the words on the beach below, how she would turn to him and in his face see that they were meant for her.

"Take a picture to show your grandchildren," she had said to him, lightly as she could, and walked away, thinking that he couldn't imagine how quickly the time would pass, how the grandfather he'd become would be, in part, the kid he was now: tanned, strong, crazy in love.

Astro barked once, jarring her back into the present. She'd stopped without quite realizing it, and he'd brought a stick and laid it at her feet. She laughed, threw it. Then started forward again, preparing herself to see Tom when she rounded the point.

But he wasn't there. She walked a little further, to the sculptures she'd described, and sat on the hollowed-out tree trunk to wait for him. This was farther than she usually walked, so she was not surprised to see that the sculptures had changed since the last time she passed. They were always different, though they didn't change as much in the winter as they did in summer when sunbathers ventured to this remote part of the beach, came upon them, and stopped to add a few stones or take some away.

There were two today, maybe twenty feet apart. They were shoulder-high, pillar-like, made of big, flat stones laid carefully one upon the other – eight or so at the base, narrowing to a single flat stone with a round boulder perched on top, like a head. Their rounded planes suggested facial features, and they had been turned so that the two figures seemed to be looking at each other across the distance between them, rooted there, yearning.

She looked at her watch. Five past eight. What if Tom had changed his mind? She hadn't checked her e-mails this morning. A message could be there, waiting for her: thinking it through, he'd realized it was not a good idea for him to come.

She fixed her gaze on the waves coming in, hoping the enduring rhythm would help bring her mind into a state of calm. But her thoughts raced and soon she gave up, took the birding binoculars she kept in the pocket of her coat and trained them toward Monarch Beach.

There he was coming toward her, head down against the cold, his hands jammed into the pockets of his parka. He disappeared into a scoop of shoreline then emerged again, jogging now, coming closer and closer until she dropped the binoculars because she didn't need them to see him anymore, and just stood as still as the sculptures behind her until, reaching her, he opened his arms and took her in. Astro barked once, then wagged his tail, observing them with a quizzical expression.

Tom laughed, bent and ruffled his fur. "Fuck, it's cold," he said. "Beautiful, though." He stepped back and looked at her. "You, too. You look beautiful."

"Don't," she said, tears springing to her eyes.

"Sorry," he said, drawing her close again. "Jane, I'm sorry. Nora. What can I do?"

"I have no idea," she said. "Be real? Convince me I'm not invisible?"

"Hey," he said. "What's not real about the two of us on this fucking freezing cold beach together?"

Which made her smile, made her feel real, fully present in her own life for the first time since Claire had gone away.

They sat down on the log and watched the sun play on the water for a long time, Astro at their feet. When she finally spoke, it was to tell him about the young man on the beach spelling with the stones. She wasn't sure why.

"Why didn't we get married?" Tom said, when she was through. "I mean, it wasn't like I didn't know you were the person I wanted to be with forever. I knew that the first day. Why didn't we ever even talk about it?"

"I thought about it sometimes," Nora said. "Thought, eventually, we probably would. But those couple of years after graduation, when everybody else was getting married, Bridget was so miserable about Pete and it seemed to me that our getting married, too, would have made her feel even worse. That was partly it, for me. Then there was the idea of having a wedding. What were the options there? Your parents meeting my family? Not inviting my family at all? I felt so horrible already about just . . . abandoning them the way I did, and to get married and not invite them to the wedding –

"I *felt* married to you – which I convinced myself was what really mattered."

"I know," Tom said. "It never occurred to me that we wouldn't stay together. So, why hurry – right? We had all the time in the world to make it legal." He smiled, ruefully. "Jesus, we were stupid then. Anyway. Tell me what happened with Charlie and Claire."

She stumbled tearfully through an account of all that had happened from Thanksgiving night, when she told Charlie about Bobby serving in Vietnam, to Claire's exit on New Year's Day. "Charlie will never forgive me for driving her away," she said. "Never. He didn't want me to tell her at all. And now I think, he was right. I was being selfish. It was for me, really. Telling. I'd convinced myself I had to tell them the truth. That I was doing it for *them*. But all it did was create total devastation – for everybody."

"Bullshit," Tom said. "Don't run that trip on yourself. You did the right thing, the only thing you could do. They'll see that, eventually."

"Claire, maybe," Nora said. "Charlie?"

"I don't know Charlie," Tom said. "I don't know the two of you together. But you've been married – what? Twenty years? Surely, that counts for a lot. He'll come around. Won't he?"

"The problem is," she said, crying again, "Our whole life together was built on the fact that neither one of us ever wanted to look back – and I can't not look back anymore. Charlie still doesn't want to look back. He's scared to death of it. I don't even know if he can."

"You love him," Tom said.

Nora nodded, covered her face with her hands.

"Then, probably, eventually, you can work things out."

She looked up, looked at him – as familiar to her, as real as her own lost self. "I love Charlie, with Claire. I love the three of us together, the family we've been. But – "

Tom waited.

"I never, ever loved Charlie completely, *just* Charlie, the way I loved you. It was just one more thing I lied about – only that lie was the worst kind, because I was also lying to myself. What am I supposed to do with that?"

An ore boat appeared on the horizon and they sat, quietly, watching it make its slow progress southward. The waves washed in, gray-green, depositing tiny, glittering shards of ice along the shore. It was cold, getting colder. Nora shivered, and Tom drew her close.

"What if you went back with me?" he asked.

She shivered again, though this time not from the cold.

"I've got a studio apartment in the attic of my house. I never rent it; I don't want the hassle. You could use it for a little while. As long you want. The new semester just started. Maybe if you're close, if you could talk to Claire a little bit at a time –

"I know," he said. "There's the problem of what she's going to think about me. But we're not . . . I don't think either one of us is ready to – "

"No," Nora said. "No."

"Then if you're going to tell Claire the truth about everything, don't you think she could believe you were telling the truth when you said she was the reason you'd come back with me? It *would* be the reason."

She didn't think Claire would believe it; she wasn't sure she completely believed it herself. But the thought of seeing Claire, putting her arms around her as she had done when Claire was a little girl, being there if Claire needed to cry or to rage at her –

"Look, if you think it's a bad idea – "

"No," she said. "I mean, what would a good idea be? I can't keep on with Charlie the way we've been, especially knowing we're never going to agree about what's best for Claire in all this. Maybe if I go, maybe if she'll talk to me – "

"So, okay," he said. "Let's give it a try."

He stood, pulled her up – and kept hold of her hand as they walked back to the beach parking lot, where his truck was parked. Astro hopped in first, sniffed the passenger seat thoroughly before Nora could nudge him out of the way and climb in herself.

"He smells Maxine – my dog. She's usually the one who sits there."

"Oh," Nora said, shocked by the realization that she'd be leaving Astro, too, when she went. He sat on the seat between them, looking at her, his head cocked. She reached to scratch behind his ears, which he loved and which usually calmed him, but he ducked away to lay his head on her shoulder, as if to hold her in place, and she put her arm around him and petted him, running her hand repeatedly from the top of his head, down his back.

"It's okay, buddy," she said.

Tom glanced at her, started the engine. It was still early, the town deserted as they drove up Main Street – past the Friendly Tavern and Diane's dark shop. Past the Hummingbird Café, its blue neon coffee cup glowing. The nursing home, where Jo slept.

"Which way?" he asked when they got to the highway.

Nora directed him and he turned right, onto the gray ribbon of road she'd traveled countless times toward home. Yesterday's snow, still untouched, sparkled in the fields and on the boughs of the pines.

"Beautiful country," Tom said, and she nodded, her eyes burning with tears.

Charlie was in the kennel run, bent over, a half-dozen dogs jumping up all around him, begging for the treats he always kept in his jacket pocket. He stood when the truck pulled into the driveway, watched as Astro bound out of it and headed toward him, his tail wagging wildly. Then Nora.

"I know what you're going to tell me," he said, when she reached him. "Don't bother. Just go. Okay? Just goddamn it, go."

"I'm going to Bloomington to try to talk to Claire. That's all. Charlie – "

But he turned and walked away from her, Astro trotting behind him.

Inside, she was surprised to see how completely she'd cleaned the kitchen before she left to meet Tom: every surface clear, the dishwasher loaded – as if she'd known she would not have time to clean it up after her walk, as she usually did. She paused briefly at the door to the sunroom, thinking the geraniums probably needed water – but why bother? Once she was gone, Charlie would either care for them or not. So she kept on, upstairs, past Jo's bedroom, where Charlie's books and music CDs were in a clutter on the bedside table, to their own room at the end of the hall.

They'd borrowed a suitcase from Diane when they took Claire to Bloomington last summer, Nora suddenly remembered, and there was nothing to pack her clothes in but a couple of beach totes and an old pink duffel bag Claire used for sleepovers when she was a little girl. She filled them quickly, with whatever was at hand. Last, she tucked in her favorite picture of Claire – seven years old, wearing overalls and a baseball cap, her two front teeth missing. A smile on her face as big as the sun.

Nora slept most of the way back to Bloomington, waking now and then, disoriented – not by the sight of Tom at the wheel beside her, so familiar and dear, but in remembering, a heartbeat later, that it had not always been this way. They talked a little when she surfaced – Tom talked. He had a second apartment, he said, above his garage. He told her about Kate and her son, Cody, who lived there – rent-free after he realized that Kate made just enough money, waitressing, to go back to school if rent weren't an issue.

"I figured, a couple of years – what's the big deal? It's not like I need the money. She's a good kid, a hard worker. And I get a kick out of Cody. He's eight. He loves to hang out in the garage and hand me shit when I'm working on my cars. Or sit on my motorcycle. I get him root beer in bottles and keep it in the little fridge out there. So, you know, we can have a few beers together."

He drove steadily, stopping only once at a gas station, where they fueled up, took a bathroom break, and got sandwiches to eat on the road. Late in the afternoon, he turned on the radio, found an NPR station.

"Bulking up for Baghdad," the announcer said, and launched into a story about the troop build-up in the Persian Gulf. Attacking Iraq now was all the more crucial in light of North Korea's recent claim to possess nuclear weapons, according to President Bush – this despite analysts' warnings that North Korea had far greater capacity to wreak havoc than Saddam Hussein, even if the inspectors did turn up the weapons of mass destruction that so far remained elusive.

"Fucking asshole," Tom said.

Entering Bloomington, they saw the occasional antiwar bumper sticker. "War Is Not the Answer," "Think! It's Patriotic," "Yee-haw Is Not a Foreign Policy," "What Would Jesus Bomb?" Kids driving, mostly – stuff piled high in the back seats. Bass thumping. Pulled up to a stoplight, you could hear it – even with the windows closed. Heading back for the new semester.

Claire and Dylan might be on the road, too, coming back from his home in Cincinnati. Never in a million years could she have imagined that a time would come when she'd have no idea about her daughter's plans. Thank God for Dylan, she thought. At least she wasn't alone. He was a good boy, solid – and he loved her. He'd help her through all this. She wondered how he had explained Claire's sudden appearance to his family, this girlfriend they'd never met. Had he told them the truth about why she'd come; if he had, would it make them think Claire was somehow . . . unsuitable? Had Claire told him everything? Nora hoped she had.

They were quiet driving the last few miles; darkness had fallen by the time they turned onto Kirkwood Avenue. Students roamed up and down the street, some hand-in-hand, some in groups, laughing, probably catching up with each other after break. A boy whizzed by on a bicycle, his head bent into the cold. Tom turned onto North Grant Street, drove a few blocks, and pulled into the driveway of a wood-frame house. There was a light on in the upstairs apartment, one illuminating the narrow iron stairway that hugged the side of the house.

"I turned the heat on before I left," he said. "In case – "

"Thanks," Nora said.

He opened his door. "I don't know about you, but I'm starving again. Let's go to my place first; I'll fix us something. Then I'll take you upstairs."

Maxine bounded to the door when they entered, wagging her tail wildly. She barked half-heartedly at the sight of Nora, but leaned into her hand when Nora bent to scratch her ears. Then sniffed up and down her jeans. Astro, Nora thought, missing him.

"We're not talking gourmet here," Tom said, retrieving deli packages, a loaf of bread and two Miller Lites from the refrigerator.

"Good." She laughed. "You being a gourmet cook could've tipped me right over the edge."

He fixed them turkey sandwiches, spooned coleslaw from a plastic container, set out a bag of chips. He held up one of the beers and cocked his head slightly toward her. She nodded, took it from him, popped the tab. She couldn't remember the last time she'd had a beer – she and Charlie always drank wine – but it tasted good, familiar. The smell of it brought back Saturday night parties at the Sigma Chi house, Tom's room there, the old farmhouse Pete rented out in the country, picnics in Brown County – everything.

There was a school picture of a little boy on the refrigerator, some drawings of cars and motorcycles, one of a man and a boy – stick figures with big smiling faces, under a yellow sun.

"Cody," Tom said, when he noticed her looking at them. "The kid I told you about. I have a whole drawer full of pictures he's made for me."

"He loves you," she said.

"Yeah. He does."

"There was a whole unit in my child psych class on kids' pictures, how you could know so much about them by looking at what they drew. The size of people, where they're placed. You can see what they're noticing, too." She smiled. "When Claire was maybe five, she started drawing all of her people with these gargantuan eyelashes. She went through this hilarious phase of drawing dogs with little circles on their butts with poop falling out of them."

Tom laughed. "What's she like? Claire?"

Nora showed him Claire's senior picture, which she kept in her wallet.

"She looks like you," he said.

"Her face," Nora said. "But she's got long limbs, like Charlie's. She's got his hands, too – beautiful, beautiful hands, with long fingers and perfect oval nails she keeps cut short because she plays the cello. Freckles, which you can't see in the picture. She blushes when she gets excited or upset, which she hates, even though it actually makes her look prettier. She cries at the sight of a hurt animal, but never, ever when she's hurt herself. Then she withdraws, broods."

"Like you used to," Tom said.

It startled her to realize that this was true. "I hated to cry," she said. "I still do. I feel – stripped away."

Silence fell between them; Maxine watched Tom attentively.

He smiled. "Think she wants me to tell her what she's supposed to do with you?"

"There's a sixty-four thousand dollar question," she said.

"Yeah, well, my guess is it won't be the last. What am I supposed to do with you, Jane?"

"Nora," she said. "Tom, I need to be Nora. For Claire – "

"Right," he said. "Of course – "

"She'll need that, I think. No matter what happens."

He nodded. "It's pretty. Nora. I'll get used to it. Come on," he said. "I'll take you up to the apartment."

She held the rail following him upstairs because she felt light-headed, faint. He opened the door, told her what she needed to know, then handed her the key ring, which also had a key to his house on it. "It's pretty spare in here," he said. "Feel free to come down to the house whenever you want." He hesitated a long moment, his hand on the doorknob. Then he was gone.

The space was spare, as he had said: just one room, a kitchenette, and a tiny bathroom. There was a foldout couch, which he'd had made up for her, an armchair and end table, a dresser. A Formica dinette table and two mismatched chairs. The walls were white, the ceiling was sloped low on two sides with dormers built into it, long window seats below, which Tom had shown her could be used for extra storage. It was exactly the kind of attic refuge she'd read about in books, coveted, when she was a girl, Nora thought – a room to dream in, to while away lazy afternoons imagining what your grown-up life would turn out to be.

26

"Hazy Shade of Winter"

She slept poorly and missed the lake when she woke – knowing it was there, knowing she could step outside and walk across the meadow to the path through the forest that would take her to the shoreline in moments. She missed the sight of Astro, all coiled energy, bursting into the morning.

It was still dark outside. The clock on the bedside table said six o'clock: the time she always woke up. Tom left for work around eight-thirty, he'd told her. He'd always hated getting up in the morning, she remembered. Always slept till the last possible moment, then dragged himself from bed like a gut-shot bear, grumbling, till he'd had his coffee. Had he ever gotten used to it?

She got up, dressed. She put her few things away, sat down in the armchair, stood up again and paced the little apartment. Move, her body told her. So she slipped out, tiptoed down the stairs, and set out walking. She might have been Jane, she thought, hurrying down the street after Bridget on that long-ago night, a girl huddled against the cold, hurrying toward what would turn out to be her life. She let her feet carry her to the place at the edge of campus where she had stood, watching Bridget disappear into the trees. Then across University Avenue, up a brick path through the woods toward where she remembered the ROTC building had stood.

Nora didn't expect to see it, of course. But she was surprised not to find some evidence that it had been there once – a flat place, perhaps, a cluster of trees obviously younger than those around them, or even a new building replacing it. She picked a spot near where it must have been, stood, waited to feel – what? But she felt nothing, just cold. And a little foolish, though she told herself this wasn't something she had planned to do. She continued on the path, which eventually wound its way to Third Street, where the big fraternity houses loomed like castles in the gauzy light of the streetlamps.

There was a Starbucks open on University Avenue, and she bought a latte to take back to the apartment. Once there, she crept back up the stairs and closed the door behind her. She didn't turn on a light. She sat down in the armchair and sipped her coffee, watching the sky slowly lighten. At eight-twenty, she heard the engine of a car start and looked out the window to see the little boy, Cody, run across the yard, his backpack bumping, his arms waving – heading for Tom like a ball for a glove. Kate was out of the car, scraping the ice from the windshield.

Not exactly a kid, Nora thought. She looked to be in her early thirties, dark and slim, with a smile so dazzling that Nora could see it from where she sat. Tom walked toward her, his hand on Cody's shoulder, Maxine zooming back and forth between them until Tom reached the car and settled Cody into the backseat. He and Kate stood talking for a moment. She glanced upward, toward the apartment. Tom nodded.

Was there something more than friendship between them, Nora suddenly wondered? Tom hadn't said there was, but he hadn't said there wasn't, either. Or, if not Kate, someone else? Someone who might also know he'd gone up to Michigan and was waiting right now to hear whether or not she had come back with him? A woman he'd expect her to get to know, to be with? How would she be able to do that?

Maxine barked once when she heard Nora turn the key in the lock, but greeted her, tail wagging, as if it were perfectly normal for her to be here. Tom had left a note on the kitchen table. "Made coffee. Not much in the refrigerator, but help yourself to whatever you can find. How about lunch? If I don't hear from you, I'll meet you at noon at the Uptown Cafe. It's on Kirkwood, near the old Indiana Theater. Take care."

Nora poured a cup of coffee. No half-and-half in the refrigerator and the coffee was strong; Tom always made coffee too strong. But she drank it anyway, wandering through the empty house. The living room, with its big flat-screen TV, wall-to-ceiling bookshelves flanking the fireplace, black leather couches, and a deep, comfortable black leather reading chair. A guest room doubled as a study, with more bookshelves and the old oak desk they'd bought together when Tom started law school. A clinically neat bathroom – and in the medicine cabinet, no evidence of anyone but Tom. His bedroom, spare – and, in the closet, no evidence of anyone but him, either.

Which didn't necessarily mean anything, she knew.

Resolutely, she returned to Tom's study, picked up the phone and called Diane.

"My God! Nora! I've been trying to get you for an hour!" Diane said, when she answered. "Did you get my message? Didn't Mo tell you when she got to the clinic?" Then rushed on, before Nora could answer. "He's here! The baby! Carah went into the hospital around midnight last night and he was born at six this morning. Henry Wade, don't you love that? Oh, my God. You won't believe how beautiful he is!

"Nora?" she said, after a few moments had passed. "Are you there?"

"I am," Nora said. "But not . . . I mean – Diane, I'm at Tom's house, in Bloomington."

"What?" Diane said, after a long, stunned silence.

"I didn't plan to come. I'd made up my mind not even to e-mail Tom anymore because – well, I don't need to explain that. But Charlie's been horrible since Claire left. He won't help me with Claire, he won't even talk to me, and I got so, I don't know, distraught that I e-mailed him. Tom. He came. It was his idea for me to go back with him and see if I could get Claire to talk to me.

"I'm not staying with him," Nora added. "I mean, in his house. He's got an attic apartment. I'm staying there. Anyway. I should have called when I got here last night. But – Charlie didn't tell Mo?"

"If he did, he swore her to secrecy because she didn't tell me. And she seemed okay when I talked to her last night, not like – but Nora, why didn't you tell me how bad things were with Charlie before now?"

"I don't know, I couldn't. And you've been so excited about the baby," Nora said. "I didn't want to spoil that with the stupid mess I've gotten myself into. And now I've – "

"Don't even go there," Diane said. "Believe me, nothing could spoil how I feel about this baby. Or Carah. Nothing! I'm just – sorry. I mean, that all this is so hard. Have you called her yet? Claire?"

"No. I don't even know if she'll talk to me. What if she – "

"One thing at a time, Nora. Call her, then – "

"You don't think she'll talk to me, do you? Which, okay, didn't even occur to me till right now. God. I should have called you before I left."

"Because you think I'd have talked you out of going?" Diane asked. "I'm not sure I would have tried – "

"Because you don't think Charlie will ever forgive me, no matter what I do from here on in? That he even can forgive me?"

"I don't know what I think," Diane said. "Except that you've got to find a way to talk to Claire and at least you're doing something – and whatever happens because of it will . . . happen. Then you'll know.

"Meanwhile, you need to stay in touch with me. I mean it. And don't think there's any chance of ditching me if things don't work out so well. There's no fucking way under the sun I'm letting you do that. Call Claire. Now. Give me Tom's number," she added.

Nora gave it to her.

"Okay, then. Call me tonight and tell me what happened."

When they'd hung up, Nora sat, the phone in her hand, until the dial tone reverted to loud beeping. Then she set it in the cradle and sat, trying to work up the nerve to call Claire. It was still early, which meant she might still be in her room. Or she could have spent the night with Dylan, in his apartment. For all Nora knew, she might spend every night there. Maybe they'd gotten up early this morning to drive back from Cincinnati and were still on the road.

She'd call Charlie first, she decided. She knew he wouldn't answer, but it hadn't occurred to her that it would be her own voice she would hear on the answering machine, speaking to her from her own kitchen.

You've reached the Quillens . . .

She opened her mouth to leave a message, but her voice wouldn't work and she pressed the "off" button on the phone, paced a while, then took a deep breath and called Claire's cell phone number.

"Hey!" Claire's voice said. "Leave a message. I'll call you back."

"Honey, I'm in Bloomington," she managed to say. "Please. Can we talk?"

She left Tom's number, realizing too late that if Claire called and she wasn't there, she'd hear his voice on the answering machine.

"It's not me," he said, when she told him this at lunch. "It's one of those robot voices. So you don't have to worry about that. But, you know, you could also just go over to the dorm. See if she'll come down and talk to you. Or leave a note."

"A note," she said.

"Yeah. Remember? That thing people did before e-mail. Something simple: 'I love you. I'm here. Can we talk?'

"I realize I don't know jack shit about dealing with kids," he added.

"Right. I'm the expert," she said.

He grinned. "A joke. Promising."

Surprising herself, she grinned back at him.

"Come on," he said. "I'll show you my office. You can write a note there."

It was spacious, with a window overlooking the square, which was still busy with workers going to and from lunch, the occasional shopper, lawyers shivering across to the courthouse in their suit jackets. There was a wall of oak file cabinets, another of floor-to-ceiling shelves lined with law books. His diplomas, framed in black, were hung above his desk.

He handed her a legal pad and pen and gestured toward one of the client chairs. "Simple," he said. "Remember?"

He'd always been good at that, she thought: simple – and wrote more or less what he had suggested in the restaurant. *Claire. I've come to Bloomington hoping that we can talk. Would you please call me at this number? I love you.* XOXO *Mom*

"Okay," she said. "Do you have any plain envelopes? Without your return address?"

"Oh," Tom said – and came up with one.

Nora made her way back toward campus and through the university gates, threading her way toward Claire's dorm among throngs of students bundled up in bright parkas, on their way to class. She kept an eye out: any one of them might be her daughter. But she reached the dorm without seeing Claire, left the envelope with the desk attendant, and walked back to Tom's house to wait for her call. But no call came.

In the next days, she walked Maxine for hours at a time, hoping for a glimpse of Claire, a chance to catch her off-guard and see something revealing in Claire's first sight of her. And Claire loved dogs. Surely, she wouldn't be able to resist bending to pet Maxine and ruffle her ears. One vulnerable moment, Nora thought. Just that.

She stopped sometimes and stood in the trees near Ballantine Hall, where virtually everyone had at least one class each semester. Sometimes she sat on a bench near the music building, listening for the sound of cellos, or hovered near the Union. She felt as invisible among the students as she had felt on that summer day in People's Park, before her life had begun to unravel.

27

"High out of Time"

Tom had bought his house because of the three-and-a-half-car garage, he said – so big it took up most of the backyard. Inside, there was a stereo, cable TV, a little refrigerator full of beer and soda. A workbench, shelves of automotive products. Mechanics toolboxes with the tools fanned out neatly in the drawers. The Corvette, the GTO, the truck, the Harley, each one gleaming. Pete had lived in the apartment above it for a long time, until his inheritance allowed him to buy a small house of his own, and Tom had rented it until he decided he didn't like people living so close to him. It had remained empty until he offered it to Kate.

She was waiting tables at The Regulator when Tom met her. Cody's father had disappeared with another woman, one without a child, and she was living with another single mother with whom she traded childcare, taking a class a semester, barely making ends meet. More than once, she'd come home after a late shift to find Cody and her housemate Rosemary's daughter asleep in front of the television and Rosemary drunk, in bed with a man she'd been seeing whom Kate did not like or trust. Her parents who had plenty of money refused to give her any help at all.

"She'd sinned, having Cody 'out of wedlock,'" Tom told Nora. "If she can't make it through school, if she can't get decent childcare for Cody and the two of them are driving around on icy roads in a crap car with bald tires, hey, it's not their problem." So he'd given Kate the use of the apartment, bought her a decent used car, and found her a day job flexible enough to allow her to take several classes each semester, for which he paid the tuition.

"And just in case you think anything between us but that . . ." he added, "there's not. Never has been. I made up my mind a long time ago to never date a woman too young to remember Che Guevara. I'm serious," he said, when Nora laughed. "She's old enough to be my daughter."

As for what Kate knew about Nora, Tom said he had told her that they'd been close in college and had rediscovered one another when Nora's daughter started her freshman year at IU this fall. Said daughter was having some difficulties. That's why Nora was here.

All this had been to prepare Nora for dinner at Kate's house that night.

When they arrived, Cody barreled into Tom for a hug, then turned to look at Nora and said, "My mom told me you knew Tom since before I was born!"

"Cody!" Kate said, casting an apologetic look toward Nora.

"It's true," he said. "You – "

"It is, indeed, true." Tom grinned. "And no secret. My friend Nora is as old as I am."

"Wait a minute." Nora grinned back at him. "I'm one whole year younger than Tom – and he'd better not forget it."

"How old – "

"Stop!" Kate said, but she was laughing. "Sorry. He's just a little obsessed with age right now. Cody, show Tom and Nora your new *Rescue Hero* while I get dinner on the table. I know they're just dying to see it."

He took each of them by the hand and led them to the bedroom he and Kate shared – everything in it a little boy's bedroom, from the shelves of toys and books to the twin beds covered with Star Wars bedspreads.

"What are *Rescue Heroes*?" Nora asked.

"Like 9/11," Cody said. "The guys who save everybody. Tom got me this." He took a truck from one of the shelves. "It's the URV."

"Ultimate Robot Vehicle," Tom explained.

"Robots," Nora said. "Cool!"

Cody beamed. "Yeah. Here's my new guy." He held up an action figure dressed like a fireman, put him in the cockpit of the vehicle, and picked up a remote control device. "See. This URV goes anywhere. Even in very dangerous territory." He pressed a button to make the vehicle move across the floor and narrated a series of imaginary events voice that made Nora remember Claire playing with her *My Little Pony* figures at the same age.

"You guys want to play?" Cody asked.

"Another time, buddy," Tom said. "Right now I'm headed for your mom's pot roast. I'm starving."

Kate gathered them at a prettily set table, and served up the meal.

She smiled when Nora said she thought the apartment was charming.

"Garage sales," she said.

She had a knack for putting things together. Except for the single bedroom and a bathroom, the apartment was one big room, with lemon-yellow walls hung with art posters and a cozy chintz sofa that Kate told Nora she'd slipcovered herself. She was studying textile design, something she'd been fascinated with since she was a child, watching her grandmother embroider and needlepoint. Her study corner in the apartment was cluttered with brightly colored yarns and bits of beautiful fabric. A basket of knitting sat on the floor, next to a cranberry easy chair, an estate sale find. She made extra money making sweaters and IU afghans that she sold on consignment in a knitting shop.

"She likes you," Tom said later, walking her to the steps of her apartment.

"You thought she wouldn't?"

"No. It's just, Kate – "

"Adores you," Nora finished for him. "She's worried I'm going to hurt you somehow."

"She's attached to me." He smiled. "It's nice, kind of like having my own daughter. And, yeah, she's probably worried about me getting hurt. But I figure you can't really get into something like we've gotten into without somebody getting hurt, can you? I'm not hurt, so far. And you're okay – well, as okay as you can be under the circumstances. Right?"

"I am. I think. So far."

"Well, then," he said.

Nora hugged herself against the chill, watched the frosty clouds of her own breath mingle with Tom's in the darkness. He was hatless, his bare hands shoved into his jacket pockets. But they stood there until Tom finally bent, kissed her lightly on the cheek, then took her shoulders and turned them toward the stairs. "You're freezing," he said. "Go in. I'll see you tomorrow."

Alone in the attic apartment, Nora couldn't shake the image of the four of them at the dinner table; anyone looking in would have assumed they were a family, she thought – a happy family enjoying each other at the end of the day. She and Kate talking about domestic things; Cody bending Tom's ear about *Rescue Heroes* and basketball. She looked across the yard to Kate's lit windows and imagined her putting Cody to bed, then settling into her studies.

She was old enough to be his daughter, Tom had said. She was old enough to be their daughter. If they'd stayed together there might be a girl like Kate, made of the two of them – loved by them as deeply and fiercely as she and Charlie loved Claire. It took her breath away to think of it. The image of such a girl was so strong it seemed like a memory from a parallel life, one that had been playing out all these years while she lived her life in Michigan.

How would she be different if she had come back? And Tom? He seemed, essentially, unchanged to her. His silver hair, his aged face still caught her by surprise sometimes. The hint of sadness that surfaced now and then, his resigned acceptance of the world as it was pained her, though she told herself such feelings were inevitable to growing older. All those years she had not known him pained her, too. Who he had been in his thirties and forties? What had he thought and dreamed? How and when had he remembered her? She'd filled up those years in her own life loving Charlie and Claire, yet the time seemed somehow insubstantial to her now, a future in which the three of them would be a happy family again as lost as the life she might have had with Tom.

She had called Charlie several times, but he hadn't answered the phone, hadn't responded to the messages she'd left – or to the letter she'd sent that first week. As for Claire, she'd finally sent an e-mail that said, "Mom. Please stop calling me. I can't talk to you now. I really can't. I have no idea what to say."

"Now," Diane said, when Nora called to report this, in tears. "She's saying can't talk to you now, she's not saying she can't ever talk to you. I know it's hard, but, trust me, you just need to leave her be."

She continued to take Maxine for long walks every morning, but she avoided campus, where she might run into Claire, exploring the neighborhoods that fanned out in every direction. Blocks of student housing, giving way to blocks of neatly kept bungalows, enclaves of stately homes where professors and town professionals lived their lives. Walking back down Kirkwood Street, toward Tom's, she often stopped to talk to Pete, who sat in his usual place strumming his guitar, pretty much regardless of the weather.

"Jane," he'd say – and she allowed it.

She'd sit down beside him and they'd talk awhile, Maxine leaning her head into Pete's leg, looking up at him, until he set his guitar down to scratch her ears. He was the one she could talk to about Bridget, maybe because it was the two of them who'd loved her best, who'd feel in some way responsible for what had happened to her for the rest of their lives.

He had loved Bridget, he assured Nora again and again. He regretted how things had turned out between them, she was just so – he didn't know how to explain how it got to be that when he was with her he felt like he was drowning.

"You guys were better," he said. "You and Tom."

"Because I wanted to drown, I wanted to lose myself in someone else," Nora said. "Which wasn't good, in the end."

"Yeah, well, it was still better. You guys were friends, you know? Easy together. You're easy together now."

They were – and in the continuing silence from Charlie and Claire, Nora was left to live in the present moment with him, to be drawn into his life. Most days she met him for lunch someplace near the square; they went to movies together; hung out with his friends on pool night at The Regulator. They went to movies, watched IU basketball on TV. They talked. Tom was affectionate toward her, linking arms with her as they walked, sometimes kissing her lightly on her cheek or forehead, pulling her into a quick embrace when it was time for her to go back to her apartment each evening.

There, Bridget returned to her, in dreams. The dream of Bridget falling backward into the flames; the dream of following her that Christmas Eve, beneath the black bowl of sky. But happy dreams, too, bits and pieces of their lives all jumbled up so that time and place made their own history. Bridget's grin, her laugh, her voice.

Alone in the attic apartment, Nora had conversations with Bridget in her head.

You shouldn't have followed me that night. It was stupid. I didn't want to be saved, so how could you have saved me?

I couldn't just let you go when I knew –

You should have. Look what a fucking mess you made of things.

Not a total mess. Bridget, you don't know Claire.

You wouldn't either if –

Don't say that. I can't think about that.

Of course you can't. You never could let yourself think about anything that might get in the way of who you thought you wanted to be. To be honest, Jane, it used to drive me crazy the way you always tried to hide where you came from. Did you think Tom and Pete and I didn't figure it out? Did you think we'd care?

I was afraid . . .

You were always afraid, you haven't changed. So are you ever going to do anything about it? You know something? I'm glad Pete saw you. I'm glad everything fell apart because maybe, maybe you'll open your freaking eyes and see what you've seen all along. You hold all the cards with Tom, you always held all the cards with Tom. You decide.

But I did decide. I chose Charlie.

Bridget went silent then, leaving her alone to contemplate the wreck she'd made of her life, the hurt that could never be undone. "Who loves me?" Charlie had asked that night in the Hummingbird Café when she had told him everything. "Isn't that the real problem? I don't know who you are."

The first week of February, Nora sat at the bar at The Regulator, nursing a bottle of beer, half-watching Tom play pool with Pete, half-watching Colin Powell on the television mounted in the corner of the room. The contrast fascinated her: Tom, in jeans and a sweatshirt, leaning over the pool table, cue poised, utterly absorbed in the game; Powell, in his dark suit and red power tie, leaning into the camera, his index finger raised in accusation.

"This terror network is teaching its operatives how to produce Ricin and other poisons," Powell said. "Let me remind you how Ricin works. Less than a pinch – imagine a pinch of salt . . ." He paused, his eyes narrowing. "Less than a pinch of Ricin – eating just this amount in your food – would cause shock, followed by circulatory failure. Death comes within seventy-two hours, and there is no antidote. There is no cure. It is fatal."

"This is such total bullshit," Nora said. "He should be ashamed."

The woman sitting next to her raised her beer, tipped it toward Nora. "Asshole," she said.

When the pool game was over, Tom pulled up a bar stool and sat down. "Goddamn it," he said, cheerfully. "He beats me every fucking time. Look at him!" He nodded toward Pete, who'd taken on a burly guy in a Harley tee shirt and was moving methodically around the table, making one perfect shot after another. "He's unconscious."

"He's got a little more time to practice than most people," Nora said.

"True." Tom laughed. "You've got a point there."

On the television, Colin Powell continued cataloging the imminent dangers to the U.S. The camera panned the curved tables where the UN representatives sat, listening intently, then returned to him. "Given Saddam Hussein's history of aggression," he said, "given what we know of his grandiose plans . . ."

They watched awhile, then the woman sitting next to them said, "The truth is, 9/11 was the best thing that ever happened to them. You've got to admit it's brilliant how they've used it to scare the shit out of people so they can do whatever they want."

Tom shrugged, signaled for another beer. "People are idiots," he said.

Powell's voice disappeared into the buzz of conversation, the laughter, the Eagles playing on the sound system. "Desperado." Nora remembered driving cross-country alone in one of the awful beater cars she owned after leaving Tom, listening to that song on the radio. When, exactly – or where – she couldn't remember. Just the chronic ache of loneliness she lived with then, the sense that she belonged nowhere, with no one. That there would never again be a place where she might feel at home. She had turned off the radio that day, driven on for miles in absolute silence. Afterward, if she listened to the radio, she tuned to a station with music that carried no memories with it. Then all those years with Charlie, the radio tuned to classical music on NPR.

She thought of him now, saw him sitting in his favorite chair, oblivious to everything except Beethoven or the Bach *Goldberg Variations* he so loved booming from the stereo, as loud as he wanted it to be – and Charlie loved music loud. It was a trait Nora had always found odd and endearing in a person who lived so quietly, most comfortable in the shadows, and some part of her longed for the countless evenings she'd spent sitting near him, a book in her lap, abandoned to the beauty of the music surrounding them.

"You got quiet," Tom said, walking home. "I know. What's to say? Jesus, though, I'm beginning to feel like I could be a bona fide revolutionary this time. You know what we need here, don't you? The draft. Call up all those chicken-shit Congressmen's kids and the kids of all these corporate CEOs set to make billions of dollars on government contracts. Call up the fucking Bush twins, for that matter – "

Nora stopped. "It's not that. Iraq."

Tom stopped, too. "What then?" he asked.

"I was thinking about Charlie," she said. "Thinking he was probably listening to music while that speech was going on, probably still is, right now, and maybe he'll turn the late news on and hear about it, but probably he won't. And he's always going to be that way. It's a big part of what I loved about him, you know? Our world together was so small and safe. But that's not really love, is it?

"Or not enough. Not now. Even if I wanted to go back, even if I wanted to try to work things out, the fact remains that I lied to him about who I was. I can't fix that; I don't think he can forgive me for it. I lied to myself, marrying him when I knew how I would always, always feel about you. Which is the real problem, isn't it? That still I love you. That I can't lie to myself about it anymore. I can't – "

"Jane." He drew her to him, brushed her lips with his fingertips to quiet her, then kissed her – and she fell back into her body, came home to it, only then realizing, how fully she had been away.

28

"The Sunshine of Your Love"

On a shelf in Tom's basement there was a box marked "Jane," filled with the things she'd left behind the night of the bombing. Her birth certificate, her high school yearbooks, her college diploma. The leather ring binder she'd splurged on her freshman year, worn from years of use, neatly organized with notes from her last semester of classes – and extra packages of paper, narrow-ruled. Yellowed with age. A dozen or so battered, annotated paperbacks she had particularly loved, an odd assortment – everything from *Pride and Prejudice* to *Black Like Me*. The hardback copy of *Little Women* a favorite uncle had given her for Christmas when she was in the fourth grade, its thin pages worn as soft as cloth from reading and rereading it. The ratty, washed-out IU sweatshirt she'd bought when she was a freshman and had never been able to part with.

Photographs. Fraternity dances: Tom and herself, Bridget and Pete, arms wound around each other, grinning. Pictures of herself with Bridget mugging for the camera, time passing in the clothes they wore – wheat jeans and madras shirts to embroidered bell-bottom jeans and hippy blouses. One Bridget had taken at Bean Blossom: Tom standing behind Jane, his arms wrapped around her, Lake Lemon shimmering in the background, ringed by trees in autumn color. They leaned into the frame of the picture, sun-struck, smiling.

There were Bobby's letters and the letter Daniel Pettus had sent to her when her student teaching was done, the brown, ruled paper it was written on crinkled at the edges. There were class pictures from every year she'd taught, the reports on ancient Egypt she'd meant to grade over Christmas break, still in the canvas bag she carried back and forth to school each day. The sight of the children's handwriting, their voices on the page brought them back to her so vividly – and the sorrow she had felt at disappearing so suddenly and completely from their lives. They were grown now, well into their thirties. What had become of them?

She and Tom had kissed their way home that first night, hesitating only for a moment before going inside. "Jesus," he said. "I feel like I did that day I went over to the dorm to see if you really wanted to go out with me."

She smiled. "I did want to," she said. "What I'm thinking about is that first time, at Pete's. Remember that?"

He kissed her again, turned the key in the lock. "Oh, yeah," he said. "I remember."

They made love, slept, finally, in each other's arms – Maxine, curled up at the foot of the bed, having observed them intently through it all, her head cocked, as if to say, "What's going on here, anyway?"

The next morning, Tom had brought the box up from the basement and set it before her. Opening it, taking out the objects one by one, Nora felt like an archaeologist of her own life. Each thing Tom had saved, an artifact that might have been lost forever. Each one a small, tangible piece of what her life once was – and might have been.

The sight of the children's handwriting had brought back winter mornings in her classroom, the sense of anticipation she'd always felt as the yellow school buses pulled into the parking lot. The pure joy of the children entering the room, surrounding her like a flock of beautiful birds. She remembered in her body the utter confidence she had felt teaching, the knowledge that being with the children was the single thing in her whole life that was absolutely good and right – and she was struck with an overpowering sense of loss for what she had believed would be her life's work. Washed with longing for that place and time, the sense of purpose and possibility she'd felt in her classroom, the lives of her students in her hands.

"You can teach again, if you want to," Tom said, when she dissolved into tears trying to explain this. "You have a savings account, remember? And nearly thirty years of interest on whatever was in it. More than enough to take any classes you'd need to take to renew your license."

She was shocked to realize the money was still there, taken aback by the possibility of resuming a teaching career after all these years – and cried harder.

"Jane," Tom said. "Nora. Nora. You can do anything. Nothing. I don't care. I'm just saying the money's there for when you need it."

"But I don't know what I want to do. I can't even imagine – "

"You don't have to. You know you've got the money; we'll go from there."

We, Nora thought – and remembered how, to Tom, they had been "we" from the start.

"I'm coming," Diane said, when Nora finally told her that she'd moved down to Tom's house. "I mean, is it okay if I come? I'm going to Chicago to see Henry this weekend, how about if I come down afterward? Nora, we need to talk."

When she got there late Sunday afternoon, she hugged Nora hard. Letting go, she held out her hand to Tom. "Listen," she said. "I'm not here to try to drag her back to Michigan, in case that's what you're thinking."

"No," he said. "No, I didn't think that."

But something changed in his face that made Nora think that, until that moment, he had. "Can I get you a beer?" he asked Diane. "A glass of wine?"

"A beer would be fabulous. First, though – " She took a small photo album from the depths of her bag and held it out to him. "You'll want to fully admire Henry, the wonder-child."

He laughed, paged through it obediently, Nora peering over his shoulder.

"Clearly a genius," he pronounced.

"He's perfect." Nora smiled.

"Well," Diane said. "I knew it was the right thing to drive down here and see you." And had them laughing within minutes, telling about Mo's encounter with her ex-husband, Bob.

"They instantly took against each other, no surprise, but I'm sitting there watching the two of them glower at each other, thinking, Hey, Bob, asshole, you're the one who dropped in with no invitation, why don't you just get the hell out of here, and it suddenly strikes me as hilarious that the two great loves of my life are Republicans. Not that Bob was exactly – oh, well. You know what I mean. I married him, for whatever that's worth. Though I was pregnant," she added, to Tom.

"Still. I do vaguely remember being in love with him. Or misplaced lust. Whatever.

"Mo's coming around, though," she went on. "God knows, I've been working on her night and day. Even she admits the Colin Powell thing was a debacle. And the Brits and their phony dossier? Totally absurd. I'll tell you, though. Northern Michigan is full of 'patriots.' Every other car with a flag stuck on it somewhere and those idiotic bumper stickers."

"They're everywhere," Tom said.

They walked to the square for dinner, Diane and Tom still talking about Iraq, Nora happy at the new sound their familiar voices mingling made.

"I just needed to see you with him," Diane said to Nora over coffee in Tom's kitchen after he'd gone to work the next morning. "I couldn't think about you, I couldn't think about anything until – " Her voice went wobbly. "I like him. Tom. You're different with him. It's like you're standing in the sun. But what are you going to do about it?"

"I don't know what to do. All I know is I can't even think about walking away from him again, I don't want to think about it. But I don't know what that means. And I feel so horrible about – " Nora took a deep breath, blew it out. "Tell me about Charlie," she said.

"There's not much to tell," Diane said. "He won't talk about it, not even to Mo. He goes on through the days the way he always has, except you're not there. He keeps Astro with him all the time, that's the only thing different. It's awful, you know? Not that I'm saying – "

"What? It's not my fault? I should go back? It is my fault; I should go back. I have to, eventually. I know that. But – "

"It's Claire I'm worried about," Diane said. "That's the other reason I came. She won't talk to you, I have no idea what she and Charlie talk about, if they've talked about this at all, and both Mo and I are afraid she'll come home for spring break and be shocked by the shape he's in. Plus, somebody needs to see her, see how she is.

"Do you think she'd talk to me?" she went on. "I mean, what if I just call her? I'm her co-godmother, for Pete's sake. What's she going to do, hang up on me?"

"She might," Nora said.

"Well, if she does, she does."

"Go for it," Nora said. "It can't hurt to give it a try."

Diane took out her cell phone, hit Claire's number on speed dial.

"Hey, Claire," she said, after a few moments. "It is. Well, I just knew you were probably thinking, why doesn't somebody call me up and give me a full report on that baby! Oh, my gosh, Claire, he is so – amazing." She described Henry, laughed. "Of course, it would be virtually impossible for any child to be cuter than you were, but I've got to say he's right up there. I can't wait for you to see him. Honey, how are you?"

She was quiet a while, listening. "Mmmm," she said, occasionally. Or, "I know."

Nora got up, poured another cup of coffee, straightened the newspaper Tom had left on the table.

"Listen, can I come see you?" Diane asked. "I probably should have said this right off, but I was just so glad to hear your voice and I – well, I'm here, in Bloomington. With your mom." She glanced at Nora, raised an eyebrow hopefully.

Then she said, "It's okay. I totally understand. I'll come alone. Just tell me where." She paused. "Right. I'm sure I can find it."

Diane punched the "off" button and put the phone back in her bag. "We're meeting in an hour. At the Student Union, in the Commons, wherever that is."

"Oh, God," Nora said. "That's where I met Tom."

"Well," Diane said. "I sure as hell won't tell her that. So, okay, let's get dressed and walk ourselves into some kind of state of – okay, calm would be too much to ask. We'll just walk. Then you can take me to the Commons and we'll figure out a place to meet afterwards.

"How did she sound?" Nora asked.

Diane shrugged. "A little lost. Pissed. But – "

"I know," Nora said. "Why wouldn't she be?"

They set out walking soon afterwards, bundled up in their parkas. It was overcast and gray, the cars on Kirkwood Avenue filthy with the salt and slush kicked up from the street. The Petoskey stone Nora had picked up the morning she met Tom on the beach was still in her pocket. She'd forgotten to throw it back into the lake. She fingered it now, wondering what Lake Michigan looked like this morning. Blue, silver, green, gray. She thought about how in the coldest weather ice balls – some as big as snowmen – formed near the shore, bobbling in the water, how the beach looked marbled sometimes, tan and white with melting snow.

They'd walked through the campus gates by then. There was the old library, where she and Tom had studied sometimes that first year. The Student Union, Wylie Hall, where she had sat enthralled, listening to Professor Berkowitz lecture about *The Canterbury Tales.* Past Ballantine Hall, they took the path down through the woods that Nora used to walk to class from her dorm. No voices, no scales coming from the closed windows of the music building. The greenhouse windows at Jordan Hall were fogged over, showing only the occasional gargantuan palm leaf pressed against the glass. Students hurried past them, bent into the cold.

They made their way back to the Union twenty minutes before Claire would arrive. There was music playing on the jukebox in the Commons – something Nora didn't recognize. Dim light seeped in through the narrow leaded windows, slanting wanly across the wooden tables.

"Where were you?" Diane asked. "When you met Tom?"

"Where the Burger King kitchen is now. They've changed everything. He and Pete went out that same revolving door over there just after I met him, though. I remember that. And Bridget and I being all whipped up into a frenzy because they'd just asked us to a party at the fraternity house the next night."

"God, do you believe how fucking old we are?" Diane asked.

They arranged to meet at the Starbucks just across from the university gates when Diane was finished talking with Claire. Nora couldn't just go sit, though. She walked a while longer, glad for the raw, wet wind that made her face sting. She wished she had thought to bring Tom's iPod, which she'd borrowed other mornings when she walked. He had hundreds of old songs on it that played randomly. She never knew what would come up, what memories would come with it. If they were too painful, all she had to do was touch the button for a new song and the memories it brought, which – with luck – would be happier, or at least easier to bear.

Surely, everyone felt this way to some degree by the time they'd reached their fifties. Surely, everyone had memories they tried to avoid. But if you'd led a life in which the same memories were free to float up again and again, maybe the edges wore away, the worst parts receding over time. It seemed impossible to her now that she had been able to forget so much for so long. Would she have just died someday, all those painful memories still buried inside her, if Claire had made a different choice?

She thought of the guilt she'd felt at Claire's age, insisting that her parents give her something they could not afford, how she couldn't forgive her mother for the sacrifice she'd made so she could to college. For the small, struggling life she led that made such sacrifice necessary. She shivered, not only from the cold. What if Claire never forgave her letting her have what she wanted, when she had known full well all that might be lost because of it?

Knowing, too, what – who – she might find.

At Starbucks, she bought a large latte and held it in her hands for the warmth. A table opened up near the window and she sat down, rubbing a circle on the glass, hoping Claire might walk Diane to the gates and she might at least catch a glimpse of her. It was foolish to hope that the two of them would appear and walk, smiling, toward the café together; still, hope flared up and she could not quite extinguish it.

She breathed in the smell of coffee and cinnamon, held her gaze on the gates until Diane appeared, alone, and made her way across the street. She put her palm on the cold window, as if this would somehow focus her thoughts, then drew it back again and put both hands in her lap.

"I'm sorry," Diane said, sinking into the chair beside her, unwinding the scarf from around her neck. "I didn't say so, but I thought I could get her to come talk to you. I was sure of it. Shit. Nora, I've probably only made you feel worse."

Nora shook her head.

"Because you couldn't feel worse," Diane said. "Believe me. I know."

"Exactly why I'm glad you came, no matter what," Nora said. "You're the only one who has any idea what this is like. Tom doesn't. He can't."

Diane leaned toward her, eyes brimming with tears. "The thing is, Nora – she's going home; Dylan's taking her this weekend."

"For spring break? I knew they had it early, but – "

"No. To stay. Well, for now."

"Stay?" Nora asked. "But she can't do that. Her classes – "

"She dropped out the first week, moved out of the dorm," Diane said. "She's been staying with Dylan. He came, after we'd been talking for a while – he was probably there all along and I just didn't see him. He told me she'd already made up her mind to do it before she got to Cincinnati. Poor kid, he looked beat. He tried to talk her out of it, he said – "

"And Charlie's letting her do this? Goddamn him," Nora said. "He's the one who insisted she had to come here in the first place. It was so perfect for her. No other place would do. Now he's just going to let her throw it all away.

"What's wrong with him?" she went on. "It didn't have to be like this. If he'd helped me when I said I had to tell her – but no. He refused to deal with it at all. Like it would just go away if we – "

She stopped when she realized that the women at the table next to theirs had stopped talking and were staring at her.

"He doesn't know," Diane said, quietly.

"Oh." Nora put her hands to her face. "Oh, God. What should I do?"

"I don't think there's anything you can do. She's determined to go. You could come back with me." She looked at Nora. "But unless you think you and Charlie might get back together, there's a good chance it would make things worse. I don't know, maybe it would be a good thing for just the two of them to be together right now. Dylan will stay through spring break; he's coming again for the summer; and Claire's planning to come back to Bloomington with him in the fall. By then – "

"What?" Nora asked. "By then, what?"

"You'll have a better idea of what your life is going to be – and maybe Claire will be more willing to consider where she can fit into it."

"Maybe not, though." Nora said.

Diane sighed. "Come on. You knew this part wasn't going to be easy."

Tears streamed down Nora's face and she blotted them with a napkin. "I know," she said. "I know. But it never once occurred to me when I decided to come back to Bloomington with Tom that Claire wouldn't be here. Near me."

29

"MacArthur Park"

Nora remembered a summer evening, dusk, lightning bugs flickering all around her. She was nine, maybe ten years old, standing in a vacant lot at the edge of her neighborhood, watching cars go by on the interstate, her hand lifted in a wave, imagining that a nice car with a happy family in it would pull over, and someone inside would open the door and beckon for her to come with them. It didn't matter where they were going. Just one step away from where was now and she knew, in time, she would be able find her way into the world she'd read about in books. She was sure of it. New York, Paris, London, Rome. The watery streets of Venice. Cathedrals, pyramids. Fields of heather, snow-capped mountains. Tulips as far as the eye could see.

Later, when darkness fell, and her parents sent her to bed, she propped a library book against her bent legs, pulled the covers up into a tent and read with a flashlight. She did this almost every night of her childhood, traveling by words. She made lists of things she didn't know or understand in a notebook and looked them up in the encyclopedia at school. What, exactly, was a moor? Were unicorns real? Was a hair shirt really made of hair? She puzzled over how whole civilizations could just get buried. How long did it take, she wondered? Didn't people living nearby notice? Now the answer to this question seemed perfectly clear. They were buried by life itself, as it proceeded relentlessly forward.

In the weeks since Claire left Bloomington, Nora had spent whole days, still in her nightgown and robe, just sitting in Tom's leather chair in a kind of dream state, fascinated by the workings of her own mind. At any given moment, her brother might appear, grimy and annoying; her sisters, their blond heads bent, doing their homework at the dinette table. The four of them might be crowded together in the backseat of the family car, the kids in their pajamas, their hair still wet from their baths, on their way to the Dairy Queen where they went sometimes on summer evenings. Her father driving, her mother, happy in the moment, her bent arm resting in the open window to catch the breeze. She'd feel claustrophobic, if it were her turn in the middle; agitated, not knowing herself until the last moment whether she would ask, as she too often did, for a sundae or milkshake or just settle for the nickel cone she knew her parents could afford. The perfect curl of ice cream at the tip of those cones, she remembered that – and the pleasure of licking it off, at the same time thinking the curl on a ten-cent cone would have been bigger, thus an even greater pleasure.

She would get away from this small, stupid life, she had promised herself again and again. She would not live as her parents did. Her father, his music on the radio all that was left of whatever dreams he might have had; her mother with no apparent dreams at all, except the happiness of her children. If she had only known then how hard it was, what it felt like to have a child upon whose happiness so much of your life hinged, Nora thought, she might have been kinder to her mother all those years ago. If she could have known how foolish she would turn out to be. How she'd just walk away from her dreams because she was afraid to face up to what she'd done and, in the end, settle for a life every bit as small as – and so much less honest than – her parents' had been. And worse, having made that life with its implicit commitments and promises, she'd be seriously considering walking away again, knowing it would wreak havoc in her daughter's life. Something that, for all her failures, Nora knew her own mother never would have done. It would have been inconceivable to her.

Sometimes, lost in her thoughts, Nora didn't even hear Tom come home from work and he would find her in the darkening living room, a cup of coffee grown cold in her hands. He would kneel beside her, place his hand on her shoulder, as if to ground her.

"Nora," he'd say.

But his voice speaking her name sounded strange to her; she could tell he still felt strange saying it. He would always think of her as Jane.

The foreboding she felt as war in Iraq grew closer, more inevitable, deepened her confusion and despair. Massive peace demonstrations around the world, petitions against the war flooded the internet, claims of faulty intelligence made by imminently trustworthy people did nothing to stop the clock ticking toward the showdown that most believed, for better or worse, had been planned for in the days after 9/11.

When it finally came, Nora and Tom watched, mesmerized: the president at the podium in his dark business suit, behind him a long, empty, red-carpeted corridor. Clever planning, they agreed: the image of him framed by the doorway, strong, silent, completely alone. When he spoke, the arrogant, in-your-face tone of the past months was gone and in its place the voice of reason. No smart-ass comments about "Freedom fries," no bragging about shock and awe, no threats about evil empires.

"My fellow citizens," he said. "Events in Iraq have now reached the final days of decision." Then, lying as Lyndon Johnson and Richard Nixon had done before him, made his case for war.

In the morning, Nora turned on *The Today Show* to find that, though the war had not officially started, a logo had been assigned to it – and, beneath that logo, flanked by a huge map of the Middle East, Katie Couric, in a black suit, interviewed two generals, who touted amazing, "intelligent" bombs and, with obvious difficulty, restrained their enthusiasm describing the MOAB: "Mother of All Bombs."

"A last resort," one said.

"Of course, we hope not to use it," said the other

They made Nora think of watching *Apocalypse Now* with Tom a few nights before. Robert Duvall waxing eloquent about the smell of napalm in the morning.

The whole broadcast mirrored the surreal quality of that movie as it proceeded. Duvall himself was on the show, teaching Katie how to tango – revealing spike heels and lacy black tights beneath the surprisingly short skirt of the black suit she'd worn in the presence of the generals. There was a feature on Saddam's luxury bunker, another on arms brokering – dozens of men in a Baghdad gun store testing the heft of shoulder-held weapons, one of them cocking a pistol toward the camera "USA," he said, grinning. Another on a Chinook-flying grandmother with gray, coiffed hair, an American flag pin on her Army fatigues.

In Rockefeller Plaza, the usual screamers competed for a moment onscreen.

"Hey, Al! I'm twenty-one today!" a kid called.

His friend held up a cardboard Wisconsin Badger.

But Al headed for a woman holding up a baby in a pink snowsuit.

"This is an antiwar baby," she said into the microphone, and he backed away.

Back in the studio, Elmo reassured the children. "Do you ever feel upset when you see or hear something scary?" he asked in his sweet, scratchy little voice. "Elmo does, too! Talk to a grown-up! Draw a picture! Tell a story! Or – " He waved his fuzzy red arms wildly and hollered, "Wubawubawuba!"

"Stay calm," a human citizen of *Sesame Street* advised parents. "Keep a routine."

"Give them a big kiss, too!" Elmo said.

Perhaps strangest of all, there were regular updates on a *Today* employee undergoing a colonoscopy. "She's under conscious sedation," the doctor said. "Relaxed, comfortable. But she *thinks* she's awake, she wants to talk." He smiled. "That's what conscious sedation is."

Nora made herself get up, get dressed, and she took Maxine for a long walk. It was quiet on campus, students home for spring break. A lone girl stood, coatless, shivering, at the university gates holding a piece of poster board on which she'd written in black magic marker:

"Bush lies. Remember Vietnam."

It made Nora furious. And ashamed. If she'd been better, smarter – if their whole generation had been better, smarter, more committed to doing what was right – there'd be no need for the girl to be standing there in quiet, lonely protest of what they'd allowed the world to become. She walked on until she was so exhausted that she came back to the house and slept until the sound of Tom's key in the door woke her that evening.

"Are you all right?" he asked.

She told him about seeing the girl that morning.

"And you felt *ashamed* about that?" he asked.

She looked up sharply at the undercurrent of anger in his voice.

"She shouldn't have been the only one. I should – "

"You should what?" he asked. "It certainly went well the last time you decided to try to stop a war. And now you think you should do it again? For Christ's sake, would you quit this?" he went on, before she could try to explain. "You always did this, always indulged yourself in it. Stupid shame and guilt. And over what? Wanting something better than what your parents had, that's where it started – "

"My parents," she said. "What are you talking about?"

"I'm talking about getting your shit together," he said. "I'm talking about . . . oh, *fuck*."

He went to the refrigerator, got a beer, and twisted off the cap. "As far as I can tell, the only thing you've done since Claire went back to Michigan is sit here all day and relive every single thing you've ever done wrong in your whole life."

"I've done a lot wrong." Nora took a deep breath, tried to get control of her voice. "I've got a lot to think about. I have to figure out – "

"What?" Tom asked. "How you're going to punish yourself for it? For how long?

"Jane – " The anger drained from his voice when he spoke her true name, and when he came to her, wordlessly drew her to him, Nora's tears finally came. They ran down her face, soaking Tom's shirt, her hair. Maxine came and sat at their feet, her head on Tom's knee, and he petted her to reassure her.

"Listen," he said, eventually. "We haven't talked about your family. Whether your parents are still alive, whether you might want to try to contact them. You're probably nowhere near ready for that. Maybe you never will be. But you need to think about all that stuff with your family. I mean it. You did this when you were eighteen, this . . . beating up on yourself over what you wanted. Come on, everybody wants a better life than what their parents had. Parents want it for their kids. You do, for Claire. *Your* parents wanted it. They were proud of you for going to school – "

"Don't say that," Nora sobbed. "Please. Don't."

Tom disentangled himself from her, got up, and turned on every lamp in the room, as if this might make her see what he needed her to see. But the light hurt her eyes, and she held her hands against them.

When he spoke again, his voice was hurt and weary, and she kept her hands to her face to avoid looking at him. "All these years, I've never, ever doubted what I felt about you," he said. "I never doubted that we'd have stayed together if Bridget hadn't come that Christmas, if things hadn't come down the way they did.

"But, man, I don't know. Lately, I find myself thinking maybe we wouldn't have made it, after all. The way you were so determined not to be happy. The way you felt guilty about everything. What happened to Bridget was your fault. *Vietnam* was your fault. Now you think this stupid war is your fault, too.

"It's not your fucking fault!" he said. "Okay?

"You can wreck the rest of your life over it if you want. You can indulge yourself, being guilty and ashamed. But, you know something? Punishing yourself the way you did when Bridget died – not coming back – punished me, too. It wrecked *my* life for a long time. Which is okay. I mean, I understand it – and I'm fine. Or I was, until I saw you."

He sank back to the couch, beside her, but did not touch her this time. "I love you," he said. "You still, *still* have no fucking idea how much I love you. But I'm in way over my head here. I can't do this again. I can't watch you do it. I won't."

She sat in stunned silence at what had just passed between them, watched him hunch over and begin to cry, his shoulders heaving. Images of the gathering war flickered on the television: people milling in the streets of Baghdad, Saddam Hussein looking defiant, bombers lined up on an airstrip in Kuwait. Twenty-four more hours, and the bombing would begin. Tom was right: there was nothing she could do about it. He was right about the other thing too: they could not go on as they were.

"Tom." She touched his shoulder and he turned to her. "I have to go back to Michigan. For now, anyway. I can't just walk away from my life again."

"I know," he said. "I'll take you in the morning."

30

"Carry On"

They set out, news of the war on the car radio. The bombing had begun; you could hear the rat-tat-tat of gunfire, Baghdad exploding behind the measured voices of reporters describing the city now under siege. Nora felt numb to it, though. She was remembering how she'd felt, years ago, riding home on the Greyhound bus after the weekend at Pete's house, thinking of Tom, of making love with him for the first time. Thinking that if she could just stay in that moment she wouldn't miss him so desperately, she wouldn't think about how long it seemed before school started and they would be together again.

She glanced at him, lost in his own thoughts, and remembered making love with him last night, too – so fiercely and for so long that when it was over they both lay back, exhausted, spent. She had never felt the way she felt then: there and not there in the same intense measure. Her body an instrument with which she felt, finally, she had said to Tom all she had wanted and needed to say. Whatever happened, she would have the memory of that, she told herself. But it didn't seem anywhere near enough to her.

In the middle of the night, she had awakened and slipped out of bed to e-mail Diane that she was coming – half so she wouldn't back out, she thought. Tom stirred and reached for her, and she went back to the warm bed. "Whatever happens, you're not going to disappear on me again," he whispered, drawing her near. "Right?"

"Right," she said.

"Okay, then. We can do this." He yawned, rubbed slow circles on her shoulders, and sleep took her toward the morning.

It had been spring-like in Bloomington when they left, crocuses popping in Tom's yard. If you looked closely, you could see a slight swelling on the branches of the maple trees getting ready to bud. In another few weeks, they'd be offering up those little green bouquets. North of Grand Rapids, though, there was still snow in the fields, and the sky was heavy and gray, promising more to come. At Manistee, there was the first glimpse of the lake, pewter, with silvered choppy waves. Onekema, Arcadia, Frankfort. Route 22, slow-going in the autumn – tourists gawking at the spectacle of changing leaves – was nearly deserted this afternoon. It hugged the western scoop of Crystal Lake, plunged farther north through deep forest. It passed River Rental, closed up and desolate, the Platte River icy at the edges. Soon, a sign said, "Monarch, eleven miles."

They passed the turnoff to Nora's house, drove on into town. It was late afternoon by then and, though the sun would not actually set for another hour or so, the windows in the houses they passed were lamp-lit against the gloom. Diane's shop, usually brightly lit, was dark; the CLOSED sign on the door. But her car was there, and a slice of light outlined the door to the back room, where Nora knew she waited.

She and Tom sat a moment, the engine still on. They had decided he'd just drop her off at Diane's shop, then turn around and head south, stop when he got tired – though Nora suspected he'd drive on home.

"You've got my cell phone," he said.

She nodded.

"I'll get a new one tomorrow and send you the number. Call. Or e-mail. Let me know."

"I will. I promise."

He leaned over, kissed her. "You're doing the right thing," he said. "You'll be okay. *We* will."

Nora took a deep breath, then opened the door of the truck, flooding the cab with light, and raised her hand to wave. Tom raised his hand, too, held it against hers, palm-to-palm.

"Okay, then," he said.

She grabbed her bag, got out, and closed the door, casting him in darkness again. She was glad it was an ugly afternoon, glad there was nobody on the street to see her stand and watch the truck make its way up Main Street and disappear around the corner, nobody to watch her walk between the buildings to the back door of the shop.

"You look shell-shocked," Diane said, drawing her in.

"I am. Listen, I'm really sorry to put you in the middle of this. But I didn't know what else to do. I didn't think I could go . . . home."

"God. Don't worry about that," Diane said. "Where's Tom?"

"He's gone. I – we – thought anything else would have made things worse. Ha! Like they could get worse," Nora said, sinking into one of Diane's wicker chairs.

"Hey, things can always get worse," Diane said, cheerily – which made Nora laugh, in spite of herself. Exactly, she knew, what Diane had intended.

"So – " Diane settled into the other wicker chair. "Can I boss you around?"

"Please," Nora said. "Someone should."

"All right, then." She sat down in the other chair. "Mo and I are leaving for Florida to see Betty the day after tomorrow – "

"Going to see Betty?" Nora echoed. "*Together?*"

"Yes," Diane said. "Can you believe it? Anyway. We'll be gone a week, and you can house sit for us. That way you can get a feel for the way things are with Charlie and Claire without exactly being there."

"Where's Mo with all this?" Nora asked.

"You know Mo." She smiled. "It's a step-by-step thing with her. When I got the e-mail this morning, I knew what we needed to do. But I waited to tell her until she got home from the clinic; I knew she'd feel bad being with Charlie, knowing you were on your way back. It would have made her mad at both of us."

"You mean, madder than she already is, right?" Nora asked.

"Well," Diane waved the question away. "You said Tom wouldn't stay, so I told her you'd have dinner with us, stay at our house while we were gone – like we'd really have let you stay in a motel! I also told her you'd let Charlie and Claire know you were here. She wouldn't have to be the one to tell them. Okay? Nora?"

Nora's teeth had begun to chatter; she'd grown suddenly cold. "I have to," she said. "I know. Mo shouldn't have to do that. But – is it really okay for me to come home with you? Are you sure?"

"You're coming," Diane said. "Mo's fixing dinner right now. She's expecting us. You can't avoid her forever." She reached for the phone and offered it to Nora. "Want to just get it over with? The longer you wait – "

Nora took the phone, punched in the familiar numbers. It rang a few times, then Claire answered. "Honey?" Nora said. "Claire?"

"Mom?" Claire said.

"Yes, I – "

"What?" Diane asked, when Nora didn't go on.

"She hung up," Nora said.

"Shit." Diane frowned. "Shit," she said again. "Well, it's no surprise. Call back. She probably won't answer and you can leave a message. It's all you can do."

Nora dialed the number again, half afraid to hear her own voice on the answering machine. But Claire had changed the message, which upset her even more.

"Hi, you've reached the Quillens. Please leave a message after the beep."

"Claire, I'm – " She stopped herself before saying "home." "I'm at Diane's shop. I just got here, nobody but Diane knew that I was coming and I wanted you to know – "

Claire was listening, she knew. Maybe Charlie, too. Nora waited, half because she didn't know what to say next, half hoping one of them would pick up the phone and talk to her.

"Well, like I said, I'm here," went on, into the silence. "I'd just like for us to talk, if we can. I'll be – "

When Diane saw that she was unable go on, she took the phone. "Claire, it's Diane," she said. "We're going to my house now. That's where we'll be. Claire? Would you pick up?" She waited a moment, but when Claire did not respond she set the phone back into the cradle.

She looked at Nora, shrugged. "Okay," she said. "Well, they know."

Nora woke at dawn the next morning to the sound of the waves crashing onto the shore and went to the window of the guest room she had helped Diane decorate last summer. A lone figure walked at the edge of the water, stopping now and then to pick up a stone and turn it over in her hand. Mary Matson, Nora saw. Mary walked every morning, as she once had, and occasionally they'd pass and exchange pleasantries, Mary going one way, Nora the other. What would Mary say if they met this morning, she wondered? Would she speak at all? Would anyone in town speak to her? They had taken her in years ago because Jo and Charlie loved her; but it was a small town, after all, their town. Leaving Charlie, she'd betrayed them all.

She retreated from the window and lay back on the bed, listening to the rise and fall of Mo and Diane's voices as they got up and began the day. Soon, there was the smell of coffee. The clink of dishware being set on the table. Diane knocked lightly on her door. "You're up, right? Come have breakfast."

Nora wrapped herself in the robe Diane had left on the bathroom hook for her and padded out to the kitchen in her stocking feet. Mo was dressed in jeans and a big white fisherman's sweater, briskly efficient, fully awake; Diane was in blue flannel pajamas with pink cows on them, still disheveled, yawning.

She rolled her eyes. "One of the many compromises we've made to keep our love alive," she said, as Mo spooned oatmeal into the three bowls she'd set on the table. "We always start the day with a good breakfast – as opposed to, say, luxuriating in bed till the last possible moment and grabbing a Pop Tart on our way out the door.

"We used to have bacon and eggs," she went on, dreamily. "Waffles. Cinnamon rolls. Then we turned fifty and she became a food Nazi. Like, we'll live forever if we eat oatmeal. Like we'd *want* to live forever, eating oatmeal. I hate fucking oatmeal."

"Quiet," Mo said again, spooning on strawberries, but she was smiling.

Nora didn't like oatmeal much herself, but she ate it – and gratefully, because Mo had made and offered it; because, despite a tense reunion the night before and more than a few anxious moments talking about what the next days might bring, Mo had seemed genuinely glad to see her. She'd been shocked at Charlie's stubborn refusal to talk to Nora at all since she'd left, Diane had confided, driving to the house the night before – not even about Claire. Upset at his willingness to allow Claire to stay holed up with him at the farmhouse, when she ought to be at school – or, at the very least, out now and then with people her own age.

"She'll never tell you that," Diane said. "You know Mo. She's loyal as a dog. But – "

"I hate it that I spoiled something between them," Nora said. "They've been friends so long. It's been so important to both of them."

"It doesn't hurt Mo to see things the way they really are," Diane said. "It's good for her, good for both of us. If it makes you feel any better, your getting into such a mess seems to have jolted Mo every which way – and, in my view, all for the good. I mean, the two of us going to see Betty? Who'd have thought! Not that I'm exactly looking forward to it. It's warm there and it's still freezing cold here; that's what I keep telling myself."

Still, Nora felt bad about it. After they'd eaten, she watched Mo make her lunch and put it in the backpack she carried to the clinic every day. "What will you do?" she asked. "I mean, when you see Charlie this morning?"

"What I do every day," she said, putting on her jacket. "Give him a hug and say, 'Okay, let's get to it.'" She shrugged. "If he wants to say anything about the fact that you're here, he'll say it. If he doesn't, he won't. I never rush Charlie, you know? I learned that a long time ago. I just wait."

"Is he okay?" Nora asked – the question she'd been afraid to ask the night before.

"No," Monique said, simply. "But he wasn't before, was he? I just didn't realize it." She hefted her backpack onto her shoulder before Nora could say anymore, brushed Diane's cheek with a kiss and left.

"Here." Diane thrust a sheaf of photographs toward her. "Look at Henry. You can't possibly be unhappy looking at Henry. He looks a little like a lizard, don't you think? A really handsome lizard. And extremely intelligent."

"He's beautiful," Nora said.

"Yes, he is," Diane said. "And without a single one of Bob's bad genes. I'm absolutely sure of it. Look at him! Don't you think Grace-the-misnamed has been wiped totally clear of the genetic tableau?"

"Clearly gone," Nora said. "No trace whatsoever."

Diane poured a third cup of coffee. "Want to know the really funny thing? Mo's been sending Betty pictures of Henry and she's absolutely thrilled about him. She actually knit him a little blanket. Betty! Can you believe it? The grandchild she never had." She smiled, fully awake now. "We never know what's going to happen, do we? Really, in fifty-five years that's all I've been able to figure out at all."

"I wish Jo could – "

"I know," Diane said. "But I'll tell you, Nora, she's just not there. Mo and I go over a couple of times a week to check in on her, but she has no idea who we are. She seems comfortable, she doesn't seem afraid – which is, I guess, the best you can hope for. But, *God*."

"Does Charlie go?"

Diane shook her head. "Not much. Weirdly, I think he's mad at her. You know, I've thought a lot about what he told you about Vietnam – seeing the guy get thrown out of the helicopter, doing nothing. Was there any single thing Jo thought was more important than being good? Could she have believed for ten seconds that Charlie ever did anything really wrong? *Ever*? No way! If you want a little junior psychology here, I don't think he did anything so awful in Vietnam, I think it was what he didn't do that got him all screwed up – but either way he never could have talked about it with Jo. He'd never have risked disappointing her. So she went on assuming he was perfect, and he soldiered on, trying to be perfect, which was what he thought she needed him to be." Diane sipped her coffee, thoughtfully. "Maybe she did need that. Maybe she couldn't have dealt with whatever he might have told her about what happened there. I don't know. And I don't mean to overanalyze. Or criticize Jo. It's just, sometimes when things change, what you always thought was true . . . shifts.

"I just mean to say, I guess it makes sense he'd be angry. Jo always protected him, ran interference for him, made things right. Now she's there, but not there. She can't help him. He doesn't know what to do."

"Do you think he'd want me back," Nora asked. "If I'd come?"

"Only if you could come back and both of you act as if nothing had happened – and, to be honest, in my most selfish mode that's exactly what I want. We could all sit out in the gazebo in the summer and drink wine and not talk about Iraq – or anything else that matters. We could dote on Claire, and Carah and Henry when they visit. You know, just drift into old age and decrepitness together. I missed you when you were gone. I mean, I love Mo – but you're my best friend. You always get my jokes, you always think I'm funny. You gossip. Mo never gossips! Oh, shit." She wiped away tears. "I don't mean to lay a guilt trip on you. And it's not like you won't still be my best friend, whatever you do. Right? I mean, that's a given."

"It's a given," Nora said. "Another given is that if Jo were still here, still herself, none of this would have happened in the first place. I never, ever could have brought myself to do anything I knew would hurt her or, worse, make her think less of me. I'd never have started up anything with Tom, never in a million years considered going off with him, which probably tells you more than anything how not right Charlie and I were all along. How not right I was.

"So I've got to get right. Whatever that turns out to be – or mean."

"Well, then," Diane said, rising. "I will change from my cow pajamas into something more serious and comb my hair, so that I can be the best possible help to you."

31

"Get Together"

Diane had planned to close the shop while she and Monique were in Florida; business was slow in March, anyway. But she accepted gratefully when Nora offered to keep it open. It would be good for both of them, Nora said. No customers would be turned away, and she'd have something to do to pass the time, waiting and hoping to hear from Claire.

She walked the shoreline in the early mornings, going as far as the hollowed-out tree where she had met Tom in January. There, she'd sit awhile in the weak spring sunshine and watch the waves break and recede. Just days ago, driving north with him, it had been winter. Snow everywhere – deep, sparkling, white. Now the snow was shrinking away from the trees and bushes, leaving circles of brown earth. The dune grasses were beginning to show, some with bits of green in them. The beach parking lot was squishy with mud.

It was a relief to sit in the quiet shop all day. It was a cheerful place, full of the work of dozens of artists who lived in the area. Scarves and beautiful woven throws in rainbow colors, whimsical ceramics, jewelry made of feathers and stones, cuddly dolls with embroidered faces. The lake in every season was there in watercolors and photographs. Mobiles turned lazily in the light breath of heat coming from the ceiling registers. Nora brought one of the wicker chairs from the back room and set it near the front window, where she sat – sometimes hours at a time – a book open her lap, gazing out on Main Street, half-hoping, half-fearing to catch a glimpse of Charlie or Claire. It seemed odd to her that their lives could be so calamitously different and the street scene she looked out on so completely unchanged. Macbeth's Grocery, the post office, the Friendly Tavern, the ice cream store. The cozy little public library that had long ago been the one-room schoolhouse.

Nights, alone in Mo and Diane's house, she woke, disoriented, her heart racing. Where, *who* was she? If she couldn't go back to sleep, she'd drag herself from bed, pull on the robe Diane had lent her and go into the family room, where she'd touch the space bar of the computer and the screen would blink and glow with light.

She did not write to Tom. She did that in the mornings, from the computer at Diane's shop. At night wrote to herself – everything, anything she could remember. Long, rainy afternoons in the library of her childhood – light seeping through the high windows into the cozy basement room lined with books and herself at one of the scarred tables, a book open before her. *The Moffats, Little House in the Big Woods, The Five Little Peppers and How They Grew.* Books about happy families. She had devoured them, carrying them home in the basket of her bicycle, disappearing into them, relegating her real family to the edges of her consciousness.

If she wrote long enough, if she wrote without flinching, finally, she began to feel her soul take on weight. She began to believe that, in time, she would be able to explain what had happened to her when she was young – how she had lost her path, her love, her self – and to believe that Claire would listen.

A little over a week into the war, U.S. troops crept toward Baghdad in sandstorms of epic proportion. The news was grim: convoys ambushed, a downed helicopter, terrified soldiers captured and shown on Iraqi television. No grateful Iraqis crowding the side of the roads to greet them as predicted by Rumsfeld and Wolfowitz, no flowers thrown into their paths.

Meanwhile, Baghdad continued to burn, pummeled by U.S. bombers. Nora switched off *The Today Show* and set out walking earlier than usual to avoid the disturbing images of people's lives in ruin. She walked quickly, fueled by anger, past the tree trunk where she usually sat, past the stone sculptures, until she calmed down and the world around her became more real and compelling than the world on the screen. Later, she wondered if she had known where she was going all along – though, at the time, she rounded the point and reached what used to be the end point of her morning walks thinking only of how lovely and improbable the dunes were: sand mountains, rising to the sky.

She kept on until she came to the break in the trees high above her, the entrance to the forest path that led home – and, suddenly, there was Astro bounding down the dune. She fell to her knees, opened her arms to him, and he danced around her, whimpering, licking her face. He rolled over, panting, and when Nora scratched his stomach she could have sworn that he was smiling. She bent and nuzzled him. He smelled of dog and dirt and water.

"Astro!"

Nora looked up and saw Claire at the top of the dune.

"Astro!" she shouted again. "You come back here. Right now!"

Astro looked at her, his tail wagging. He looked at Nora with an inquisitive expression.

"Go," she said. But, of course, he wouldn't.

He looked back and forth between Nora and Claire, who called for him again. Barked, as if to protest the position they'd put him in.

Nora stood, took hold of his collar. "Come on, buddy," she said, and started up the dune with him. Her legs burned, having grown unaccustomed to the pull of the sand in the months she'd been away, and she was winded by the time she reached the top.

"He does this every morning," Claire said, accusingly. "Looking for you."

"Oh – " Nora's heart plunged at the thought of it and at the sight of her daughter, so unexpectedly there before her, flushed with anger and from running through the woods after Astro. So beautiful. She could not take her eyes from her.

"What are you doing here?" Claire asked. "If you were planning to come visit us – "

"No," Nora said. "I mean, I – "

"Because Dad doesn't want to see you and, really, neither do I." She bent to clip on the leash, brushing Nora's hand where it still held Astro's collar.

"I know," Nora said. "But, honey, can't we – "

"No," Claire said. "I've got stuff to do. Mo's gone this week; plus, I'm doing all the work you used to do. Come on," she said to Astro, who ducked his head at the tone of her voice and went with her. But he stopped when they reached the place where the path turned, looked back to where Nora stood and barked once, as if he thought that might make her follow.

He was waiting on Mo and Diane's porch when she got home from the shop that evening. When he saw her get out of the car, he put his head between his paws and gazed up at her with an apologetic expression. His tail thumped hopefully, and when she knelt to stroke his fur, he turned his head so that her hand was exactly in the spot behind his ears, where he loved to be scratched.

He must be hungry, she thought. It was exactly the time she had always fed him. Could he know that? Was that why he'd come?

He was a dog. He couldn't really be trying to bring the family back together.

She sat down on the porch step, petted him, trying to decide what to do. She could call and tell Claire and Charlie that she was bringing him home, or she could just go. If she simply appeared, they'd have to talk to her; they'd be too surprised not to. Nora took a deep breath, grabbed Astro's collar as she had earlier that morning, and walked to the car with him.

She opened the door and he hopped in, his tail wagging at the prospect of a ride. She smiled, thinking of the Gary Larson cartoon Claire loved: a highway full of dogs, driving, their heads stuck out of the car windows, their ears flying back in the wind. The caption: "If dogs could drive." It had been on their refrigerator so long it was yellow with age; it was probably still there, she thought – and rolled the window down for Astro, despite the fact that the temperature had dropped and it was quite a wintry evening.

She drove up Main Street to Highway 22, then south through the pine forests to the turn-off toward home. It was dusk, the landscape every shade of gray, except for the slender, arched trunks of the white birches at the forest's edge, gleaming in the last light.

"Beautiful country," Tom had said, driving the same road a few months before.

Oh, it was. She looked out at the tall pines, never-changing, their tips a long, serrated line against the pewter sky. At that moment, she loved this place that had sheltered her for so many years more than she had ever loved it and, at the same time, understood – this was the trade-off, this was what she would lose. It was Charlie's place, his home. His town, his woods, his meadow, his lake. None of it had ever belonged to her, really. She'd give it all up, everything – but not until he spoke to her, not until he agreed to do whatever he could do to keep her from losing Claire.

She was shaking when she pulled into the driveway. Charlie was just closing the clinic, and Astro barked once when he saw him start across the yard. Nora opened the car door and he leapt out, raced toward him. Charlie reached into his pocket for a dog treat and, as he bent to offer it, caught sight of Nora approaching in the fading light. He stood straight up.

"He was at Mo and Diane's house when I got back from the shop," she said. "I guess he followed my scent there. I saw him when I was walking this morning."

"Claire told me," Charlie said. "She – "

He looked weary, Nora thought. Thinner, old.

"I don't know what to do with her," he said. "I was wrong to let her come back. I – "

Anger rippled across his face, but only briefly.

"I'm resigned to this," he said. "You and – Tom. Whatever – "

She took a step toward him, but he stepped back – as if afraid of her, she thought.

"What do you want?" he asked.

"Nothing," she said. "Claire. That's all. I just want you to help me talk to her."

He brushed the heel of his hand across his eyes, glanced up to her lit bedroom window. "Go to her, then," he said. "I think she's been waiting for you since this morning."

Nora looked at him and, for a moment, thought maybe she could love him again. She could try. Shouldn't she try? But when he turned abruptly and retreated from her, back into the clinic, she knew it was impossible. There were things he kept hidden in his heart – and to make a real marriage he would have to reveal them. Something he could not or would not do.

Night had settled in by now, and the house was completely dark, except for Claire's lit window. Nora did not turn on any lights as she made her way through the kitchen, down the hall. It was easier that way, the vestiges of her old life ghostly around her. The stairs creaked just past the landing. She reached the top, where she had turned so many times toward the comfort of the cozy room she and Charlie shared. The door was open, the bed made. There was her reading chair, shadowy in the moonlight, the clutter of books she'd left behind still on the table beside it. Charlie had moved into Jo's room, she saw, as she turned the other way and walked past it.

Claire's door was closed. Nora knocked lightly, pushed it open a crack and peered inside. She was fast asleep, her face blotchy from crying, a yellow Lab puppy curled at her feet. It raised its head, looked drowsily at Nora, then sighed and tucked back into itself. Claire was covered with the red and white afghan Diane had made for her to take to college, one corner of it clutched in her hand and pulled up against her cheek. It was exactly the same way she used to sleep with the flannel blanket she'd carried everywhere until she went to kindergarten, Nora remembered. She did not think. Just went in and laid down beside her daughter, put her arms around her and waited until she stirred.

"Claire," she whispered, and held her, still, though Claire grew rigid against her.

"Where's Dad?" she asked.

"In the clinic. I talked to him. He sent me up to you. Honey – "

"No," Claire said, weeping now. "I can't talk. What could I say?"

Nora held fast to her, drew her even closer, which Claire allowed. "You don't have to talk," she said. "We don't. Not now, not till you're ready. But, Honey – " Now her own voice was thick with tears. "I find I simply can't go on not being your mother any longer. I just can't. So could we just stay here a little while? Just you and me – and see how that makes us feel?"

She felt Claire hiccough and nod against her chest. Nora reached over and turned out the lamp, then stroked her daughter's wet cheeks, combed her fingers through her long, tangled hair until Claire sighed a long, deep sigh and slept again, exhausted, in her arms.

32

"Let it Be"

Charlie was sitting at the kitchen table with a cup of coffee when she came downstairs, his posture erect, both hands gripping the mug as if to ground him there.

"Don't say you're sorry," he said. "Just don't say *that.*"

She didn't say anything. She didn't want to talk to him now, but she poured a cup of coffee for herself and sat down in her place across from him.

"How is she?" he asked.

"Sad. Sleeping. We didn't talk. I just – " She shook her head, pressed her knuckles against her eyes for moment. "Charlie, please. What are we going to do about – "

"I accept that you felt you had to tell me . . . what you did," he said. "But I'll never be able to accept your telling Claire. You did, though, and it's going to take both of us to figure out what to do about it. I don't want to talk it to death," he said. "I just want us to make a plan."

"My plan is to be near her," Nora said. "Not talk. Not yet. Just be. If the apartment over the Hummingbird is still empty, I'll stay there – assuming that's okay with you."

He nodded.

Astro got up from his sheepskin pillow, padded over to sit next to Nora, his tail thumping slowly. Hopefully, she thought.

"He's a mess, too," Charlie said, but not unkindly. "He's your dog, it turns out. You should take with him with you."

She felt weak with gratitude, she wanted to put her arms around him and tell him that she loved him, loved the part of Claire that was him, and the family they had been. But it would have been worse than trying to tell him she was sorry.

"The puppy – " she began.

He shrugged, smiled a little. "Yo-Yo Ma – which seems to have morphed to Monty somehow. She's training him. She means to take him back to school with her in the fall. He's going to be a great dog," he said – and became himself again, telling her why.

Back at Diane's, Astro sniffed all of Nora's belongings thoroughly, probably scenting Maxine. When she woke the next morning, he jumped down from the bed where he'd been sleeping beside her and positioned himself just inside the door, facing in, his head on his paws, as if he could keep her there.

"Walk?" she asked, after she'd drunk a cup of coffee, showered and dressed.

He leapt up, tail wagging, and followed her joyously out into the cold, running circles around her until they got to the beach, at which point he ran ahead of her, for home.

Nora walked slowly, breathing in the wet lake air, memorizing the upward scoop of dunes to the overhanging cliffs above, the brittle grasses, the graceful pattern of white birches against the lightening sky. There was still ice as far out as she could see, drifts frozen into what looked like icebergs near the horizon, ruffles of frozen waves near the shore.

She passed the stone sculptures where she had met Tom, stopped, and looked back, remembering the sight of him jogging toward her. She'd talked to him the night before, told him about Claire, about Charlie giving her Astro.

"It was good of him," Tom said. "Things are going to be okay."

"Maybe," she said. "If I can follow the never-talk-about-anything-that-matters rule."

"You can talk to me about stuff that matters. You need to do that. Deal?"

"Deal," she said.

She walked on until she reached the familiar break in the trees, where she followed Astro up the dune, through the woods to the meadow. The farmhouse might have been on a Christmas card, she thought, surrounded by snow-iced pine trees, smoke curling up from the chimney. Astro bounded toward the sound of dogs barking in the run. Charlie looked up and raised his hand when he saw her coming behind him.

"There's coffee inside," he said, when she reached him.

Claire sat at the kitchen table in her pajamas, eating toast and jam, her hair still tangled from sleeping, her eyes puffy from yesterday's tears. Monty greeted them, rolling over at the sight of Astro, who nudged him playfully. Nora scooped up the puppy, nuzzled him, and sat down in her usual place.

"He's lovely," she said to her daughter.

Claire nodded.

Nora knew she didn't dare say that she was sorry, or try to explain – anything. She kept the puppy in her lap to keep from going to Claire and holding her as she'd done the night before.

"Would you like some coffee?" Claire asked. "I could fix you some toast."

"I'd love that," Nora said, though she wasn't hungry.

Claire got up, poured the coffee into the yellow mug Nora always used; then fixed the toast, buttered it, and slathered it with black raspberry jam.

"I miss Grandma's jam," she said, setting the plate in front of Nora. "I always think of it. Every morning. It's stupid, you know? I mean, *toast* making me sad?"

It's always the little things, Nora wanted to say. The yellow mug, the row of cookbooks on the shelf, the summer geraniums leggy but still surviving on the sun porch. Instead, she offered up the puppy, and Claire took him and buried her face in his fur, weeping.

"Honey – " Nora said. "Claire."

But Claire shook her head, took a deep breath, and collected herself. "I've been taking Monty over to the nursing home to see her," she said. "She doesn't pet him or anything, but she likes it if I put him near her. I can tell. It's sad, Mom. How she is. Dad won't even go there."

"I'll go," Nora said. "Can we go together?"

"Okay," Claire said.

Nora had avoided the nursing home since she'd come back, worried that she might get a cool reception, but Jo's caregivers were visibly glad to see her, and if they had an opinion about her separation from Charlie it wasn't evident.

Claire headed toward Jo's room, carrying Monty in her arms, stopping so folks in wheelchairs and on walkers could pet and marvel over him. Nora followed slowly, her anxiety about seeing Jo compounded by the stale scent of the place, the low murmur of suffering and complaint. She had prepared herself for the worst, but the sight of Jo shocked her nonetheless: skin and bones, chalk-white, her mouth frozen into a perfect "O." Jo's eyes fluttered open at the sound of her voice, but her expression remained blank. Monty curled cooperatively into himself when Claire placed him on the bed near Jo's chest. Jo watched as Claire bent closer to her, her fingers twitched when Claire lifted her hand and put it on the puppy. Muscle memory, Claire thought, from petting all the dogs she'd loved in her life.

As they were leaving, the head nurse signaled Nora into her office. Jo had been fighting colds and infections since she'd been sick at Christmas-time, she said. She didn't have a living will. The doctor had tried to talk to Charlie about what he wanted them to do if she became ill enough to need resuscitation. But Charlie continued to avoid such a conversation.

"Would you talk to him?" she asked.

Nora lied and said she would, knowing that, right now, she couldn't even risk trying.

Later that day, Claire helped her load some things into Diane's car to take to the apartment over the Hummingbird Café. Clothes, mostly. Books, sheets, towels. Astro's bed. Claire didn't offer to go with her, and Nora didn't ask. Climbing the stairs to the apartment, she had remembered following Jo up all those years ago, the relief of setting her duffel bag down in a clean space. She remembered the patch of late-summer sunlight on the bed, the starched eyelet curtains at the window. Had she really believed she could simply shed the person she'd been?

Diane had invited her to stay on in the guest room, but Nora declined. She was glad to have a place to be alone, where she could think things through, where she could feel comfortable calling Tom whenever she felt like it, where she could set the old photograph of the two of them at Bean Blossom on her bedside table and look at it when she needed courage, needed to remember who she was.

She made herself be patient. Mornings, she walked Astro to their – Charlie's – house. After a quietly companionable breakfast with Claire, she helped Claire train Monty and they talked about how adorable he was, how smart. Sometimes the two of them drove into Traverse City together to see a movie or shop and then talked about the movie or their purchases, Claire now and then forgetting herself and saying something about Dylan – what movies he loved, something funny he'd said. She and Charlie and Claire shared meals and talked about all of the above, plus music, plus the weather.

Ice-out on Lake Michigan came in April, with its creaking and thumping and moaning, the sharp cracks as chunks of ice broke into glittering islands, the suck and gurgle of water reasserting itself, rippling into ponds that grew larger each day. Claire had been frightened of it as a little girl, the low whistling and banging and hissing were like a scary movie, she said. But Charlie taught her to listen to it, to hear it as a kind of symphony and, in time, ice-out had become something she loved. Something the three of them had always walked down to witness together, standing at the shore amidst the Brobdingnagian chunks of ice that washed up on the beach, as clear and bright as diamonds.

She did not talk about the Pentagon-staged rescue of Jessica Lynch, a pretty young soldier who was Claire's age, or the toppling of Saddam's statue in Baghdad, or the looting and violence there, except to Diane and Tom.

"Freedom is untidy," Donald Rumsfeld pronounced. "Stuff happens."

Spring came. The fields and meadows greened up, the trees leafed out, swaths of violets and trillium blanketed the forest floor. Charlie continued to keep a careful distance from her, his determination to live in the present moment unwavering. Had he purged her from the Museum of Charlie in his mind, she wondered, and, if so, how had he accomplished this? Her own mind reeled with memories so vivid that she was constantly distracted, surfacing with surprise to see him, a man in his fifties, or Claire grown into a young woman. Jo in the nursing home, blank and suffering.

When the call came, she was the one to answer it: Jo had awakened feverish, with chest pain and respiratory distress that the doctor had diagnosed as acute onset pneumonia. They needed Charlie's permission to admit her to the hospital in Traverse City. They should be prepared to consider what measures should be taken to save her life.

"Of course they should take her to the hospital if she needs to go." Charlie said, when she went out to the clinic to find him. "But for Christ's sake, do we need to talk about . . . the *other* right now? She might come out of this just fine." And he glared at her, as if daring her to say what she was thinking: *And would that be a* good *thing?*

He was ominously silent on the way to the hospital. Entering Jo's room, where she lay tethered to an IV, breathing in oxygen through a nasal catheter, he stopped short, shocked at the sight of her, then walked out again. Claire followed him; Nora didn't dare. She pulled a chair up to Jo's bedside and sat down, brushed her tangled hair away from her damp forehead. Jo was hot and clammy to the touch, her breathing labored. The hand that wasn't restrained by the IV scrabbled on the bedcovers; it felt skeletal when Nora lifted and stilled it, folding it into her own.

She bent close to Jo, kissed her cheek and, in a low voice, told her everything.

Jo's eyes remained closed, her body motionless. There was no recognizable sign that she'd heard a word Nora said. But Nora had read that some people who'd been near death and survived vividly remembered the sense of floating above the scene of their own demise, observing panicked doctors and grieving loved ones with an equanimity that puzzled them upon re-entering their bodies.

"I love you," she whispered. "We'll be all right. I promise."

When the doctor arrived to examine Jo, she joined Charlie and Claire in the waiting room. Charlie pointedly concentrated on the magazine he was leafing through. Claire's eyes were fixed on whatever game show was on the television, but when Nora sat down beside her and gave her a brief hug, she allowed it. When a nurse appeared perhaps fifteen minutes later to escort them to the conference room where the doctor was waiting, Charlie stayed both of them with a glance, rose, and followed her, alone.

"I told Dad, she's not here anymore," Claire said, tearfully. "She wouldn't want to be this way. Not knowing us, not even knowing herself."

But it was Mo who finally convinced him to accept that fact Jo was dying, who sat vigil with him until Jo finally took her last breath, and stayed beside him through the funeral and until the last person had left the reception at the Hummingbird Café.

"You know Mo," Diane said a few days afterward. "She's going to take care of Charlie forever. You don't have to worry about that. And all you had to do was look at Claire and Dylan at the funeral to see he's the one who's going to make sure she's okay. When he comes back next week for summer break, forget about seeing much of Claire, no matter how well you've been getting along.

"So what about *your* life, Nora?" she asked. "What are you going to do about that?"

33

"Here, There and Everywhere"

On the first of May, President Bush had swaggered in full flight regalia from the jet that landed him on the aircraft carrier *Abraham Lincoln,* grinning, giving the thumbs up to the hundreds of sailors lining the flight deck under a banner that proclaimed "Mission Accomplished."

"Combat operations in Iraq have ended," he announced. "In the battle of Iraq, the United States and our allies have prevailed."

But troop strength remained essentially the same, fierce battles continued to rage, the death count rose. One hundred thirty-eight Americans had been killed by the Fourth of July, a third of them after Bush's pronouncement. Thousands of Iraqi civilians had died in air strikes and explosions, were injured or displaced. So far, not a single WMD had been found.

Recently, a taped message from Saddam Hussein, who remained at large, had urged guerilla fighters to continue their resistance to the U.S.-led occupation.

"Bring them on," President Bush responded. "We're not leaving until we accomplish the task, and the task is going to be a free country led by the Iraqi people." He offered no timetable for the withdrawal of American forces.

"Oh!" Nora said. "I guess he forgot the war was over. Not to mention the fact that he went AWOL from the Reserves when it looked like he might get sent to Vietnam."

Tom glanced at her sharply.

"Don't worry," she said. "I know I'm not responsible for it. I'm just saying . . ."

He smiled. "Okay, then. Progress."

They were sitting in a restaurant on Front Street in Traverse City, half-watching the news on the TV above the bar, half-watching the townspeople and tourists there for the Cherry Festival pass by on their way to the park along the lakeshore to watch the annual air show. They waved little American flags, wore tee shirts and baseball caps plastered with flags and stars and eagles. "American Patriot," "In God We Trust," "These Colors Don't Run." Usually, the air show featured the Navy's Blue Angels in a festive, conspicuous display of aerobatic maneuvers. This year it was the Air Force, with a tactical demonstration of the aircraft being used in Iraq, including a simulated weapons deployment.

"Fun and games," Tom said.

He paid the check and they walked, hand-in-hand, in the opposite direction of the crowd, toward Nora's apartment. She could not stop looking at him. They had talked every day since she'd come back in March but had waited until this weekend to see each other. It had made her feel young again, the way she'd felt waiting for him that long ago summer, and her first sight of him the day before had brought back the boy leaning against a post at the bus station, waiting for her bus to arrive. The sense that life, everything was still all before them.

"It is," he said, when she told him that. "It's just going to be a little shorter than we planned."

The first planes screamed into the sky as they walked, and Nora shuddered, imagining what it must be like to see them coming at you for real, how you'd draw your children to you, try to shelter them, knowing only luck would save them – or God or fate, if you believed in either.

"You're quiet," Tom said. "Are you worried about Claire?"

"A little. And Diane in Chicago, doing the same thing, waiting for Rose. She's coming to dinner at Carah's tonight – Rose is. Diane's a wreck about it. I know," she added. "Like me worrying about any of it really helps."

The apartment still smelled of the cherry pie she'd baked that morning and of the little doll pies she'd made for Claire. One of four apartments in an old Victorian house, it belonged to a friend of Diane's, an artist who was in France on a fellowship through the summer. It was on the second floor, airy: white walls hung with her abstract Michigan landscapes; shelves that held driftwood and Petoskey stones, birds' nests, dried flowers, and branches with bright red winter berries. A bay window overlooked the neighborhood, and after she had made a pitcher of lemonade and set out the plates for the pie, Nora sat in the window seat and watched for Claire and Dylan to come up the street after the air show.

She had moved to Traverse City after Jo's death to stay close to her daughter, found a part- time job at a bookstore to keep busy, and started seeing a therapist, an older woman who listened intently and whose questions and observations turned out to be very much like Tom's.

"Talk," Dr. Whiting would say, when she arrived each Tuesday afternoon.

And Nora did, surprised by how easy it was to tell the secrets she'd held so close to her, how her whole body lightened as the words they were made of flew out of her mouth and into the air. She talked to Claire, too, more cautiously – and often with a heavy heart. She was still looking for the words to explain that she would give Claire her life, but, even if she wanted to, she couldn't give Claire her whole and only heart. The heart gives itself away. You can't control it.

She had to go slowly. She had to *be* there. Their best times were when they didn't try to talk at all – when Claire drove over and they went to a movie, took a picnic lunch to the beach and sat reading together, or walked down by the marina to look at the boats. When Dylan returned for summer break, the two of them came together.

He was different from last summer, more man than boy. Their relationship was different, too, seasoned by Claire's troubles, but the "we" of them seemed stronger for it – which Charlie felt as loss, but for which Nora was grateful. What more could you wish for your child than the kind of happiness real love brings, the exclusive friendship, the grounding? And it made her believe that, if she was patient, the time would come when she'd be able to say, "Tom and I were in love that way when we were young," and Claire would be able to listen.

Now here they came toward the apartment, talking, Claire's arms waving. They were still talking, coming up the stairs, and Claire's first words when Nora opened the door were, "Mom. That . . . *stealth bomber.* Did you see it? Oh, my God," she rattled on, before Nora could answer. "It was awful. Like a humongous bat. Like *death* coming right at you."

"Everyone's cheering and we're, like, 'Shit'!" Dylan said. "We need comfort food – hot pie, with ice cream melting on it. Seriously. That thing scared the crap out of both of us."

"Whatever they're doing with that thing, wherever, is wrong," Claire said, quietly.

Then she came in and held her hand out to Tom.

Nora had the odd sense of a camera rolling, recording a rehearsed scene – the introductions, Tom's inevitable comment that Claire looked like her mother and Claire deciding to smile, and Dylan leavening the moment saying he had a friend who said you should look at your girlfriend's mother before making any major commitments and he figured he was good to go there, and Tom saying no doubt about that. Nora playing her part, serving the pie and ice cream and lemonade, being surprised by Dylan saying, you know they ought to shove W out of the Green Zone and see how long he survives, and Claire agreeing, saying you were right, Mom, last summer, how you were so upset about the war.

Nora was in the film, but outside, watching, listening, too. Claire and Dylan holding hands under the table, Tom scratching Astro's ears, asking Claire and Dylan about their studies and about their jobs at River Rental and drawing out of them that they planned to come back and live here when they finished college, maybe teach at Interlochen if they could get on there, whatever, they'd find something.

Then Nora saying, "Well, it's a wonderful, magical place to live your life," not trusting her voice to say more than that.

Dishes in the sink, hugs and handshakes, the door closing behind them.

"It was okay, right?" Tom asked.

"Yes," she said. "*Yes.*"

He smiled. "Next?"

Next there would be Tom meeting Charlie and Mo. There would be writing to her parents, who Tom had learned were still alive, in the same house, and the move back to Bloomington in the fall. There'd be problems that could not be solved, sorrows that would never, ever go away. The war would go on and there would be other corrupt wars, too, and she'd be angry about them all, which was all right because she didn't ever want not to be angry about something so wrong. As an antidote, she would make herself remember the children she had taught so long ago, how their struggles humbled her, how their gratitude for even the smallest kindness broke her heart and at the same time made her feel hopeful that she could make some difference in the world.

She wanted that hope in her life again.

Right now, though, the rest of the long weekend stretched out before them. They'd rest a while, maybe make love, then in the early evening pack a picnic supper and drive a road lined with cherry orchards to a secret beach she knew. When the air began to chill, they'd climb the huge dune behind it, a grueling, steep climb – hearts pounding, thighs burning, sand collecting in their shoes – and when they reached the top they'd turn and see the spectacular scoop of shoreline curving to a blue-gray distance in either direction. Soon the sun would flare up and make its glittery path across the water, then sink into the horizon, trailing tatters of pink and orange, its last rays like long fingers raking the clouds. The color would drain from the trees and sand and grasses; the water would go glassy and opaque. And night would fall, showering them with stars.

BARBARA SHOUP is the author of six previous novels and co-author of two books about the creative process. A native Hoosier, she is the Executive Director of the Writers' Center of Indiana, an Associate Faculty member at IUPUI, and an Associate Editor for OV Books. She lives in Indianapolis.